FORFEIT AND BLOOD SPORT

Also by Dick Francis in Pan Books

THE SPORT OF QUEENS
(autobiography)

LESTER: The Official
Biography

DEAD CERT
NERVE
FOR KICKS
ODDS AGAINST
FLYING FINISH
ENQUIRY
RAT RACE
BONECRACK
SMOKESCREEN
SLAY-RIDE
KNOCK DOWN
HIGH STAKES
IN THE FRAME
RISK
TRIAL RUN
WHIP HAND
REFLEX
TWICE SHY
BANKER
THE DANGER
PROOF
BREAK IN
BOLT
HOT MONEY
THE EDGE
STRAIGHT
LONGSHOT
COMEBACK
DRIVING FORCE
DECIDER
WILD HORSES
COME TO GRIEF
TO THE HILT
10lb PENALTY
FIELD OF THIRTEEN
SECOND WIND
SHATTERED

Dick Francis has written forty-one international bestsellers and is widely acclaimed as one of the world's finest thriller writers. His awards include the Crime Writers' Association's Cartier Diamond Dagger for his outstanding contribution to the crime genre, and an honorary Doctorate of Humane Letters from Tufts University of Boston. In 1996 Dick Francis was made a Mystery Writers of America Grand Master for a lifetime's achievement and in 2000 he received a CBE in the Queen's Birthday Honours list.

Dick Francis

FORFEIT AND BLOOD SPORT

PAN BOOKS

Forfeit first published 1968 by Michael Joseph
First published by Pan Books 1970
Blood Sport first published 1967 by Michael Joseph
First published by Pan Books 1969

This omnibus edition published 2004 by Pan Books
an imprint of Pan Macmillan Ltd
Pan Macmillan, 20 New Wharf Road, London N1 9RR
Basingstoke and Oxford
Associated companies throughout the world
www.panmacmillan.com

ISBN 0330 43266 4

1 3 5 7 9 8 6 4 2

A CIP catalogue record for this book is available from
the British Library.

Typeset by Intype London Limited
Printed and bound in Great Britain by
Mackays of Chatham plc, Chatham, Kent

FORFEIT

CHAPTER ONE

The letter from *Tally* came on the day Bert Checkov died. It didn't look like trouble; just an invitation from a glossy to write an article on the Lamplighter Gold Cup. I flicked it across the desk to the Sports Editor and went on opening the mail which always accumulated for me by Fridays. Luke-John Morton grunted and stretched out a languid hand, blinking vacantly while he listened to someone with a lot to say on the telephone.

'Yeah . . . yeah. Blow the roof off,' he said.

Blowing the roof off was the number one policy of *The Sunday Blaze*, bless its cold heart. Why didn't I write for *The Sunday Times*, my wife's mother said, instead of a rag like *The Sunday Blaze*? They hadn't needed me, that was why. She considered this irrelevant, and when she couldn't actively keep it quiet, continued to apologize to every acquaintance for my employment. That the *Blaze* paid twenty-eight per cent more than *The Times*, and that her daughter was expensive, she ignored.

I slit open a cheap brown envelope and found some nut had written to say that only a vicious unscrupulous bum like myself would see any good in the man I had defended last Sunday. The letter was written on lavatory paper and spite oozed from it like marsh gas. Derry Clark read it over my shoulder and laughed.

'Told you you'd stir them up.'

'Anything for an unquiet life,' I agreed.

Derry wrote calm uncontroversial articles each week assessing form and firmly left the crusading rebel stuff to me. My back, as he constantly pointed out, was broader than his.

Eight more of my other correspondents proved to be thinking along the same general lines. All anonymous, naturally. Their problems, I reflected, dumping their work in the waste basket, were even worse than mine.

'How's your wife?' Derry said.

'Fine, thanks.'

He nodded, not looking at me. He'd never got over being embarrassed about Elizabeth. It took some people that way.

Luke-John's conversation guttered to a close. 'Sure . . . sure. Phone it through by six at the latest.' He put down the receiver and focused on my letter from *Tally*, his eyes skidding over it with professional speed.

'A study in depth . . . how these tarty magazines love that phrase. Do you want to do it?'

'If the fee's good.'

'I thought you were busy ghosting Buster Figg's autobiography.'

'I'm hung up on chapter six. He's sloped off to the Bahamas and left me no material.'

'How far through his horrid little life have you got?' His interest was genuine.

'The end of his apprenticeship and his first win in a classic.'

'Will it sell?'

'I don't know,' I sighed. 'All he's interested in is money, and all he remembers about some races is the starting price. He gambled in thousands. And he insists I put his biggest bets in. He says they can't take away his licence now he's retired.'

Luke-John sniffed, rubbing a heavily freckled hand across the prominent tendons of his scrawny neck, massaging his walnut-sized larynx, dropping the heavy eyelid hoods while he considered the letter from *Tally*. My contract with the *Blaze* was restrictive: books were all right, but I couldn't write articles for any other paper or magazine without Luke-John's permission, which I mostly didn't get.

Derry pushed me out of his chair and sat in it himself. As I spent only Fridays in the office, I didn't rate a desk and usurped my younger colleague's whenever he wasn't looking. Derry's desk held a comprehensive reference library of form books in the top three drawers and a half-bottle of vodka, two hundred purple hearts and a pornographic film catalogue in the bottom one. These were window dressing only. They represented the wicked fellow Derry would like to be, not the lawful, temperate, semi-detached man he was.

I perched on the side of his desk and looked out over the Friday morning clatter, a quarter-acre of typewriters and telephones going at half speed as the week went on towards Sunday. Tuesdays the office was dead: Saturdays it buzzed like flies squirted with DDT. Fridays I felt part of it. Saturdays I went to the races. Sundays and Mondays, officially off. Tuesdays to Thursdays, think up some galvanizing subject to write about, and write it. Fridays, take it in for Luke-John, and then for the editor, to read and vet.

Result, a thousand words a week, an abusive mailbag, and a hefty cheque which didn't cover my expenses.

Luke-John said, 'Are you or Derry doing the Lamplighter?'

Without giving me a second Derry jumped in. 'I am.'

'That all right with you, Ty?' Luke-John asked dubiously.

'Oh sure,' I said. 'It's a complicated handicap. Right up his street.'

Luke-John pursed his thin lips and said with unusual generosity, '*Tally* says they want background stuff, not tips . . . I don't see why you shouldn't do it, if you want to.'

He scribbled a large OK, at the bottom of the page and signed his name. 'But of course,' he added, 'if you dig up any dirt, keep it for *us*.'

Generous, be damned, I thought wryly. Luke-John's soul belonged to the *Blaze* and his simple touchstone in all decisions was, 'Could it possibly, directly or indirectly, benefit the paper?' Every member of the sports section had at some time or other been ruthlessly sacrificed on his altar. For cancelled holidays, smashed appointments, lost opportunities, he cared not one jot.

'Sure,' I said mildly. 'And thanks.'

'How's your wife?' he asked.

'Fine, thanks.'

He asked every week without fail. He had his politenesses, when it didn't cost the *Blaze*. Maybe he really cared. Maybe he only cared because when she wasn't 'fine' it affected my work.

I pinched Derry's telephone and dialled the number.

'*Tally* magazine, can I help you?' A girl's voice, very smooth, West Ken, and bored.

'I'd like to talk to Arnold Shankerton.'

'Who's calling?'

'James Tyrone.'

'One moment, please.' Some clicks and a pause. 'You're through.'

An equally smooth, highly sophisticated tenor voice proclaimed itself to be Arnold Shankerton, Features. I thanked him for his letter and said I would like to accept his commission. He said that would be very nice in moderately pleased tones and I gently added, 'If the price is right naturally.'

'Naturally,' he conceded. 'How much do you want?'

Think of a number and double it. 'Two hundred guineas, plus expenses.'

Luke-John's eyebrows rose and Derry said, 'You'll be lucky.'

'Our profit margin is small,' Shankerton pointed out a little plaintively. 'One hundred is our absolute limit.'

'I pay too much tax.'

His sigh came heavily down the wire. 'A hundred and fifty, then. And for that it'll have to be good.'

'I'll do my best.'

'Your best,' he said, 'would scorch the paper. We want the style and the insight but not the scandal. Right?'

'Right,' I agreed without offence. 'How many words?'

'It's the main feature. Say three thousand five hundred, roughly speaking.'

'How about pictures?'

'You can have one of our photographers when you're ready. And within reason, of course.'

'Of course,' I said politely. 'When do you want it by?'

'We go to press on that edition . . . let's see . . . on November twentieth. So we'd like your stuff on the morning of the seventeenth, at the very latest. But the earlier the better.'

I looked at Derry's calendar. Ten days to the seventeenth.

'All right.'

'And when you've thought out how you'd like to present it, send us an outline.'

'Will do,' I said: but I wouldn't. Outlines were asking for trouble in the shape of editorial alterations. Shankerton could, and would, chop at the finished article to his heart's content, but I was against him getting his scissors into the embryo.

Luke-John skimmed the letter back and Derry picked it up and read it.

'In depth,' he said, sardonically. 'You're used to the deep end. You'll feel quite at home.'

'Yeah,' I agreed absentmindedly. Just what *was* depth, a hundred and fifty guineas worth of it?

I made a snap decision that depth in this case would be the background people, not the stars.

The stars hogged the headlines week by week. The background people had no news value. For once, I would switch them over.

Snap decisions had got me into trouble once or twice in the past. All the same, I made this one. It proved to be the most trouble-filled of the lot.

*

Derry, Luke-John, and I knocked off soon after one and walked down the street in fine drizzle to elbow our way into the bar of The Devereux in Devereux Court opposite the Law Courts.

Bert Checkov was there, trying to light his stinking old pipe and burning his fingers on the matches. The shapeless tweed which swathed his bulk was as usual scattered with ash and as usual his toecaps were scuffed and grey. There was more glaze in the washy blue eyes than one-thirty normally found there: an hour too much, at a rough guess. He'd started early.

Luke-John spoke to him and he stared vaguely back. Derry bought us a half-pint each and politely asked Bert to have one, though he'd never liked him.

'Double scotch,' Bert mumbled, and Derry thought of his mortgages and scowled.

'How's things?' I asked, knowing that this too was a mistake. The Checkov grumbles were inexhaustible.

For once, however, the stream was damned. The watery eyes focused on me with an effort and another match sizzled on his skin. He appeared not to notice.

'Gi' you a piesh o' advish,' he said, but the words stopped there. The advice stayed in his head.

'What is it?'

'Piesh o' advish.' He nodded solemnly.

Luke-John raised his eyes to the ceiling in an exasperation that wasn't genuine, for old-time journalists like Bert he had an unlimited regard which no amount of drink could quench.

'Give him the advice, then,' Luke-John suggested. 'He can always do with it.'

The Checkov gaze lurched from me to my boss. The Checkov mouth belched uninhibitedly. Derry's pale face twisted squeamishly, and Checkov saw him. As a gay lunch, hardly a gas. Just any Friday, I thought: but I was wrong. Bert Checkov was less than an hour from death.

Luke-John, Derry, and I sat on stools round the bar counter and ate cold meat and pickled onions, and Bert Checkov stood swaying behind us, breathing pipe smoke and whisky fumes down our necks. Instead of the usually steady rambling flow of grousing to which we were accustomed, we received only a series of grunts, the audible punctuation of the inner Checkov thoughts.

Something on his mind. I wasn't interested enough to find out what. I had enough on my own.

Luke-John gave him a look of compassion and another whisky, and the alcohol washed into the pale blue eyes like a tide, resulting in pin-point pupils and a look of blank stupidity.

'I'll walk him back to his office,' I said abruptly. 'He'll fall under a bus if he goes on his own.'

'Serve him right,' Derry said under his breath, but carefully so that Luke-John shouldn't hear.

We finished lunch with cheese and another half-pint. Checkov lurched sideways and spilt my glass over Derry's knee and the pub carpet. The carpet soaked it up good-temperedly, which was more than could be said for Derry. Luke-John shrugged, resignedly, half laughing, and I finished what was left of my beer with one swallow, and I steered Bert Checkov through the crowd and into the street.

'Not closing time yet,' he said distinctly.

'For you it is, old chum.'

He rolled against the wall, waving the pipe vaguely in his chubby fist. 'Never leave a pub before closing. Never leave a story while it's hot. Never leave a woman on her doorstep. Paragraphs and skirts should be short and pheasants and breasts should be high.'

'Sure,' I said sighing. Some advice.

I took his arm and he came easily enough out on to the Fleet Street pavement. His tottering progress up towards the City end produced several stares but no actual collisions. Linked together we crossed during a lull in the traffic and continued eastwards under the knowing frontages of the *Telegraph* and the black glass *Express.* Fleet Street had seen the lot: no news value in an elderly racing correspondent being helped back from lunch with a skinful.

'A bit of advice,' he said suddenly, stopping in his tracks. 'A bit of advice.'

'Yes?' I said patiently.

He squinted in my general direction.

'We've come past the *Blaze.*'

'Yeah.'

He tried to turn me round to retrace our steps.

'I've business down at Ludgate Circus. I'm going your way today,' I said.

'Zat so?' He nodded vaguely and we shambled on. Ten more paces. He stopped again.

'Piece of advice.'

He was looking straight ahead. I'm certain that he saw nothing at all. No bustling street. Nothing but what was going on inside his head.

I was tired of waiting for the advice which showed no signs of materializing. It had begun to drizzle again. I took his arm to try and get him moving along the last fifty yards to his paper's florid front door. He wouldn't move.

'Famous last words,' he said.

'Whose?'

'Mine. Naturally. Famous last words. Bit of advice.'

'Oh sure,' I sighed. 'We're getting wet.'

'I'm not drunk.'

'No.'

'I could write my column any time. This minute.'

'Sure.'

He lurched off suddenly, and we made it to his door. Three steps and he'd be home and dry.

He stood in the entrance and rocked unsteadily. The pale blue eyes made a great effort towards sobering up, but the odds were against it.

'If anyone asks you,' he said finally, 'don't do it.'

'Don't do what?'

An anxious expression flitted across his pallid fleshy

face. There were big pores all over his nose, and his beard was growing out in stiff black millimetres. He pushed one hand into his jacket pocket, and the anxiety turned to relief as he drew it out again with a half-bottle of scotch attached.

‘’Fraid I’d forgotten it,’ he mumbled.

‘See you then, Bert.’

‘Don’t forget,’ he said. ‘That advice.’

‘Right.’ I began to turn away.

‘Ty?’

I was tired of him. ‘What?’

‘You wouldn’t let it happen to you, I know that . . . but sometimes it’s the strong ones get the worst clobbering . . . in the ring, I mean . . . they never know when they’ve taken enough . . .’

He suddenly leaned forward and grasped my coat. Whisky fumes seeped up my nose and I could feel his hot breath across the damp air.

‘You’re always broke, with that wife of yours. Luke-John told me. Always bloody stony. So don’t do it . . . don’t sell your sodding soul . . .’

‘Try not to,’ I said wearily, but he wasn’t listening.

He said, with the desperate intensity of the very drunk, ‘They buy you first and blackmail after . . .’

‘Who?’

‘Don’t know . . . Don’t sell . . . don’t sell your column.’

‘No,’ I sighed.

'I *mean* it.' He put his face even closer. 'Never sell your column.'

'Bert . . . Have you?'

He closed up. He pried himself off me and went back to rocking. He winked, a vast caricature of a wink.

'Bit of advice,' he said nodding. He swivelled on rubbery ankles and weaved an unsteady path across the lobby to the lifts. Inside he turned round and I saw him standing there under the light clutching the half-bottle and still saying over and over, 'Bit of advice, bit of advice.'

The doors slid heavily across in front of him. Shrugging, puzzled a little, I started on my way back to the *Blaze*. Fifty yards along, I stopped off to see if the people who were servicing my typewriter had finished it. They hadn't. Call back Monday, they said.

When I stepped out into the street again a woman was screaming.

Heads turned. The high-pitched agonized noise pierced the roar of wheels and rose clean above the car horns. With everyone else, I looked to see the cause.

Fifty yards up the pavement a knot of people was rapidly forming and I reflected that in this particular place droves of regular staff reporters would be on the spot in seconds. Nevertheless, I went back. Back to the front door of Bert's paper, and a few steps farther on.

Bert was lying on the pavement. Clearly dead. The

shining fragments of his half-bottle of whisky scattered the paving slabs around him, and the sharp smell of the spilt spirit mixed uneasily with the pervading diesel.

'He fell. He fell.' The screaming woman was on the edge of hysterics and couldn't stop shouting. 'He fell. I saw him. From up there. He fell.'

Luke-John said 'Christ' several times and looked badly shocked. Derry shook out a whole lot of paper clips on to his desk and absentmindedly put them back one by one.

'You're sure he was dead?' he said.

'His office was seven floors up.'

'Yeah.' He shook his head disbelievingly. 'Poor old boy.' Nil nisi bonum. A sharp change of attitude.

Luke-John looked out of the *Blaze* window and down along the street. The smashed remains of Bert Checkov had been decently removed. The pavement had been washed. People tramped unknowingly across the patch where he had died.

'He was drunk,' Luke-John said. 'Worse than usual.'

He and Derry made a desultory start on the afternoon work. I had no need to stay as the editor had OK'd my copy, but I hung around anyway for an hour or two, not ready to go.

They had said in Bert's office that he came back paralytic from lunch and simply fell out of the window. Two girl secretaries saw him. He was taking a drink out of the neck of the bottle of whisky, and he suddenly staggered against the window, which swung open, and he toppled out. The bottom of the window was at hip height. No trouble at all for someone as drunk as Bert.

I remembered the desperation behind the bit of advice he had given me.

And I wondered.

CHAPTER TWO

Three things immediately struck you about the girl who opened the stockbroker Tudor door at Virginia Water. First, her poise. Second, her fashion sense. Third, her colour. She had honey-toast skin, large dark eyes, and a glossy shoulder-length bounce of black hair. A slightly broad nose and a mouth to match enhanced a landscape in which Negro and Caucasian genes had conspired together to do a grand job.

'Good afternoon,' I said. 'I'm James Tyrone. I telephoned . . .'

'Come in,' she nodded. 'Harry and Sarah should be back at any minute.'

'They are still playing golf?'

'Mm.' She turned, smiled slightly, and gestured me into the house. 'Still finishing lunch, I expect.'

It was three thirty-five. Why not?

She led me through the hall (well-polished parquet, careful flowers, studded leather umbrella stand) into a chintz and chrysanthemum sitting-room. Every window in the house was a clutter of diamond-shaped leaded lights which might have had some point when glass could only be made in six-inch squares and had to be joined together to get anywhere. The modern imitation obscured the light and the view and was bound to infuriate window cleaners. Harry and Sarah had opted also for uncovered dark oak beams with machine-made chisel marks. The single picture on the plain cream walls made a wild contrast: a modern impressionistic abstract of some cosmic explosion, with the oils stuck on in lumps.

'Sit down.' She waved a graceful hand at a thickly cushioned sofa. 'Like a drink?'

'No, thank you.'

'Don't journalists drink all day?'

'If you drink and write, the writing isn't so hot.'

'Ah yes,' she said, 'Dylan Thomas said he had to be stone cold for any good to come of it.'

'Different class,' I smiled.

'Same principle.'

'Absolutely.'

She gave me a long inspection, her head an inch tilted to one side and her green dress lying in motionless folds down her slender body. Terrific legs in the latest in stockings ended in shiny green shoes with gold buckles, and the only other accessory on display was a broad-strapped gold watch on her left wrist.

'You'll know me again,' she said.

I nodded. Her body moved subtly inside the green dress.

She said slowly, with more than simple meaning. 'And I'll know you.'

Her voice, face, and manner were quite calm. The brief flash of intense sexual awareness could have been my imagination. Certainly her next remark held no undertone and no invitation.

'Do you *like* horses?'

'Yes, I do,' I said.

'Six months ago I would have said the one place I would never go would be to a race meeting.'

'But you go now?'

'Since Harry won Egocentric in that raffle, life has changed in this little neck of the woods.'

'That,' I said, 'is exactly what I want to write about.'

I was on *Tally* business. Background to the Lamplighter. My choice of untypical racehorse owners, Harry and Sarah Hunterson, came back at that point from their Sunday golf-course lunch, sweeping in with them a breeze compounded of healthy links air, expensive cigar smoke, and half-digested gin.

Harry was big, sixtyish, used to authority, heavily charming, and unshakably Tory. I guessed that he read the *Telegraph* and drove a three-litre Jaguar. With automatic transmission, of course. He gave me a hearty handshake and said he was glad to see his niece had been looking after me.

'Yes, thank you.'

Sarah said, 'Gail dear, you didn't give Mr Tyrone a drink.'

'He didn't want one.'

The two women were coolly nice to each other in civilized voices. Sarah must have been about thirty years older, but she had worked hard at keeping nature at bay. Everything about her looked careful, from the soft gold rinse via the russet-coloured dress to the chunky brown golfing shoes. Her well-controlled shape owed much to the drinking man's diet, and only a deep sag under the chin gave the game away. Neither golf nor gin had dug wrinkles anywhere except round her eyes. Her mouth still had fullness and shape. The wrappings were good enough to hold out hopes of a spark-striking mind, but these proved unrealistic. Sarah was all-of-a-piece, with attitudes and opinions as tidy and well-ordered and as imitative as her house.

Harry was easy to interview in the aftermath of the nineteenth hole.

'I bought this raffle ticket at the Golf Club dance, you see. Some chap was there selling them, a friend of a friend, you know, and I gave him a quid. Well, you know how it is at a dance. For charity, he said. I thought a quid was a bit steep for a raffle ticket, even if it was for a horse. Though I didn't want a horse, mind you. Last thing I wanted. And then damn me if I didn't go and win it. Bit of a problem, eh? To suddenly find yourself saddled with a racehorse?' He laughed, expecting a reward for his little joke.

I duly obliged. Sarah and Gail were both wearing the expressions which meant they had heard him say saddled with a racehorse so often that they had to grit their teeth now at each repetition.

'Would you mind,' I said, 'telling me something of your background and history?'

'Life story, eh?' He laughed loudly, looking from Sarah to Gail to collect their approval. His head was heavily handsome though a shade too fleshy round the neck. The bald sunburned crown and the well-disciplined moustache suited him. Thread veins made circular patches of colour on his cheeks. 'Life story,' he repeated. 'Where shall I start?'

'Start from birth,' I said, 'and go on from there.'

Only the very famous who have done it too often, or the extremely introverted, or the sheer bloody-minded, can resist such an invitation. Harry's eyes lit up, and he launched forth with enthusiasm.

Harry had been born in a Surrey suburb in a detached house a size or two smaller than the one he now owned. He had been to a day school and then a minor public school and was turned down by the army because as soon as he left school he had pleurisy. He went to work in the City, in the head office of a finance company, and had risen from junior clerk to director, on the way using occasional snippets of information to make himself modest capital gains via the stockmarket. Nothing shady, nothing rash: but enough so that there should be no drop in his standard of living when he retired.

He married at twenty-four and five years later a

lorry rammed his car and killed his wife, his three-year-old daughter, and his widowed mother. For fifteen years, much in demand at dinner parties, Harry 'looked around'. Then he met Sarah in some Conservative Party committee rooms where they were doing voluntary work addressing pamphlets for a by-election, and they had married three months later. Below the confident fruitiness of successful Harry's voice there was an echo of the motivation of this second marriage. Harry had begun to feel lonely.

As lives went, Harry's had been uneventful. No *Blaze* material in what he had told me, and precious little for *Tally*. Resignedly, I asked him if he intended to keep Egocentric indefinitely.

'Yes, yes, I think so,' he said. 'He has made quite a remarkable difference to us.'

'In what way?'

'It puts them several notches up in lifemanship,' Gail said coolly. 'Gives them something to boast about in pubs.'

We all looked at her. Such was her poise that I found it impossible to tell whether she meant to be catty or teasing, and from his uncertain expression, so did her uncle. There was no ducking it, however, that she had hit to the heart of things, and Sarah smoothly punished her for it.

'Gail dear, would you go and make tea for all of us?'

Gail's every muscle said she would hate to. But she stood up ostentatiously slowly, and went.

'A dear girl,' Sarah said. 'Perhaps sometimes a little trying.' Insincerity took all warmth out of her smile, and she found it necessary to go on, to make an explanation that I guessed she rushed into with every stranger at the first opportunity.

'Harry's sister married a barrister . . . such a clever man, you know . . . but, well . . . *African*.'

'Yes,' I said.

'Of course we're *very* fond of Gail, and as her parents have gone back to his country since it became independent, and as she was born in England and wanted to stay here, well, we . . . well, she lives here with us.'

'Yes,' I said again. 'That must be very nice for her.'

Sad, I thought, that they felt any need to explain. Gail didn't need it.

'She teaches at an art school in Victoria,' Harry added. 'Fashion drawing.'

'Fashion *design*,' Sarah corrected him. 'She's really quite good at it. Her pupils win prizes, and things like that.' There was relief in her voice now that I understood, and she was prepared to be generous. To do her justice, considering the far-back embedded prejudices she clearly suffered from, she had made a successful effort. But a pity the effort showed.

'And you,' I said, 'how about your life? And what do you think of Egocentric?'

She said apologetically that her story wasn't as interesting as Harry's. Her first husband, an optician, had died a year before she met Harry, and all she had done, apart from short excursions into voluntary work, was keep house for the two of them. She was glad Harry had won the horse, she liked going to the races as an owner, she thought it exciting to bet, but ten shillings was her usual, and she and Gail had found it quite fun inventing Harry's racing colours.

'What are they?'

'White with scarlet and turquoise question marks, turquoise sleeves, red cap.'

'They sound fine,' I smiled. 'I'll look out for them.'

Harry said his trainer was planning to fit in one more race for Egocentric before the Lamplighter, and maybe I would see him then. Maybe I would, I said, and Gail brought in the tea.

Harry and Sarah rapidly downed three cups each, simultaneously consulted their watches, and said it was time to be getting along to the Murrows' for drinks.

'I don't think I'll come,' Gail said. 'Tell them thanks, but I have got some work to do. But I'll come and fetch you, if you like, if you think it might be better not to drive home. Give me a ring when you're ready.'

The Murrow drinks on top of the golf club gin were a breathalyser hazard in anyone's book. Harry and Sarah nodded and said they would appreciate it.

'Before you go,' I said, 'could you let me see any newspaper cuttings you have? And any photographs?'

'Certainly, certainly,' Harry agreed. 'Gail will show them to you, won't you, honey? Must dash now, old chap, the Murrows, you know . . . President of the golf club. Nice to have met you. Hope you've got all the gen you need . . . don't hesitate to call if you want to know anything else.'

'Thank you,' I said, but he was gone before I finished. They went upstairs and down, and shut the front door, and drove away. The house settled into quiet behind them.

'They're not exactly alcoholic,' Gail said. 'They just go eagerly from drink to drink.'

Gail's turn to explain. But in her voice, only objectivity: no faintest hint of apology, as there had been in Sarah's.

'They enjoy life,' I said.

Gail's eyebrows rose. 'Do you know,' she said, 'I suppose they do. I've never really thought about it.'

Self-centred, I thought. Cool. Unaffectionate. Everything I disliked in a woman. Everything I needed one to be. Much too tempting.

'Do you want to see those photographs?' she asked.

'Yes, please.'

She fetched an expensive leather folder and we went through them one by one. Nothing in the few clippings that I hadn't learnt already. None of the photographs were arresting enough for *Tally*. I said I'd come back one day soon, with a photographer. Gail put the folder away and I stood up to go.

'It'll be two hours yet before they ring up from the Murrows. Stay and have that drink now?'

I looked at my watch. There was a train every thirty minutes. I supposed I could miss the next. There was Elizabeth. And there was Gail. And it was only an hour.

'Yes,' I said. 'I will.'

She gave me beer and brought one for herself. I sat down again on the sofa and she folded herself gracefully on to a large velvet cushion on the floor.

'You're married, of course?'

'Yes,' I agreed.

'The interesting-looking ones always are.'

'Then why aren't you?'

Her teeth flashed liquid white in an appreciative smile. 'Ah . . . marriage can wait.'

'How long?' I asked.

'I suppose . . . until I find a man I can't bear to part with.'

'You've parted with quite a few?'

'Quite a few.' She nodded and sipped her beer, and looked at me over the rim. 'And you? Are you faithful to your wife?'

I felt myself blink. I said carefully, 'Most of the time.'

'But not always?'

'Not always.'

After a long considering pause she said one short word.

'Good.'

'And is that,' I asked, 'a philosophic comment, or a proposition?'

She laughed. 'I just like to know where I stand.'

'Clear eyed and wide awake . . .?'

'I hate muddle,' she nodded.

'And emotional muddle especially?'

'You're so right.'

She had never loved, I thought. Sex, often. Love, never. Not what I liked, but what I wanted. I battened down the insidious whisper and asked her, like a good journalist, about her job.

'It serves.' She shrugged. 'You get maybe one authentic talent in every hundred students. Mostly their ambition is five times more noticeable than their ideas.'

'Do you design clothes yourself?'

'Not for the rag trade. Some for myself, and for Sarah, and for the school. I prefer to teach. I like being able to turn vaguely artistic ignorance into competent workmanship.'

'And to see your influences all along Oxford Street?'

She nodded, her eyes gleaming with amusement. 'Five of the biggest dress manufacturers now have old students of mine on their design staff. One of them is so individual that I can spot his work every time in the shop windows.'

'You like power,' I said.

'Who doesn't?'

'Heady stuff.'

'All power corrupts?' She was sarcastic.

'Each to his own corruption,' I said mildly. 'What's yours, then?'

She laughed. 'Money, I guess. There's a chronic shortage of the folding stuff in all forms of teaching.'

'So you make do with power.'

'If you can't have everything,' she nodded, 'you make do with *something*.'

I looked down into my beer, unable to stop the contraction I could feel in my face. Her words so completely summed up my perennial position. After eleven years I was less resigned to it than ever.

'What are you thinking about?' she asked.

'Taking you to bed.'

She gasped. I looked up from the flat brown liquid ready for any degree of feminine outrage. I could have mistaken her.

It seemed I hadn't. She was laughing. Pleased.

'That's pretty blunt.'

'Mm.'

I put down the beer and stood up, smiling. 'Time to go,' I said, 'I've a train to catch.'

'After that? You can't go after that.'

'Especially after that.'

For answer she stood up beside me, took hold of my hand, and put my fingers into the gold ring at the top of the zipper down the front of her dress.

'Now go home,' she said.

'We've only known each other three hours,' I protested.

'You were aware of me after three minutes.'

I shook my head. 'Three seconds.'

Her teeth gleamed. 'I like strangers.'

I pulled the ring downwards and it was clearly what she wanted.

Harry and Sarah had a large white fluffy rug in front of their fireplace. I imagined it was not the first time Gail had lain on it. She was brisk, graceful, unembarrassed. She stripped off her stockings and shoes, shook off the dress, and stepped out of the diminutive green bra and panties underneath it. Her tawny skin looked warm in the gathering dusk, and her shape took the breath away.

She gave me a marvellous time. A generous lover as well as practised. She knew when to touch lightly, and when to be vigorous. She had strong internal muscles, and she knew how to use them. I took her with passionate gratitude, a fair substitute for love.

When we had finished I lay beside her on the rug and felt the released tension weighing down my limbs in a sort of heavy languorous weakness. The world was a million light-years away and I was in no hurry for it to come closer.

'Wow,' she said, half breathless, half laughing. 'Boy, you sure needed that.'

'Mm.'

'Doesn't your wife let you . . .?'

Elizabeth, I thought. Oh God, Elizabeth. I must sometimes. Just sometimes.

The old weary tide of guilt washed back. The world closed in.

I sat up and stared blindly across the darkening room. It apparently struck Gail that she had been less than tactful, because she got up with a sigh and put her clothes on again, and didn't say another word.

For better or worse, I thought bitterly. For richer, for poorer. In sickness and in health keep thee only unto her as long as you both shall live. I will, I said.

An easy vow, the day I made it. I hadn't kept it. Gail was the fourth girl in eleven years. The first for nearly three.

'You'll miss your train,' she observed prosaically, 'if you sit there much longer.'

I looked at my watch, which was all I had on. Fifteen minutes.

She sighed. 'I'll drive you along to the station.'

We made it with time to spare. I stepped out of the car and politely thanked her for the lift.

'Will I see you again?' she said. Asking for information. Showing no anxiety. Looking out at me through the open window of the estate car outside Virginia Water station she was giving a close imitation of any suburban wife doing the train run. A long cool way from the rough and tumble on the rug. Switch on, switch off. The sort of woman I needed.

'I don't know,' I said indecisively. The signal at the end of the platform went green.

'Goodbye,' she said calmly.

'Do Harry and Sarah,' I asked carefully, 'always play golf on Sundays?'

She laughed, the yellow station lighting flashing on teeth and eyes.

'Without fail.'

'Maybe . . .'

'Maybe you'll ring, and maybe you won't.' She nodded. 'Fair enough. And maybe I'll be in, and maybe I won't.' She gave me a lengthy look which was half smile and half amused detachment. She wouldn't weep if I didn't return. She would accommodate me if I did. 'But don't leave it too long, if you're coming back.'

She wound up the window and drove off without a wave, without a backward glance.

The green electric worm of a train slid quietly into the station to take me home. Forty minutes to Waterloo. Underground to King's Cross. Three-quarters of a mile to walk. Time to enjoy the new ease in my body. Time to condemn it. Too much of my life was a battlefield in which conscience and desire fought constantly for the upper hand: and whichever of them won, it left me the loser.

Elizabeth's mother said with predictable irritation, 'You're late.'

'I'm sorry.'

I watched the jerks of her crossly pulling on her

gloves. Overcoat and hat had already been in place when I walked in.

'You have so little consideration. It'll be nearly eleven when I get back.'

I didn't answer.

'You're selfish. All men are selfish.'

There was no point in agreeing with her, and no point in arguing. A disastrous and short-lived marriage had left hopeless wounds in her mind which she had done her best to pass on to her only child. Elizabeth, when I first met her, had been pathologically scared of men.

'We've had our supper,' my mother-in-law said. 'I've stacked the dishes for Mrs Woodward.'

Nothing could be more certainly relied upon to upset Mrs Woodward than a pile of congealed plates first thing on Monday morning.

'Fine,' I said, smiling falsely.

'Goodbye, Elizabeth,' she called.

'Goodbye, Mother.'

I opened the door for her and got no thanks.

'Next Sunday, then,' she said.

'That'll be nice.'

She smiled acidly, knowing I didn't mean it. But since she worked as a receptionist-hostess in a health farm all week, Sunday was her day for seeing Elizabeth. Most weeks I wished she would leave us alone, but that Sunday it had set me free to go to Virginia

Water. From the following Sunday, and what I might do with it, I wrenched my thoughts away.

When she had gone I walked across to Elizabeth and kissed her on the forehead.

'Hi.'

'Hi yourself,' she said. 'Did you have a good afternoon?'

Straight jab.

'Mm.'

'Good . . . Mother's left the dishes again,' she said.

'Don't worry, I'll do them.'

'What would I do without you!'

We both knew the answer to that. Without me, she would have to spend the rest of her life in a hospital ward, a prisoner with no possibility of escape. She couldn't breathe without the electrically driven pump which hummed at the foot of her high bed. She couldn't cut up her own food or take herself to the bathroom. Elizabeth, my wife, was ninety per cent paralysed from poliomyelitis.

CHAPTER THREE

We lived over a row of lock-up garages in a mews behind Gray's Inn Road. A development company had recently knocked down the old buildings opposite, letting in temporary acres of evening sunshine, and was now at the girder stage of a block of flats. If these made our place too dark and shut in when they were done, I would have to find us somewhere else. Not a welcome prospect. We had moved twice before and it was always difficult.

Since race trains mostly ran from London, and to cut my travelling time down to a minimum, we lived two minutes' walk from the *Blaze*. It had proved much better, in London, to live in a backwater than in a main street: in the small mews community the neighbours all knew about Elizabeth and looked up to her window and waved when they passed, and a lot of them came upstairs for a chat and to bring our shopping.

The district nurse came every morning to do Elizabeth's vapour rubs to prevent bed sores, and I did them in the evenings. Mrs Woodward, a semi-trained but unqualified nurse, came Mondays to Saturdays from nine-thirty to six, and was helpful about staying longer if necessary. One of our main troubles was that Elizabeth could not be left alone in the flat even for five minutes in case there was an electricity failure. If the main current stopped, we could switch her breathing pump over to a battery, and we could also operate it by hand: but someone had to be there to do it quickly. Mrs Woodward was kind, middle-aged, reliable, and quiet, and Elizabeth liked her. She was also very expensive, and since the welfare state turns a fish-faced blind eye on incapacitated wives, I could claim not even so much as a tax allowance for Mrs Woodward's essential services. We had to have her, and she kept us poor: and that was that.

In one of the garages below the flat stood the old Bedford van which was the only sort of transport of any use to us. I had had it adapted years ago with a stretcher-type bed so that it would take Elizabeth, pump, batteries, and all, and although it meant too much upheaval to go out in it every week, it did sometimes give her a change of scenery and some country air. We had tried two holidays by the sea in a caravan, but she had felt uncomfortable and insecure, and both times it had rained, so we didn't bother any more. Day trips were enough, she said. And although she enjoyed them, they exhausted her.

Her respirator was the modern cuirass type: a Spirashell: not the old totally enclosed iron lung. The Spirashell itself slightly resembled the breastplate of a suit of armour. It fitted over the entire front of her chest, was edged with a thick roll of latex, and was fastened by straps round her body. Breathing was really a matter of suction. The pump, which was connected to the Spirashell by a thick flexible hose, alternately made a partial vacuum inside the shell, and then drove air back in again. The vacuum period pulled Elizabeth's chest wall outwards, allowing air to flow downwards into her lungs. The air-in period collapsed her chest and pushed the used breaths out again.

Far more comfortable, and easier for everyone caring for her than a box respirator, the Spirashell had only one drawback. Try how we might, and however many scarves and cardigans we might stuff in round the edges, between the latex roll and her nightdress, it was eternally draughty. As long as the air in the flat was warm it no longer worried her. Summer was all right. But the cold air continually blowing on to her chest not surprisingly distressed her. Cold also reduced to nil the small movements she had retained in her left hand and wrist, and on which she depended for everything. Our heating bills were astronomical.

In the nine and a half years since I had extricated her from hospital we had acquired almost every gadget invented. Wires and pulleys trailed all round the flat. She could read books, draw the curtains, turn on and off the lights, the radio, and television, use the telephone, and type letters. An electric box of tricks called

Possum did most of these tasks. Others worked on a system of levers set off by the feather-light pressure of her left forefinger. Our latest triumph was an electric pulley which raised and rotated her left elbow and forearm, enabling her to eat some things on her own, without always having to be fed. And with a clipped-on electric toothbrush, she could now brush her own teeth.

I slept on a divan across the room from her with a bell beside my ear for when she needed me in the night. There were bells, too, in the kitchen and bathroom, and the tiny room I used for writing in, which with the large sitting-room made up the whole of the flat.

We had been married three years, and we were both twenty-four, when Elizabeth caught polio. We were living in Singapore, where I had a junior job in the Reuter's office, and we flew home for what was intended to be a month's leave.

Elizabeth felt ill on the flight. The light hurt her eyes, and she had a headache like a rod up the back of her neck, and a stabbing pain in her chest. She walked off the aircraft at Heathrow and collapsed halfway across the tarmac, and that was the last time she ever stood on her feet.

Our affection for each other had survived everything that followed. Poverty, temper, tears, desperate frustrations. We had emerged after several years into our comparative calms of a settled home, a good job, a reasonably well-ordered existence. We were firm close friends.

But not lovers.

We had tried, in the beginning. She could still feel of course, since polio attacks only the motor nerves, and leaves the sensory nerves intact. But she couldn't breath for more than three or four minutes if we took the Spirashell right off, and she couldn't bear any weight or pressure on any part of her wasted body. When I said, after two or three hopeless attempts, that we would leave it for a while she had smiled at me with what I saw to be enormous relief, and we had rarely even mentioned the subject since. Her early upbringing seemed to have easily reconciled her to a sexless existence. Her three years of thawing into a satisfying marriage might never have happened.

On the day after my trip to Virginia Water I set off as soon as Mrs Woodward came and drove the van north-east out of London and into deepest Essex. My quarry this time was a farmer who had bred gold dust in his fields in the shape of Tiddely Pom, ante-post favourite for the Lamplighter Gold Cup.

Weeds luxuriantly edged the pot-holed road which led from a pair of rotting gateless gateposts into Victor Roncey's farmyard. The house itself, an undistinguished arrangement of mud-coloured bricks, stood in a drift of sodden unswept leaves and stared blankly from symmetrical grubby windows. Colourless paint peeled quietly from the woodwork and no smoke rose from the chimneys.

I knocked on the back door, which stood half open, and called through a small lobby into the house, but there was no reply. A clock ticked with a loud cheap mechanism. A smell of wellington boots richly acquainted with cowpat vigorously assaulted the nose. Someone had dumped a parcel of meat on the edge of the kitchen table from which a thread of watery blood, having by-passed the newspaper wrapping, was making a small pink pool on the floor.

Turning away from the house I wandered across the untidy yard and peered into a couple of outbuildings. One contained a tractor covered with about six years' mud. In another, a heap of dusty-looking coke rubbed shoulders with a jumbled stack of old broken crates and sawn-up branches of trees. A larger shed housed dirt and cobwebs and nothing else.

While I hovered in the centre of the yard wondering how far it was polite to investigate, a large youth in a striped knitted cap with a scarlet pom-pom came round a corner at the far end. He also wore a vast sloppy pale blue sweater, and filthy jeans tucked into heavy-weight gum boots. Fair haired, with a round weather-beaten face, he looked cheerful and uncomplicated.

'Hullo,' he said. 'You want something?' His voice was light and pleasant, with a touch of local accent.

'I'm looking for Mr Roncey.'

'He's round the roads with the horses. Better call back later.'

'How long will he be?'

'An hour, maybe,' he shrugged.

'I'll wait, then, if you don't mind,' I said, gesturing towards my van.

'Suit yourself.'

He took six steps towards the house and then stopped, turned round, and came back.

'Hey, you wouldn't be that chap who phoned?'

'Which chap?'

'James Tyrone?'

'That's right.'

'Well, for crying out loud why didn't you say so? I thought you were a traveller . . . come on into the house. Do you want some breakfast?'

'Breakfast?'

He grinned. 'Yeah. I know it's nearly eleven. I get up before six. Feel peckish again by now.'

He led the way into the house through the back door, did nothing about the dripping meat, and added to the wellington smell by clumping across the floor to the farthest door, which he opened.

'Ma?' he shouted. 'Ma.'

'She's around somewhere,' he said, shrugging and coming back. 'Never mind. Want some eggs?'

I said no, but when he reached out a half-acre frying pan and filled it with bacon I changed my mind.

'Make the coffee,' he said, pointing.

I found mugs, powdered coffee, sugar, milk, kettle and spoons all standing together on a bench alongside the sink.

'My ma,' he explained grinning, 'is a great one for the time and motion bit.'

He fried six eggs expertly and gave us three each, with a chunk of new white bread on the side.

We sat at the kitchen table, and I'd rarely tasted anything so good. He ate solidly and drank coffee, then pushed his plate away and lit a cigarette.

'I'm Peter,' he said. 'It isn't usually so quiet around here, but the kids are at school and Pat's out with Pa.'

'Pat?'

'My brother. The jockey of the family. Point-to-points, mostly, though. I don't suppose you would know of him?'

'I'm afraid not.'

'I read your column,' he said. 'Most weeks.'

'That's nice.'

He considered me, smoking, while I finished the eggs. 'You don't talk much, for a journalist.'

'I listen,' I said.

He grinned. 'That's a point.'

'Tell me about Tiddely Pom, then.'

'Hell, no. You'll have to get Pa or Pat for that. They're crazy on the horses. I just run the farm.' He watched my face carefully. I guessed for surprise, since in spite of being almost my height he was still very young.

'You're sixteen?' I suggested.

'Yeah.' He sniffed, disgusted. 'Waste of effort, though, really.'

'Why?'

'Why? Because of the bloody motorway, that's why. They've nearly finished that bloody three-lane monster and it passes just over there, the other side of our ten-acre field.' He gestured towards the window with his cigarette. 'Pa's going raving mad wondering if Tiddely Pom'll have a nervous breakdown when those heavy lorries start thundering past. He's been trying to sell the place for two years, but no one will have it, and you can't blame them, can you?' Gloom settled on him temporarily. 'Then, see, you never know when they'll pinch more of our land, they've had fifty acres already, and it doesn't give you much heart to keep the place right, does it?'

'I guess not,' I said.

'They've talked about knocking our house down,' he went on. 'Something about it being in the perfect position for a service station with restaurants and a vast car park and another slip road to Bishops Stortford. The only person who's pleased about the road is my brother Tony, and he wants to be a rally driver. He's eleven. He's a nut.'

There was a scrunch and clatter of hooves outside, coming nearer. Peter and I got to our feet and went out into the yard, and watched three horses plod up the bumpy gravel drive and rein to a halt in front of us. The rider of the leading horse slid off, handed his reins to the second, and came towards us. A trim, wiry man in his forties with thick brown hair and a mustard-coloured moustache.

'Mr Tyrone?'

I nodded. He gave me a brisk hard handshake in harmony with his manner and voice and then stood back to allow me a clear view of the horses.

'That's Tiddely Pom, that bay.' He pointed to the third horse, ridden by a young man very like Peter, though perhaps a size smaller. 'And Pat, my son.'

'A fine-looking horse,' I said insincerely. Most owners expected praise: but Tiddely Pom showed as much high quality to the naked eye as an uncut diamond. A common head, slightly U-necked on a weak shoulder, and herring-gutted into the bargain. He looked just as uncouth at home as he did on a racecourse.

'Huh,' snorted Roncey. 'He's not. He's a doer, not a looker. Don't try and butter me up. I don't take to it.'

'Fair enough,' I said mildly. 'Then he's got a common head and neck, a poor shoulder, and doesn't fill the eye behind the saddle either.'

'That's better. So you do know what you're talking about. Walk him round the yard, Pat.'

Pat obliged. Tiddely Pom stumbled around with the floppy gait that once in a while denotes a champion. This horse, bred from a thoroughbred hunter mare by a premium stallion, was a spectacular jumper endowed with a speed to be found nowhere in his pedigree. When an ace of this sort turned up unexpectedly it took the owner almost as long as the public to realize it. The whole racing industry was unconsciously geared against the belief that twenty-two carat stars could come from tiny owner-trained stables. It had taken Tiddely Pom three seasons to become known, where from a big fashionable public stable he would have been newsworthy in his first race.

'When I bred him I was hoping for a point-to-point horse for the boys,' Roncey said. 'So we ran him all one season in point-to-points and apart from one time Pat fell off he didn't get beat. Then last year we thought we would have a go in hunter 'chases as well, and he went and won the Foxhunters' at Cheltenham.'

'I remember that,' I said.

'Yes. So last year we tried him in open handicaps, smallish ones . . .'

'And he won four out of six,' I concluded for him.

'It's your job to know, I suppose. Pat,' he shouted. 'Put him back in his box.' He turned to me again. 'Like to see the others?'

I nodded, and we followed Pat and the other two horses across the yard and round the corner from which Peter had originally appeared.

Behind a ramshackle barn stood a neat row of six well-kept wooden horse boxes with shingle roofs and newly painted black doors. However run down the rest of the farm might be, the stable department was in tip-top shape. No difficulty in seeing where the farmer's heart lay: with his treasure.

'Well now,' Roncey said. 'We've only the one other racehorse, really, and that's Klondyke, that I was riding just now. He ran in hunter 'chases in the spring. Didn't do much good, to be honest.' He walked along to the second box from the far end, led the horse in and tied it up. When he took the saddle off I saw that Klondyke was a better shape than Tiddely Pom, which was saying little enough, but the health in his coat was conspicuous.

'He looks well,' I commented.

'Eats his head off,' said Roncey, dispassionately, 'and he can stand a lot of work, so we give it to him.'

'One-paced,' observed Pat regretfully over my shoulder. 'Can't quicken. Pity. We won just the two point-to-points with him. No more.'

There was the faintest glimmer of satisfaction in the laconic voice, and I glanced at him sideways. He saw me looking and wiped the expression off his face but not before I had seen for certain that he had mixed feelings about the horses' successes. While they progressed to National Hunt racing proper, he didn't. Older amateur riders had been engaged, and then professionals. The father–son relationship had needles in it.

'What do you have in the other boxes?' I asked Roncey, as he shut Klondyke's door.

'My old grey hunter at the end, and two hunter mares here, both in foal. This one, Piglet, she's the dam of Tiddely Pom of course; she's in foal to the same sire again.'

Unlikely, I thought, that lightning would strike twice.

'You'll sell the foal,' I suggested.

He sniffed. 'She's in the farm accounts.'

I grinned to myself. Farmers could train their horses and lose the cost in the general farm accounts, but if they sold one it then came under the heading of income and was taxed accordingly. If Roncey sold either Tiddely Pom or his full brother, nearly half would go to the Revenue.

'Turn the mares out, Joe,' he said to his third rider, a patient-looking old man with skin like bark, and we watched while he set them loose in the nearest field. Peter was standing beside the gate with Pat: bigger, more assured, with far fewer knots in his personality.

'Fine sons,' I said to Roncey.

His mouth tightened. He had no pride in them. He made no reply at all to my fishing compliment, but instead said, 'We'll go into the house and you can ask me anything you want to know. For a magazine, you said?'

I nodded.

'Pat,' he shouted. 'You give these three horses a good strapping and feed them and let Joe get on with the hedging. Peter, you've got work to do. Go and do it.'

Both his boys gave him the blank acquiescing look

which covers seething rebellion. There was a perceptible pause before they moved off with their calm accepting faces. Lids on a lot of steam. Maybe one day Roncey would be scalded.

He led the way briskly back across the yard and into the kitchen. The meat still lay there dripping. Roncey by-passed it and gestured me to follow him through the far door into a small dark hall.

'Madge?' he shouted. 'Madge?'

Father had as little success as son. He shrugged in the same way and led me into a living-room as well worn and untidy as the rest of the place. Drifts of clutter, letters, newspapers, clothing, toys, and indiscriminate bits of junk lay on every flat surface, including the chairs and the floor. There was a vase of dead and dessiccated chrysanthemums on a window sill, and some brazen cobwebs networked the ceiling. Cold ash from the day before filled the grate. A toss-up, I thought, whether one called the room lived-in or squalid.

'Sit down if you can find somewhere,' Roncey said. 'Madge lets the boys run wild in the house. Not firm enough. I won't have it outside, of course.'

'How many do you have?'

'Boys? Five.'

'And a daughter?' I asked.

'No,' he said abruptly. 'Five boys.'

The thought didn't please him. 'Which magazine?'

'*Tally*,' I said. 'They want background stories to the

Lamplighter, and I thought I would give the big stables a miss and shine a bit of the spotlight on someone else for a change.'

'Yes, well,' he said defensively, 'I've been written up before, you know.'

'Of course,' I said soothingly.

'About the Lamplighter, too. I'll show you.' He jumped up and went over to a knee-hole desk, pulled out one of the side drawers bodily, and brought it across to where I sat at one end of the sofa. He put the drawer in the centre, swept a crumpled jersey, two beaten-up dinky cars and a gutted brown paper parcel on to the floor, and seated himself in the space.

The drawer contained a heap of clippings and photographs all thrust in together. No careful sticking into expensive leather folders, like the Huntersons.

My mind leapt to Gail. I saw Roncey talking to me but I was thinking about her body. Her roundnesses. Her fragrant pigmented skin. Roncey was waiting for an answer and I hadn't heard what he'd asked.

'I'm sorry,' I said.

'I asked if you know Bert Checkov.' He was holding a lengthy clipping with a picture alongside and a bold headline, 'Back Tiddely Pom NOW.'

'Yes . . . and no,' I said uncertainly.

'How do you mean?' he said brusquely. 'I should have thought you would have known him, being in the same business.'

'I did know him. But he died. Last Friday.'

I took the clipping and read it while Roncey went through the motions of being shocked, with the indifference uppermost in his voice spoiling the effect.

Bert Checkov had gone to town with Tiddely Pom's chances in the Lamplighter. The way he saw it, the handicapper had been suffering from semi-blindness and mental blocks to put Tiddely Pom into the weights at ten stone seven, and all punters who didn't jump on the bandwagon instantly needed to be wet nursed. He thought the ante-post market would open with generous odds, but urged everyone to hurry up with their shirts, before the bookmakers woke up to the bonanza. Bert's pungent phraseology had given Roncey's horse more boost than a four stage rocket.

'I didn't know he'd written this,' I admitted. 'I missed it.'

'He rang me up only last Thursday and this was in the paper on Friday. That must have been the day you said he died. In point of fact I didn't expect it would appear. When he telephoned he was, to my mind, quite drunk.'

'It's possible,' I conceded.

'I wasn't best pleased about it either.'

'The article?'

'I hadn't got my own money on, do you see? And there he went, spoiling the price. When I rang up my bookmaker on Friday he wouldn't give me more than a hundred to eight, and today they've even made him favourite at eight to one, and there's still nearly three weeks to the race. Fair enough he's a good horse, but he's not Arkle. In point of fact I don't understand it.'

'You don't understand why Checkov tipped him?'

He hesitated. 'Not to that extent, then, let's say.'

'But you do hope to win?'

'Hope,' he said. 'Naturally, I hope to win. But it's the biggest race we've ever tried . . . I don't *expect* to win, do you see?'

'You've as good a chance as any,' I said. 'Checkov had his column to fill. The public won't read half-hearted stuff, you have to go all out for the positive statement.'

He gave me a small tight smile laced with a sneer for the soft option. A man with no patience or sympathy for anyone else's problems, not even his sons'.

The sitting-room door opened and a large woman in a sunflower dress came in. She had thick fair down on her legs but no stockings, and a pair of puffed ankles bulged over the edges of some battered blue bedroom slippers. Nevertheless she was very light on her feet and she moved slowly, so that her progress seemed to be a weightless drift: no mean feat considering she must have topped twelve stone.

A mass of fine light brown hair hung in an amorphous cloud round her head, from which a pair of dreamy eyes surveyed the world as though half asleep. Her face was soft and rounded, not young, but still in a way immature. Her fantasy life, I guessed uncharitably, was more real to her than the present. She had been far away in the past hour, much farther than upstairs.

'I didn't know you were in,' she said to Roncey.

He stood up several seconds after me. 'Madge, this is James Tyrone. I told you he was coming.'

'Did you?' She transferred her vague gaze to me. 'Carry on, then.'

'Where have you been?' Roncey said. 'Didn't you hear me calling?'

'Calling?' She shook her head. 'I was making the beds, of course.' She stood in the centre of the room, looking doubtfully around at the mess. 'Why didn't you light the fire?'

I glanced involuntarily at the heap of ashes in the grate, but she saw them as no obstacle at all. From a scratched oak box beside the hearth she produced three firelighters and a handful of sticks. These went on top of the ashes, which got only a desultory poke. She struck a match, lit the firelighters, and made a wigwam of coal. The new fire flared up good temperedly on the body of the old while Madge took the hearth brush and swept a few cinders out of sight behind a pile of logs.

Fascinated, I watched her continue with her housework. She drifted across to the dead flowers, opened the window, and threw them out. She emptied the water from the vase after them, then put it back on the window sill and shut the window.

From behind the sofa where Roncey and I sat she

pulled a large brown cardboard box. On the outside was stencilled Kellogg's Cornflakes, 12 ↔ Family Six and on the inside it was half filled with the same sort of jumble which was lying around the room. She wafted methodically around in a large circle taking everything up and throwing it just as it came into the box, a process which took approximately three minutes. She then pushed the box out of sight again behind the sofa and plumped up the seat cushions of two armchairs on her way to the door. The room, tidy and with the brightly blazing fire, looked staggeringly different. The cobwebs were still there but one felt it might be their turn tomorrow. Peter was right. Ma had got the time and motion kick completely buttoned up; and what did it matter if the motive was laziness.

Roncey insisted that I should stay to lunch and filled in the time beforehand with a brisk but endless account of all the horses he had ever owned. Over lunch, cold beef and pickles and cheese and biscuits served at two-thirty on the kitchen table, it was still he who did all the talking. The boys ate steadily in silence and Madge contemplated the middle distance with eyes which saw only the scenes going on in her head.

When I left shortly afterwards Pat asked for a lift into Bishops Stortford and braved his father's frown to climb into the front seat of the van. Roncey shook hands firmly as before and said he hoped to receive a free copy of *Tally*. 'Of course,' I said. But *Tally* were notoriously mean: I would have to send it myself.

He waved me out of the yard and told Pat brusquely to come straight back on the four o'clock bus, and we were barely out through the sagging gateposts before Pat unburdened himself of a chunk of bottled resentment.

'He treats us like children . . . Ma's no help, she never listens . . .'

'You could leave here,' I pointed out. 'You're what – nineteen?'

'Next month. But I can't leave and he knows it. Not if I want to race. I can't turn professional yet, I'm not well enough known and no one would put me up on their horses. I've got to start as an amateur and make a name for myself, Pa says so. Well, I couldn't be an amateur if I left home and got an ordinary job somewhere, I couldn't afford all the expenses and I wouldn't have any time.'

'A job in a stable . . .' I suggested.

'Do me a favour. The rules say you can't earn a salary in any capacity in a racing stable and ride as an amateur, not even if you're a secretary or an assistant or anything. It's bloody unfair. And don't say I could get a job as a lad and do my two and have a professional licence, of course I could. And how many lads ever get as far as jockeys, doing that? None. Absolutely none. You know that.'

I nodded.

'I do a lad's work now, right enough. Six horses, we've got, and I do the bloody lot. Old Joe's the only labour we've got on the whole farm, except us, believe it or not. Pa's always got a dozen jobs lined up for him. And I wouldn't mind the work, and getting practically no pay, I really wouldn't, if Pa would let me ride in anything except point-to-points, but he won't, he says I haven't enough experience, and if you ask me he's making bloody sure I never get enough experience . . . I'm absolutely fed up, I'll tell you straight.'

He brooded over his situation all the way into Bishops Stortford. A genuine grievance, I thought. Victor Roncey was not a father to help his sons get on.

CHAPTER FOUR

They held the inquest on Bert Checkov on that Monday afternoon. Verdict: Misadventure. Dead drunk he was, said the girl typists who saw him fall. Dead drunk.

And after he hit the pavement, just dead.

When I went into the office on Tuesday morning, Luke-John and Derry were discussing whether or not to go to the funeral on the Wednesday.

'Croxley,' Derry said. 'Where's that?'

'Near Watford,' I said. 'On the Metropolitan Line. A straight run into Farringdon Street.'

'What Fleet Street needs,' said Derry gloomily, 'is a tube station a lot nearer than blooming Farringdon. It's three-quarters of a mile if it's an inch.'

'If you're right, Ty, we can manage it easily,' Luke-John said authoritatively. 'We should all go, I think.'

Derry squinted at the small underground map in his diary. 'Croxley. Next to Watford. What do you know?'

I'd had a girl at Watford once. The second one. I'd spent a lot of time on the Metropolitan Line while

Elizabeth was under the impression I was extra busy in the *Blaze*. Guilt and deceit were old familiar travelling companions. From Watford, from Virginia Water, from wherever.

'Ty,' Luke-John was saying sharply.

'Huh?'

'The funeral is at two-thirty. An hour, say, to get there . . .?'

'Not me,' I said. 'There's this *Tally* article to be done. It'll take me at least another two days in interviews.'

He shrugged. 'I'd have thought . . .'

'What depths have you plumbed so far?' Derry asked. He was sitting with his feet up on the desk. No work in a Sunday paper on Tuesday.

'The Roncey family,' I said. 'Tiddely Pom.'

Derry sniffed. 'Ante-post favourite.'

'Will he be your tip?' I asked with interest.

'Shouldn't think so. He's won a few races but he hasn't beaten much of any class.'

'Bert tipped him strongly. Wrote a most emphatic piece about catching the odds now before they shorten. He wrote it last Thursday; it must have been straight after the handicap was published in the racing calendar: and it was in his paper on Friday. Roncey showed me the clipping. He said Bert was drunk when he rung up.'

Luke-John sighed. Derry said decisively, 'That does it, then. If Bert tipped him, I'm not going to.'

'Why not?'

'Bert's heavy long-distance tips were nearly always non-starters.'

Luke-John stretched his neck until the tendons stood out like strings, and massaged his nobbly larynx. 'Always the risk of that, of course. It happens to everyone.'

'Do you mean that seriously?' I asked Derry.

'Oh sure. Sorry about your *Tally* article and all that,' he grinned, 'but I'd say just about the time it's published you'll find Tiddely Pom has been taken out of the Lamplighter.'

Derry twiddled unconcernedly with a rubber band and Luke-John shuffled absentmindedly through some papers. Neither of them felt the shiver travelling down my spine.

'Derry,' I said. 'Are you sure?'

'Of what?'

'That Bert always tipped non-starters for big races.'

Derry snapped the band twice in his fingers. 'To be precise, if you want me to be precise, Bert tipped a higher percentage of big-race non-starters than anyone else in the street, and he has been at his best in this direction, or worst, or at any rate his most consistent, during the past year. He'd blow some horse up big, tell everyone to back it at once, and then wham, a day or two before the race it would be scratched.'

'I've never noticed,' said Luke-John forbiddingly, as if it couldn't have happened without.

Derry shrugged. 'Well, it's a fact. Now, if you want

to know something equally useless about that puffed-up Connersley of the *Sunday Hemisphere*, he has a weird habit of always tipping horses which start with his own initial, C. Delusions of grandeur, I imagine.'

'You're having us on,' Luke-John said.

Derry shook his head. 'Uhuh. I don't just sit here with my eyes shut, you know. I read the newspapers.'

'I think,' I said suddenly, 'I will fetch my typewriter.'

'Where is it?'

Over my shoulder on the way back to the door I said, 'Being cleaned.'

This time the typewriter was ready. I collected it and went farther along the street, to Bert's paper. Up in the lift, to Bert's department. Across the busy floor to the sports desk. Full stop beside the assistant sports editor, a constant racegoer, a long-known bar pal.

'Ty! What's the opposition doing here?'

'Bert Checkov,' I said.

We discussed him for a while. The assistant sports editor was hiding something. It showed in half-looks, unfinished gestures, an unsuccessfully smothered embarrassment. He said he was shocked, shattered, terribly distressed by Bert's death. He said everyone on the paper would miss him, the paper would miss him, they all felt his death was a great loss. He was lying.

I didn't pursue it. Could I, I asked tentatively, have a look at Bert's clippings book? I would very much like to reread some of his articles.

The assistant sports editor said kindly that I had little to learn from Bert Checkov or anyone else for that matter, but to go ahead. While he got back to work I sorted out the record racks at the side of the room and eventually found three brown paper clippings books with Bert's work stuck into the pages.

I took my typewriter out of its carrying case and left it lying on an inconspicuous shelf. The three clippings books went into the carrying case, though I had to squeeze to get it shut, and I walked quietly and unchallenged out of the building with my smuggled goods.

Luke-John and Derry goggled at the books of cuttings.

'How on earth did you get them out? And why on earth do you want them?'

'Derry,' I said, 'can now set about proving that Bert always tipped non-starters in big races.'

'You're crazy,' Luke-John said incredulously.

'No,' I said regretfully. 'If I'm right, the *Blaze* is on the edge of the sort of scandal it thrives on. A circulation explosion. And all by courtesy of the sports section.'

Luke-John's interest sharpened instantly from nil to needles.

'Don't waste time then, Derry. If Ty says there's a scandal, there's a scandal.'

Derry gave me a sidelong look. 'Our truffle hound on the scent, eh?' He took his feet off the desk and resignedly got to work checking what Bert had forecast against what had actually happened. More and more form books and racing calendars were brought out, and Derry's written lists slowly grew.

'All right,' he said at last. 'Here it is, just as I said. These books cover the last three years. Up till eighteen months ago he tipped runners and non-runners in about the same proportion as the rest of us poor slobs. Then he went all out suddenly for horses which didn't run when it came to the point. All in big races, which had ante-post betting.' He looked puzzled. 'It can't be just coincidence, I do see that. But I don't see the point.'

'Ty?' said Luke-John.

I shrugged. 'Someone has been working a fiddle.'

'Bert wouldn't.' His voice said it was unthinkable.

'I'd better take these books back before they miss them,' I said, packing them again into the typewriter case.

'Ty!' Luke-John sounded exasperated.

'I'll tell you when I come back,' I said.

There was no denunciation at Bert's office. I returned the books to their shelf and retrieved my typewriter, and thanked the assistant sports editor for his kindness.

'You still here? I thought you'd gone.' He waved a friendly hand. 'Any time.'

'All right,' said Luke-John truculently when I got

back to the *Blaze*. 'I won't believe Bert Checkov was party to any fiddle.'

'He sold his soul,' I said plainly. 'Like he told me not to.'

'Rubbish.'

'He sold his column. He wrote what he was told to write.'

'Not Bert. He was a newspaper man, one of the old school.'

I considered him. His thin face looked obstinate and pugnacious. Loyalty to an old friend was running very strong.

'Well then,' I said slowly, 'Bert wrote what he was forced to write.'

A good deal of the Morton tension subsided and changed course. He wouldn't help to uncover a scandal an old friend was responsible for, but he'd go the whole way to open up one he'd been the victim of.

'Clever beast,' said Derry under his breath.

'Who forced him?' Luke-John said.

'I don't know. Not yet. It might be possible to find out.'

'And *why?*'

'That's much easier. Someone has been making an ante-post book on a certainty. What Bert was doing . . . being forced to do . . . was persuading the public to part with their money.'

They both looked contemplative. I started again,

explaining more fully. 'Say a villain takes up bookmaking. It can happen, you know.'

Derry grinned. 'Say one villain hits on a jolly scheme for making illegal gains in a foolproof way with very little effort. He only works it on big races which have ante-post betting, because he needs at least three weeks to rake in enough to make it worth the risk. He chooses a suitable horse, and he forces Bert to tip it for all his column's worth. Right? So the public put their money on, and our villain sticks to every penny that comes his way. No need to cover himself against losses. He knows there won't be any. He knows he isn't going to have to pay out on that horse. He knows it's going to be scratched at or after the four-day forfeits. Very nice fiddle.'

After a short silence Derry said, 'How does he know?'

'Ah well,' I said, shrugging. 'That's another thing we'll have to find out.'

'I don't believe it,' Luke-John said sceptically. 'All that just because Bert tipped a few non-starters.'

Derry looked dubiously at the lists he had made. 'There were too many non-starters. There really were.'

'Yes,' I said.

'But you *can't* have worked out all that just from what I said, from just that simple casual remark . . .'

'No,' I agreed. 'There was something else, of course. It was something Bert himself said, last Friday, when I walked back with him from lunch. He wanted to give me a piece of advice.'

'That's right,' Derry said. 'He never came out with it.'

'Yes he did. He did indeed. With great seriousness. He told me not to sell my soul. Not to sell my column.'

'No,' Luke-John said.

'He said, "First they buy you and then they blackmail you." '

Luke-John said, 'No,' again automatically.

'He was very drunk,' I said. 'Much worse than usual. He called the advice he was giving me his famous last words. He went up in the lift with a half-bottle of whisky, he walked right across his office, he drank from the bottle, and without a pause he fell straight out of the window.'

Luke-John put his freckled fingers on his thin mouth and when he spoke his voice was low, protesting, and thick, 'No . . . my *God*.'

After leaving the *Blaze* I collected the van and drove down to a racing stable in Berkshire to interview the girl who looked after the best-known horse in the Lamplighter.

Zig Zag was a household name, a steeplechaser of immense reputation and popularity, automatic headline material: but any day the cracks would begin to show, since he would be turning eleven on January the first.

The Lamplighter, to my mind, would be his last bow as grand old man before the younger brigade shouldered him out. Until Bert Checkov had rammed home the telling difference in weights, Zig Zag, even allotted a punitive twelve stone ten pounds, had been the automatic choice for ante-post favourite.

His girl groom was earnest and devoted to him. In her twenties, unsophisticated, of middling intelligence, Sandy Willis's every sentence was packed with pithy stable language which she used unselfconsciously, and which contrasted touchingly with her essential innocence. She showed me Zig Zag with proprietary pride and could recite, and did, his every race from the day he was foaled. She had looked after him always, she said, ever since he came into the yard as a leggy untried three-year-old. She didn't know what she'd do when he was retired, racing wouldn't be the same without him somehow.

I offered to drive her into Newbury to have tea in a café or an hotel, but she said no, thank you, she wouldn't have time because the evening work started at four. Leaning against the door of Zig Zag's box she told me about her life, hesitantly at first, and then in a rush. Her parents didn't get on, she said. There were always rows at home, so she'd cleared out pretty soon after leaving school, glad to get away, her old man was so mean with the housekeeping and her mum did nothing but screech, nag, nag, at him mostly but at her too and her two kid sisters, right draggy the whole thing was, and she hoped Zig Zag would be racing at Kempton on Boxing Day so she'd have a good excuse not to go home for Christmas. She loved her work, she loved Zig Zag, the racing world was the tops, and no, she wasn't in any hurry to get married, there were always boys around if she wanted them and honestly whoever would swop Zig Zag for a load of draggy housework, especially if it turned out like her mum and dad . . .

She agreed with a giggle to have her photograph taken if Zig Zag could be in the picture too, and said she hoped that *Tally* magazine would send her a free copy.

'Of course,' I assured her, and decided to charge all free copies against expenses.

When I left her I walked down through the yard and called on the trainer, whom I saw almost every time I went racing. A businesslike man in his fifties, with no airs and few illusions.

'Come in, Ty,' he said. 'Did you find Sandy Willis?'

'Thank you, yes. She was very helpful.'

'She's one of my best lads.' He waved me to an armchair and poured some oak-coloured tea out of a silver pot. 'Sugar?' I shook my head. 'Not much in the upstairs department, but her horses are always jumping out of their skins.'

'A spot of transferred mother love,' I agreed. I tasted the tea. My tongue winced at the strength of the tannin.

Norton Fox poured himself another cup and took three deep swallows.

'If I write her up for *Tally*,' I said, 'you won't do the dirty on me and take Zig Zag out of the Lamplighter at the last minute?'

'I don't plan to.'

'Twelve stone ten is a prohibitive weight,' I suggested.

'He's won with twelve thirteen.' He shrugged. 'He'll never come down the handicap.'

'As a matter of interest,' I said, 'what happened to Brevity just before the Champion Hurdle?'

Norton clicked his tongue in annoyance. 'You can rely on it, Zig Zag will *not* be taken out at the last minute. At least, not for no reason, like Brevity.'

'He was favourite, wasn't he?' I knew he was, I'd checked carefully from Derry's list. 'What exactly happened?'

'I've never been so furious about anything.' The eight-month-old grievance was still vivid in his voice. 'I trained that horse to the minute. To the minute. We always had the Champion Hurdle as his main target. He couldn't have been more fit. He was ready to run for his life. And then what? Do you know what? I declared him at the four-day stage, and the owner, the *owner*, mark you, went and telephoned Weatherbys two days later and cancelled the declaration. Took the horse out of the race. I ask you! And on top of that, he hadn't even the courtesy, or the nerve probably, to tell me what he'd done, and the first I knew of it was when Brevity wasn't in the overnight list of runners. Of course I couldn't believe it and rang up Weatherbys in a fury and they told me old Dembley himself had struck his horse out. And I still don't know why. I had the most God almighty row with him about it and all he would say was that he had decided not to run, and that was that. He never once gave me a reason. Not one, after all that planning and all that work. I told him to take his horses away, I was so angry. I mean, how can you train for a man who's going to do that to you? It's impossible.'

'Who trains for him now?' I asked sympathetically.

'No one. He sold all three of his horses, including Brevity. He said he'd had enough of racing, he was finished with it.'

'You wouldn't still have his address?' I asked.

'Look here, Ty, you're not putting all that in your wretched paper.'

'No,' I assured him. 'Just one day I might write an article on owners who've sold out.'

'Well . . . yes, I still have it.' He copied the address from a ledger and handed it to me. 'Don't cause any trouble.'

'Not for you,' I said. Trouble was always Luke-John's aim, and often mine. The only difference was that I was careful my friends shouldn't be on the receiving end. Luke-John had no such difficulties. He counted no one, to that extent, a friend.

Mrs Woodward and Elizabeth were watching the news on television when I got back. Mrs Woodward took a quick look at her watch and made an unsuccessful attempt at hiding her disappointment. I had beaten her to six o'clock by thirty seconds. She charged overtime by the half hour, and was a shade over businesslike about it. I never got a free five minutes: five past six and it would have cost me the full half hour. I understood that it wasn't sheer miserliness. She was a widow whose teenage son had a yearning to be a doctor, and as far as I could see it would be mainly Tyrone who put him through medical school.

The time-keeping war was conducted with maximum politeness and without acknowledgement that it existed. I simply synchronized our two clocks and my watch with the BBC time signal every morning, and paid up with a smile when I was late. Mrs Woodward gave me a warmer welcome at ten past six than at ten to, but never arrived a minute after nine-thirty in the mornings. Neither of us had let on to Elizabeth how acutely the clock was watched.

Mrs Woodward was spare and strong, with a little of her native Lancashire in her voice and a lot in her character. She had dark hair going grey, rich brown eyes, and a determined jaw line which had seen her through a jilting fiancé and a work-shy husband. Unfailingly gentle to Elizabeth, she had never yet run out of patience, except with the vacuum cleaner, which occasionally regurgitated where it should have sucked.

In our flat she wore white nylon overalls which she knew raised her status from home-help in the eyes of visitors, and I saw no reason to think any worse of her for it. She took off the overall and hung it up, and I helped her into the dark blue coat she had been wearing every single day for at least three years.

'Night, Mr Tyrone. Night, luv,' she said, as she always said. And as always I thanked her for coming, and said I'd see her in the morning.

'Did you have a good day?' Elizabeth asked, when I kissed her forehead. Her voice sounded tired. The Spirashell tugged her chest up and down in a steady rhythm, and she could only speak easily on the outgoing breaths.

'I went to see a girl about a horse,' I said, smiling, and told her briefly about Sandy Willis and Zig Zag. She liked to know a little of what I'd been doing, but her interest always flagged pretty soon, and after so many years I could tell the exact instant by the microscopic relaxation in her eye muscles. She rarely said she was tired and had had enough of anything because she was afraid I would think her complaining and querulous and find her too much of a burden altogether. I couldn't persuade her to say flatly 'Stop, I'm tired.' She agreed each time I mentioned it that she would, and she never did.

'I've seen three of the people for the *Tally* article,' I said. 'Owner, owner-trainer, and stable girl. I'm afraid after supper I'd better make a start on the writing. Will you be all right watching television?'

'Of course . . .' She gave me the sweet brilliant smile which made every chore for her possible. Occasionally I spotted her manufacturing it artificially, but no amount of reassurance seemed able to convince her that she needn't perform tricks for me, that I wouldn't shove her back into hospital if she lost her temper, that I didn't need her to be angelic, that she was safe with me, and loved, and, in fact very much wanted.

'Like a drink?' I said.

'Love one.'

I poured us both a J and B with Malvern Water, and took hers over and fastened it into a holder I'd rigged up, with the bent drinking straw near to her mouth. Using that she could drink in her own time, and a lot less got spilt on the sheets. I tasted appreciatively the pale fine Scotch, slumping into the big armchair beside her bed, sloughing off the day's travelling with a comfortable feeling of being at home. The pump's steady soft thumping had its usual soporific effect. It sent most of our visitors fast asleep.

We watched a brain-packed quiz game on television and companionably answered most of the questions wrong. After that I went into the kitchen and looked at what Mrs Woodward had put out for supper. Plaice coated with bread crumbs, a bag of frozen chips, one lemon. Stewed apples, custard. Cheddar cheese, square crackers. The Woodward views on food didn't entirely coincide with my own. Stifling thoughts of underdone steak I cooked the chips in oil and the plaice in butter, and left mine to keep hot while I helped Elizabeth. Even with the new pulley gadget some foods were difficult: the plaice broke up too easily and her wrist got tired, and we ended up with me feeding her as usual.

While I washed the dishes I made coffee in mugs, fixed Elizabeth's into the holder, and took mine with my typewriter into the little room which would have been a child's bedroom if we'd ever had a child.

The *Tally* article came along slowly, its price tag reproaching me for every sloppy phrase. The Huntersons, the Ronceys, Sandy Willis. Dissect without hurting, probe but leave whole. Far easier, I thought resignedly, to pick them to bits. Good for *Tally*'s sales too. Bad for the conscience, lousy for the Huntersons, the Ronceys, Sandy Willis. To tell all so that the victim liked it . . . this was what took the time.

After two hours I found myself staring at the wall, thinking only of Gail. With excruciating clearness I went through in my mind every minute of that uninhibited love making, felt in all my limbs and veins an echo of passion. Useless to pretend that once was enough, that the tormenting hunger had been anaesthetized for more than a few days. With despair at my weakness I thought about how it would be on the next Sunday. Gail with no clothes on, graceful and firm.

Gail smiling with my hands on her breasts, Gail fluttering her fingers on the base of my spine.

The bell rang sharply above my head. One ring: not urgent. I stood up slowly, feeling stupid and ashamed. Day-dreaming like Madge Roncey. Just as bad. Probably much worse.

Elizabeth was apologetic. 'Ty, I'm sorry to interrupt you . . .'

How can I do it, I thought. And knew I would.

'My feet are awfully cold.'

I pulled out the hot water bottle, which had no heat left. Her feet were warm enough to the touch, but that meant nothing. Her circulation was so poor that her ankles and feet ached with cold if not constantly warmed from outside.

'You should have said,' I protested.

'Didn't want to disturb you.'

'Any time,' I said fiercely. 'Any time.' And preferably twenty minutes ago. For twenty minutes she'd suffered her cold feet and all I'd done was think of Gail.

I filled her bottle and we went through her evening routine. Rubs with surgical spirit. Washing. Bedpan.

Her muscles had nearly all wasted to nothing so that her bones showed angularly through the skin, and one had to be careful when lifting her limbs, as pressure in some places hurt her. That day Mrs Woodward had painted her toe nails for her instead of only her fingernails as usual.

'Do you like it?' she said. 'It's a new colour, Tawny Pink.'

'Pretty,' I nodded. 'It suits you.'

She smiled contentedly. 'Sue Davis brought it for me. She's a pet, that girl,'

Sue and Ronald Davis lived three doors away: married for six months and it still showed. They had let their euphoria spill over on to us. Sue brought things in to amuse Elizabeth and Ronald used his rugger-bred strength to carry the pump downstairs when we went out in the van.

'It matches my lipstick better than the old colour.'

'Yes, it does,' I agreed.

When we married she had had creamy skin and hair as glossy as new-peeled conkers. She had sun-browned agile limbs, and a pretty figure. The transition to her present and for ever state had been as agonizing for her mentally as it had been physically, and at one point of that shattering progress I was aware she would have killed herself if even that freedom hadn't been denied her.

She still had a good complexion, fine eyebrows, and long-lashed eyes, but the russet lights had turned to grey in both her irises and her hair, as if the colour had drained away with the vitality. Mrs Woodward was luckily expert with shampoo and scissors and I too had long grown accurate with a lipstick, so that Elizabeth always turned a groomed and attractive head to the world and could retain at least some terrifically important feminine assurance.

I settled her for the night, slowing the rate of breathing pump a little and tucking the covers in firmly round her chin to help with the draught. She slept in the same half sitting propped-up position as she spent the days: the Spirashell was too heavy and uncomfortable if she lay down flat, beside not dragging as much air into her lungs.

She smiled when I kissed her cheek. 'Goodnight, Ty.'

'Goodnight, honey.'

'Thanks for everything.'

'Be my guest.'

Lazily I pottered round the flat, tidying up, brushing my teeth, re-reading what I'd written for *Tally* and putting the cover on the typewriter. When I finally made it to bed Elizabeth was asleep, and I lay between the lonely sheets and thought about Bert Checkov and the non-starters like Brevity in the Champion Hurdle, planning in detail the article I would write for the *Blaze* on Sunday.

Sunday.

Inevitably, inexorably, every thought led back to Gail.

CHAPTER FIVE

I telephoned to Charles Dembley, the ex-owner of Brevity, on Wednesday morning, and a girl answered, bright fresh voice, carefree, and inexperienced.

'Golly, did you say Tyrone? *James* Tyrone? Yes, we do have your perfectly frightful paper. At least we used to. At least the gardener does, so I often read it. Well, of course come down and see Daddy, he'll be frightfully pleased.'

Daddy wasn't.

He met me outside his house, on the front step, a smallish man nearing sixty with a grey moustache and heavy pouches under his eyes. His manner was courteous stonewall.

'I am sorry you have had a wasted journey, Mr Tyrone. My daughter Amanda is only fifteen and is apt to rush into things . . . I was out when you telephoned, as I expect she told you. I hope you will forgive her. I have absolutely nothing to say to you. Nothing at all. Good afternoon, Mr Tyrone.'

There was a tiny twitch in one eyelid and the finest

of dews on his forehead. I let my gaze wander across the front of his house (genuine Georgian, not too large, unostentatiously well kept) and brought it gently back to his face.

'What threat did they use?' I asked. 'Amanda?'

He winced strongly and opened his mouth.

'With a fifteen-year-old daughter,' I commented, 'one is dangerously vulnerable.'

He tried to speak but achieved only a croak. After clearing his throat with difficulty he said, 'I don't know what you're talking about.'

'How did they set about it?' I asked. 'By telephone? By letter? Or did you actually see them face to face?'

His expression was a full giveaway, but he wouldn't answer.

I said, 'Mr Dembley, I can write my column about the last-minute unexplained withdrawal of favourites, mentioning you and Amanda by name, or I can leave you out of it.'

'Leave me out,' he said forcefully. 'Leave me out.'

'I will,' I agreed, 'if in return you will tell me what threat was made against you, and in what form.'

His mouth shook with a mixture of fear and disgust. He knew blackmail when he heard it. Only too well.

'I can't trust you.'

'Indeed you can,' I said.

'If I keep silent you will print my name and they will think I told you anyway . . .' He stopped dead.

'Exactly,' I said mildly.

'You're despicable.'

'No,' I said. 'I'd simply like to stop them doing it to anyone else.'

There was a pause. Then he said, 'It *was* Amanda. They said someone would rape her. They said I couldn't guard her twenty-four hours a day for years on end. They said to make her safe all I had to do was call Weatherbys and take Brevity out of the Champion Hurdle. Just one little telephone call, against my daughter's . . . my daughter's health. So I did it. Of course I did. I had to. What did running a horse in the Champion Hurdle matter compared with my daughter?'

What indeed.

'Did you tell the police?'

He shook his head. 'They said . . .'

I nodded. They would.

'I sold all my horses, after,' he said. 'There wasn't any point going on. It could have happened again, any time.'

'Yes.'

He swallowed. 'Is that all?'

'No . . . Did they telephone, or did you see them?'

'It was one man. He came here, driven by a chauffeur. In a Rolls. He was, he seemed to me, an educated man. He had an accent, I'm not sure what it was, perhaps Scandinavian, or Dutch, something like that. Maybe even Greek. He was civilized . . . except for what he said.'

'Looks?'

'Tall . . . about your height. Much heavier, though. Altogether thicker, more flesh. Not a crook's face at all. I couldn't believe what I was hearing him say. It didn't fit the way he looked.'

'But he convinced you,' I commented.

'Yes.' He shuddered. 'He stood there watching me while I telephoned to Weatherbys. And when I'd finished he simply said, "I'm sure you've made a wise decision, Mr Dembley," and he just walked out of the house and the chauffeur drove him away.'

'And you've heard no more from him at all?'

'No more. You will keep your bargain, too, like him?'

My mouth twisted. 'I will.'

He gave me a long look. 'If Amanda comes to any harm through you, I will see it costs you . . . costs you . . .' He stopped.

'If she does,' I said, 'I will pay.'

An empty gesture. Harm couldn't be undone, and paying wouldn't help. I would simply have to be careful.

'That's all,' he said. 'That's all.' He turned on his heel, went back into his house, and shut the front door decisively between us.

For light relief on the way home I stopped in Hampstead to interview the man who had done the handicap for the Lamplighter. Not a well-timed call. His wife had just decamped with an American colonel.

'Damn her eyes,' he said. 'She's left me a bloody note.' He waved it under my nose. 'Stuck up against the clock, just like a ruddy movie.'

'I'm sorry,' I said.

'Come in, come in. What do you say to getting pissed?'

'There's the unfortunate matter of driving home.'

'Take a taxi, Ty, be a pal. Come on.'

I looked at my watch. Four-thirty. Half an hour to home, counting rush hour traffic. I stepped over the threshold and saw from his relieved expression that company was much needed. He already had a bottle out with a half-full glass beside it, and he poured me one the same size.

Major Colly Gibbons, late forties, trim, intelligent, impatient, and positive. Never suffered fools gladly and interrupted rudely when his thoughts leaped ahead, but was much in demand as a handicapper, as he had a clear comprehensive view of racing as a whole, like a master chess player winning ten games at once. He engineered more multiple dead heats than anyone else in the game; the accolade of his profession and a headache to the interpreters of photo finishes.

'A bloody colonel,' he said bitterly. 'Out-ranked, too.'

I laughed. He gave me a startled look and then an unwilling grin.

'I suppose it *is* funny,' he said. 'Silly thing is, he's very like me. Looks, age, character, everything. I even like the guy.'

'She'll probably come back,' I said.

'Why?'

'If she chose a carbon copy of you, she can't hate you all that much.'

'Don't know as I'd have her,' he said aggressively. 'Going off with a bloody colonel, and a Yank at that.'

His pride was bent worse than his heart: none the less painful. He sloshed another stiff whisky into his glass and asked me why, as a matter of interest, I had come. I explained about the *Tally* article, and, seeming to be relieved to have something to talk about besides his wife, he loosened up with his answers more than I would normally have expected. For the first time I understood the wideness of his vision and the grasp and range of his memory. He knew the form book for the past ten years by heart.

After a while I said, 'What can you remember about ante-post favourites which didn't run?'

He gave me a quick glance which would have been better focused three drinks earlier. 'Is this for *Tally*, still?'

'No,' I admitted.

'Didn't think so. Question like that's got the *Blaze* written all over it.'

'I won't quote you.'

'Too right you won't.' He drank deeply, but seemed

no nearer oblivion. 'Put yourself some blinkers on and point in another direction.'

'Read what I say on Sunday,' I said mildly.

'Ty,' he said explosively. 'Best to keep out.'

'Why?'

'Leave it to the authorities.'

'What are they doing about it? What do they know?'

'You know I can't tell you,' he protested. 'Talk to the *Blaze*! I'd lose my job.'

'Mulholland went to jail rather than reveal his sources.'

'All journalists are not Mulholland.'

'Same secretive tendencies.'

'Would you,' he said seriously, 'go to jail?'

'It's never cropped up. But if my sources want to stay unrevealed, they stay unrevealed. If they didn't who would tell me anything?'

He thought it over. 'Something's going on,' he said at last.

'Quite,' I said. 'And what are the authorities doing about it?'

'There's no evidence . . . look, Ty, there's nothing you can put your finger on. Just a string of coincidences.'

'Like Bert Checkov's articles?' I suggested.

He was startled. 'All right, then. Yes. I heard it on good authority that he was going to be asked to explain them. But then he fell out of the window . . .'

'Tell me about the non-runners,' I said.

He looked gloomily at the note from his wife, which he still clutched in his hand. He took a deep swallow and shrugged heavily. The caution barriers were right down.

'There was this French horse, Polyxenes, which they made favourite for the Derby. Remember? All last winter and spring there was a stream of information about it, coming out of France . . . how well he was developed, how nothing could stay with him on the gallops, how he made all the three-year-olds look like knock-kneed yearlings? Every week, something about Polyxenes.'

'I remember,' I said. 'Derry Clark wrote him up for the *Blaze*.'

Colly Gibbons nodded. 'So there we are. By Easter, six to one favourite for the Derby. Right? They leave him in through all the forfeit stages. Right? They declare him at the four-day declarations. Right? Two days later he's taken out of the race. Why? He knocked himself out at exercise and his leg's blown up like a football. Can't run a lame horse. Too bad, everybody who'd backed him. Too bad. All their money down the drain. All right. Now I'll tell you something, Ty. That Polyxenes, I'll never believe he was all that good. What had he ever done? Won two moderate races as a two-year-old at St Cloud. He didn't run this year before the Derby. He didn't run the whole season in the end. They said his leg was still bad. I'll tell you what I think.

He never was good enough to win the Derby, and from the start they never meant him to run.'

'If he were as bad as that they could have run him anyway. He wouldn't have won.'

'Would you risk it, if you were them? The most fantastic outsiders *have* won the Derby. Much more certain not to run at all.'

'Someone must have made thousands,' I said slowly.

'More like hundreds of thousands.'

'If they know it's going on, why don't the racing authorities do something about it?'

'What *can* they do? I told you, no evidence. Polyxenes *was* lame, and he stayed lame. He was seen by dozens of vets. He had a slightly shady owner, but no shadier than some of ours. Nothing, absolutely nothing, could be proved.'

After a pause I said, 'Do you know of any others?'

'God, Ty, you're a glutton. Well . . . yes . . .'

Once started, he left little out. In the next half-hour I listened to the detailed case histories of four more ante-post favourites who hadn't turned up on the day. All could have been bona-fide hard-luck stories. But all, I knew well, had been over-praised by Bert Checkov.

He ran down, in the end, with a faint look of dismay.

'I shouldn't have told you all this.'

'No one will know.'

'You'd get information out of a deaf mute.'

I nodded. 'They can usually read and write.'

'Go to hell,' he said. 'Or rather, don't. You're four behind me, you aren't trying.' He waved the bottle in my general direction and I went over and took it from him. It was empty.

'Got to go home,' I said apologetically.

'What's the hurry?' He stared at the letter in his hand. 'Will your wife give you gip if you're late? Or will she be running off with some bloody Yankee colonel?'

'No,' I said unemotionally. 'She won't.'

He was suddenly very sober. '*Christ*, Ty . . . I forgot.'

He stood up, as steady as a rock. Looked forlornly round his comfortable wifeless sitting-room. Held out his hand.

'She'll come back,' I said uselessly.

He shook his head. 'I don't think so.' He sighed deeply. 'Anyway, I'm glad you came. Needed someone to talk to, you know. Even if I've talked too much . . . better than getting drunk alone. And I'll think of you, this evening. You . . . and your wife.'

I got hung up in a jam at Swiss Cottage and arrived home at eight minutes past seven. An hour and a half's overtime. Mrs Woodward was delighted.

'Isn't she sweet?' Elizabeth said when she had gone. 'She never minds when you are late. She never complains about having to stay. She's so nice and kind.'

'Very,' I said.

As usual I spent most of Thursday at home, writing Sunday's article. Mrs Woodward went out to do the week's shopping and to take and collect the laundry.

Sue Davis came in and made coffee for herself and Elizabeth. Elizabeth's mother telephoned to say she might not come on Sunday, she thought she could be getting a cold.

No one came near Elizabeth with a cold. With people on artificial respiration, colds too often meant pneumonia, and pneumonia too often meant death.

If Elizabeth's mother didn't come on Sunday, I couldn't go to Virginia Water. I spent too much of the morning unproductively trying to persuade myself it would be better if the cold developed, and knowing I'd be wretched if it did.

Luke-John galloped through the article on non-starting favourites, screwed his eyes up tight and leaned back on his chair with his face to the ceiling. Symptoms of extreme emotion. Derry reached over, twitched up the typewritten sheets and read them in his slower intense short-sighted-looking way. When he'd finished he took a deep breath.

'Wowee,' he said. 'Someone's going to love this.'

'Who?' said Luke-John, opening his eyes.

'The chap who's doing it.'

Luke-John looked at him broodingly. 'As long as he can't sue, that's all that matters. Take this down to the lawyers and make sure they don't let it out of their sight.'

Derry departed with a folded carbon copy of the article and Luke-John permitted himself a smile.

'Up to standard, if I may say so.'

'Thanks,' I said.

'Who told you all this?'

'Couple of little birds.'

'Come off it, Ty.'

'Promised,' I said. 'They could get their faces pushed in, one way or another.'

'I'll have to know. The editor will want to know.'

I shook my head. 'Promised.'

'I could scrub the article altogether . . .'

'Tut, Tut,' I said. 'Threats now?'

He rubbed his larynx in exasperation. I looked round the vast busy floor space, each section, like the sports desk, collecting and sorting out its final copy. Most of the feature stuff went down to the compositors on Fridays, some even on Thursdays, to be set up in type. But anything like a scoop stayed under wraps upstairs until after the last editions of the Saturday evening papers had all been set up and gone to press. The compositors were apt to make the odd ten quid by selling a red-hot story to reporters on rival newspapers. If the legal department and the editor both cleared my article, the print shop wouldn't see it until too late to do them any good. The *Blaze* held its scandalous disclosures very close to its chest.

Derry came down from the lawyers without the article.

'They said they'd have to work on it. They'll ring through later.'

The *Blaze* lawyers were of Counsel standard on the

libel laws. They needed to be. All the same they were true *Blaze* men with 'publish and be damned' engraved on their hearts. The *Blaze* accountants allowed for damages in their budget as a matter of course. The *Blaze*'s owner looked upon one or two court cases a year as splendid free advertising, and watched the sales graphs rise. There had however been four actions in the last six months and two more were pending. A mild memo had gone round, saying to cool it just a fraction. Loyal for ever, Luke-John obeyed even where he disapproved.

'I'll take this in to the editor,' he remarked. 'See what he says.'

Derry watched his retreating back with reluctant admiration.

'Say what you like, the sports pages sell this paper to people who otherwise wouldn't touch it with gloves on. Our Luke-John, for all his stingy little ways, must be worth his weight in gumdrops.'

Our Luke-John came back and went into a close huddle with a soccer correspondent. I asked Derry how the funeral had been, on the Wednesday.

'A funeral's a funeral.' He shrugged. 'It was cold. His wife wept a lot. She had a purple nose, blue from cold and red from crying.'

'Charming.'

He grinned. 'Her sister told her to cheer up. Said how lucky it was Bert took out all that extra insurance.'

'He did what?'

'Yeah. I thought you'd like that. I chatted the sister up a bit. Two or three weeks ago Bert trebled his life insurance. Told his wife they'd be better off when he retired. Sort of self-help pension scheme.'

'Well, well,' I said.

'So it had to be an accident,' Derry nodded. 'In front of witnesses. The insurance company might not have paid up if he'd fallen out of the window with no one watching.'

'I wonder if they'll contest it.'

'Don't see how they can, when the inquest said misadventure.'

The editor's secretary came back with my piece. The editor's secretary was an expensive package tied up with barbed wire. No one, reputedly, had got past the prickles to the goodies.

The editor had scrawled 'OK on the lawyer's say so' across the top of the page. Luke-John stretched out a hand for it, nodded in satisfaction, and slid it into the lockable top drawer of his desk, talking all the while to the soccer man. There was no need for me to stay longer. I told Derry I'd be at home most of the day if they wanted me and sketched a goodbye.

I was halfway to the door when Luke-John called after me.

'Ty . . . I forgot to tell you. A woman phoned, wanted you.'

'Mrs Woodward?'

'Uhuh. Let's see, I made a note . . . oh yes, here it

is. A Miss Gail Pominga. Would you ring her back. Something about *Tally* magazine.'

He gave me the slip of paper with the telephone number. I went across to the under-populated news desk and picked up the receiver. My hands were steady. My pulse wasn't.

'The Western School of Art. Can I help you?'

'Miss Pominga . . .'

Miss Pominga was fetched. Her voice came on the line, as cool and uninvolved as at the railway station.

'Are you coming on Sunday?' Crisp. Very much to the point.

'I want to.' Understatement. 'It may not be possible to get away.'

'Well . . . I've been asked out to lunch.'

'Go, then,' I said, feeling disappointment lump in my chest like a boulder.

'Actually, if you are coming I will stay at home.'

Damn Elizabeth's mother, I thought. Damn her and her cold.

'I want to come. I'll come if I possibly can,' I said.

There was a short silence before she said, 'When can you let me know for sure?'

'Not until Sunday, really. Not until I go out to catch the train.'

'Hmm . . .' She hesitated, then said decisively, 'Ring me in any case, whether you can come or whether you can't. I'll fix it so that I can still go to lunch if you aren't coming.'

'That marvellous,' I said, with more feeling than caution.

She laughed. 'Good. Hope to see you, then. Any time after ten. That's when Harry and Sarah go off to golf.'

'It would be eleven-thirty or so.'

She said, 'All right,' and 'Goodbye,' and disconnected. I went home to write up Colly Gibbons for *Tally* and to have lunch with Elizabeth and Mrs Woodward. It was fish again: unspecified variety and not much flavour. I listened to Elizabeth's sporadic conversation and returned her smiles and hoped fiercely not to be there with her forty-eight hours later. I ate automatically, sightlessly. By the end of that meal, treachery tasted of salt.

CHAPTER SIX

Time was running short, *Tally*-wise. With their deadline only two days ahead I went to Heathbury Park races on Saturday to meet Dermot Finnegan, an undistinguished jockey with an undistinguished mount in the Lamplighter.

For a while I couldn't understand a word he said, so impenetrable was his Irish accent. After he had sipped unenthusiastically at a cup of lunch-counter coffee for ten minutes he relaxed enough to tell me he always spoke worse when he was nervous, and after that we got by with him having to repeat some things twice, but not four or five times, as at the beginning.

Once past the language barrier, Dermot unveiled a resigned wit and an accepting contented way of life. Although by most standards his riding success was small, Dermot thought it great. His income, less than a dustman's, seemed to him princely compared with the conditions of his childhood. His father had fed fourteen children on the potatoes he had grown on two and a half exhausted acres. Dermot, being neither the strong eldest nor the spoilt youngest, had usually had to shove for his share and hadn't always got it. At nineteen he tired of the diet and took his underdeveloped physique across the sea to Newmarket, where an Irish accent, irrespective of previous experience, guaranteed him an immediate job in the labour-hungry racing industry.

He had 'done his two' for a while in a flat-racing stable, but couldn't get a ride in a flat race because he hadn't been apprenticed. Philosophically he moved down the road to a stable which trained jumpers as well, where the 'Governor' gave him a chance in a couple of hurdle races. He still worked in the same stable on a part-time basis, the 'Governor' still put him up as his second string jockey. How many rides? He grinned, showing spaces instead of teeth. Some seasons, maybe thirty. Two years ago, of course, it was only four, thanks to breaking his leg off a brainless divil of a knock-kneed spalpeen.

Dermot Finnegan was twenty-five, looked thirty. Broken-nosed and weatherbeaten, with bright sharp blue eyes. His ambition, he said, was to take a crack at Aintree. Otherwise he was all right with what he had: he wouldn't want to be a classy top jockey, it was far too much responsibility. 'If you only ride the scrubbers round the gaffs at the back end of the season, see, no one expects much. Then they gets a glorious surprise if you do come in.'

He had ridden nineteen winners in all, and he could

remember each of them in sharp detail. No, he didn't think he would do much good in the Lamplighter, not really, as he was only in it because his stable was running there. 'I'll be on the pacemaker, sure. You'll see me right up there over the first, and maybe for a good while longer, but then my old boy will run out of steam and drop out of the back door as sudden as an interrupted burglar, and if I don't have to pull him up it'll be a bloody miracle.'

Later in the afternoon I watched him start out on some prospective ten-year-old dog-meat in a novice chase. Horse and rider disappeared with a flurry of legs into the second open ditch, and when I went to check on his injuries some time after the second race I met Dermot coming out of the ambulance room wearing a bandage and a grin.

'It's only a scratch,' he assured me cheerfully. 'I'll be there for the Lamplighter sure enough.'

Further investigation led to the detail of a fingernail hanging on by a thread. 'Some black divil' had leant an ill-placed hoof on the Finnegan hand.

To complete the *Tally* round-up I spent the last half of the afternoon in the clerk of the course's office, watching him in action.

Heathbury Park, where the Lamplighter was to be held a fortnight later, had become under his direction one of the best organized courses in the country. Like the handicapper, he was ex-forces, in his case RAF, which was unusual in that the racing authorities as a rule leant heavily towards the Army and the Navy for their executives.

Wing Commander Willy Ondroy was a quiet effective shortish man of forty-two who had been invalided out after fracturing his skull in a slight mishap with a Vulcan bomber. He still, he said, suffered from blackouts, usually at the most inconvenient, embarrassing, and even obscene moments.

It wasn't until after racing had finished for the day that he was really ready to talk, and even then he dealt with a string of people calling into his office with statistics, problems, and keys.

The Lamplighter was his own invention, and he was mostly proud of it. He'd argued the Betting Levy Board into putting up most of the hefty stake money, and then drawn up entry conditions exciting enough to bring a gleam to the hardest-headed trainer's eye. Most of the best horses would consequently be coming. They should draw an excellent crowd. The gate receipts would rise again. They'd soon be able to afford to build a warm modern nursery-room, their latest project, to attract young parents to the races by giving them somewhere to park their kids.

Willy Ondroy's enthusiasm was of the enduring, not the bubbling kind. His voice was as gentle as the expression in his amber eyes, and only the small self-mockery in his smile gave any clue to the steel within. His obvious lack of any need to assert his authority in any forceful way was finally explained after I'd dug, or tried to dig, into his history. A glossed over throw-away phrase about a spot of formation flying turned out to be his version of three years as a Red Arrow, flying two feet away from the jet pipe of the aircraft in front. 'We did two hundred displays in one year,' he said apologetically. 'Entertaining at air shows. Like a concert party on Blackpool pier, no difference really.'

He had been lucky to transfer to bombers when he was twenty-six, he said. So many RAF fighter and formation pilots were grounded altogether when their reaction times began to slow. He'd spent eight years on bombers, fifteen seconds knowing he was going to crash, three weeks in a coma, and twenty months finding himself a civilian job. Now he lived with his wife and twelve-year-old twins in a house on the edge of the racecourse, and none of them wanted to change.

I caught the last train when it was moving and made a start on Dermot and Willy Ondroy on the way back to London.

Mrs Woodward departed contentedly at a quarter to seven, and I found she had for once left steaks ready in the kitchen. Elizabeth was in good spirits. I mixed us a drink each and relaxed in the armchair, and only after a strict ten minutes of self denial asked her casually if her mother had telephoned.

'No, she hasn't.' She wouldn't have.

'So you don't know if she's coming?'

'I expect she'll ring, if she doesn't.'

'I suppose so,' I said. Damn her eyes, couldn't she at least settle it, one way or another?

Trying to shut my mind to it I worked on the *Tally* article; cooked the supper; went back to *Tally*; stopped to settle Elizabeth for the night; and returned to the typewriter until I'd finished. It was then half past two. A pity, I thought, stretching, that I wrote so slowly, crossed out so much. I put the final version away in a drawer with only the fair copy to be typed the next day. Plenty of time for that even if I spent the rest of it on the primrose path making tracks for Gail.

I despised myself. It was five before I slept.

Elizabeth's mother came. Not a sniffle in sight.

I had spent all morning trying to reconcile myself to her non-appearance at ten-fifteen, her usual time of arrival. As on past occasions, I had turned a calm and everyday face to Elizabeth and found I had consciously to stifle irritation at little tasks for her that normally I did without thought.

At ten-seventeen the door bell rang, and there she was, a well-groomed good-looking woman in her mid-fifties with assisted tortoiseshell hair and a health farm figure. When she showed surprise at my greeting I knew I had been too welcoming. I damped it down a little to more normal levels and saw that she felt more at home with that.

I explained to her, as I had already done to Elizabeth, that I still had people to interview for *Tally*, and by ten-thirty I was walking away down the mews feeling as though a safety valve was blowing fine. The sun was shining too. After a sleepless night, my conscience slept.

Gail met me at Virginia Water, waiting outside in the estate car. 'The train's late,' she said calmly, as I sat in beside her. No warm, loving, kissing hello. Just as well, I supposed.

'They work on the lines on Sunday. There was a delay at Staines.'

She nodded, let in the clutch, and cruised the three-quarters of a mile to her uncle's house. There she led the way into the sitting-room and without asking poured two beers.

'You aren't writing today,' she said, handing me the glass.

'No.'

She gave me a smile that acknowledged the purpose of my visit. More businesslike about sex than most women. Certainly no tease. I kissed her mouth lightly, savouring the knowledge that the deadline of the Huntersons' return was three full hours ahead.

She nodded as if I'd spoken. 'I approve of you,' she said.

'Thanks.'

She smiled, moving away. Her dress that day was of a pale cream colour which looked wonderful against the gilded coffee skin. She was no darker, in fact, than many southern Europeans or heavily sun-tanned English: her mixed origin was distinct only in her face. A well-proportioned, attractive face, gathering distinction from the self-assurance within. Gail, I imagined, had had to come to terms with herself much earlier and more basically than most girls. She had done almost too good a job.

A copy of *The Sunday Blaze* lay on the low table, open at the sports page. Editors or sub-editors write all the headlines, and Luke-John had come up with a beauty. Across the top of my page, big and bold, it said, 'Don't back Tiddely Pom – YET'. Underneath, he'd left in word for word every paragraph I'd written. This didn't necessarily mean he thought each word was worth its space in print, but was quite likely because there weren't too many advertisements that week. Like all newspapers, the *Blaze* lived on advertising: if an advertiser wanted to pay for space, he got it, and out went the deathless prose of the columnists. I'd lost many a worked-on sentence to the late arrival of spiels on Whosit's cough syrup or Wammo's hair tonic. It was nice to see this intact.

I looked up at Gail. She was watching me.

'Do you always read the sports page?' I asked.

She shook her head. 'Curiosity,' she said. 'I wanted to see what you'd written. That article . . . it's disturbing.'

'It's meant to be.'

'I mean, it leaves the impression that you know a great deal more than you've said, and it's all bad, if not positively criminal.'

'Well,' I said, 'it's always nice to hear one has done exactly what one has intended.'

'What usually happens when you write in this way?'

'Repercussions? They vary from a blast from the racing authorities about minding my own business to abusive letters from nut cases.'

'Do wrongs get righted?'

'Very occasionally.'

'Sir Galahad,' she mocked.

'No. We sell more papers. I apply for a raise.'

She laughed with her head back, the line of her throat leading tautly down into her dress. I put out my hand and touched her shoulder, suddenly wanting no more talk.

She nodded at once, smiling, and said, 'Not on the rug. More comfortable upstairs.'

Her bedroom furnishings were pretty but clearly Sarah's work. Fitted cupboards, a cosy armchair, book shelves, a lot of pale blue carpet, and a single bed.

At her insistence, I occupied it first. Then while I watched, like the time before, she took off her clothes. The simple, undramatized, unselfconscious undressing was more ruthlessly arousing than anything one could ever pay to see. When she had finished she stood still for a moment near the window, a pale bronze naked girl in a shaft of winter sun.

'Shall I close the curtains?'

'Whichever you like.'

She screwed my pulse rate up another notch by stretching up to close them, and then in the mid-day dusk she came to bed.

At three she drove me back to the station, but a train pulled out as we pulled in. We sat in the car for a while, talking, waiting for the next one.

'Do you come home here every night?' I asked.

'Quite often not. Two of the other teachers share a flat, and I sleep on their sofa a night or two every week, after parties, or a theatre, maybe.'

'But you don't want to live in London all the time?'

'D'you think it's odd, that I stay with Harry and Sarah? Quite frankly, it's because of money. Harry won't let me pay for living here. He says he wants me to stay. He's always been generous. If I had to pay for everything myself in London my present standard of living would go down with a reverberating thump.'

'Comfort before independence,' I commented mildly.

She shook her head. 'I have both.' After a considering pause she said, 'Do you live with your wife? I mean, have you separated, or anything?'

'No, we've not separated.'

'Where does she think you are today?'

'Interviewing someone for my *Tally* article.'

She laughed. 'You're a bit of a bastard.'

Nail on the head. I agreed with her.

'Does she know you have . . . er . . . outside interests? Has she ever found you out?'

I wished she would change the subject. However, I owed her quite a lot, at least some answers, which might be the truth and nothing but the truth, but would certainly not be the whole truth.

'She doesn't know,' I said.

'Would she mind?'

'Probably.'

'But if she won't . . . sleep with you . . . well, why don't you leave her?'

I didn't answer at once. She went on, 'You haven't any children, have you?' I shook my head. 'Then what's to stop you? Unless, of course, you're like me.'

'How do you mean?'

'Staying where the living is good. Where the money is.'

'Oh . . .' I half laughed, and she misunderstood me.

'How can I blame you,' she sighed, 'when I do it myself? So your wife is rich . . .'

I thought about what Elizabeth would have been condemned to without me: to hospital ward routine, hospital food, no privacy, no gadgets, no telephone, lights out at nine and lights on at six, no free will at all, for ever and ever.

'I suppose you might say,' I agreed slowly, 'that my wife is rich.'

Back in the flat I felt split in two, with everything familiar feeling suddenly unreal. Half my mind was still down in Surrey. I kissed Elizabeth and thought of Gail. Depression had clamped down like drizzle in the train and wouldn't be shaken off.

'Some man wants to talk to you,' Elizabeth said. 'He telephoned three times. He sounded awfully angry.'

'Who?'

'I couldn't understand much of what he said. He was stuttering.'

'How did he get our number?' I was irritated, bored; I didn't want to have to deal with angry men on the telephone. Moreover our number was ex-directory, precisely so that Elizabeth should not be bothered by this sort of thing.

'I don't know. But he did leave his number for you to ring back, it was the only coherent thing he said.'

Elizabeth's mother handed me a note pad on which she had written down the number.

'Victor Roncey,' I said.

'That's right,' agreed Elizabeth with relief. 'That sounds like it.'

I sighed, wishing that all problems, especially those of my own making, would go away and leave me in peace.

'Maybe I'll call him later,' I said. 'Right now I need a drink.'

'I was just going to make some tea,' said Elizabeth's mother reprovingly, and in silent fury I doubled the quantity I would normally have taken. The bottle was nearly empty. Gloomy Sunday.

Restlessly I took myself off into my writing-room and started the clean unscribbled-on retype for *Tally*, the mechanical task eventually smoothing out the rocky tensions of my guilt-ridden return home. I couldn't afford to like Gail too much, and I did like her. To come to love someone would be too much hell altogether. Better not to visit Gail again. I decided definitely not to. My body shuddered in protest, and I knew I would.

Roncey rang again just after Elizabeth's mother had left.

'What the devil do you mean about this . . . this trash in the paper? Of course my horse is going to run. How dare you . . . how dare you suggest there's anything shady going on?'

Elizabeth had been right: he was stuttering still, at seven in the evening. He took a lot of calming down to the point of admitting that nowhere in the article was it suggested that he personally had anything but good honest upright intentions.

'The only thing is, Mr Roncey, as I said in the article, that some owners have in the past been pressurized into not running their horses. This may even happen to you. All I was doing was giving punters several good reasons why they would be wiser to wait until half an hour before big races to put their money on. Better a short starting price than losing their money in a swindle.'

'I've read it,' he snapped. 'Several times. And no one, believe me, is going to put any pressure on *me*.'

'I very much hope not,' I said. I wondered whether his antipathy to his elder sons extended to the smaller ones; whether he would risk their safety or happiness for the sake of running Tiddely Pom in the Lamplighter. Maybe he would. The stubborn streak ran through his character like iron in granite.

When he had calmed down to somewhere near reason I asked him if he'd mind telling me how he'd got my telephone number.

'I had the devil's own job, if you want to know. All that ex-directory piffle. The enquiries people refused point blank to tell me, even though I said it was urgent. Stupid, I call it, but I wasn't to be put off by that. If you want to know, your colleague on the paper told me. Derrick Clark.'

'I see,' I said resignedly, thinking it unlike Derry to part so easily with my defences. 'Well, thank you. Did the *Tally* photographer find you all right?'

'He came on Friday. I hope you haven't said anything in *Tally* about . . .' His anger was on its way up again.

'No,' I said decisively. 'Nothing like that at all.'

'When can I be sure?' He sounded suspicious.

'That edition of *Tally* is published on the Tuesday before the Lamplighter.'

'I'll ask for an advance copy from the editor. Tomorrow. I'll demand to see what you've written.'

'Do that,' I agreed. Divert the buck to Arnold Shankerton. Splendid.

He rang off still not wholly pacified. I dialled Derry's number and prepared to pass the ill temper along to him.

'*Roncey?*' He said indignantly. 'Of course I didn't give your number to Roncey.' His baby girl was exercising her lungs loudly in the background. 'What did you say?'

'I said, who *did* you give it to?'

'Your wife's uncle.'

'My wife hasn't got any uncles.'

'Oh Christ. Well, he said he was your wife's uncle, and that your wife's aunt had had a stroke, and that he wanted to tell you, but he'd lost your number.'

'Lying crafty bastard,' I said with feeling. 'And he accused me of misrepresenting facts.'

'I'm sorry, Ty.'

'Never mind. Only check with me first, next time, huh? Like we arranged.'

'Yeah. Sure. Sorry.'

'How did he get hold of your number, anyway?'

'It's in the *Directory of the British Turf*, unlike yours. My mistake.'

I put the receiver back in its special cradle near to Elizabeth's head and transferred to the armchair, and we spent the rest of the evening as we usually did, watching the shadows on the goggle box. Elizabeth never tired of it, which was a blessing, though she complained often about the shut-downs in the day time between all the child-orientated programmes. Why couldn't they fill them, she said, with interesting things for captive adults.

Later I made some coffee and did the vapour rubs and other jobs for Elizabeth, all with a surface of tranquil domesticity, going through my part with my thoughts somewhere else, like an actor at the thousandth performance.

On the Monday morning I took my article to the *Tally* offices and left the package at the reception desk, virtuously on the deadline.

After that I caught the race train to Leicester, admitting to myself that although it was technically my day off I did not want to stay in the flat. Also the Hundersons' raffle horse Egocentric was to have its pre-Lamplighter warm-up which gave me an excellent overt reason for the journey.

Raw near-mist was doing its best to cancel the proceedings and only the last two fences were visible. Egocentric finished fourth without enough steam left to blow a whistle, and the jockey told the trainer that the useless bugger had made a right bloody shambles of three fences on the far side and couldn't jump for peanuts. The trainer didn't believe him and engaged a different jockey for the Lamplighter. It was one of those days.

The thin Midland crowd of cloth caps and mufflers strewed the ground with betting slips and newspapers and ate a couple of hundredweight of jellied eels out of little paper cups. I adjourned to the bar with a colleague from the *Sporting Life*, and four people commented on my non-starters with varying degrees of belief. Not much of a day. One, on the whole, to forget.

The journey home changed all that. When I forget it, I'll be dead.

CHAPTER SEVEN

Thanks to having left before the last race I had a chance in the still empty and waiting train of a forward-facing window-seat in a non-smoker. I turned the heating to 'hottest', and opened the newspaper to see what Spyglass had come up with in the late editions.

'Tiddely Pom will run, trainer says. But is your money really safe?'

Amused, I read to the end. He'd cribbed most of my points and rehashed them. Complimentary. Plagiarism is the sincerest form of flattery.

The closed door to the corridor slid open and four bookmaker's clerks lumbered in, stamping their feet with cold and discussing some luckless punter who had lost an argument over a betting slip.

'I told him to come right off it, who did he think he was kidding? We may not be archangels, but we're not the ruddy mugs he takes us for.'

They all wore navy blue overcoats which after a while they shed on the luggage racks. Two of them shared a large packet of stodgy-looking sandwiches and the other two smoked. They were all in the intermediate thirty-forties, with London-Jewish accents in which they next discussed their taxi drive to the station in strictly non Sabbath day terms.

'Evening,' they said to me, acknowledging I existed, and one of them gestured with his cigarette to the non-smoking notice on the window and said, 'OK with you, chum?'

I nodded, hardly taking them in. The train rocked off southwards, the misty day turned to foggy night, and five pairs of eyeballs fell gently shut.

The door to the corridor opened with a crash. Reluctantly I opened one eye a fraction, expecting the ticket collector. Two men filled the opening, looking far from bureaucratic. Their effect on my four fellow travellers was a spine-straightening mouth-opening state of shock. The larger of the newcomers stretched out a hand and pulled the blinds down on the insides of the corridor-facing windows. Then he gave the four clerks a contemptuous comprehensive glance, jerked his head towards the corridor and said with simplicity, 'Out.'

I still didn't connect any of this as being my business, not even when the four men meekly took down their navy blue overcoats and filed out into the train. Only when the large man pulled out a copy of the *Blaze* and pointed to my article did I have the faintest prickle on the spine.

'This is unpopular in certain quarters,' remarked the larger man. Thick sarcastic Birmingham accent. He pursed his lips, admiring his own heavy irony. 'Unpopular.'

He wore grubby overalls from shoes to throat, with above that a thick neck, puffy cheeks, a small wet mouth, and slicked-down hair. His companion, also in overalls, was hard and stocky with wide eyes and a flat-topped head.

'You shouldn't do it, you shouldn't really,' the large man said. 'Interfering and that.'

He put his right hand into his pocket and it reappeared with a brass ridge across the knuckles. I glanced at the other man. Same thing.

I came up with a rush, grabbing for the communication cord. Penalty for improper use, twenty-five pounds. The large man moved his arm in a professional short jab and made havoc of my intention.

They had both learned their trade in the ring, that much was clear. Not much else was. They mostly left my head alone, but they knew where and how to hit to hurt on the body, and if I tried to fight off one of them, the other had a go. The most I achieved was a solid kick on the smaller man's ankle which drew from him four letters and a frightening kidney punch. I collapsed on to the seat. They leant over me and broke the Queensberry Rules.

It crossed my mind that they were going to kill me, that maybe they weren't meaning to, but they were killing me. I even tried to tell them so, but if any sound came out, they took no notice. The larger one hauled me bodily to my feet and the small one broke my ribs.

When they let go I crumpled slowly on to the floor and lay with my face against cigarette butts and the screwed-up wrappings of sandwiches. Stayed quite motionless, praying to a God I had no faith in not to let them start again.

The larger one stooped over me.

'Will he cough it?' the smaller one said.

'How can he? We ain't ruptured nothing, have we? Careful, aren't I? Look out the door, time we was off.'

The door slid open and presently shut, but not for a long time was I reassured that they had completely gone. I lay on the floor breathing in coughs and jerky shallow breaths, feeling sick. For some time it seemed in a weird transferred way that I had earned such a beating not for writing a newspaper article but because of Gail; and to have deserved it, to have sinned and deserved it, turned it into some sort of expurgation. Pain flowed through me in a red-hot tide, and only my guilt made it bearable.

Sense returned, as sense does. I set about the slow task of picking myself up and assessing the damage. Maybe they had ruptured nothing: I had only the big man's word for it. At the receiving end it felt as though they had ruptured pretty well everything, including self-respect.

I made it up to the seat, and sat vaguely watching the lights flash past, fuzzy and yellow from fog. Eyes half shut, throat closing with nausea, hands nerveless and weak. No one focus of pain, just too much. Wait, I thought, and it will pass.

I waited a long time.

The lights outside thickened and the train slowed down. London. All change. I would have to move from where I sat. Dismal prospect. Moving would hurt.

The train crept into St Pancras and stopped with a jerk. I stayed where I was, trying to make the effort to stand up and not succeeding, telling myself that if I didn't get up and go I could be shunted into a siding for a cold uncomfortable night, and still not raking up the necessary propulsion.

Again the door slid open with a crash. I glanced up, stifling the beginnings of panic. No man with heavy overalls and knuckleduster. The guard.

Only when I felt the relief wash through me did I realize the extent of my fear, and I was furious with myself for being so craven.

'The end of the line,' the guard was saying.

'Yeah,' I said.

He came into the compartment and peered at me. 'Been celebrating, have you, sir?' He thought I was drunk.

'Sure,' I agreed. 'Celebrating.'

I made the long-delayed effort and stood up. I'd been quite right about it. It hurt.

'Look, mate, do us a favour and don't throw up in here,' said the guard urgently.

I shook my head. Reached the door. Rocked into the corridor. The guard anxiously took my arm and helped me down on to the platform, and as I walked carefully away I heard him behind me say to a bunch of porters, half laughing, 'Did you see that one? Greeny grey and sweating like a pig. Must have been knocking it back solid all afternoon.'

I went home by taxi and took my time up the stairs to the flat. Mrs Woodward for once was in a hurry for me to come, as she was wanting to get home in case the fog thickened. I apologized. 'Quite all right, Mr Tyrone, you know I'm usually glad to stay . . .' The door closed behind her and I fought down a strong inclination to lie on my bed and groan.

Elizabeth said, 'Ty, you look terribly pale,' when I kissed her. Impossible to hide it from her completely.

'I fell,' I said. 'Tripped. Knocked the breath out of myself, for a minute or two.'

She was instantly concerned; with the special extra anxiety for herself apparent in her eyes.

'Don't worry,' I comforted her. 'No harm done.'

I went into the kitchen and held on to the table. After a minute or two I remembered Elizabeth's pain-killing tablets and took the bottle out of the cupboard. Only two left. There would be. I swallowed one of them, tying a mental knot to remind me to ring the doctor for another prescription. One wasn't quite enough, but better than nothing. I went back into the big room and with a fair stab at normality poured our evening drinks.

By the time I had done the supper and the jobs for Elizabeth and got myself undressed and into bed, the main damage had resolved itself into two or possibly three cracked ribs low down on my left side. The rest slowly subsided into a blanketing ache. Nothing had ruptured, like the man said.

I lay in the dark breathing shallowly and trying not to cough, and at last took time off from simply existing to consider the who and why of such a drastic roughing up, along with the pros and cons of telling Luke-John. He'd make copy of it, put it on the front page, plug it for more than it was worth, write the headlines himself. My feelings would naturally be utterly disregarded as being of no importance compared with selling papers. Luke-John had no pity. If I didn't tell him and he found out later, there would be frost and fury and a permanent atmosphere of distrust. I couldn't afford that. My predecessor had been squeezed off the paper entirely as a direct result of having concealed from Luke-John a red-hot scandal in which he was involved. A rival paper got hold of it and scooped the *Blaze*. Luke-John never forgave, never forgot.

I sighed deeply. A grave mistake. The cracked ribs stabbed back with unnecessary vigour. I spent what could not be called a restful, comfortable, sleep-filled night, and in the morning could hardly move. Elizabeth watched me get up and the raw anxiety twisted her face.

'Ty!'

'Only a bruise or two, honey. I told you, I fell over.'

'You look . . . hurt . . .'

I shook my head. 'I'll get the coffee . . .'

I got the coffee. I also looked with longing at Elizabeth's last pill, which I had no right to take. She still suffered sometimes from terrible cramp, and on these occasions had to have the pills in a hurry. I didn't need any mental knots to remind me to get some more. When Mrs Woodward came, I went.

Doctor Antonio Perelli wrote the prescription without hesitation and handed it across.

'How is she?'

'Fine. Same as usual.'

'It's time I went to see her.'

'She'd love it,' I said truthfully. Perelli's visits acted on her like champagne. I'd met him casually at a party three years earlier, a young Italian doctor in private practice in Welbeck Street. Too handsome, I'd thought at once. Too feminine, with those dark, sparkling, long-lashed eyes. All bedside manner and huge fees, with droves of neurotic women patients paying to have their hands held.

Then just before the party broke up someone told me he specialized in chest complaints, and not to be put off by his youth and beauty, he was brilliant; and by coincidence we found ourselves outside on the pavement together, hailing the same taxi, and going the same way.

At the time I had been worried about Elizabeth. She had to return to hospital for intensive nursing every time she was ill, and with a virtual stamping out of polio, the hospitals geared to care for patients on artificial respiration were becoming fewer and fewer. We had just been told she could not expect to go back any more to the hospital that had always looked after her.

I shared the taxi with Perelli and asked him if he knew of anywhere I could send her quickly if she ever needed it. Instead of answering directly he invited me into his tiny bachelor flat for another drink, and before I left he had acquired another patient. Elizabeth's general health had improved instantly under his care and I paid his moderate fees without a wince.

I thanked him for the prescription and put it in my pocket.

'Ty . . . are the pills for Elizabeth, or for you?'

I looked at him, startled. 'Why?'

'My dear fellow, I have eyes. What I see in your face is . . . severe.'

I smiled wryly. 'All right. I was going to ask you. Could you put a bit of strapping on a couple of ribs?'

He stuck me up firmly and handed me a small medicine glass containing, he said, disprins dissolved in nepenthe, which worked like a vanishing trick: now you feel it, now you don't.

'You haven't told Elizabeth?' he said anxiously.

'Only that I fell and winded myself.'

He relaxed, moving his head in a gesture of approval. 'Good.'

It had been his idea to shield her from worries which ordinary women could cope with in their stride. I had thought him unduly fussy at first, but the strict screening he had urged had worked wonders. She had become far less nervous, much happier, and had even put on some badly needed weight.

'And the police? Have you told the police?'

I shook my head and explained about Luke-John.

'Difficult. Um. Suppose you tell this Luke-John simply that those men threatened you? You'll not be taking your shirt off in the office.' He smiled in the way that made Elizabeth's eyes shine. 'These two men, they will not go about saying they inflicted so much damage.'

'They might,' I frowned, considering. 'It could be a good idea if I turned up in perfect health at the races today and gave them the lie.'

With an assenting gesture he mixed me a small bottle full of disprin and nepenthe. 'Don't eat much,' he said, handing it over. 'And only drink coffee.'

'OK.'

'And do nothing that would get you another beating like this.'

I was silent.

He looked at me with sad understanding. 'That is too much to give up for Elizabeth?'

'I can't just . . . crawl away,' I protested. 'Even for Elizabeth.'

He shook his head. 'It would be best for her. But . . .' He shrugged, and held out his hand in good-bye. 'Stay out of trains, then.'

I stayed out of trains. For ninety-four minutes. Then I caught the race train to Plumpton and travelled down safely with two harmless strangers and a man I knew slightly from the BBC.

Thanks to Tonio's mixture I walked about all day and talked and laughed much the same as usual. Once I coughed. Even that caused only an echo of a stab. For maximum effect I spent a good deal of my time walking about the bookmakers' stalls, inspecting both their prices and their clerks. The fraternity knew something had happened. Their heads swivelled as I passed and they were talking behind my back, nudging each other. When I put ten shillings on a semi-outsider with one of them he said, 'You feeling all right, chum?'

'Why not?' I said in surprise. 'It's a nice enough day.'

He looked perplexed for a second, and then shrugged. I walked on, looking at faces, searching for a familiar one. The trouble was I'd paid the four clerks in the compartment so little attention that I wasn't sure I'd recognize any one of them again, and I wouldn't have done, if he hadn't given himself away. When he saw me looking at him, he jerked, stepped down off his stand, and bolted.

Running was outside my repertoire. I walked quietly up behind him an hour later when he had judged it safe to go back to his job.

'A word in your ear,' I said at his elbow.

He jumped six inches. 'It was nothing to do with me.'

'I know that. Just tell me who the two men were. Those two in overalls.'

'Do me a favour. Do I want to end up in hospital?'

'Twenty quid?' I suggested.

'I dunno about that . . . How come you're here today?'

'Why not?'

'When those two've seen to someone . . . they stay seen to.'

'Is that so? They seemed pretty harmless.'

'No, straight up,' he said curiously, 'didn't they touch you?'

'No.'

He was puzzled.

'A pony. Twenty-five quid,' I said. 'For their names, or who they work for?'

He hesitated. 'Not here, mate. On the train.'

'Not on the train.' I was positive. 'In the press box. And now.'

He got five minutes off from his grumbling employer and went in front of me up the stairs to the eyrie allotted to newspapers. I gave a shove-off sign to the only press man up there, and he obligingly disappeared.

'Right,' I said. 'Who were they?'

'They're Brummies,' he said cautiously.

'I know that. You could cut their accents.'

'Bruisers,' he ventured.

I stopped myself just in time from telling him I knew that too.

'They're Charlie Boston's boys.' It came out in a nervous rush.

'That's better. Who's Charlie Boston?'

'So who hasn't heard of Charlie Boston? Got some betting shops, hasn't he, in Birmingham and Wolverhampton and such like.'

'And some boys on race trains?'

He looked more puzzled than ever. 'Don't you owe Charlie no money? So what did they want, then? It's usually bad debts they're after.'

'I've never heard of Charlie Boston before, let alone had a bet with him.' I took out my wallet and gave him five fivers. He took them with a practised flick and stowed them away in a pocket like Fort Knox under his left armpit. 'Dirty thieves,' he explained. 'Taking precautions, aren't I?'

He scuttled off down the stairs, and I stayed up in the press box and took another swig at my useful little bottle, reflecting that when Charlie Boston unleashed his boys on me he had been very foolish indeed.

Luke-John reacted predictably with a bridling 'They can't do that to the *Blaze*' attitude.

Wednesday morning. Not much doing in the office. Derry with his feet up on the blotter, Luke-John elbow deep in the dailies' sports pages, the telephone silent, and every desk in the place exhibiting the same feverish inactivity.

Into this calm I dropped the pebble of news that two men, adopting a threatening attitude, had told me not to interfere in the non-starters racket. Luke-John sat up erect like a belligerent bull frog, quivering with satisfaction that the article had produced tangible results. With a claw hand he pounced on the telephone.

'Manchester office? Give me the sports desk . . . That you, Andy? Luke Morton. What can you tell me about a bookmaker called Charlie Boston? Has a string of betting shops around Birmingham.'

He listened to a lengthy reply with growing intensity.

'That adds up. Yes. Yes. Fine. Ask around and let me know.'

He put down the receiver and rubbed his larynx. 'Charlie Boston changed his spots about a year ago. Before that he was apparently an ordinary Birmingham bookmaker with about six shops and a reasonable reputation. Now, Andy says he's expanded a lot and become a bully. He says he's been hearing too much about Charlie Boston lately. Seems he hires two ex-boxers to collect unpaid debts from his credit customers, and as a result of all this he's coining it.'

I thought it over. Charlie Boston of Birmingham with his betting shops and bruisers didn't gel at all with the description Dembley had given me of a quiet gentleman in a Rolls with a chauffeur and a Greek, Dutch, or Scandinavian accent. They even seemed an unlikely pair of shoulder to shoulder partners. There might of course be two separate rackets going on, and if so, what happened if they clashed? And by which of them had Bert Checkov been seduced? But if they were all one outfit, I'd settle for the Rolls gent as the brains and Charlie Boston the muscles. Setting his dogs on me had been classic muscle-bound thinking.

Luke-John's telephone rang and he reached out a hand. As he listened his eyes narrowed and he turned his head to look straight at me.

'What do you mean, he was pulped? He certainly was not. He's here in the office at this moment and he went to Plumpton races yesterday. What your paper needs is a little less imagination . . . If you don't believe me, talk to him yourself.' He handed me the receiver, saying with a grimace, 'Connersley. Bloody man.'

'I heard,' said the precise malicious voice on the phone, 'that some Birmingham heavies took you to pieces on the Leicester race train.'

'A rumour,' I said with boredom. 'I heard it myself yesterday at Plumpton.'

'According to my informant you couldn't have gone to Plumpton.'

'Your informant is unreliable. Scrap him.'

A small pause. Then he said, 'I can check if you were there.'

'Check away.' I put the receiver down with a brusque crash and thanked my stars I had reached Luke-John with my version first.

'Are you planning a follow-up on Sunday?' he was asking. Connersley had planted no suspicions: was already forgotten. 'Hammer the point home. Urge the racing authorities to act. Agitate. You know the drill.'

I nodded. I knew the drill. My bruises gave me a protesting nudge. No more, they said urgently. Write a nice mild piece on an entirely different, totally innocuous subject.

'Get some quotes,' Luke-John said.

'OK.'

'Give with some ideas,' he said impatiently. 'I'm doing all your ruddy work.'

I sighed. Shallowly and carefully. 'How about us making sure Tiddely Pom starts in the Lamplighter? Maybe I'll go fix it with the Ronceys . . .'

Luke-John interrupted, his eyes sharp. 'The *Blaze* will see to it that Tiddely Pom runs. Ty, that's genius.

Start your piece with that. The *Blaze* will see to it . . . Splendid. Splendid.'

Oh God, I thought. I'm the world's greatest bloody fool. Stay out of race trains, Tonio Perelli had said. Nothing about lying down on the tracks.

CHAPTER EIGHT

Nothing had changed at the Ronceys'. Dead leaves, cobwebs, still in place. No dripping meat on the kitchen table: two unplucked pheasants sagged with limp necks there instead. The sink overflowed with unwashed dishes and the wellington smell had intensified.

I arrived unannounced at two-thirty and found Roncey himself out in the yard watching Pat and the old man saw up a large hunk of dead tree. He received me with an unenthusiastic glare but eventually took me through into the sitting-room with a parting backwards instruction to his son to clean out the tackroom when he'd finished the logs.

Madge was lying on the sofa, asleep. Still no stockings, still the blue slippers, still the yellow dress, very dirty now down the front. Roncey gave her a glance of complete indifference and gestured me to one of the armchairs.

'I don't need help from the *Blaze*,' he said, as he'd said outside in the yard. 'Why should I?'

'It depends on how much you want Tiddely Pom to run in the Lamplighter.'

'Of course he's going to run.' Roncey looked aggressive and determined. 'I told you. Anyone who tries to tell me otherwise has another think coming.'

'In that case,' I said mildly, 'one of two things will happen. Either the men operating the racket will abandon the idea of preventing Tiddely Pom from running, as a result of all the publicity they've been getting. Or they will go ahead and stop him. If they've any sense they'll abandon the idea. But I don't see how one can count on them having any sense.'

'They won't stop him.' Pugnacious jaw, stubborn eyes.

'You can be sure they will, one way or another, if they want to.'

'I don't believe you.'

'But would you object to taking precautions, just in case? The *Blaze* will foot the bills.'

He stared at me long and hard. 'This is not just a publicity stunt to cover your sensation-hunting paper with glory?'

'Dual purpose,' I said. 'Half for you and betting public. Half for us. But only one object: to get Tiddely Pom safely off in the Lamplighter.'

He thought it over.

'What sort of precautions?' he said at last.

I sighed inwardly with mixed feelings, a broken-ribbed skier at the top of a steep and bumpy slope, with only myself to thank.

'There are three main ones,' I said. 'The simplest is a letter to Weatherbys, stating your positive intention to run in the Lamplighter, and asking them to check carefully with you if they should receive any instructions to strike out the horse either before or after the four-day declaration stage next Tuesday. You do realize, don't you, that I or anyone else could send a telegram or a telex striking out the horse, and you would have a bit of a job getting him put back again?'

His mouth dropped open. '*Anyone?*'

'Anyone signing your name. Of course. Weatherbys receive hundreds of cancellations a week. They don't check to make sure the trainer really means it. Why should they?'

'Good God,' he said, stunned. 'I'll write at once. In fact I'll ring them up.' He began to stand up.

'There won't be that much urgency,' I said. 'Much more likely a cancellation would be sent in at the last moment, in order to allow as much time as possible for ante-post bets to be made.'

'Oh . . . quite.' A thought struck him as he sat down again. 'If the *Blaze* declares it is going to make Tiddely Pom safe and then he *doesn't* run for some reason, you are going to look very silly.'

I nodded. 'A risk. Still . . . We'll do our best. But we do need your whole-hearted cooperation, not just your qualified permission.'

He made up his mind. 'You have it. What next?'

'Tiddely Pom will have to go to another stable.'

That rocked him. 'Oh no.'

'He's much too vulnerable here.'

He swallowed. 'Where, then?'

'To one of the top trainers. He will still be expertly prepared for the race. He can have the diet he's used to. We'll give you a report on him every day.'

He opened and shut his mouth several times, speechless.

'Thirdly,' I said, 'your wife and at least your three youngest sons must go away for a holiday.'

'They can't,' he protested automatically.

'They must. If one of the children were kidnapped, would you set his life against running Tiddely Pom?'

'It isn't possible,' he said weakly.

'Just the threat might be enough.'

Madge got up and opened her eyes. They were far from dreamy. 'Where and when do we go?' she said.

'Tomorrow. You will know where after you get there.'

She smiled with a vivid delight. Fantasy had come to life. Roncey himself was not enchanted.

'I don't like it,' he said frowning.

'Ideally, you should all go. The whole lot of you,' I said.

Roncey shook his head. 'There are the other horses, and the farm. I can't leave them. And I need Pat here, and Peter.'

I agreed to that, having gained the essentials. 'Don't tell the children they are going,' I said to Madge. 'Just keep them home from school in the morning, and someone will call for you at about nine. You'll need only country clothes. And you'll be away until after the race on Saturday week. Also, please do not on any account write any letters straight to here, or let the children send any. If you want to write, send the letters to us at the *Blaze*, and we will see that Mr Roncey gets them.'

'But Vic can write to us?' Madge said.

'Of course . . . but also via the *Blaze*. Because he won't know where you are.'

They both protested, but in the end saw the sense of it. What he didn't know, he couldn't give away, even by accident.

'It won't only be people working the racket who might be looking for them,' I explained apologetically. 'But one or two of our rival newspapers will be hunting for them, so as to be able to black the *Blaze*'s eye. And they are quite skilled at finding people who want to stay hidden.'

I left the Ronceys looking blankly at each other and drove the van back to London. It seemed a very long way, and too many aches redeveloped on the journey. I'd finished Tonio's mixture just before going into the office in the morning and was back on Elizabeth's pills, which were not as good. By the time I got home I was tired, thirsty, hurting, and apprehensive.

Dealt with the first three: armchair and whisky. Contemplated the apprehension, and didn't know which would be worse, another encounter with the Boston boys or a complete failure with Tiddely Pom. It would likely be one or the other. Could even be both.

'What's the matter, Ty?' Elizabeth looked and sounded worried.

'Nothing.' I smiled at her. 'Nothing at all, honey.'

The anxious lines relaxed in her face as she smiled back. The pump hummed and thudded, pulling air into her lungs. My poor, poor Elizabeth. I stretched my hand over and touched her cheek in affection, and she turned her head and kissed my fingers.

'You're a fantastic man, Ty,' she said. She said something like it at least twice a week. I twitched my nose and made the usual sort of answer, 'You're not so bad yourself.' The disaster that a virus had made of our lives never got any better. Never would. For her it was total and absolute; for me there were exits, like Gail. When I took them, the guilt I felt was not just the ordinary guilt of an unfaithful husband, but that of a deserter. Elizabeth couldn't leave the battlefield; but when it got too much for me, I just slid out and left her.

At nine o'clock the next morning Derry Clark collected Madge and the three Roncey boys in his own Austin and drove them down to Portsmouth and straight on to the Isle of Wight car ferry.

At noon I arrived at the farm with a car and Rice

trailer borrowed from the city editor, whose daughter went in for show jumping. Roncey showed great reluctance at parting with Tiddely Pom, and loaded the second stall of the trailer with sacks of feed and bales of hay, adding to these the horse's saddle and bridle, and also three dozen eggs and a crate of beer. He had written out the diet and training regime in four-page detail scattered with emphatic underlinings. I assured him six times that I would see the new trainer followed the instructions to the last full stop.

Pat helped with the loading with a twisted smile, not unhappy that his father was losing control of the horse. He gave me a quick look full of ironic meaning when he saw me watching him, and said under his breath as he humped past with some hay, 'Now he knows what it feels like.'

I left Victor Roncey standing disconsolately in the centre of his untidy farmyard watching his one treasure depart, and drove carefully away along the Essex lanes, heading west to Berkshire. About five miles down the road I stopped near a telephone box and rang up the Western School of Art.

Gail said, 'Surprise, surprise.'

'Yes,' I agreed. 'How about Sunday?'

'Um.' She hesitated. 'How about tomorrow?'

'Won't you be teaching?'

'I meant,' she explained, 'tomorrow night.'

'Tomorrow . . . *all* night?'

'Can you manage it?'

I took so deep a breath that my sore ribs jumped. It depended on whether Mrs Woodward could stay, as she sometimes did.

'Ty?' she said. 'Are you still there?'

'Thinking.'

'What about?'

'What to tell my wife.'

'You slay me,' she said. 'Is it yes or no?'

'Yes,' I said with a sigh. 'Where?'

'A hotel, I should think.'

'All right,' I agreed. I asked her what time she finished work, and arranged a meeting point at King's Cross railway station.

When I called the flat, Elizabeth answered.

'Ty? Where are you?'

'On the road. There's nothing wrong. It's just that I forgot to ask Mrs Woodward before I left if she could stay with you tomorrow night . . . so that I could go up to Newcastle ready for the races on Saturday.' Louse, I thought. Mean, stinking louse. Lying, deceiving louse. I listened miserably to the sounds of Elizabeth asking Mrs Woodward and found no relief at all in her answer.

'She says yes, Ty, she could manage that perfectly. You'll be home again on Saturday?'

'Yes, honey. Late, though.'

'Of course.'

'See you this evening.'

''Bye, Ty,' she said with a smile in her voice. 'See you.'

I drove all the way to Norton Fox's stable wishing I hadn't done it. Knowing that I wouldn't change it. Round and round the mulberry bush and a thumping headache by Berkshire.

Norton Fox looked curiously into the trailer parked in the private front drive of his house.

'So that's the great Tiddely Pom. Can't say I think much of him from this angle.'

'Nor from any other,' I agreed. 'It's good of you to have him.'

'Happy to oblige. I'm putting him in the box next to Zig Zag, and Sandy Willis can look after both of them.'

'You won't tell her what he is?' I asked anxiously.

'Of course not.' He looked resigned to my stupidity. 'I've recently bought a chaser over in Kent . . . I've just postponed collecting it a while, but Sandy and all the other lads think Tiddely Pom is him.'

'Great.'

'I'll just get my head lad to drive the trailer into the yard and unload. You said on the phone that you wanted to stay out of sight . . . come inside for a cuppa.'

Too late, after I'd nodded, I remembered the near black tea of my former visit. The same again. Norton remarked that his housekeeper had been economizing, he never could get her to make it strong enough.

'Did the *Tally* photographer get here all right?' I

asked as he came in from the yard, filled his cup, and sat down opposite me.

He nodded. 'Took dozens of pics of Sandy Willis and thrilled her to bits.' He offered me a slice of dry-looking fruit cake and when I said no, ate a large chunk himself, undeterred. 'That article of yours last Sunday,' he said past the currants, 'that must have been a bombshell in certain quarters.'

I said, 'Mm, I hope so.'

'Brevity . . . that Champion Hurdler of mine . . . that was definitely one of the non-starters you were talking about, wasn't it? Even though you didn't mention it explicitly by name?'

'Yes, it was.'

'Ty, did you find out *why* Dembley struck his horse out, and then sold out of racing altogether?'

'I can't tell you why, Norton,' I said.

He considered this answer with his head on one side and then nodded as if satisfied. 'Tell me one day, then.'

I smiled briefly. 'When and if the racket is extinct.'

'You go on the way you are, and it will be. If you go on exposing it publicly, the ante-post market will be so untrustworthy that we'll find ourselves doing as the Americans do, only betting on a race on the day of the race, and never before. They don't have any off-the-course betting at all, over there, do they?'

'Not legally.'

He drank in big gulps down to the tea leaves. 'Might

shoot our attendances up if punters had to go to the races to have a bet.'

'Which would shoot up the prize money too . . . did you see that their champion jockey earned well over three million dollars last year? Enough to make Gordon Richards weep.'

I put down the half-finished tea and stood up. 'Must be getting back, Norton. Thank you again for your help.'

'Anything to prevent another Brevity.'

'Send the accounts to the *Blaze*.'

He nodded. 'And ring the sports desk every day to give a report, and don't speak to anyone except you or Derry Clark or a man called Luke-John Morton. Right?'

'Absolutely right,' I agreed. 'Oh . . . and here are Victor Roncey's notes. Eggs and beer in Tiddely Pom's food every night.'

'I've one owner,' Norton said, 'who sends his horse champagne.'

I drove the trailer back to the city editor's house, swapped it for my van, and went home. Ten to seven on the clock. Mrs Woodward was having a grand week for overtime and had cooked chicken à la king for our supper, leaving it ready and hot. I thanked her. 'Not at all, Mr Tyrone, a pleasure I'm sure. Ta ta, luv, see you tomorrow, I'll bring my things for stopping the night.'

I kissed Elizabeth, poured the drinks, ate the

chicken, watched a TV programme, and let a little of the day's tension trickle away. After supper there was my Sunday article to write. Enthusiasm for the project: way below zero. I went into the writing-room determined to put together a calm played-down sequel to the previous week, with a sober let's-not-rush-our-fences approach. Somewhere along the line most of these good intentions vanished. Neither Charlie Boston nor the foreign gent in the Rolls was going to like the result.

Before setting off to the office in the morning I packed an overnight bag, with Elizabeth reminding me to take my alarm clock and a clean shirt.

'I hate it when you go away,' she said. 'I know you don't go often, probably not nearly as much as you ought to. I know you try not to get the faraway meetings . . . Derry nearly always does them, and I feel so guilty because his wife has those tiny children to look after all alone . . .'

'Stop worrying,' I said, smiling. 'Derry likes to go.' I had almost convinced myself that I really was taking the afternoon train to Newcastle. Gail was hours away, unreal. I kissed Elizabeth's cheek three times and dearly regretted leaving her. Yet I left.

Luke-John and Derry were both out of the office when I arrived. Luke-John's secretary handed me a large envelope which she said had come for me by hand just after I left on Wednesday. I opened it. The galley-proofs of my *Tally* article: please would I read and OK immediately.

'*Tally* telephoned for you twice yesterday,' Luke-John's secretary said. 'They go to press today. They wanted you urgently.'

I read the article. Arnold Shankerton had changed it about here and there and had stamped his own slightly pedantic views of grammar all over it. I sighed. I didn't like the changes, but a hundred and fifty guineas plus expenses softened the impact.

Arnold Shankerton said in his perfectly modulated tenor, with a mixture of annoyance and apology, 'I'm afraid we've had to go ahead and print, as we hadn't heard from you.'

'My fault. I've only just picked up your letter.'

'I see. Well, after I'd worked on it a little I think it reads very well, don't you? We're quite pleased with it. We think it will be a success with our readers. They like that sort of intimate human touch.'

'I'm glad,' I said politely. 'Will you send me a copy?'

'I'll make a note of it,' he said suavely. I thought I would probably have to buy one on a bookstall. 'Let me have your expenses. Small, I hope?'

'Sure,' I agreed. 'Tiny.'

Luke-John and Derry came back as I disconnected and Luke-John, without bothering to say good morning, stretched out a hand for my Sunday offering. I took it out of my pocket and he unfolded it and read it.

'Hmph,' he said. 'I expected a bit more bite.'

Derry took one of the carbon copies from me and read it.

'Any more bite and he'd have chewed up the whole page,' he said, disagreeing.

'Couldn't you emphasize a bit more that only the *Blaze* knows where Tiddely Pom is?' Luke-John said. 'You've only implied it.'

'If you think so.'

'Yes, I do think so. As the *Blaze* is footing the bills we want all the credit we can get.'

'Suppose someone finds him . . . Tiddely Pom?' I asked mildly. 'Then we'd look right nanas, hiding him, boasting about it, and then having him found.'

'No one will find him. The only people who know where he is are us three and Norton Fox. To be more precise, only you and Fox know *exactly* where he is. Only you and Fox know which in that yard full of sixty horses is Tiddely Pom. Neither of you is going to tell anyone else. So how is anyone going to find him? No, no, Ty. You make that article absolutely definite. The *Blaze* is keeping the horse safe, and only the *Blaze* knows where he is.'

'Charlie Boston may not like it,' Derry observed to no one in particular.

'Charlie Boston can stuff it,' Luke-John said impatiently.

'I meant,' Derry explained, 'that he might just send

his thug-uglies to take Ty apart for so obviously ignoring their keep-off-the-grass.'

My pal. Luke-John considered the possibility for two full seconds before shaking his head. 'They wouldn't dare.'

'And even if they did,' I said, 'it would make a good story and you could sell more papers.'

'Exactly.' Luke-John started nodding and then looked at me suspiciously. 'That was a joke?'

'A feeble one.' I sighed, past smiling.

'Change the intro, then, Ty. Make it one hundred per cent specific.' He picked up a pencil and put a line through the first paragraph. Read the next, rubbed his larynx thoughtfully, let that one stand. Axed the next. Turned the page.

Derry watched sympathetically as the pencil marks grew. It happened to him, too, often enough. Luke-John scribbled his way through to the end and then returned to the beginning, pointing out each alteration that he wanted made. He was turning my moderately hard-hitting original into a bulldozing battering ram.

'You'll get me slaughtered,' I said, and meant it.

I worked on the rewrite most of the morning, fighting a rearguard action all the way. What Luke-John finally passed was a compromise between his view and mine, which still left me so far out on a limb as to be balancing on twigs. Luke-John took it in to the editor, stayed there while he read it, and brought it triumphantly back.

'He liked it. Thinks it's great stuff. He liked Derry's piece yesterday too, summing up the handicap. He told me the sports desk is a big asset to the paper.'

'Good,' Derry said cheerfully. 'When do we get our next raise?'

'Time for a jar at The Devereux,' Luke-John suggested, looking at his watch. 'Coming today, Ty?'

'Norton Fox hasn't rung through yet.'

'Call him then.'

I telephoned to Fox. Tiddely Pom was fine, ate his feed the previous evening, had settled in well, had done a mile at a working canter that morning, and no one had looked at him twice. I thanked him and relayed the news to Roncey, who sounded both agitated and depressed.

'I don't like it,' he said several times.

'Do you want to risk having him at home?'

He hesitated, then said, 'I suppose not. No. But I don't like it. Don't forget to ring tomorrow evening. I'll be at Kempton races all afternoon.'

'The sports editor will ring,' I assured him. 'And don't worry.'

He put the receiver down saying an explosive 'Huh.' Luke-John and Derry were already on the way to the door and I joined them to go to lunch.

'Only a fortnight since Bert Checkov died,' observed Derry, sitting on a bar stool. 'Only ten days since we spotted the non-starters. Funny.'

Hilarious. And eight more days to go to the

Lamplighter. This Monday, I decided, I would stay safely tucked away at home.

'Don't forget,' I said to Derry. 'Don't tell anyone my phone number.'

'What brought that on all of a sudden?'

'I was thinking about Charlie Boston. My address isn't in the phone book . . .'

'Neither Derry nor I will give your address to anyone,' Luke-John said impatiently. 'Come off it, Ty, anyone would think you were frightened.'

'Anyone would be so right,' I agreed, and they both laughed heartily into their pints.

Derry was predictably pleased that I wanted to go to Newcastle instead of Kempton, leaving the London meeting for once for him.

'Is it all right?' he said, embarrassed. 'With your wife, I mean?'

I told him what Elizabeth had said, but as usual anything to do with her made him uncomfortable. Luke-John said dutifully, 'How is she?' and I said 'Fine.'

I kicked around the office all the afternoon, arranging a travel warrant to Newcastle, putting in a chit for expenses for Heathbury Park, Leicester, and Plumpton, and collecting the cash from Accounts. Luke-John was busy with a football columnist and the golfing correspondent, and Derry took time off from working out his tips for every meeting in the following week to tell me about taking the Roncey kids to the Isle of Wight.

'Noisy little devils,' he said disapprovingly. 'Their mother has no control over them at all. She seemed to be in a dream most of the time. Anyway, none of them actually fell off the ferry, which was a miracle considering Tony, that was the eldest one, was trying to lean over far enough to see the paddles go round. I told him they were under the water. Made no difference.'

I made sympathetic noises, trying not to laugh out of pity for my ribs. 'They were happy enough, then?'

'Are you kidding? No school and a holiday at the sea? Tony said he was going to bathe, November or no November. His mother showed no signs of stopping him. Anyway, they settled into the boarding house all right though I should think we shall get a whacking bill for damage, and they thought it tremendous fun to change their names to Robinson, no trouble there. They thought Robinson was a smashing choice, they would all pretend they were cast away on a desert island . . . Well, I tell you, Ty, by the time I left them I was utterly exhausted.'

'Never mind. You can look forward to bringing them back.'

'Not me,' he said fervently. 'Your turn for that.'

*

At four I picked up my suitcase and departed for King's Cross. The Newcastle train left at five. I watched it go.

At five forty-eight she came up from the Underground, wearing a beautifully cut darkish-blue coat and carrying a creamy-white suitcase. Several heads turned to look at her, and a nearby man who had been waiting almost as long as I had watched her steadfastly until she reached the corner where I stood.

'Hullo,' she said. 'Sorry I'm late.'

'Think nothing of it.'

'I gather,' she said with satisfaction, 'that you fixed your wife.'

CHAPTER NINE

She moved against me in the warm dark and put her mouth on the thin skin somewhere just south of my neck. I tightened my arms round her, and buried my nose in her clean, sweet-scented hair.

'There's always something new,' she said sleepily. 'Broken ribs are quite a gimmick.'

'I didn't feel them.'

'Oh yes you did.'

I stroked my hands slowly over her smooth skin and didn't bother to answer. I felt relaxed and wholly content. She had been kind to my ribs, gentle to my bruises. They had even in an obscure way given her pleasure.

'How did it happen?'

'What?'

'The black-and-blue bit.'

'I lost an argument.'

She rubbed her nose on my chest. 'Must have been quite a debate.'

I smiled in the dark. The whole world was inside

the sheets, inside the small private cocoon wrapping two bodies in intimate primeval understanding.

'Ty?'

'Mm?'

'Can't we stay together all weekend?'

I said through her hair, 'I have to phone in a report from Newcastle. Can't avoid it.'

'Damn the *Blaze*.'

'There's Sunday, though.'

'Hurrah for the Golf Club.'

We lay quiet for a long while. I felt heavy with sleep and fought to stay awake. There were so few hours like this. None to waste.

For Gail time was not so precious. Her limbs slackened and her head slid down on to my arm, her easy breath fanning softly against my chest. I thought of Elizabeth lying closely curled against me like that when we were first married, and for once it was without guilt, only with regret.

Gail woke of her own accord a few hours later and pulled my wrist round to look at the luminous hands on my watch.

'Are you awake?' she said. 'It's ten to six.'

'Do you like it in the morning?'

'With you, Ty, any time.' Her voice smiled in the darkness. 'Any old time you care to mention.'

I wasn't that good. I said, 'Why?'

'Because you're normal, maybe. Nice bread and

butter love.' She played the piano down my stomach. 'Some men want the weirdest things . . .'

'Let's not talk about them.'

'OK,' she said. 'Let's not.'

I caught the Newcastle express at eight o'clock with ten seconds in hand. It was a raw cold morning with steam hissing up from under the train. Hollow clanking noises and unintelligible station announcements filled the cars, and bleary-eyed shiving passengers hurried greyly through the British Standard dawn.

I took my shivering bleary-eyed self into the dining car and tried some strong black coffee, but nothing was going to shift the dragging depression which had settled in inexorably as soon as I left Gail. I imagined her as I had left her, lying warm and luxuriously lazy in the soft bed and saying Sunday was tomorrow. We could start again where we'd left off. Sunday was certainly tomorrow, but there was Saturday to get through first. From where I sat it looked like a very long day.

Four and a half hours to Newcastle. I slept most of the way, and spent the rest remembering the evening and night which were gone. We had found a room in a small private hotel near the station and I had signed the register Mr and Mrs Tyrone. No one there had shown any special interest in us; they had presently shown us to a clean uninspiring room and given us the key, had asked if we wanted early tea, and said they were sorry they didn't do dinner, there were several good restaurants round about. I paid them in advance, explaining that I had an early train to catch. They smiled, thanked me, withdrew, asked no questions, made no comment. Impossible to know what they guessed.

We talked for a while and then went out to a pub for a drink and from there to an Indian restaurant where we took a long time eating little, and an even longer time drinking coffee. Gail wore her usual air of businesslike poise and remained striking-looking even when surrounded by people of her own skin colour. I, with my pale face, was in a minority.

Gail commented on it. 'London must be the best place in the world for people like me.'

'For anyone.'

She shook her head. 'Especially for people of mixed race. In so many countries I'd be on the outside looking in. I'd never get the sort of job I have.'

'It never seems to worry you, being of mixed race,' I said.

'I accept it. In fact I wouldn't choose now to be wholly white or wholly black, if I could alter it. I am used to being me. And with people like you, of course, it is easy, because you are unaffected by me.'

'I wouldn't say that, exactly,' I said, grinning.

'Damn it, you know what I mean. You don't mind me being brown.'

'You're brown and you're beautiful. A shattering combination.'

'You're not being serious,' she complained.

'And you're glossy to the bone.'

Her lips curved in amusement. 'If you mean I've a hard core instead of a soft centre, then I expect you're right.'

'And one day you'll part from me without a twinge.'

'Will we part?' No anxiety, no involvement.

'What do you think?'

'I think you wouldn't leave your wife to live with me.'

Direct, no muddle, no fluffy wrappings.

'Would you?' she asked, when I didn't quickly answer.

'I'll never leave her.'

'That's what I thought. I like to get things straight. Then I can enjoy what I have, and not expect more.'

'Hedging your bets.'

'What do you mean?' she asked.

'Insuring against disappointment.'

'When people desperately want what they can never have, they *suffer*. Real grinding misery. That's not for me.'

'You will be luckier than most,' I said slowly, 'if you can avoid it altogether.'

'I'll have a damned good try.'

One day uncontrollable emotion would smash up all that organized level-headedness. Not while I was around, if I could help it. I prized it too much. Needed her to stay like that. Only while she demanded so little could I go on seeing her, and since she clearly knew it, we had a good chance of staying clearly on the tightrope for as long as we wanted.

With the coffee we talked, as before, about money. Gail complained that she never had enough.

'Who has?' I said sympathetically.

'Your wife, for one.' There was a faint asperity in her voice, which made me stifle my immediate impulse to deny it.

'Sorry,' she said almost at once. 'Shouldn't have said that. What your wife has is quite irrelevant. It's what I haven't got that we're talking about. Such as a car of my own, a sports car, and not having to borrow Harry's all the time. And a flat of my own, a sunny one overlooking the park. Never having to budget every penny. Buying lavish presents for people if I feel like it. Flying to Paris often for a few days, and having a holiday in Japan . . .'

'Marry a millionaire,' I suggested.

'I intend to.'

We both laughed, but I thought she probably meant it. The man she finally didn't part with would have to have troubles with his surtax. I wondered what she would do if she knew I could only afford that dinner and the hotel bill because *Tally*'s fee would be plugging for a while the worst holes in the Tyrone economy. What would she do if she knew that I had a penniless paralysed wife, not a rich one. On both counts, wave a rapid goodbye, probably. For as long as I could, I wasn't going to give her the opportunity.

I missed the first Newcastle race altogether and only reached the press stand halfway through the second. Delicate probes among colleagues revealed that nothing dramatic had happened in the hurdle race I had spent urging the taxi driver to rise above twenty. Luke-John would never know.

After the fourth race I telephoned through a report, and another after the fifth, in which one of the top northern jockeys broke his leg. Derry came on the line and asked me to go and find out from the trainer who would be riding his horse in the Lamplighter instead, and I did his errand thanking my stars I had had the sense actually to go to Newcastle, and hadn't been tempted to watch the racing on television and phone through an 'on-the-spot' account from an armchair three hundred miles away, as one correspondent of my acquaintance had been known to do.

Just before the last race someone touched my arm. I turned. Colly Gibbons, the handicapper, looking harassed and annoyed.

'Ty. Do me a favour.'

'What?'

'You came by train? First class?'

I nodded. The *Blaze* wasn't mean about comfort.

'Then swap return tickets with me.' He held out a slim booklet which proved to be an air ticket, Newcastle to Heathrow.

'There's some damn meeting been arranged here which I shall have to go to after this race,' he explained. 'And I won't be able to catch the plane. I've only just found out . . . it's most annoying. There's a later train . . . I particularly want to get to London tonight.'

'Done,' I said. 'Suits me fine.'

He smiled, still frowning simultaneously. 'Thanks. And here are the keys to my car. It's in the multi-storey park opposite the Europa building.' He told me its number and position. 'Drive yourself home.'

'I'll drive to your house and leave the car there,' I said. 'Easier than bringing it over tomorrow.'

'If you're sure . . .' I nodded, giving him my train ticket.

'A friend who lives up here was going to run me back to the airport,' he said. 'I'll get him to take you instead.'

'Have you heard from your wife?' I asked.

'That's just it . . . she wrote to say we'd have a trial reconciliation and she'd be coming home today. If I stay away all night she'll never believe I had a good reason . . . She'll be gone again.'

'Miss the meeting,' I suggested.

'It's too important, especially now I've got your help. I suppose you couldn't explain to her, if she's there, that I'm on my way?'

'Of course,' I said.

So the friend whisked me off to the airport and I flew to Heathrow, collected the car, drove to

Hampstead, explained to Mrs Gibbons, who promised to wait, and arrived home two and a half hours early. Elizabeth was pleased, even if Mrs Woodward wasn't.

Sunday morning. Elizabeth's mother didn't come.

Ten-fifteen, ten-thirty. Nothing. At eleven someone telephoned from the health farm and said they were so sorry, my mother-in-law was in bed with a virus infection, nothing serious, don't worry, she would ring her daughter as soon as she was a little better.

I told Elizabeth. 'Oh well,' she said philosophically, 'we'll have a nice cosy day on our own.'

I smiled at her and kept the shocking disappointment out of my face.

'Do you think Sue Davies would pop along for a moment while I get some whisky?' I asked.

'She'd get it for us.'

'I'd like to stretch my legs . . .'

She smiled understandingly and rang Sue, who came at twelve with flour down the sides of her jeans. I hurried round corners to the nearest phone box and gave the Huntersons' number. The bell rang there again and again, but no one answered. Without much hope I got the number of Virginia Water station and rang there: no, they said, there was no young woman waiting outside in an estate car. They hadn't seen one all morning. I asked for the Huntersons' number again. Again, no reply.

Feeling flat I walked back to our local pub and

bought the whisky, and tried yet again on the telephone too publicly installed in the passage there.

No answer. No Gail.

I went home.

Sue Davis had read out to Elizabeth my piece in the *Blaze*.

'Straight between the eyeballs,' she observed cheerfully. 'I must say, Ty, no one would connect the punch you pack in that paper with the you we know.'

'What's wrong with the him you know?' asked Elizabeth with real anxiety under the surface gaiety. She hated people to think me weak for staying at home with her. She never told anyone how much nursing she needed from me: always pretended Mrs Woodward did everything. She seemed to think that what I did for her would appear unmanly to others; she wanted in public a masculine never-touch-the-dishes husband, and since it made her happy I played that role except when we were alone.

'Nothing's wrong with him,' Sue protested. She looked me over carefully. 'Nothing at all.'

'What did you mean, then?' Elizabeth was smiling still, but she wanted an answer.

'Oh . . . only that this Ty is so quiet, and that one . . .' she pointed to the paper, 'bursts the eardrums.' She put her head on one side, summing me up, then turned to Elizabeth with the best of motives and said: 'This one is so gentle . . . that one is tough.'

'Gentle nothing,' I said, seeing the distress under

Elizabeth's laugh. 'When you aren't here, Sue, I throw her round the room and black her eyes regularly on Fridays.' Elizabeth relaxed, liking that. 'Stay for a drink,' I suggested to Sue, 'now that I've fetched it.'

She went, however, back to her half-baked Yorkshire pudding, and I avoided discussing what she had said by going out to the kitchen and rustling up some omelettes for lunch. Elizabeth particularly liked them, and could eat hers with the new feeding gadget, up to a point. I helped her when her wrist tired, and made some coffee and fixed her mug in its holder.

'Do you really know where the horse is?' she asked.

'Tiddely Pom? Yes, of course.'

'Where is it?'

'Dark and deadly secret, honey,' I said. 'I can't tell anyone, even you.'

'Oh, go on,' she urged. 'You know I won't tell either.'

'I'll tell you next Sunday.'

Her nose wrinkled. 'Thanks for nothing.' The pump heaved away, giving her breath. 'You don't think anyone would try to . . . well . . . *make* you tell. Where he is, I mean.' More worry, more anxiety. She couldn't help it. She was always on the edge of a precipice, always on the distant look-out for anything which would knock her over.

'Of course not, honey. How could they?'

'I don't know,' she said; but her eyes were full of horrors.

'Stop fussing,' I said with a smile. 'If anyone threatened me with anything really nasty, I'd say quick enough where he is. No horse is worth getting in too deep for.' Echoes of Dembley. The matrix which nurtured the germ. No one would sacrifice themselves or their families for the sake of running a horse.

Elizabeth detected the truth in my voice and was satisfied. She switched on the television and watched some fearful old movie which bored me to death. Three o'clock came and went. Even if I'd gone to Virginia Water, I would have been on the way back again. And I'd had Friday night. Rare, unexpected Friday night. Trouble was, the appetite grew on what it fed on, as someone else once said. The next Sunday was at the wrong end of a telescope.

Drinks, supper, jobs for Elizabeth, bed. No one else called, no one telephoned. It crossed my mind once or twice as I lazed in the armchair in our customary closed-in little world, that perhaps the challenge implicit in my column had stirred up, somewhere, a hive of bees.

Buzz buzz, busy little bees. Buzz around the *Blaze*. And don't sting me.

I spent all Monday in and around the flat. Washed the van, wrote letters, bought some socks, kept off race trains from Leicester.

Derry telephoned twice to tell me (*a*) that Tiddely Pom was flourishing, and (*b*) the Roncey children had sent him a stick of peppermint rock.

'Big deal,' I said.

'Not bad kids.'

'You'll enjoy fetching them.'

He blew a raspberry and hung up.

Tuesday morning I walked to the office. One of those brownish late November days, with saturated air and a sour scowl of fog to come. Lights shone out brightly at 11 a.m. People hurried along Fleet Street with pinched, mean eyes working out whose neck to scrunch on the next rung of the ladder, and someone bought a blind man's matches with a poker chip.

Luke-John and Derry wore moods to match.

'What's the matter?' I asked mildly.

'Nothing's happened,' Derry said.

'So?'

'So where's our reaction?' Luke-John enquired angrily. 'Not a letter. No one's phoned, even. Unless,' he brightened, 'unless Charlie Boston's boys have called on you with a few more threats?'

'They have not.'

Relapse into gloom for the sports desk. I alone wasn't sorry the article had fallen with a dull thud. If it had. I thought it was too soon to be sure. I said so.

'Hope you're right, Ty,' Luke-John said sceptically. 'Hope it hasn't all been a coincidence . . . Bert Checkov and the non-starters . . . hope the *Blaze* hasn't wasted its time and money for nothing on Tiddely Pom . . .'

'Charlie Boston's boys were not a coincidence.'

'I suppose not.' Luke-John sounded as though he

thought I might have misunderstood what the Boston boys had said.

'Did your friend in Manchester find out any more about Charlie B?' I asked.

Luke-John shrugged. 'Only that there was some talk about his chain of betting shops being taken over by a bigger concern. But it doesn't seem to have happened. He is still there, anyway, running the show.'

'Which bigger concern?'

'Don't know.'

To pass the time we dialled four of the biggest London bookmaking businesses which had chains of betting shops all over the country. None of them admitted any immediate interest in buying out Charlie Boston. But one man was hesitant, and when I pressed him, he said, 'We did put out a feeler, about a year ago. We understood there was a foreign buyer also interested. But Boston decided to remain independent and turned down both offers.'

'Thanks,' I said, and Luke-John commented that that took us a long way, didn't it. He turned his attention crossly to a pile of letters which had flooded in contradicting one of the football writers, and Derry began to assess the form for the big race on Boxing Day. All over the vast office space the Tuesday picking of teeth and scratching of scabs proceeded without haste, the slow week still lumbering. Tuesday was gossip day. Wednesday, planning. Thursday, writing. Friday, editing. Saturday, printing. Sunday, *Blaze* away. And on

Mondays the worked-on columns lit real fires or wrapped fish and chips. No immortality for a journalist.

Tuesday was also *Tally* day. Neither at home nor at the office had a copy come for me by post. I went downstairs to the next-door magazine stand, bought one, and went back inside the *Blaze*.

The pictures were off-beat and rather good, the whole article well presented. One had to admit that Shankerton knew his stuff. I forgave him his liberties with my syntax.

I picked up Derry's telephone and got through to the *Tally* despatch department. As expected, they didn't send free copies to the subjects of any articles: not their policy. Would they send them? Oh sure, give us the addresses, we'll let you have the bill. I gave them the six addresses, Huntersons, Ronceys, Sandy Willis, Colly Gibbons, Dermot Finnegan, Willie Ondroy.

Derry picked up the magazine and plodded through the article, reading at one third Luke-John's wide-angled speed.

'Deep, deep,' he said ironically, putting it down. 'One hundred and fifty fathoms.'

'Sixty will go in tax.'

'A hard life,' Derry sighed. 'But if you hadn't picked on Roncey, we would never have cottoned on to this non-starter racket.'

Nor would I have had any cracked ribs. With them, though, the worst was over. Only coughing, sneezing, laughing, and taking running jumps were sharply undesirable. I had stopped eating Elizabeth's pills. In another week, the cracks would have knitted.

'Be seeing you,' I said to Derry. Luke-John waved a freckled farewell hand. Carrying *Tally* I went down in the lift and turned out of the front door up towards the Strand, bound for a delicatessen shop which sold Austrian apple cake which Elizabeth liked.

Bought the cake. Came out into the street. Heard a voice in my ear. Felt a sharp prick through my coat abeam the first lumbar vertebra.

'It's a knife, Mr Tyrone.'

I stood quite still. People could be stabbed to death in busy streets and no one noticed until the body cluttered up the fairway. Killers vanished into crowds with depressing regularity.

'What do you want?' I said.

'Just stay where you are.'

Standing on the Fleet Street pavement, holding a magazine and a box of apple cake. Just stay where you are. For how long?

'For how long?' I said.

He didn't answer. But he was still there, because his knife was. We stood where we were for all of two minutes. Then a black Rolls rolled to a silent halt at the kerb directly opposite where I stood. The door to the back seat swung open.

'Get in,' said the voice behind me.

I got in. There was a chauffeur driving, all black

uniform and a stolid acne-scarred neck. The man with the knife climbed in after me and settled by my side. I glanced at him, I knew I'd seen him somewhere before, didn't know where. I put *Tally* and the apple cake carefully on the floor. Sat back. Went for a ride.

CHAPTER TEN

We turned north into the Aldwych and up Drury Lane to St Giles Circus. I made no move towards escape, although we stopped several times at traffic lights. My companion watched me warily, and I worked on where I had seen him before and still came up with nothing. Up Tottenham Court Road. Left, right, left again. Straight into Regent's Park and round the semi-circle. Stopped smoothly at the turnstile entrance to the Zoo.

'Inside,' said my companion, nodding.

We stepped out of the car, and the chauffeur quietly drove off.

'You can pay,' I remarked.

He gave me a quick glance, tried to juggle the money out of his pocket one-handed, and found he couldn't manage it if he were to be of any use with his knife.

'No,' he said. 'You pay. For us both.'

I paid, almost smiling. He was nowhere near as dangerous as he wanted to be thought.

We checked through the turnstiles. 'Where now?' I said.

'Straight ahead. I'll tell you.'

The Zoo was nearly empty. On that oily Tuesday November lunch time, not even the usual bus loads from schools. Birds shrieked mournfully above the aviary and a notice board said the vultures would be fed at three.

A man in a dark overcoat and black homburg hat was sitting on a seat looking towards the lions' outdoor compounds. The cages were empty. The sun-loving lions were inside under the sun lamps.

'Over there,' said my companion, nodding.

We walked across. The man in the black homburg watched us come. Every line of his clothes and posture spoke of money, authority, and high social status, and his manner of irritating superiority would have done credit to the Foreign Office. As Dembley had said, his subject matter was at variance with his appearance.

'Did you have any trouble?' he asked.

'None at all,' said the knife man smugly.

A bleak expression crept into pale grey eyes as cold as the stratosphere. 'I am not pleased to hear it.'

The accent in his voice was definite but difficult. A thickening of some consonants, a clipping of some vowels.

'Go away, now,' he said to the knife man. 'And wait.'

My nondescript abductor in his nondescript raincoat nodded briefly and walked away, and I nearly remembered where I'd seen him. Recollection floated up, but not far enough.

'You chose to come,' the man in the homburg said flatly.

'Yes and no.'

He stood up. My height, but thicker. Yellowish skin, smooth except for a maze of wrinkles round his eyes. What I could see of his hair was nearly blond, and I put his age down roughly as five or six years older than myself.

'It is cold outside. We will go in.'

I walked with him round inside the Big Cats' House, where the strong feral smell seemed an appropriate background to the proceedings. I could guess what he wanted. Not to kill: that could have been done in Fleet Street or anywhere on the way. To extort. The only question was how.

'You show too little surprise,' he said.

'We were waiting for some . . . reaction. Expecting it.'

'I see.' He was silent, working it out. A bored-looking tiger blinked at us lazily, claws sheathed inside rounded pads, tail swinging a fraction from side to side. I sneered at him. He turned and walked three paces and three paces back, round and round, going nowhere.

'Was last week's reaction not enough for you?'

'Very useful,' I commented. 'Led us straight to Charlie Boston. So kind of you to ask. That makes you a sidekick of his.'

He gave me a blazingly frosty glare. 'I *employ* Boston.'

I looked down, not answering. If his pride were as easily stung as that he might give me more answers than I gave him.

'When I heard about it I disapproved of what they did on the train. Now, I am not so sure.' His voice was quiet again, the voice of culture, diplomacy, tact.

'You didn't order it, then?'

'I did not.'

I ran my hand along the thick metal bar which kept visitors four feet away from the animals' cages. The tiger looked tame, too gentle to kill. Too indifferent to maul, to maim, to scrape to the bone.

'You know what we want,' said the polite tiger by my side. 'We want to know where you have hidden the horse.'

'Why?' I said.

He merely blinked at me.

I sighed. 'What good will it do you? Do you still seriously intend to try to prevent it from running? You would be much wiser to forget the whole thing and quietly fold your tent and steal away.'

'You will leave that decision entirely to me.' Again, the pride stuck out a mile. I didn't like it. Few enemies were as ruthless as those who feared a loss of face. I began to consider before how wide an acquaintanceship the face had to be preserved. The wider, the worse for me.

'Where is it?'

'Tiddely Pom?' I said.

'Tiddely Pom.' He repeated the name with fastidious disgust. 'Yes.'

'Quite safe.'

'Mr Tyrone, stop playing games. You can't hide for ever from Charlie Boston.'

I was silent. The tiger yawned, showing a full set of fangs. Nasty.

'They could do more damage next time,' he said.

I looked at him curiously, wondering if he seriously thought I would crumble under so vague a threat. He stared straight back and was unmoved when I didn't answer. My heart sank slightly. More to come.

'I suspected,' he said conversationally, 'when I heard that you were seen at Plumpton races the day following Boston's ill-judged attack, that physical pressure would run us into too much difficulty in your case. I see that this assessment was correct. I directed that a different lever should be found. We have, of course, found it. And you will tell us where the horse is hidden.'

He took out the black crocodile wallet and removed from it a small sheet of paper, folded once. He gave it to me. I looked. He saw the deep shock in my face and he smiled in satisfaction.

It was a photo-copy of the bill of the hotel where I had stayed with Gail. Mr and Mrs Tyrone, one double room.

'So you see, Mr Tyrone, that if you wish to keep

this interesting item of news from your wife, you must give us the address we ask.'

My mind tumbled over and over like a dry-cleaning machine and not a useful thought came out.

'So quiet, Mr Tyrone? You really don't like that, do you? So you will tell us. You would not want your wife to divorce you, I am sure. And you have taken such pains to deceive her that we are certain you know she would throw you out if she discovered this . . .' He pointed to the bill. 'How would she like to know that your mistress is coloured? We have other dates, too. Last Sunday week, and the Sunday before that. Your wife will be told it all. Wealthy women will not stand for this sort of thing, you know.'

I wondered numbly how much Gail had sold me for.

'Come along, Mr Tyrone. The address.'

'I need time,' I said dully.

'That's right,' he said calmly. 'It takes time to sink in properly, doesn't it? Of course you can have time. Six hours. You will telephone us at precisely seven o'clock this evening.' He gave me a plain white card with numbers on it. 'Six hours is all, Mr Tyrone. After that, the information will be on its way to your wife, and you will not be able to stop it. Do you clearly understand?'

'Yes,' I said. The tiger sat down and shut its eyes. Sympathetic.

'I thought you would.' He moved away from me

towards the door. 'Seven o'clock precisely. Good day, Mr Tyrone.'

With erect easy assurance he walked straight out of the Cat House, turned a corner, and was gone. My feet seemed to have become disconnected from my body. I was going through the disjointed floating feeling of irretrievable disaster. A disbelieving part of my mind said that if I stayed quite still the nutcracker situation would go away.

It didn't, of course. But after a while I began to think normally instead of in emotional shock waves; began to look for a hole in the net. I walked slowly away from the tiger, out into the unwholesome air and down towards the gate, all my attention turned inward. Out of the corner of my eye I half caught sight of my abductor in his raincoat standing up a side path looking into an apparently empty wire-netted compound, and when I'd gone out of the turnstile on to the road it hit me with a thump where I'd seen him before. So significant a thump that I came to a rocking halt. Much had urgently to be understood.

I had seen him at King's Cross station while I waited for Gail. He had been standing near me: had watched her all the way from the Underground until she had reached me. Looking for a lever. Finding it.

To be watching me at King's Cross, he must have followed me from the *Blaze.*

Today, he had picked me up outside the *Blaze.*

I walked slowly, thinking about it. From King's

Cross in the morning I had gone on the train to Newcastle, but I hadn't come back on my return ticket. Colly Gibbons had. I'd taken that unexpected roundabout route home, and somewhere, maybe back at Newcastle races, I'd shaken off my tail.

Someone also must either have followed Gail, or have gone straight into the hotel to see her after I had left. I baulked at thinking she would sell me out with my imprint still on our shared sheets. But maybe she would. It depended on how much they had offered her, I supposed. Five hundred would have tempted her mercenary heart too far.

No one but Gail could have got a receipt from the hotel. No one but Gail knew of the two Sunday afternoons. No one but Gail thought my wife was rich. I coldly faced the conclusion that I had meant little to her. Very little indeed. My true deserts. I had sought her out because she could dispense sex without involvement. She had been consistent. She owed me nothing at all.

I reached the corner and instinctively turned my plodding steps towards home. Not for twenty paces did I realize that this was a desperate mistake.

Gail didn't know where I lived. She couldn't have told them. They didn't know the true facts about Elizabeth: they thought she was a rich woman who would divorce me. *They picked me up this morning outside the* Blaze . . . At the same weary pace I turned right at the next crossing.

If the man in the black homburg didn't know where I lived, the Raincoat would be following to find out. Round the next corner I stopped and looked back through the thick branches of a may bush, and there he was, hurrying. I went on slowly as before, heading round imperceptibly towards Fleet Street.

The Homburg Hat had been bluffing. He couldn't tell Elizabeth about Gail, because he didn't know where to find her. Ex-directory telephone. My address in none of the reference books. By sheer luck I twice hadn't led them straight to my own front door.

All the same, it couldn't go on for ever. Even if I fooled them until after the Lamplighter, one day, somehow, they would tell her what I'd done.

First they buy you, then they blackmail, Bert Checkov had said. Buy Gail, blackmail me. All of a piece. I thought about blackmail for three long miles back to the *Blaze.*

Luke-John and Derry were surprised to see me back. They made no comment on a change in my appearance. I supposed the inner turmoil didn't show.

'Have any of the crime reporters a decent pull with the police?' I asked.

Derry said, 'Jimmy Sienna might have. What do you want?'

'To trace a car number.'

'Someone bashed that ancient van of yours?' Luke-John asked uninterestedly.

'Hit and run,' I agreed with distant accuracy.

'We can always try,' Derry said with typical helpfulness. 'Give me the number, and I'll go and ask him.'

I wrote down for him the registration of Homburg Hat's Silver Wraith.

'A London number,' Derry remarked. 'That might make it easier.' He took off across the room to the crime desk and consulted a mountainous young man with red hair.

I strolled over to the deserted news desk and with a veneer of unconcern over a thumping heart dialled the number Homburg Hat had told me to ring at seven. It was three-eighteen. More than two hours gone out of six.

A woman answered, sounding surprised.

'Are you sure you have the right number?' she said.

I read it out to her.

'Yes, that's right. How funny.'

'Why is it funny?'

'Well, this is a public phone box. I had just shut the door and was going to make a call when the phone started ringing . . . Are you *sure* you have the right number?'

'I can't have,' I said. 'Where is this phone box, exactly?'

'It's one of a row in Piccadilly underground station.'

I thanked her and rang off. Not much help.

Derry came back and said Jimmy Sienna was doing what he could, good job it was Tuesday, he was bored and wanted something to pass the time with.

I remembered that I had left my copy of *Tally* and Elizabeth's cake on the floor of the Rolls. Debated whether or not to get replacements. Decided there was no harm in it, and went out and bought them. I didn't see Raincoat, but that didn't mean he wasn't there or that they hadn't swapped him for someone I wouldn't know.

Derry said Jimmy Sienna's police friend was checking the registration number but would use his discretion as to whether it was suitable to pass on to the *Blaze*. I sat on the side of Derry's desk and bit my nails.

Outside, the fog which had been threatening all day slowly cleared right away. It would. I thought about unobserved exits under the bright Fleet Street lights.

At five, Luke-John said he was going home, and Derry apologetically followed. I transferred myself to Jimmy Sienna's desk and bit my nails there instead. When he too was lumbering to his feet to leave, his telephone finally rang. He listened, thanked, scribbled.

'There you are,' he said to me. 'And good luck with the insurance. You'll need it.'

I read what he'd written. The Silver Wraith's number had been allocated to an organization called 'Hire Cars Lucullus'.

*

I left the *Blaze* via the roof. *Tally*, apple cake, and mending ribs complicated the journey, but after circumnavigating ventilation shafts and dividing walls I walked sedately in through the fire door of the next-door newspaper, a popular daily in the full flood of going to press.

No one asked me what I was doing. I went down in the lift to the basement and out to the huge garage at the rear where rows of yellow vans stood ready to take the wet ink bundles off to the trains. I knew one of the drivers slightly, and asked him for a lift.

'Sure, if you want Paddington.'

'I do.' I wanted anywhere he was going.

'Hop in, then.'

I hopped in, and after he was loaded he drove briskly out of the garage, one indistinguishable van among a procession. I stayed with him to Paddington, thanked him, and backtracked home on the underground, as certain as I could be that no one had followed.

I beat Mrs Woodward to six by two minutes but had no heart for the game.

From six-thirty to seven I sat in the armchair holding a glass of whisky and looking at Elizabeth, trying to make up a beleagured mind.

'Something worrying you, Ty,' she said, with her ultra-sensitive feeling for trouble.

'No, honey.'

The hands galloped round the clock. At seven o'clock precisely I sat absolutely still and did nothing at all. At five past I found I had clenched my teeth so hard that I was grinding them. I imagined the telephone box in Piccadilly Circus, with Homburg Hat or Raincoat or the chauffeur waiting inside it. Tiddely Pom was nothing compared with Elizabeth's peace of mind, and yet I didn't pick up the receiver. From seven onwards the clock hands crawled.

At half past Elizabeth said again, with detectable fear, 'Ty, there *is* something wrong. You never look so . . . so bleak.'

I made a great effort to smile at her as usual, but she wasn't convinced. I looked down at my hands and said with hopeless pain, 'Honey, how much would it hurt you if I went . . . and slept with a girl?'

There was no answer. After an unbearable interval I dragged my head up to look at her. Tears were running down her cheeks. She was swallowing, trying to speak.

From long, long habit I pulled a tissue out of the box and wiped her eyes, which she couldn't do for herself.

'I'm sorry,' I said uselessly. 'I'm sorry . . .'

'Ty . . .' She never had enough breath for weeping. Her mouth strained open in her need for more air.

'Honey, don't cry. Don't cry. Forget I said it. You

know I love you, I'd never leave you, Elizabeth, honey, dear Elizabeth, don't cry . . .'

I wiped her eyes again and cursed the whim which had sent me down to the Huntersons for *Tally*. I could have managed without Gail. Without anyone. I had managed without for most of eleven years.

'Ty.' The tears stopped. Her face looked less strained. 'Ty.' She gulped, fighting for more breath. 'I can't bear to think about it.'

I stood beside her, holding the tissue, wishing she didn't have to.

'We never talk about sex,' she said. The Spirashell heaved up her chest, let it drop, rhythmically. 'I don't want it any more . . . you know that . . . but sometimes I remember . . . how you taught me to like it . . .' Two more tears welled up. I wiped them away. She said, 'I haven't ever asked you . . . about girls . . . I couldn't, somehow.'

'No,' I said slowly.

'I've wondered sometimes . . . if you ever have, I mean . . . but I didn't really want to know . . . I know I would be too jealous . . . I decided I'd never ask you . . . because I would want you to say yes . . . and yet I know that's selfish . . . I've always been told men are different, they need women more . . . is it true?'

'Elizabeth,' I said helplessly.

'I didn't expect you ever to say anything . . . after all these years . . . yes, I would be hurt, if I knew . . . I couldn't help it . . . Why did you ask me? I wish you hadn't.'

'I would never have said anything,' I said with regret, 'but someone is trying to blackmail me.'

'Then . . . you *have* . . .?'

'I'm afraid so.'

'Oh.' She shut her eyes. 'I see.'

I waited, hating myself. The tears were over. She never cried for long. She physically couldn't. If she progressed into one of her rare bursts of rebellious anger she would utterly exhaust herself. Most wives could scream or throw things. Elizabeth's furies were the worse for being impotent. It must have been touch and go, because when she spoke her voice was low, thick, and deadly quiet.

'I suppose you couldn't afford to be blackmailed.'

'No one can.'

'I know it's unreasonable of me to wish you hadn't told me. To wish you hadn't done it at all. Any man who stays with a paralysed wife ought to have *something* . . . So many of them pack up and leave altogether . . . I know you say you never will and I do mostly believe it, but I must be such an unbearable burden to you . . .'

'That,' I said truthfully, 'is just not true.'

'It must be. Don't tell me . . . about the girl.'

'If I don't, the blackmailer will.'

'All right . . . get it over quickly . . .'

I got it over quickly. Briefly. No details. Hated

myself for having to tell her, and knew that if I hadn't, Homburg Hat wouldn't have stopped his leverage with the whereabouts of Tiddely Pom. Blackmailers never did. Don't sell your soul, Bert Checkov said. Don't sell your column. Sacrifice your wife's peace instead.

'Will you see her again?' she asked.

'No.'

'Or . . . anyone else?'

'No.'

'I expect you will,' she said. 'Only if you do . . . don't tell me . . . Unless of course someone tries to blackmail you again . . .'

I winced at the bitterness in her voice. Reason might tell her that total lifelong celibacy was a lot to demand, but emotion had practically nothing to do with reason, and the tearing emotions of any ordinary wife on finding her husband unfaithful hadn't atrophied along with her muscles. I hadn't expected much else. She would have to have been a saint or a cynic to have laughed it off without a pang, and she was neither of those things, just a normal human being trapped in an abnormal situation. I wondered how suspicious she would be in future of my most innocent absences; how much she would suffer when I was away. Reassurance, always tricky, was going to be doubly difficult.

She was very quiet and depressed all evening. She wouldn't have any supper, wouldn't eat the apple cake. When I washed her and did the rubs and the other intimate jobs I could almost feel her thinking about the other body my hands had touched. Hands, and much else. She looked sick and strained, and for almost the first time since her illness, embarrassed. If she could have done without me that evening, she would have.

I said, meaning it, 'I'm sorry, honey.'

'Yes.' She shut her eyes. 'Life's just bloody, isn't it.'

CHAPTER ELEVEN

The uncomfortable coolness between Elizabeth and myself persisted in the morning. I couldn't go on begging for a forgiveness she didn't feel. At ten I said I was going out, and saw her make the first heart-rending effort not to ask where.

'Hire Cars Lucullus' hung out in a small plushy office in Stratton Street, off Piccadilly. Royal blue Wilton carpet, executive-type acre of polished desk, tasteful prints of vintage cars on dove grey walls. Along one side, a wide gold-upholstered bench for wide gold-upholstered clients. Behind the desk, a deferential young man with Uriah Heep eyes.

For him I adopted a languid voice and my best imitation of the homburg hat manners. I had, I explained, left some property in one of his firm's cars, and I hoped he could help me get it back.

We established gradually that no, I had not hired one of their cars, and no, I did not know the name of the man who had, he had merely been so kind as to give me a lift. Yesterday.

Ah. Then had I any idea which car . . .?

A Rolls-Royce, a Silver Wraith.

They had four of those. He briefly checked a ledger, though I suspected he didn't need to. All four had been out on hire yesterday. Could I describe the man who had given me a lift? 'Certainly. Tallish, blondish, wearing a black homburg. Not English. Possibly South African.'

'Ah. Yes.' He had no need to consult the ledger this time. He put his spread fingertips carefully down on the desk. 'I regret, sir, I cannot give you his name.'

'But surely you keep records?'

'This gentleman puts great store on privacy. We have been instructed not to give his name and address to anyone.'

'Isn't that a bit odd?' I said, raising eyebrows.

He considered judicially. 'He is a regular customer. We would, of course, give him any service he asked for, without question.'

'I suppose it wouldn't be possible to . . . um . . . purchase the information?'

He tried to work some shock into his deference. It was barely skin deep.

'Was your lost property very valuable?' he asked.

Tally and apple cake. 'Very,' I said.

'Then I am sure our client will return it to us. If you

would let us have your own name and address, perhaps we could let you know?'

I said the first name I thought of, which nearly came out as Kempton Park. 'Kempton Jones. 31 Cornwall Street.'

He wrote it down carefully on a scratch pad. When he had finished, I waited. We both waited.

After a decent interval he said, 'Of course, if it is really important, you could ask in the garage . . . they would let you know as soon as the car comes in, whether your property is still in it.'

'And the garage is where?' The only listed number and address of the Lucullus Cars had been the office in Stratton Street.

He studied his fingertips. I produced my wallet and resignedly sorted out two fivers. The twenty-five for the bookmaker's clerk's information about Charlie Boston's boys I had put down to expenses and the *Blaze* had paid. This time I could be on my own. Ten pounds represented six weeks' whisky, a month's electricity, three and a half days of Mrs Woodward, one and a half weeks' rent.

He took it greedily, nodded, gave me a hypocritical obsequious smile, and said, 'Radmor Mews, Lancaster Gate.'

'Thanks.'

'You do understand, sir, that it's more than my job is worth to give you our client's name?'

'I understand,' I said. 'Principles are pretty things.'

Principles were luckily not so strongly held in Radnor Mews. The foreman sized me up and another tenner changed hands. Better value for money this time.

'The chauffeur comes here to collect the car, see? We never deliver it or supply a driver. Unusual, that. Still, the client is always right, as long as he pays for it, I always say. This foreigner, see, he likes to travel in style when he comes over here. 'Course, most of our trade is like that. Americans mostly. They hire a car and a driver for a week, two weeks, maybe three. We drive them all over, see, Stratford, Broadway, the Cotswold run most often, and Scotland a good deal too. Never have all the cars in here at once, there'd hardly be room, see, four Silver Wraiths for a start, and then two Austin Princesses, and three Bentleys and a couple of large Wolseleys.'

I brought him back gently to the Silver Wraith in question.

'I'm telling you, aren't I?' he protested. 'This foreign chap, he takes a car, always a Rolls mind you, though of course not always the same one, whenever he's over here. Started coming just over a year ago, I'd say. Been back several times, usually just for three or four days. Longer this time, I'd say. Let's see, the chauffeur came for a car last week. I could look it up . . . Wednesday. Yes, that's right. What they do, see, is the chauffeur flies over first, picks up the car and then drives out to

Heathrow to fetch his gent off the next flight. Neat, that. Shows money, that does.'

'Do you know where they fly from?'

'From? Which country? Not exactly. Mind, I think it varies. I know once it was Germany. But usually farther than that, from somewhere hot. The chauffeur isn't exactly chatty, but he's always complaining how cold it is here.'

'What is the client's name?' I asked patiently.

'Oh sure, hang on a minute. We always put the booking in the chauffeur's name, see, it's easier, being Ross. His gent's name is something chronic. I'll have to look back.'

He went into his little boarded cubicle of an office and looked back. It took him nearly twenty minutes, by which time he was growing restive. I waited, making it plain I would wait all day. For ten pounds he could keep on looking. He was almost as relieved as I was when he found it.

'Here it is, look.' He showed me a page in a ledger, pointing to a name with a black-rimmed fingernail. 'That one.'

There was a pronunciation problem, as he'd said.

Vjoersterod.

'Ross is easier,' the foreman repeated. 'We always put Ross.'

'Much easier,' I agreed. 'Do you know where I could find them, or where they keep the car while they're in England?'

He sniffed immediately, shutting the ledger with his finger in the page.

'Can't say as I do, really. Always a pretty fair mileage on the clock, though. Goes a fair way in the three or four days, see? But then that's regular with our cars, most times. Mind you, I wouldn't say that this Ross and his gent go up to Scotland, not as far as that.'

'Birmingham?' I suggested.

'Easily. Could be, easily. Always comes back immaculate, I'll say that for Ross. Always clean as a whistle. Why don't you ask in the front office, if you want to find them?'

'They said they couldn't help me.'

'That smarmy crumb,' he said disgustedly, 'I'll bet he knows, though. Give him his due, he's good at that job, but he'd sell his grandmother if the price was right.'

I started to walk in the general direction of Fleet Street, thinking. Vjoersterod had to be the real name of Homburg Hat. Too weird to be an alias. Also, the first time he had hired a Silver Wraith from Hire Cars Lucullus he would have had to produce cast iron references and a passport at least. The smarmy crumb was no fool. He wouldn't let five thousand pounds' worth of machinery be driven away without being certain he would get it back.

Vjoersterod. South African of Afrikaner stock.

Nothing like Fleet Street if one wanted information. The only trouble was, the man who might have heard of Vjoersterod worked on the racing page of a deadly rival to the *Blaze*. I turned into the first telephone box and rang his office. Sure, he agreed cautiously, he would meet me in the Devereux for a pint and a sandwich. He coped manfully with stifling any too open speculation about what I wanted. I smiled, and crossed the road to catch a bus. A case of who pumped who. He would be trying to find out what story I was working on, and Luke-John would be slightly displeased if he were successful and scooped the *Blaze*.

Luke-John and Derry were both among the crowd in the Devereux. Not so, Mike de Jong. I drank a half-pint while Luke-John asked me what I planned to write for Sunday.

'An account of the Lamplighter, I suppose.'

'Derry can do that.'

I lowered my glass, shrugging. 'If you like.'

'Then you,' said Luke-John, 'can do another follow-up to the Tiddely Pom business. Whether he wins or loses, I mean. Give us a puff for getting him to the starting gate.'

'He isn't there yet,' I pointed out.

Luke-John sniffed impatiently. 'There hasn't been a vestige of trouble. No reaction at all. We've frightened them off, that's what happened.'

I shook my head, wishing we had. Asked about the reports on Tiddely Pom and the Roncey children.

'All OK,' said Derry cheerfully. 'Everything going smoothly.'

Mike de Jong appared in the doorway, a quick, dark, intense man with double strength glasses and a fringe of black beard outlining his jaw. Caution rolled over him like a sea mist when he saw who I was with, and most of the purposefulness drained out of his stride. It took too much manoeuvring to get Luke-John and Derry go to into the further bar to eat without me, and Luke-John left looking back over his shoulder with smouldering suspicion, wanting to know why.

Mike joined me, his sharp face alight with appreciation.

'Keeping secrets from the boss, eh?'

'Sometimes he's butter-fingered with other people's TNT.'

Mike laughed. The cogs whirred round in his high-speed brain. 'So what you want is private? Not for the *Blaze*?'

I dodged a direct answer. 'What I want is very simple. Just anything you may have heard about a fellow countryman of yours.'

'Who?' His accent was a carbon copy, clipped and flat.

'A man called Vjoersterod.'

There was a tiny pause while the name sank in, and then he choked on his beer. Recovered, and pretended someone had jogged his elbow. Made a playing-for-time fuss about brushing six scattered drops off his trouser leg. Finally he ran out of alibis and looked back at my face.

'Vjoersterod?' His pronunciation was subtly different from mine. The real thing.

'That's right,' I agreed.

'Yes . . . well, Ty . . . why do you ask me about him?'

'Just curiosity.'

He was silent for thirty seconds. Then he said carefully again, 'Why are you asking about him?' Who pumped who.

'Oh, come on,' I said in exasperation. 'What's the big mystery? All I want is a bit of gen on a harmless chap who goes racing occasionally . . .'

'*Harmless.* You must be mad.'

'Why?' I sounded innocently puzzled.

'Because he's . . .' He hesitated, decided I wasn't on to a story, and turned thoroughly helpful. 'Look here, Ty, I'll give you a tip, free, gratis, and for nothing. Just steer clear of anything to do with that man. He's poison.'

'In what way?'

'He's a bookmaker, back home. Very big business, with branches in all the big cities and a whole group of them round Johannesburg. Respectable enough on the surface. Thousands of perfectly ordinary people bet with him. But there have been some dreadful rumours . . .'

'About what?'

'Oh . . . blackmail, extortion, general high-powered thuggery. Believe me, he is not good news.'

'Then why don't the police . . .?' I suggested tentatively.

'Why don't they? Don't be so naïve, Ty. They can't find anyone to give evidence against him, of course.'

I sighed. 'He seemed so charming.'

Mike's mouth fell open and his expression became acutely anxious.

'You've *met* him?'

'Yeah.'

'Here . . . in England?'

'Well, yes, of course.'

'Ty . . . for God's sake . . . keep away from him.'

'I will,' I said with feeling. 'Thanks a lot, Mike. I'm truly grateful.'

'I'd hate anyone I liked to tangle with Vjoersterod,' he said, the genuine friendship standing out clear in his eyes, unexpectedly affecting. Then with a born newspaper man's instinct for the main chance, a look of intense curiosity took over.

'What did he want to talk about with you?' he asked.

'I really don't know,' I said, sounding puzzled.

'Is he going to get in touch with you again?'

'I don't know that, either.'

'Hm . . . give me a ring if he does, and I'll tell you something else.'

'Tell me now.' I tried hard to make it casual.

He considered, shrugged, and friendship won again over journalism. 'All right. It's nothing much. Just that

I too saw him here in England; must have been nine or ten months ago, back in the spring." He paused.

'In that case,' I said, 'why ever were you so horrified when I said I'd met him?'

'Because when I saw him he was in the buffet on a race train, talking to another press man. Bert Checkov.'

With an enormous effort, I kept my mildly puzzled face intact.

Mike went on without a blink. 'I warned Bert about him later, just like I have you. In here, actually. Bert was pretty drunk. He was always pretty drunk after that.'

'What did he say?' I asked.

'He said I was three months too late.'

Mike didn't know any more. Bert had clammed up after that one indiscretion and had refused to elaborate or explain. When he fell out of the window, Mike had wondered. Violent and often unexplained deaths among people who had had dealings with Vjoersterod were not unknown, he said. When I said I had met Vjoersterod, it had shocked him. He was afraid for me. Afraid I could follow Bert down on to the pavement.

I put his mind at rest. After what he'd told me, I would be forewarned, I said.

'I wonder why he got his hooks into Bert . . .' Mike said, his eyes on the middle distance, all the cogs whirring.

'I've no idea,' I said, sighing, and distracted his attention on to another half-pint and a large ham sandwich. Luke-John's thin freckled face looked over his shoulder, and he turned to him with a typical bounce, as if all his body were made of springs.

'So how's the Gospel Maker? What's cooking on the *Blaze*?'

Luke-John gave him a thin smile. He didn't care for his Fleet street nickname; nor for puns in general. Nor, it seemed, for Mike de Jong's puns in particular. Mike received the message clearly, sketched me a farewell, and drifted over to another group.

'What did he want?' Luke-John asked sharply.

'Nothing,' I said mildly. 'Just saying hullo.'

Luke-John gave me a disillusioned look, but I knew very well that if I told him at that stage about Vjoersterod he would dig until he stumbled on the blackmail, dig again quite ruthlessly to find out how I could have been blackmailed, and then proceed to mastermind all subsequent enquiries with a stunning absence of discretion. Vjoersterod would hear his steam-roller approach clean across the country. Luke-John was a brilliant sports editor. As a field marshal his casualty list would have been appalling.

He and Derry drank around to closing time at three, by which time the crowd had reduced to Sunday writers only. I declined their invitation to go back with them to the doldrums of the office, and on reflection telephoned to the only member of the racing authorities I knew well enough for the purpose.

Eric Youll at thirty-seven was the youngest and newest of the three stewards of the National Hunt Committee, the ruling body of steeplechasing. In two years, by natural progression he would be Senior Steward. After that, reduced to the ranks until re-elected for another three-year term. As a steward he made sense because until recently he had himself ridden as an amateur, and knew at first hand all the problems and mechanics of racing. I had written him up in the *Blaze* a few times and we had been friendly acquaintances for years. Whether he either could or would help me now was nonetheless open to doubt.

I had a good deal of trouble getting through to him, as he was a junior sprig in one of the grander merchant banks. Secretaries with bored voices urged me to make an appointment.

'Right now,' I said, 'will do very well.'

After the initial shock the last voice conceded that right now Mr Youll could just fit me in. When I got there, Mr Youll was busily engaged in drinking a cup of tea and reading the *Sporting Life*. He put them both down without haste, stood up, and shook hands.

'This is unexpected,' he said. 'Come to borrow a million?'

'Tomorrow, maybe.'

He smiled, told his secretary on the intercom to bring me some tea, offered me a cigarette, and leaned back in his chair, his manner throughout one of indecision and uncertainty. He was wary of me and of the purpose of my visit. I saw that uneasy expression almost every day of my life: the screen my racing friends erected when they weren't sure what I was after, the barrier that kept their secrets from publication. I didn't mind that sort of withdrawal. Understood it. Sympathized. And never printed anything private, if I could help it. There was a very fine edge to be walked when one's friends were one's raw material.

'Off the record,' I assured him. 'Take three deep breaths and relax.'

He grinned and tension visibly left his body. 'How can I help you then?'

I waited until the tea had come and been drunk, and the latest racing news chewed over. Then, without making much of it, I asked him if he'd ever heard of a bookmaker called Vjoersterod.

His attention pin-pointed itself with a jerk.

'Is that what you've come to ask?'

'For openers.'

He drummed his fingers on the desk. 'Someone showed me your column last week and the week before . . . Stay out of it, Ty.'

'If you racing bigwigs know what's going on and who is doing it, why don't you stop him?'

'How?'

The single bald word hung in the air, cooling. It told

me a lot about the extent of their knowledge. They should have known how.

'Frankly,' I said at last, 'that's your job, not mine. You could of course ban all ante-post betting, which would knock the fiddle stone dead.'

'That would be highly unpopular with the Great British Public. Anyway your articles have hit the ante-post market badly enough as it is. One of the big firms was complaining to me bitterly about you a couple of hours ago. Their Lamplighter bets are down by more than twenty per cent.'

'Then why don't they do something about Charlie Boston?'

He blinked. 'Who?'

I took a quiet breath. 'Well, now . . . just what do the stewards know about Vjoersterod?'

'Who is Charlie Boston?'

'You first,' I said.

'Don't you trust me?' He looked hurt.

'No,' I said flatly. 'You first.'

He sighed resignedly and told me that all the stewards knew about Vjoersterod was hearsay, and scanty at that. None of them had ever actually seen him, and wouldn't know him if they did. A member of the German horse racing authorities had sent them a private warning that Vjoersterod was suspected of stage managing a series of non-starting ante-post favourites in big races in Germany, and that they had heard rumours he was now beginning to operate in England.

Pursuit had almost cornered him in Germany. He was now moving on. The British stewards had noted the alarming proportion of non-starters in the past months and were sure the German authorities were right, but although they had tried to find out the facts from various owners and trainers, they had been met with only a brick wall of silence everywhere.

'It's a year since Vjoersterod came here first,' I remarked. 'A year ago he bought out Charlie Boston's string of betting shops round Birmingham and started raking in the dough. He also found a way to force Bert Checkov to write articles which persuaded ante-post punters to believe they were on to a good thing. Vjoersterod chose a horse, Checkov wrote it up, Vjoersterod stopped it running, and bingo, the deed was done.'

His face was a mixture of astonishment and satisfaction. 'Ty, are you sure of your facts?'

'Of course I am. If you ask me, both the bookmakers and the authorities have been dead slow on the trail.'

'And how long exactly have you been on it?'

I grinned, conceding the point. I said, 'I met Vjoersterod yesterday. I referred to Charlie Boston being his partner and he told me he owned Charlie Boston. Vjoersterod wanted to know where Tiddely Pom was.'

He stared. 'Would you . . . um . . . well, if necessary, testify to that?'

'Certainly. But it would be only my word against his. No corroboration.'

'Better than anything we've had before.'

'There might be a quicker way to get results, though.'

'How?' he asked again.

'Find a way to shut Charlie Boston's shops, and you block off Vjoersterod's intakes. Without which there is no point in him waiting around to stop any favourites. If you can't get him convicted in the courts, you might at least freeze him out, back to South Africa.'

There was another long pause during which he thought complicated thoughts. I waited, guessing what was in his mind. Eventually, he said it.

'How much do you want for your help?'

'An exclusive for the *Blaze*.'

'As if I couldn't guess . . .'

'It will do,' I conceded, 'if the *Blaze* can truthfully claim to have made the ante-post market safe for punters to play in. No details. Just a few hints that but for the libel laws, all would and could be revealed.'

'Why ever do you waste your time with that dreadful rag?' he exclaimed in exasperation.

'Good pay,' I said. 'It's a good paper to work for. And it suits me.'

'I'll promise you one thing,' he said, smiling. 'If through you personally we get rid of Vjoersterod, I'll take it regularly.'

From Eric Youll's bank, I went home. If the youngest steward did his stuff, Vjoersterod's goose was on its way to the oven and would soon be cooked. He might of course one day read the *Blaze* and send someone to carve up the chef. It didn't trouble me much. I didn't believe it would happen.

Elizabeth had had Mrs Woodward put her favourite rose pink, white-embroidered sheets on the bed. I looked at her searchingly. Her hair had been done with particular care. Her makeup was flawless.

'You look pretty,' I said tentatively.

Her expression was a mixture of relief and misery. I understood with a sudden rocking wince what had led her to such scenery painting: the increased fear that if she were bitchy I would leave her. No matter if I'd earned and deserved the rough side of her tongue; I had to be placated at all costs, to be held by the best she could do to appear attractive, to be obliquely invited, cajoled, entreated to stay.

'Did you have a good day?' Her voice sounded high and near to cracking point.

'Quite good . . . how about a drink?'

She shook her head, but I poured her one all the same, and fixed it in the clip.

'I've asked Mrs Woodward to find someone to come and sit with me in the evenings,' she said. 'So that you can go out more.'

'I don't want to go out more,' I protested.

'You must do.'

'Well, I don't.' I sat down in the armchair and took a hefty mouthful of nearly neat whisky. At best, I thought, in an unbearable situation alcohol offered postponement. At worst, aggravation. And anyway it was too damned expensive, nowadays, to get drunk.

Elizabeth didn't answer. When I looked at her, I saw she was quietly crying again. The tears rolled down past her ears and into her hair. I took a tissue out of the box and dried them. Had she but known it, they were harder for me to bear than any amount of fury.

'I'm getting old,' she said. 'And you still look so young. You look . . . strong . . . and dark . . . and young.'

'And you look pale and pretty and about fifteen. So stop fretting.'

'How old is . . . that girl?'

'You said you didn't want to hear about her.'

'I suppose I don't really.'

'Forget her,' I said. 'She is of no importance. She means nothing to me. Nothing at all.' I sounded convincing, even to myself. I wished it were true. In spite of the scope of her betrayal, in a weak inner recess I ached to be able to sleep with her again. I sat with the whisky glass in my hand and thought about her on the white rug and in her own bed and in the hotel, and suffered dismally from the prospect of the arid future.

After a while I pushed myself wearily to my feet and went to fix the supper. Fish again. Mean little bits of frozen plaice. I cooked and ate them with aversion and fed Elizabeth when her wrist tired on the gadget.

All evening she kept up the pathetic attempt to be nice to me, thanking me exaggeratedly for every tiny service, apologizing for needing me to do things for her which we had both for years taken for granted, trying hard to keep the anxiety, the embarrassment, and the unhappiness out of her eyes and voice, and nowhere near succeeding. She couldn't have punished me more if she had tried.

Late that evening Tiddely Pom developed violent colic.

Norton Fox couldn't get hold of Luke-John or Derry, who had both long gone home. The *Blaze* never divulged home addresses, however urgent the enquiry. Norton didn't know my telephone number either; didn't know anyone who did.

In a state of strong anxiety, and on his vet's advice, he rang up Victor Roncey and told him where his horse was, and what they were doing to save its life.

CHAPTER TWELVE

I heard about it in the morning. Roncey telephoned at ten-thirty, when I was sitting in the writing-room looking vacantly at the walls and trying to drum up some preliminary gems for my column on Sunday. Mrs Woodward had gone out to the launderette, and Elizabeth called me to the telephone with two rings on the bell over my head: two rings for come at once but not an emergency. Three rings for 999. Four for panic.

Roncey had calmed down from the four-ring stage he had clearly been in the night before. He was calling, he said, from Norton Fox's house, where he had driven at once after being given the news. I sorted out that he had arrived at 2 a.m. to find that the vet had got Tiddely Pom over the worst, with the stoppage in the horse's gut untangling into normal function. Norton Fox had given Roncey a bed for the rest of the night, and he had just come in from seeing Tiddely Pom walk and trot out at morning exercise. The horse was showing surprisingly few ill effects from his rocky experience, and it was quite likely he would be fit enough to run in the Lamplighter on Saturday.

I listened to his long, brisk detailed saga with uncomfortable alarm. There were still two whole days before the race. Now that Roncey knew where he was, Tiddley Pom's safety was halved. When he had come to the end of the tale I asked him whether anyone had tried to find out from him at home where his horse had gone.

'Of course they did,' he said. 'Exactly as you said. Several other newspapers wanted to know. Most of them telephoned. Three or four actually turned up at the farm, and I know they asked Peter and Pat as well as me. Some of their questions were decidedly tricky. I thought at the time you'd been quite right, we might have let it slip if we'd known ourselves.'

'When did these people come to the farm? What did they look like?'

'They didn't look like anything special. Just nondescript. One of them was from the *Evening Peal*, I remember. All the enquiries were on Sunday and Monday, just after your article came out.'

'No one turned up in a Rolls?' I asked.

He laughed shortly. 'They did not.'

'Were any of your visitors tallish, thickish, blondish, with a faintly yellow skin and a slightly foreign accent?'

'None that I saw were like that. One or two saw only the boys, because they called while I was in Chelmsford. You could ask them, if you like.'

'Maybe I will,' I agreed. 'No one tried any threats?'

'No, I told your sports editor that. No one has tried any pressure of any sort. To my mind, all your elaborate precautions have been a waste of time. And now that I know where Tiddely Pom is, you may as well tell me where my family is too . . .'

'I'll think about it,' I said. 'Would you ask Norton Fox if I could have a word with him?'

He fetched Norton, who apologized for bursting open the secrecy, but said he didn't like the responsibility of keeping quiet when the horse was so ill.

'Of course not. It can't be helped,' I said. 'As long as it goes no further than Roncey himself it may not be too bad, though I'd prefer . . .'

'His sons knew, of course,' Norton interrupted. 'Though I don't suppose that matters.'

'*What?*' I said.

'Roncey told one of his sons where he was. He telephoned to him just now. He explained to me that he couldn't remember your telephone number, but he'd got it written down somewhere at home, from having rung you up before sometime. So he rang his son . . . Pat, I think he said . . . and his son found it for him. I think he, the son, asked Roncey where he was calling from, because Roncey said that as everyone had stopped enquiring about where the horse was he didn't see any harm in his son knowing, so he told him.'

'Damn it,' I said. 'The man's a fool.'

'He might be right.'

'And he might be wrong,' I said bitterly. 'Look, Norton, I suppose there was no question of Tiddely Pom's colic being a misjudged case of poisoning?'

'For God's sake, Ty . . . no. It was straightforward colic. How on earth could he have been poisoned? For a start, no one knew then who he was.'

'And now?' I asked. 'How many of your lads know now that he is Tiddely Pom?'

There was a brief, supercharged silence.

'All of them,' I said flatly.

'Some of them knew Roncey by sight,' he explained. 'And they'd all read the *Blaze*. So they put two and two together.'

One of them would soon realize he could earn a fiver by ringing up a rival newspaper. Tiddely Pom's whereabouts would be as secret as the Albert Memorial. Tiddely Pom, at that moment, was a certain non-starter for the Lamplighter Gold Cup.

Even if Victor Roncey thought that the opposition had backed out of the project, I was certain they hadn't. In a man like Vjoersterod, pride would always conquer discretion. He wouldn't command the same respect in international criminal circles if he turned out and ran just because of a few words in the *Blaze*. He wouldn't, therefore, do it.

*

At the four-day declaration stage, on the Tuesday, Roncey had confirmed with Weatherbys that his horse would be a definite runner. If he now withdrew him, as he could reasonably do because of the colic, he would forfeit his entry fee, a matter of fifty pounds. If he left his horse at Norton's still intending to run, he would forfeit a great deal more.

Because I was certain that if Tiddely Pom stayed where he was, he would be lame, blind, doped, or dead by Saturday morning.

Norton listened in silence while I outlined these facts of life.

'Ty, don't you think you are possibly exaggerating . . .?'

'Well,' I said with a mildness I didn't feel, 'how many times will you need to have Brevity – or any other of your horses – taken out of the Champion Hurdle at the last moment without any explanation, before you see any need to do something constructive in opposition?'

There was a short pause. 'Yes,' he said. 'You have a point.'

'If you will lend me your horsebox, I'll take Tiddely Pom off somewhere else.'

'Where?'

'Somewhere safe,' I said non-committally. 'How about it?'

'Oh, all right,' he sighed. 'Anything for a quiet life.'

'I'll come as soon as I can.'

'I'll repel boarders until you do.' The flippancy in his voice told me how little he believed in any threat to the horse. I felt a great urge to leave them to it, to let Roncey stew in his own indiscretion, to let Vjoersterod interfere with the horse and stop it running, just to prove I was right. Very childish urge indeed. It didn't last long, because in my way I was as stubborn as Vjoersterod. I wasn't going to turn and run from him either, if I could help it.

When I put the telephone receiver back in its special cradle, Elizabeth was looking worried and with a more normal form of anxiety.

'That Tiddely Pom,' I said lightly, 'is more trouble than a bus load of eleven-year-old boys. As I expect you gathered, I'll have to go and shift him off somewhere else.'

'Couldn't someone else do it?'

I shook my head. 'Better be me.'

Mrs Woodward was still out. I filled in the time until her return by ringing up Luke-John and giving him the news that the best laid plan had gone astray.

'Where are you taking the horse, then?'

'I'll let you know when I get there.'

'Are you sure it's necessary . . .?' he began.

'Are you,' I interrupted, 'sure the *Blaze* can afford to take any risk, after boasting about keeping the horse safe?'

'Hm.' He sighed. 'Get on with it, then.'

When Mrs Woodward came back I took the van

and drove to Berkshire. With me went Elizabeth's best effort at a fond wifely farewell. She had even offered her mouth for a kiss, which she did very rarely, as mouth to mouth kissing interfered with her frail breathing arrangements and gave her a feeling of suffocation. She liked to be kissed on the cheek or forehead, and never too often.

I spent most of the journey worrying about whether I should not after all have allowed myself to be blackmailed: whether any stand against pressure was a luxury when compared with the damage I'd done to Elizabeth's weak hold on happiness. After all the shielding, which had improved her physical condition, I'd laid into her with a bulldozer. Selfishly. Just to save myself from a particularly odious form of tyranny. If she lost weight or fretted to breakdown point it would be directly my fault; and either or both seemed possible.

A hundred and fifty guineas, plus expenses, less tax. A study in depth. *Tally* had offered me the deeps. And in I'd jumped.

On the outskirts of London I stopped to make a long and involved telephone call, arranging a destination and care for Tiddely Pom. Norton Fox and Victor Roncey were eating lunch when I arrived at the stables, and I found it impossible to instil into either of them enough of a feeling for urgency to get them to leave their casseroled beef.

'Sit down and have some,' Norton said airily.

'I want to be on my way.'

They didn't approve of my impatience and proceeded to gooseberry crumble and biscuits and cheese. It was two o'clock before they agreed to amble out into the yard and see to the shifting of Tiddely Pom.

Norton had at least had his horsebox made ready. It stood in the centre of the yard with the ramp down. As public an exit as possible. I sighed resignedly. The horsebox driver didn't like handing over to a stranger and gave me some anxious instructions about the idiosyncratic gear change.

Sandy Willis led Tiddely Pom across the yard, up the ramp, and into the centre stall of the three-stall box. The horse looked worse than ever, no doubt because of the colic. I couldn't see him ever winning any Lamplighter Gold Cup. Making sure he ran in it seemed a gloomy waste of time. Just as well, I reflected, that it wasn't to Tiddely Pom himself that I was committed, but to the principle that if Roncey wanted to run Tiddely Pom, he should. Along the lines of 'I disagree that your horse has the slightest chance, but I'll defend to the death your right to prove it.'

Sandy Willis finished tying the horse into his stall and took over where the box driver left off. Her instructions on how Tiddely Pom was to be managed were detailed and anxious. In her few days with the horse she had already identified herself with its well-being. As Norton had said, she was one of the best of his lads. I wished I could take her too, but it was useless expecting Norton to let her go, when she also looked after Zig Zag.

She said, 'He will be having proper care, won't he?'

'The best,' I assured her.

'Tell them not to forget his eggs and beer.'

'Right.'

'And he hates having his ears messed about with.'

'Right.'

She gave me a long searching look, a half smile, and a reluctant farewell. Victor Roncey strode briskly across to me and unburdened himself along similar lines.

'I want to insist that you tell me where you are taking him.'

'He will be safe.'

'Where?'

'Mr Roncey, if you know where, he is only half as safe. We've been through all this before . . .'

He pondered, his glance darting about restlessly, his eyes not meeting mine. 'Oh, very well,' he said finally, with impatience. 'But it will be up to you to make sure he gets to Heathbury Park in good time on Saturday.'

'The *Blaze* will arrange that,' I agreed. 'The Lamplighter is at three. Tiddely Pom will reach the racecourse stables by noon, without fail.'

'I'll be there,' he said. 'Waiting.'

I nodded. Norton joined us, and the two of them discussed this arrangement while I shut up the ramp with the help of the hovering box driver.

'What time do you get Zig Zag to Heathbury?' I asked Norton, pausing before I climbed into the cab.

'Midday,' he said. 'It's only thirty-two miles . . . He'll be setting off at about eleven.'

I climbed into the driving seat and looked out of the window. The two men looked back, Roncey worried, Norton not. To Norton I said, 'I'll see you this evening, when I bring the horsebox back.' To Roncey, 'Don't worry, he'll be quite safe. I'll see you on Saturday. Ring the *Blaze*, as before, if you'd like to be reassured tonight and tomorrow.'

I shut the window, sorted out the eccentric gears, and drove Tiddely Pom gently out of the yard and up the lane to the village. An hour later than I intended, I thought in disgust. Another hour for Mrs Woodward. My mind shied away from the picture of Elizabeth waiting for me to come back. Nothing would be better. Nothing would be better for a long time to come. I felt the first stirrings of resentment against Elizabeth and at least had the sense to realize that my mind was playing me a common psychological trick. The guilty couldn't stand the destruction of their self-esteem involved in having to admit they were wrong, and wriggled out of their shame by transferring it into resentment against the people who had made them feel it. I resented Elizabeth because I had wronged her. Of all ridiculous injustices. And of all ridiculous injustices, one of the most universal.

I manoeuvred the heavy horsebox carefully through

the small village and set off northeastwards on the road over the Downs, retracing the way I had come from London. Wide rolling hills with no trees except a few low bushes leaning sideways away from the prevailing wind. No houses. A string of pylons. Black furrows in a mile of plough. A bleak early December sky, a high sheet of steel-grey cloud. Cold, dull, mood-matching landscape.

There was very little traffic on the unfenced road, which served only Norton's village and two others beyond. A blue-grey Cortina appeared on the brow of the next hill, coming towards me, travelling fast. I pulled over to give him room, and he rocked past at a stupid speed for the space available.

My attention was so involved with Elizabeth that it was several seconds before the calamity got through. With a shattering jolt the casually noticed face of the Cortina's driver kicked my memory to life. It belonged to one of Charlie Boston's boys from the train. The big one. With the brass knuckles.

December couldn't stop the prickly sweat which broke out on my skin. I put my foot on the accelerator and felt Tiddely Pom's weight lurch behind me from the sudden spurt. All I could hope for was that the big man had been too occupied judging the width of his car to look up and see me.

He had, of course, had a passenger.

I looked in the driving mirror. The Cortina had gone out of sight over the hill. Charlie Boston's boys hurrying towards Norton Fox's village was no mild coincidence, but Tiddley Pom's whereabouts must have been transmitted with very little delay for them to be here already, especially if they had had to come from Birmingham. Just who, I wondered grimly, had told who where Tiddely Pom was to be found. Not that it mattered at that moment. All that mattered was to get him lost again.

I checked with the driving mirror. No Cortina. The horsebox was pushing sixty-five on a road wiser for forty. Tiddely Pom's hooves clattered inside his stall. He didn't like the swaying. He would have to put up with it until I got him clear of the Downs road, which was far too empty and far too visible from too many miles around.

When I next looked in the mirror there was a pale speck on the horizon two hills behind. It might not be them, I thought. I looked again. It was them. I swore bitterly. The speedometer needle crept to sixty-eight. That was the lot. My foot was down on the floorboards and they were gaining. Easily.

There was no town close enough to get lost in, and once on my tail they could stay there all day, waiting to find out where I took Tiddley Pom. Even in a car it would have been difficult to lose them: in a lumbering horsebox, impossible. Urgent appraisal of a depressing situation came up with only a hope that Charlie Boston's boys would again be propelled by more aggression than sense.

They were. They came up fast behind me, leaning on the horn. Maybe they thought I hadn't had time to see *them* as they went past me the other way, and wouldn't know who wanted to pass.

If they wanted to pass, they didn't want to follow. I shut my teeth. If they wanted to pass, it was now, it was here, that they meant to make certain that Tiddely Pom didn't run in the Lamplighter. What they intended to do about me was a matter which sent my mending ribs into a tizzy. I swallowed. I didn't want another hammering like the last time, and this time they might not be so careful about what they did or didn't rupture.

I held the horsebox in the centre of the road so that there wasn't room enough for their Cortina to get by. They still went on blowing the horn. Tiddely Pom kicked his stall. I took my foot some way off the accelerator and slowed the proceedings down to a more manageable forty-five. They would guess I knew who they were. I didn't see that it gave them any advantage.

A hay lorry appeared round a hill ahead with its load over-hanging the centre of the road. Instinctively I slowed still further, and began to pull over. The Cortina's nose showed sharply in the wing mirror, already up by my rear axle. I swung the horsebox back into the centre of the road, which raised flashing headlights from the driver of the advancing hay lorry. When I was far too close to a radiator to radiator confrontation he started blowing his horn furiously as well. I swung back to my side of the road when he was almost stationary from standing rigidly on his brakes, and glimpsed a furious face and a shaking fist as I swerved past. Inches to spare. Inches were enough.

The Cortina tried to get past in the short second before the horsebox was re-established on the crown of the road. There was a bump, this time, as I cut across its bows. It dropped back ten feet, and stayed there. It would only stay there, I thought despairingly, until Charlie Boston's boys had got what they came for.

Less than a mile ahead lay my likely Waterloo, in the shape of a crossroads. A halt sign. It was I who would have to halt. Either that or risk hitting a car speeding legitimately along the major road, risk killing some innocent motorist, or his wife, or his child . . . Yet if I stopped, the Cortina with its faster acceleration would pass me when I moved off again, whether I turned right, as I had intended to, or left, back to London, or went straight on, to heaven knew where.

There wouldn't be anyone at the crossroads to give me any help. No police car sitting there waiting for custom. No AA man having a smoke. No life-saving bystander of any sort. No troop of United States cavalry to gallop up in the nick of time.

I changed down into second to climb a steepish hill and forgot Norton's box driver's instructions. For a frightening moment the gears refused to mesh and the horsebox's weight dragged it almost to a standstill.

Then the cogs slid together, and with a regrettable jolt we started off again. Behind me, Charlie Boston's boys still wasted their energy and wore out their battery by almost non-stop blasts on their horn.

The horsebox trundled to the top of the hill, and there already, four hundred yards down the other side, was the crossroads.

I stamped on the accelerator. The horsebox leaped forward. Charlie Boston's boys had time to take in the scene below, and to realize that I must be meaning not to halt at the sign. In the wing mirror, I watched him accelerate to keep up, closing enough to stick to me whatever I did at the crossroads.

Two hundred yards before I got there, I stood on the brake pedal as if the road ended in an abyss ten yards ahead. The reaction was more than I'd bargained for. The horsebox shuddered and rocked and began to spin. Its rear slewed across the road, hit the verge, rocked again. I feared the whole high-topped structure would overturn. Instead, there was a thudding, crunching, anchoring crash as the Cortina bounced on and off at the rear.

The horsebox screeched and slid to a juddering stop. Upright. Facing the right way.

I hauled on the hand brake and was out of the cab on to the road before the glass from the Cortina had stopped tinkling on to the tarmac.

The grey-blue car had gone over on to its side and was showing its guts to the wind. It lay a good twenty yards behind the horsebox, and from the dented look of the roof it had rolled completely over before stopping. I walked back towards it, wishing I had a weapon of some sort, and fighting an inclination just to drive off and leave without looking to see what had happened to the occupants.

There was only one of them in the car. The big one; the driver. Very much alive, murderously angry, and in considerable pain from having his right ankle trapped and broken among the pedals. I turned my back on him and ignored his all too audible demands for assistance. Revenge, I assessed, would overcome all else if I once got within reach of his hands.

The second Boston boy had been flung out by the crash. I found him on the grass verge, unconscious and lying on his face. With anxiety I felt for his pulse, but he too was alive. With extreme relief I went back to the horsebox, opened the side door, and climbed in to take a look at Tiddely Pom. He calmly swivelled a disapproving eye in my direction and began to evacuate his bowels.

'Nothing much wrong with you, mate,' I said aloud. My voice came out squeaky with tension. I wiped my hand round my neck, tried to grin, felt both like copying Tiddely Pom's present action and being sick.

The horse really did not seem any the worse for his highly unorthodox journey. I took several deep breaths, patted his rump, and jumped down again into the road. Inspection of the damage at the back of the horsebox revealed a smashed rear light and a dent in the sturdy off rear wing no larger than a soup plate. I hoped that Luke-John would agree to the *Blaze* paying for the repairs. Charlie Boston wouldn't want to.

His unconscious boy was beginning to stir. I watched him sit up, put his hands on his head, begin to remember what had happened. I listened to his big colleague still shouting furiously from inside the car. Then with deliberate non-haste I climbed back into the cab of the horsebox, started the engine, and drove carefully away.

I had never intended to go far. I took Tiddely Pom to the safest place I could think of: the racecourse stables at Heathbury Park. There he would be surrounded by a high wall and guarded by a security patrol at night. Everyone entering racecourse stables had to show a pass: even owners were not allowed in unless accompanied by their trainer.

Willy Ondroy, consulted on the telephone, had agreed to take in Tiddely Pom, and to keep his identity a secret. The stables would in any case be open from midday and the guards would be on duty from then on: any time after that, he said, Tiddely Pom would be just one of a number of horses arriving for the following day's racing. Horses which came from more than a hundred miles away normally travelled the day before their race and stayed overnight in the racecourse stables. A distant stable running one horse on Friday and another on Saturday would send them both down on Thursday and leave them both at the racecourse stables for two nights, or possibly even three. Tiddely Pom's two nights' stay would be unremarkable and inconspicuous. The only oddity about him was that he had no lad to look after him, an awkward detail to which Willy Ondroy had promised to find a solution.

He was looking out for me and came across the grass outside the stable block to forestall me from climbing down from the cab. Instead, he opened the door on the passenger side, and joined me.

'Too many of these lads know you by sight,' he said, waving an arm to where two other horseboxes were unloading. 'If they see you, they will know you would not have brought any other horse but Tiddely Pom. And as I understand it, you don't want to land us with the security headache of a bunch of crooks trying to injure him. Right?'

'Right,' I agreed thankfully.

'Drive down this road, then. First left. In through the white gate posts, fork left, park outside the rear door of my house. Right?'

'Right,' I said again, and followed his instructions, thankful for his quick grasp of essentials and his jet formation pilot's clarity of decision.

'I've had a word with the racecourse manager,' he said. 'The stables and security are his pigeon really. Had to enlist his aid. Hope you don't mind. He's a very sound fellow, very sound indeed. He's fixing up a lad to look after Tiddely Pom. Without telling him what the horse is, naturally.'

'That's good,' I said with relief.

I stopped the horsebox and we both disembarked. The horse, Willy Ondroy said, could safely stay where he was until the racecourse manager came over for him. Meanwhile, would I care for some tea? He looked at his watch. Three-fifty. He hesitated. Or a whisky, he added.

'Why a whisky?' I asked.

'I don't know. I suppose you look as though you need it.'

'You may be right,' I said, dredging up a smile. He looked at me assessingly, but how could I tell him that I'd just risked killing two men to bring Tiddely Pom safe and unfollowed to his door. That I had been extremely lucky to get away with merely stopping them. That only by dishing out such violence had I avoided a second beating of proportions I couldn't contemplate. It wasn't really surprising that I looked as if I needed a whisky. I did. It tasted fine.

CHAPTER THIRTEEN

Norton Fox was less than pleased when I got back.

He heard me rumble into the yard and came out of his house to meet me. It was by then full dark, but there were several external lights, and more light flooded out of open stable doors as the lads bustled around with the evening chores. I parked, climbed stiffly down from the cab, and looked at my watch. Five-fifty. I'd spent two hours on a roundabout return journey to fool the box driver over the distance I'd taken Tiddely Pom. Heathbury Park and back was probably the driver's most beaten track; he would know the mileage to a hundred yards, recognize it instantly he saw it on the clock, know for a certainty where the horse was, and make my entire afternoon a waste of time.

'You're in trouble, Ty,' Norton said, reaching me and frowning. 'What in God's name were you thinking of? First the man delivering my hay gets here in a towering rage and says my horsebox drove straight at him with some maniac at the wheel and that there'd be an accident if he was any judge, and the next thing is we hear there has been an accident over by Long Barrow crossroads involving a horsebox and I've had the police here making enquiries . . .'

'Yes.' I agreed. 'I'm very sorry, Norton. Your horsebox has a dent in it, and a broken rear light. I'll apologize to the hay lorry driver. And I guess I'll have to talk to the police.'

Dangerous driving. Putting it mildly. Very difficult to prove it was a case of self-preservation.

Norton looked near to explosion. 'What on earth were you *doing*?'

'Playing cowboys and Indians,' I said tiredly. 'The Indians bit the dust.'

He was not amused. His secretary came out to tell him he was wanted on the telephone, and I waited by the horsebox until he came back, gloomily trying to remember the distinction between careless, reckless, and dangerous, and the various penalties attached. Failing to stop. Failing to report an accident. How much for those?

Norton came back less angry than he went. 'That was the police,' he said abruptly. 'They still want to see you. However, it seems the two men involved in the crash have vanished from the casualty department in the hospital and the police have discovered that the Cortina was stolen. They are less inclined to think that the accident was your fault, in spite of what the hay lorry driver told them.'

'The men in the Cortina were after Tiddely Pom,' I said flatly. 'And they damn nearly got him. Maybe you could tell Victor Roncey that there is some point to our precautions, after all.'

'He's gone home,' he said blankly. I began to walk across the dark stable yard to where I'd left my van, and he followed me, giving me directions about how to find the police station.

I stopped him. 'I'm not going there. The police can come to me. Preferably on Monday. You tell them that.'

'Why on Monday?' He looked bewildered. 'Why not now?'

'Because,' I spelled it out, 'I can tell them roughly where to find those men in the Cortina and explain what they were up to. But I don't want the police issuing any warrants before Monday, otherwise the whole affair will be *sub judice* and I won't be able to get a squeak into the *Blaze*. After all this trouble, we've earned our story for Sunday.'

'You take my breath away,' he said sounding as if I had. 'And the police won't like it.'

'For God's sake, don't tell them,' I said in exasperation. 'That was for your ears only. If and when they ask you where I am, simply say I will be getting in touch with them, and that you don't know where I live, and that they could reach me through the *Blaze*, if they want me.'

'Very well,' he agreed doubtfully. 'If you're sure. But

it sounds to me as though you're landing yourself in serious trouble. I wouldn't have thought Tiddely Pom was worth it.'

'Tiddely Pom, Brevity, Polyxenes, and all the rest . . . individually none of them was worth the trouble. That's precisely why the racket goes on.'

His disapproving frown lightened into a half-smile. 'You'll be telling me next that the *Blaze* is more interested in justice than sensationalism.'

'It says so. Often,' I agreed sardonically.

'Huh,' said Norton. 'You can't believe everything you read in the papers.'

I drove home slowly, tired and depressed. Other times, trouble had been a yeast lightening the daily bread. A positive plus factor. Something I needed. But other times, trouble hadn't bitterly invaded my marriage or earned me such a savage physical attack.

This time, although I was fairly confident that Tiddely Pom would start in his race, the successful uncovering and extermination of a racing scandal was bringing me none of the usual upsurging satisfaction. This time, dust and ashes. This time, present grief and a grey future.

I stopped on the way and rang the *Blaze*. Luke-John had left for the day. I got him at home.

'Tiddely Pom is in the racecourse stables at Heathbury,' I said. 'Guarded by an ex-policeman and a large Alsatian. The clerk of the course and the racecourse manager both know who he is, but no one else does. OK?'

'Very, I should think.' He sounded moderately pleased, but no more. 'We can take it as certain now that Tiddely Pom will start in the Lamplighter. It's made a good story, Ty, but I'm afraid we exaggerated the danger.'

I disillusioned him. 'Charlie Boston's boys were three miles from Norton Fox's stable by two-thirty this afternoon.'

'Christ,' he said. 'So it's really true . . .'

'You've looked at it so far as a stunt for the *Blaze*.'

'Well . . .'

'Well, so it is,' I agreed. 'Anyway, Charlie Boston's boys had a slight accident with their car, and they are now back to square one as they don't know where I took Tiddely Pom.'

'What sort of accident?'

'They ran into the back of the horsebox. Careless of them. I put the brakes on rather hard, and they were following a little too close.'

A shocked silence. Then he said, 'Were they killed?'

'No. Hardly bent.' I gave him an outline of the afternoon's events. Luke-John's reaction was typical and expected, and the enthusiasm was alive again in his voice.

'Keep away from the police until Sunday.'

'Sure thing.'

'This is great, Ty.'

'Yeah,' I said.

'Knock out a preliminary version tonight and bring it in with you in the morning,' he said. 'Then we can discuss it tomorrow, and you can phone me in the final touches from Heathbury after the Lamplighter on Saturday.'

'All right.'

'Oh, and give Roncey a ring, would you, and tell him the horse is only safe thanks to the *Blaze*.'

'Yes,' I said. 'Maybe I will.'

I put down the receiver and felt like leaving Roncey severely alone. I was tired and I wanted to go home. And when I got home, I thought drearily, there would be no let off, only another dose of self hate and remorse.

Roncey answered the telephone at the first ring and needed no telling. Norton Fox had already been through.

'Tiddely Pom is safe and well looked after,' I assured him.

'I owe you an apology,' he said abruptly.

'Be my guest,' I said.

'Look here, there's something worrying me. Worrying me badly.' He paused, swallowing a great deal of pride. 'Do you . . . I mean, have you any idea . . . how those men appeared so quickly on the scene?'

'The same idea as you,' I agreed. 'Your son, Pat.'

'I'll break his neck,' he said, with real and unfatherly viciousness.

'If you've any sense, you'll let him ride your horses in all their races, not just the unimportant ones.'

'What are you talking about?'

'About Pat's outsize sense of grievance. You put up anyone except him, and he resents it.'

'He's not good enough,' he protested.

'And how will he ever be, if you don't give him the experience? Nothing teaches a jockey faster than riding a good horse in a good race.'

'He might lose,' he said pugnaciously.

'He might win. When did you ever give him the chance?'

'But to give away the secret of Tiddely Pom's whereabouts . . . what would he expect to gain?'

'He was getting his own back, that's all.'

'All!'

'There's no harm done.'

'I hate him.'

'Then send him to another stable. Give him an allowance to live on and let him see if he's going to ride well enough to turn professional. That's what he wants. If you stamp on people's ambitions too hard, it's not frantically astonishing if they bite back.'

'It's a son's duty to work for his father. Especially a farmer's son.'

I sighed. He was half a century out of date and no amount of telling from me was going to change him. I said I'd see him on Sunday, and disconnected.

Like his father, I took no pleasure at all in Pat

Roncey's vengeful disloyalty. Understand, maybe. Admire, far from it.

One of the men who came to enquire at Roncey's farm must have sensed Pat's obvious disgruntlement and have given him a telephone number to ring if he ever found out where Tiddely Pom had gone, and wanted to revenge himself on his father. One might give Pat the benefit of enough doubt to suppose that he'd thought hc was only telling a rival newspaperman to the *Blaze*; but even so he must have known that a rival newspaper would spread the information to every corner of the country. To the ears which waited to hear. Exactly the same in the end. But because of the speed with which Charlie Boston's boys had reached Norton Fox's village, it must have been Raincoat or the chauffeur, or even Vjoersterod himself who had talked to Pat at the farm.

It had to be Pat. Norton Fox's stable lads might have passed the word on to newspapers, but they couldn't have told Vjoersterod or Charlie Boston because they didn't know they wanted to know, and probably didn't even know they existed.

I drove on, back to London. Parked the van in the garage downstairs. Locked up. Walked slowly and unenthusiastically up to the flat.

'Hi,' said Elizabeth brightly.

'Hi yourself.' I kissed her cheek.

It must have looked, to Mrs Woodward, a normal

greeting. Only the pain we could read in each other's eyes said it wasn't.

Mrs Woodward put on her dark blue coat and checked the time again to make sure it was ten to, not ten after. She'd had three hours extra, but she wanted more. I wondered fleetingly if I could charge her overtime to the *Blaze*.

'We've had our meal,' Mrs Woodward said. 'I've left yours ready to warm up. Just pop it in the oven, Mr Tyrone.'

'Thanks.'

''Night, then, luv,' she called to Elizabeth.

''Night.'

I opened the door for her and she nodded briskly, smiled, and said she'd be there on the dot in the morning. I thanked her appreciatively. She would indeed be there on the dot. Kind, reliable, necessary Mrs Woodward. I hoped the *Tally* cheque wouldn't be too long coming.

Beyond that first greeting Elizabeth and I could find little to say to each other. The most ordinary enquiries and remarks seemed horribly brittle, like a thin sheet of glass over a pit.

It was a relief to both of us when the door bell rang.

'Mrs Woodward must have forgotten something,' I said. It was barely ten minutes since she had left.

'I expect so,' Elizabeth agreed.

I opened the door without a speck of intuition. It swung inward with a rush, weighted and pushed by a heavy man in black. He stabbed a solid leather gloved fist into my diaphragm and when my head came forward chopped down with something hard on the back of my neck.

On my knees, coughing for breath, I watched Vjoersterod appear in the doorway, take in the scene, and walk past me into the room. A black-booted foot kicked the door shut behind him. There was a soft whistling swish in the air and another terrible thump high up between my shoulder blades. Elizabeth cried out. I staggered to my feet and tried to move in her direction. The heavy man in black, Ross, the chauffeur, slid his arm under mine and twisted and locked my shoulder.

'Sit down, Mr Tyrone,' Vjoersterod said calmly. 'Sit there.' He pointed to the tapestry-covered stool Mrs Woodward liked to knit on as there were no arms or back to get in the way of her busy elbows.

'Ty,' Elizabeth's voice rose high with fear. 'What's happening?'

I didn't answer. I felt stupid and sunk. I sat down on the stood when Ross released my arm and tried to work some control into the way I looked at Vjoersterod.

He was standing near Elizabeth's head, watching me with swelling satisfaction.

'So now we know just where we are, Mr Tyrone. Did you really have the conceit to think you could defy me and get away with it? No one does, Mr Tyrone. No one ever does.'

I didn't answer. Ross stood beside me, a pace to the rear. In his right hand he gently swung the thing he had hit me with, a short elongated pear-shaped truncheon. Its weight and crushing power made a joke of Charlie Boston's boys' knuckledusters. I refrained from rubbing the aching places below my neck.

'Mr Tyrone,' Vjoersterod said conversationally, 'where is Tiddely Pom?'

When I still didn't answer immediately he half turned, looked down, and carefully put the toe of his shoe under the switch of the electric point. From there the cable led directly to Elizabeth's breathing pump. Elizabeth turned her head to follow my eyes and saw what he was doing.

'No,' she said. It was high-pitched, terrified. Vjoersterod smiled.

'Tiddely Pom?' he said to me.

'He's in the racecourse stables at Heathbury Park.'

'Ah.' He took his foot away, put it down on the floor. 'You see how simple it is? It's always a matter of finding the right lever. Of applying the right pressure. No horse, I find, is ever worth a really serious danger to a loved one.'

I said nothing. He was right.

'Check it,' Ross said from behind me.

Vjoersterod's eyes narrowed. 'He couldn't risk a lie.'

'He wouldn't be blackmailed. He was out to get

you, and no messing. Check it.' There was advice in Ross's manner, not authority. More than a chauffeur. Less than an equal.

Vjoersterod shrugged but stretched out a hand and picked up the receiver. Telephone enquiries. Heathbury Park racecourse. The clerk of the course's house? That would do very well.

Willie Ondroy himself answered. Vjoersterod said, 'Mr Tyrone asked me to call you to check if Tiddely Pom had settled in well . . .'

He listened to the reply impassively, his pale yellow face immobile. It accounted for the fact, I thought inconsequentially, that his skin was unlined. He never smiled; seldom frowned. The only wrinkles were around his eyes, which I suppose he screwed up against his native sun.

'Thank you so much,' he said. His best Foreign Office voice, courteous and charming.

'Ask him which box the horse is in,' Ross said. 'The number.'

Vjoersterod asked. Willy Ondroy told him.

'Sixty-eight. Thank you. Goodnight.'

He put the receiver carefully back in its cradle and let a small silence lengthen. I hoped that since he had got what he came for he would decently go away again. Not a very big hope to start with, and one which never got off the ground.

He said, studying his fingernails, 'It is satisfactory, Mr Tyrone, that you do at last see the need to cooperate with me.' Another pause. 'However, in your case, I would be foolish to think that this state of affairs would last very long if I did nothing to convince you that it must.'

I looked at Elizabeth. She didn't seem to have followed Vjoersterod's rather involved syntax. Her head lay in a relaxed way on the pillow and her eyes were shut. She was relieved that I had told where the horse was: she thought that everything was now all right.

Vjoersterod followed my glance and my thought. He nodded. 'We have many polio victims on respirators in my country. I understand about them. About the importance of electricity. The importance of constant attendance. The razor edge between life and death. I understand it well.'

I said nothing. He said, 'Many men desert wives like this. Since you do not, you would care if harm came to her. Am I right? You have, in fact, just this minute proved it, have you not? You wasted so little time in telling me correctly what I wanted to know.'

I made no comment. He waited a fraction, then went smoothly on. What he said, as Dembley had found out, was macabrely at variance with the way he said it.

'I have an international reputation to maintain. I simply cannot afford to have pipsqueak journalists interfering with my enterprises and trying to hold me up to ridicule. I intend to make it clear to you once and for all, to impress upon you indelibly, that I am not a man to be crossed.'

Ross moved a pace at my side. My skin crawled. I made as good a job as I could of matching Vjoersterod's immobility of expression.

Vjoersterod had more to say. As far as I was concerned, he could go on all night. The alternative hardly beckoned.

'Charlie Boston reports to me that you have put both his men out of action. He too cannot afford such affronts to his reputation. Since all you learned from his warning attentions on the train was to strike back, we will see if my chauffeur can do any better.'

I tucked one foot under the stool, pivoted on it, and on the way to my feet struck at Ross with both hands, one to the stomach, one to the groin. He bent over, taken by surprise, and I wrenched the small truncheon out of his hand, raised it to clip him on the head.

'Ty . . .' Elizabeth's voice rose in an agonized wail. I swung round with the truncheon in my hand and met Vjoersterod's fiercely implacable gaze.

'Drop it.'

He had his toe under the switch. Three yards between us.

I hesitated, boiling with fury, wanting above anything to hit him, knock him out, get rid of him out of my life and most particularly out of the next hour of it. I couldn't risk it. One tiny jerk could cut off the current. I couldn't risk not being able to reach the switch again in time, not with Vjoersterod in front of it and Ross behind me. Under the weight of the Spirashell she would suffocate almost immediately. If I resisted any more I could kill her. He might really do it. Let her die. Leave me to explain her death and maybe even be accused of slaughtering her myself. The unwanted wife bit . . . He didn't know I knew his name or anything about him. He would think he could kill Elizabeth with reasonable safety. I simply couldn't risk it.

I put my arm down slowly and dropped the truncheon on the carpet. Ross, breathing heavily, bent and picked it up.

'Sit down, Mr Tyrone,' Vjoersterod said. 'And stay sitting down. Don't get up again. Do I make myself clear?'

He still had his toe under the switch. I sat down, seething inside, rigid outside, and totally apprehensive. Twice in a fortnight was definitely too much.

Vjoersterod nodded to Ross, who hit me solidly with the truncheon on the back of the shoulder. It sounded horrible. Felt worse.

Elizabeth cried out. Vjoersterod looked at her without pity and told Ross to switch on the television. They both waited while the set warmed up. Ross adjusted the volume to medium loud and changed the channel from a news magazine to song and dance. No neighbours, unfortunately, would call to complain about the noise. The only ones who lived near enough were out working in a nightclub.

Ross had another go with the truncheon. Instinctively I started to stand up . . . to retaliate, to escape, heaven knows.

'Sit down,' Vjoersterod said.

I looked at his toe. I sat down. Ross swung his arm and that time I fell forward off the stool on to my knees.

'Sit,' Vjoersterod said. Stiffly I returned to where he said.

'Don't,' Elizabeth said to him in a wavering voice. 'Please don't.'

I looked at her, met her eyes. She was terrified. Scared to death. And something else. Beseeching. Begging me. With a flash of blinding understanding I realized she was afraid I wouldn't take any more, that I wouldn't think she was worth it, that I would somehow stop them hurting me even if it meant switching off her pump. Vjoersterod knew I wouldn't. It was ironic, I thought mordantly, that Vjoersterod knew me better than my own wife.

It didn't last a great deal longer. It had anyway reached the stage where I no longer felt each blow separately but rather as a crushing addition to an intolerable whole. It seemed as though I had the whole weight of the world across my shoulders. Atlas wasn't even in the race.

I didn't see Vjoersterod tell Ross to stop. I had the heels of my hands against my mouth and my fingertips in my hair. Some nit on the television was advising everyone to keep their sunny side up. Ross cut him off abruptly in mid note.

'Oh God,' Elizabeth said. 'Oh God.'

Vjoersterod's smooth voice dryly comforted her. 'My dear Mrs Tyrone, I assure you that my chauffeur knows how to be a great deal more unpleasant than that. He has, I hope you realize, left your husband his dignity.'

'Dignity,' Elizabeth said faintly.

'Quite so. My chauffeur used to work in the prison service in the country I come from. He knows about humiliation. It would not have been suitable, however, to apply certain of his techniques to your husband.'

'Russia?' she asked. 'Do you come from Russia?'

He didn't answer her. He spoke to me.

'Mr Tyrone, should you try to cross me again, I would allow my chauffeur to do anything he liked. Anything at all. Do you understand?'

I was silent. He repeated peremptorily, 'Do you understand?'

I nodded my head.

'Good. That's a start. But only a start. You will also do something more positive. You will work for me. You will write for me in your newspaper. Whatever I tell you to write, you will write.'

I detached my hands slowly from my face and rested my wrists on my knees.

'I can't,' I said dully.

'I think you will find that you can. In fact you will.

You must. And neither will you contemplate resigning from your paper.' He touched the electric switch with his brown polished toe cap. 'You cannot guard your wife adequately every minute for the rest of her life.'

'Very well,' I said slowly. 'I will write what you say.'

'Ah.'

Poor old Bert Checkov, I thought drearily. Seven floors down to the pavement. Only I couldn't insure myself for enough to compensate Elizabeth for having to live for ever in a hospital.

'You can start this week,' Vjoersterod said. 'You can say on Sunday that what you have written for the last two weeks turns out to have no foundation in fact. You will restore the situation to what it was before you started interfering.'

'Very well.'

I put my right hand tentatively over my left shoulder. Vjoersterod watched me and nodded.

'You'll remember that,' he said judiciously. 'Perhaps you will feel better if I assure you that many who have crossed me are now dead. You are more useful to me alive. As long as you write what I say, your wife will be safe, and my chauffeur will not need to attend to you.'

His chauffeur, did he but know it, had proved to be a pale shadow of the Boston boys. For all my fears, it now seemed to me that the knuckledusters had been worse. The chauffeur's work was a bore, a present burden, yet not as crippling as before. No broken ribs.

No all-over weakness. This time I would be able to move.

Elizabeth was close to tears. 'How can you,' she said. 'How can you be so . . . beastly.'

Vjoersterod remained unruffled. 'I am surprised you care so much for your husband after his behaviour with that coloured girl.'

She bit her lip and rolled her head away from him on the pillow. He stared at me calmly. 'So you told her.'

There was no point in saying anything. If I'd told him where Tiddely Pom had been on Tuesday, when he first tried to make me, I would have saved myself a lot of pain and trouble. I would have saved Elizabeth from knowing about Gail. I would have spared her all this fear. Some of Bert Checkov's famous last words floated up from the past . . . 'It's the ones who don't know when to give in who get the worst clobbering . . . in the ring, I mean . . .'

I swallowed. The ache from my shoulders was spreading down my back. I was dead tired of sitting on that stool. Mrs Woodward could keep it, I thought scrappily. I wouldn't want it in the flat any more.

Vjoersterod said to Ross, 'Pour him a drink.'

Ross went over to where the whisky bottle stood on its tray with two glasses and the Malvern Water. The bottle was nearly half full. He unscrewed the cap, picked up one of the tumblers, and emptied into it all the whisky. It was filled to the brim.

Vjoersterod nodded. 'Drink it.'

Ross gave me the glass. I stared at it.

'Go on,' Vjoersterod said. 'Drink it.'

I took a breath to protest. He moved his toe towards the switch. I put the glass to my lips and took a mouthful. Jump through hoops when the man said.

'All of it,' he said. 'Quickly.'

I had eaten nothing for more than twenty-four hours. In spite of a natural tolerance, a tumbler full of alcohol on an empty stomach was not my idea of fun. I had no choice. Loathing Vjoersterod, I drank it all.

'He seems to have learned his lesson,' Ross said.

CHAPTER FOURTEEN

They stood in silence for nearly fifteen minutes, watching me. Then Vjoersterod said, 'Stand up.'

I stood.

'Turn round in a circle.'

I turned. Lurched. Staggered. Swayed on my feet.

Vjoersterod nodded in satisfaction. 'That's all, Mr Tyrone. All for today. I expect to be pleased by what you write in the paper on Sunday. I had better be pleased.'

I nodded. A mistake. My head swam violently. I overbalanced slightly. The whisky was being absorbed into my bloodstream at a disastrous rate.

Vjoersterod and Ross let themselves out unhurriedly and without another word. As soon as the door closed behind them I turned and made tracks for the kitchen. Behind me Elizabeth's voice called in a question, but I had no time to waste and explain. I pulled the tin of salt from the shelf, poured two inches of it into a tumbler and splashed in an equal amount of water.

Stirred it with my fingers. No time for a spoon. Seconds counted. Drank the mixture. It tasted like the Seven Seas rolled into one. Scorched my throat. An effort to get more than one mouthful down. I was gagging over the stuff before it did its work and came up again, bringing with it whatever of the whisky hadn't gone straight through my stomach wall.

I leaned over the sink, retching and wretched. I had lurched for Vjoersterod more than was strictly necessary, but the alcohol had in fact taken as strong and fast a hold as I had feared it would. I could feel its effects rising in my brain, disorganizing coordination, distorting thought. No possible antidote except time.

Time. Fifteen minutes, maybe, since I had taken the stuff. In ten minutes more, perhaps twenty, I would be thoroughly drunk.

I didn't know whether Vjoersterod had made me drink for any special purpose or just from bloody-mindedness. I did know that it was a horrible complication to what I had planned to do.

I rinsed my mouth out with clean water and straightened up. Groaned as the heavy yoke of bruises across my shoulders reminded me I had other troubles beside drink. Went back to Elizabeth concentrating on not knocking into the walls and doors, and picked up the telephone.

A blank. Couldn't remember the number.

Think.

Out it came. Willy Onroy answered.

'Willie,' I said. 'Move that horse out of box sixty-eight. That was the opposition you were talking to earlier. Put on all the guards you can, and move the horse to another box. Stake out sixty-eight and see if you can catch any would-be nobblers in the act.'

'Ty! Will do.'

'Can't stop, Willy. Sorry about this.'

'Don't worry. We'll see no one reaches him. I think, like you, that it's essential that he should be kept safe until the race.'

'They may be determined . . .'

'So am I.'

I put the receiver back in its cradle with his reassurance shoring me up, and met Elizabeth's horrified gaze.

'Ty,' she said faintly, 'what are you doing?'

I sat down for a moment on the arm of the chair. I felt terrible. Battered, sick and drunk.

I said, 'Listen, honey. Listen well. I can't say it twice. I can't put things back to where they were before I wrote the articles.'

'You told him you would,' she interrupted in bewilderment.

'I know I did. I had to. But I can't. I've told the stewards about him. I can't go back on that. In fact I won't. He's utter poison, and he's got to be stopped.'

'Let someone else do it.'

'That's the classic path to oppression.'

'But why you?' A protesting wail, but a serious question.

'I don't know . . . someone has to.'

'But you gave in to him . . . you let him . . .' She looked at me with wide, appalled eyes, struck by sudden realization. 'He'll come back.'

'Yes. When he finds out that Tiddely Pom has changed boxes and the whole stable is bristling with guards, he'll guess I warned them, and he'll come back. So I'm moving you out of here. Away. At once.'

'You don't mean now?'

'I do indeed.'

'But Ty . . . all that whisky . . . Wouldn't it be better to leave it until the morning?'

I shook my head. The room began spinning. I held on to the chair and waited for it to stop. In the morning I would be sore and ill, much worse than at that moment; and the morning might anyway be too late. Heathbury and back would take less than three hours in a Rolls.

'Ring up Sue Davis and see if Ron can come along to help. I'm going downstairs to get the van out, OK?'

'I don't want to go.'

I understood her reluctance. She had so little grasp on life that even a long-planned daytime move left her worried and insecure. This sudden bustle into the night seemed the dangerous course to her, and staying in a familiar warm home the safe one. Whereas they were the other way round.

'We must,' I said. 'We absolutely must.'

I stood up carefully and concentrated on walking a

straight path to the door. Made it with considerable success. Down the stairs. Opened the garage doors, started the van, and backed it out into the mews. A new set of batteries for Elizabeth's pump were in the garage. I lifted them into the van and put them in place. Waves of giddiness swept through me every time I bent my head down. I began to lose hope that I could retain any control of my brain at all. Too much whisky sloshing about in it. Too much altogether.

I went upstairs again. Elizabeth had the receiver to her ear and her eyes were worried.

'There isn't any reply. Sue and Ron must be out.'

I swore inwardly. Even at the best of times it was difficult to manage the transfer to the van on my own. This was far from the best of times.

I took the receiver out of the cradle, disconnected the Davises' vainly ringing number, and dialled that of Antonio Perelli. To my bottomless relief, he answered.

'Tonio, will you call the nursing home and tell them I'm bringing Elizabeth over.'

'Do you mean now, tonight?'

'Almost at once, yes.'

'Bronchial infection?' He sounded brisk, preparing to be reassuring, acknowledging the urgency.

'No. She's well. It's a different sort of danger. I'll tell you later. Look . . . could you possibly down tools and come over here and help me with her?'

'I can't just now, Ty. Not if she isn't ill.'

'But life and death, all the same,' I said with desperate flippancy.

'I really can't, Ty. I'm expecting another patient.'

'Oh. Well, just ring the nursing home, huh?'

'Sure,' he said. 'And . . . er . . . bring Elizabeth here on the way. Would you do that? It isn't much of a detour. I'd like just to be sure she's in good shape. I'll leave my patient for a few minutes, and just say hello to her in the van. All right?'

'All right,' I said. 'Thanks, Tonio.'

'I'm sorry . . .'

'Don't give it a thought,' I said. 'Be seeing you.'

The room whirled when I put the receiver down. I held on to the bedhead to steady myself, and looked at my watch. Couldn't focus on the dial. The figures were just a blur. I made myself see. Concentrated hard. The numbers and the hands came back sharp and clear. Ten thirty-seven. As if it mattered.

Three more trips to make up and down the stairs. Correction: five. Better start, or I'd never finish. I took the pillows and blankets off my bed, folded them as I would need them in the van, and took them down. When I'd made up the stretcher bed ready for Elizabeth, I felt an overpowering urge to lie down on it myself and go to sleep. Dragged myself back to the stairs instead.

Ridiculous, I thought. Ridiculous to try to do anything in the state I was in. Best to unscramble the eggs and go to bed. Wait till morning. Go to sleep. Sleep.

If I went to sleep I would sleep for hours. Sleep away our margin of safety. Put it into the red time-expired section. Cost us too much.

I shook myself out of it. If I walked carefully, I could stop the world spinning round me. If I thought slowly, I could still think. There was a block now somewhere between my brain and my tongue, but if the words themselves came out slurred and wrong, I still knew with moderate clarity what I had intended them to be.

'Honey,' I said to Elizabeth. 'I'm going to take the pump down first. Then you and the Shira . . . Spira.'

'You're drunk,' she said miserably.

'Not surprising,' I agreed. 'Now listen, love. You'll have to breathe on your own. Four minutes. You know you can do it eash . . . easily.' She did four minutes every day, while Mrs Woodward gave her a bed bath.

'Ty, if you drop the pump . . .'

'I won't,' I said, 'I won't . . . drop . . . the pump.'

The pump was the only one we had. There was no replacement. Always we lived in the shadow of the threat that one day its simple mechanism would break down. Spares were almost impossible to find, because respirators were an uneconomic item to the manufacturers, and they had discontinued making them. If the pump needed servicing, Mrs Woodward and I worked the bellows by hand while it was being done in the flat. Tiring for an hour. Impossible for a lifetime. If I dropped the pump and punctured the bellows, Elizabeth's future could be precisely measured.

Four minutes.

'We'd better,' I said, considering, 'pack some things for you first. Clean nightdress, f'rinstance.'

'How long . . . how long will we be going for?' She was trying hard to keep the fear out of her voice, to treat our flight on a rational, sensible basis. I admired her, understood her effort, liked her for it, loved her, had to make and keep her safe . . . and I'd never do it, I thought astringently, if I let my mind dribble on in that silly way.

How long? I didn't know how long. Until Vjoersterod had been jailed or deported. Even then, it would be safer to find another flat.

'A few days,' I said.

I fetched a suitcase and tried to concentrate on what she needed. She began to tell me, item by item, realizing I couldn't think.

'Washing things. Hair brush. Make-up. Bedsocks. Hot water bottle. Cardigans. Pills . . .' She looked with longing at the Possum machine and all the gadgets.

'I'll come soon . . . come back soon for those,' I promised. With company, just in case.

'You'll need some things yourself,' she said.

'Hm?' I squinted at her. 'Yeah . . .'

I fetched toothbrush, comb, electric razor. I would sleep in the van, dressed, on the stretcher bed. Better take a clean shirt. And a sweater. Beyond that, I couldn't be bothered. Shoved them into a grip. Packing done.

'Could you leave a note for Mrs Woodward?' she asked. 'She'll be so worried if we aren't here in the morning.'

A note for Mrs Woodward. Found some paper. Ball point pen in my pocket. Note for Mrs Woodward. 'Gone away for few days. Will write to you.' Didn't think she would be much less worried when she read that, but didn't know what else to put. The writing straggled upwards, as drunk as I felt.

'All set,' I said.

The packing had postponed the moment we were both afraid of. I looked at the pump. Its works were encased in a metal cabinet of about the size of a bed-side table, with a handle at each side for carrying. Like any large heavy box, it was easy enough for two to manage, but difficult for one. I'd done it often enough before, but not with a whirling head and throbbing bruises. I made a practice shot at picking it up, just to find out.

I found out.

Elizabeth said weakly, 'Ty . . . you can't do it.'

'Oh yes . . . I can.'

'Not after . . . I mean, it's hurting you.'

'The best thing about being drunk,' I said carefully, 'is that what you feel you don't feel, and even if you feel it you don't care.'

'What did you say?'

'Live now, hurt later.'

I pulled back her sheets and my fingers fumbled on the buckle which unfastened the Spirashell. That wouldn't do, I thought clearly. If I fumbled the buckle I'd never have a chance of doing the transfer in four minutes. I paused, fighting the chaos in my head. Sometimes in my youth I'd played a game against alcohol, treating it like an opponent, drinking too much of it and then daring it to defeat me. I knew from experience that if one concentrated hard enough it was possible to carry out quite adequately the familiar jobs one did when sober. This time it was no game. This time, for real.

I started again on the buckle, sharpening every faculty into that one simple task. It came undone easily. I lifted the Spirashell off her chest and laid it over her knees, where it hissed and sucked at the blankets.

Switched off the electricity. Unplugged the lead. Wound it on to the lugs provided. Disconnected the flexible tube which led to the Spirashell.

Committed now. I tugged the pump across the floor, pulling it on its rocky old castors. Opened the door. Crossed the small landing. The stairs stretched downwards. I put my hand on the wall to steady myself and turned round to go down backwards.

Step by step. One foot down. Lift the pump down one step. Balance it. One foot down. Lift the pump. Balance . . .

Normally, if Ron or Sue or Mrs Woodward were

not there to help, I simply carried it straight down. This time, if I did that, I would fall. I leaned against the wall. One foot down. Lift the pump down. Balance it . . . It overhung the steps. Only its back two castors were on the ground, the others out in space . . . If it fell forward, it would knock me down the stairs with it . . .

Hurry. Four minutes. Halfway down it seemed to me with an uprush of panic that the four minutes had already gone by. That I would be still on the stairs when Elizabeth died. That I would never, never get it to the bottom unless I fell down there in a tangled heap.

Step by deliberate step, concentrating acutely on every movement, I reached the ground below. Lugged the pump across the small hall, lifted it over the threshold on to the street. Rolled it to the van.

The worst bit. The floor of the van was a foot off the ground. I climbed in, stretched down, grasped the handles, and tugged. I felt as if I'd been torn apart, like the old Chinese torture of the two trees. The pump came up, in through the door, on to the floor of the van. The world whirled violently round my head. I tripped over the end of the stretcher and fell backwards still holding the pump by one handle. It rocked over, crashed on its side, broke the glass over the gauge which showed the pressures and respirations per minute.

Gasping, feeling I was clamped into a hopeless

nightmare, I bent over the pump and lifted it upright. Shoved it into its place. Fastened the straps which held it. Pushed the little wedges under its wheels. Plugged in the leads to and from the batteries. Couldn't believe I had managed it all, and wasted several seconds checking through again.

If it didn't work . . . If some of the broken glass was inside . . . If it rubbed a hole in its bellows . . . I couldn't think straight, didn't know what to do about it, hoped it would be all right.

Up the stairs. Easy without the pump. Stumbled over half the steps, reached the landing on my knees.

Elizabeth was very frightened, her eyes wide and dark, looking at death because I was drunk. When she had to do her own breathing she had no energy or air left for talking, but this time she managed one appalled, desperate word.

'Hurry.'

I remembered not to nod. Picked her up, one arm under her knees, one arm round her shoulders, pulling her towards me so that she could rest her head against my shoulder. Like one carries a baby.

She was feather light, but not light enough. She looked at my face and did my moaning for me.

'Hush,' I said. 'Just breathe.'

I went down the stairs leaning against the wall, one step at a time, refusing to fall. Old man alcohol was losing the game.

The step up into the van was awful. More trees. I

laid her carefully on the stretcher, putting her limp limbs straight.

Only the Spirashell now. Went back for it, up the stairs. Like going up a down escalator, never ending, moving where it should have been still. Picked up the Spirashell. The easiest burden. Very nearly came to grief down the stairs through tripping over the long concertina connecting tube. Stumbled into the van and thrust it much too heavily on to Elizabeth's knees.

She was beginning to labour, the tendons in her neck standing out like strings under her effort to get air.

I couldn't get the tube to screw into its connection in the pump. Cursed, sweated, almost wept. Took a deep breath, choked down the panic, tried again. The tricky two-way nut caught and slipped into a crossed thread, caught properly at last, fastened down firmly. I pressed the battery switch on the pump. The moment of truth.

The bellows nonchalantly swelled and thudded. Elizabeth gave the smallest sound of inexpressible relief. I lifted the Spirashell gently on to her chest, slipped the strap underneath her, and couldn't do up the buckle because my fingers were finally trembling too much to control. I just knelt there holding the ends tight so that the Spirashell was close enough for its vacuum to work. It pulled her chest safely up and down, up and down, filling her lungs with air. Some of the agonized apprehension drained out of her face, and some fragile colour came back.

Sixteen life-giving breaths later I tried again with the buckle. Fixed it after two more attempts. Sat back on the floor of the van, rested my elbows on my bent knees, and my head on my hands. Shut my eyes. Everything spun in a roaring black whirl. At least, I thought despairingly, at least I had to be nearly as drunk as I was going to get. Which, thanks to having got some of the stuff up, might not now be paralytic.

Elizabeth said with effortful calm, 'Ty, you aren't fit to drive.'

'Never know what you can do till you try.'

'Wait a little while. Wait till you're better.'

'Won't be better for hours.' My tongue slipped on the words, fuzzy and thick. It sounded terrible. I opened my eyes, focused carefully on the floor in front of me. The swimming gyrations in my head gradually slowed down to manageable proportions. Thought about the things I still had to do.

'Got to get the shoot . . . suitcases.'

'Wait, Ty. Wait a while.'

She didn't understand that waiting would do no good. If I didn't keep moving I would go to sleep. Even while I thought it I could feel the insidious langour tempting me to do just that. Sleep. Sleep deadly sleep.

I climbed out of the van, stood holding on to it, waiting for some sort of balance to come back.

'Won't be long,' I said. Couldn't afford to be long. She couldn't be left alone. In case.

Coordination had again deteriorated. The stairs proved worse than ever. I kept lifting my feet up far higher than was necessary, and half missing the step when I put them down. Stumbled upwards, banging into the walls. In the flat, propped up the note for Mrs Woodward so she couldn't miss it. Tucked Elizabeth's hot water bottle under my arm, carried the suitcases to the door, switched off the light, let myself out. Started down the stairs and dropped the lot. It solved the problem of carrying them, anyway. To prevent myself following them I finished the journey sitting down, lowering myself from step to step.

I picked up the hot water bottle and took it out to Elizabeth.

'I thought . . . Did you fall?' She was acutely anxious.

'Dropped the cases.' I felt an insane urge to giggle. 'S'all right.' Dropped the cases, but not the pump, not Elizabeth. Old man alcohol could stuff it.

I fetched the bags and put them on the floor of the van. Shut the doors. Swayed round to the front and climbed into the driving seat. Sat there trying very hard to be sober. A losing battle, but not yet lost.

I looked at Elizabeth. Her head was relaxed on the pillows, her eyes shut. She'd reached the stage, I supposed, when constant fear was too much of a burden and it was almost a relief to give up hope and surrender to disaster. She'd surrendered for nothing, if I could help it.

Eyes front. Method needed. Do things by numbers, slowly. Switched off the light inside the van. Suddenly very dark. Switched it on again. Not a good start. Start again.

Switched on the side lights. Much better. Switch on ignition. Check fuel. Pretty low after the run to Berkshire, but enough for five miles. Pull out the choke. Start engine. Turn out light inside van.

Without conscious thought I found the gear and let out the clutch. The van rolled forward up the mews.

Simple.

Stopped at the entrance, very carefully indeed. No one walking down the pavement, stepping out in front of me. Turned my head left and right, looking for traffic. All the lights in the road swayed and dipped. I couldn't see anything coming. Took my foot off the clutch. Turned out into the road. Gently accelerated. All clear so far.

Part of my mind was stone cold. In that area, I was sharply aware that to drive too slowly was as obvious a giveaway as meandering all over the road. To drive too fast meant no margin for a sudden stop. My reaction times were a laugh. Hitting someone wouldn't be.

As long as I kept my head still and my eyes front, it wasn't impossible. I concentrated fiercely on seeing pedestrian crossings, stationary cars, traffic lights. Seeing them in time to do something about them. I seemed to be looking down a small cone of clarity: everything in my peripheral vision was a shimmering blue.

I stopped without a jerk at some red lights. Fine. Marvellous. They changed to green. A sudden hollow void in my stomach. I couldn't remember the way. Knew it well, really. The man in the car behind began flashing his headlights. Thought of the old joke . . . What's the definition of a split second? The interval between the lights going green and the man behind hooting or flashing. Couldn't afford to sit there doing nothing. Let in the clutch and went straight on, realizing that if I strayed off course and got lost I would be sunk. The small print on my maps was for other times. Couldn't ask anyone the way, they might turn me over to the police. Breathalysers, and all that. I'd turn the crystals black.

Ten yards over the crossing I remembered the way to Welbeck Street. I hadn't gone wrong. A vote of thanks to the unconscious mind. Hip hip hooray. For God's sake mind that taxi . . . U-turns in front of drunken drivers ought to be banned . . .

Too much traffic altogether. Cars swimming out of side roads like shiny half-seen fish with yellow eyes. Cars with orange rear direction blinkers as blinding as the sun. Buses charging across to the kerb and pulling up in six feet at the stops. People running where they shouldn't cross, saving the seconds and risking the years.

Fight them all. Defeat the inefficiency of crashing. Stamp on the enemy in the blood, beat the drug confusing the brain . . . Stop the world spinning, hold tight to a straight and steady twenty miles an hour through an imaginary earthquake. Keep death off the roads. Arrive alive. Fasten your safety belts. London welcomes careful drivers . . .

I wouldn't like to do it again. Apart from the sheer physical exertion involved in keeping control of my arms and legs there was also a surging recklessness trying to conquer every care I took. An inner voice saying, 'Spin the wheel largely, go on, you can straighten out fine round the bend' and an answering flicker saying faintly, 'Careful, careful, careful, careful . . .'

Caution won. Mainly, I imagine, through distaste at what would happen to me if I were caught. Only pulling up safely at the other end could possibly justify what was to all intents a crime. I knew that, and clung to it.

Welbeck Street had receded since I went there last.

CHAPTER FIFTEEN

Tonio must have been looking out for us, because he opened the front door and came out on the pavement before I had climbed out of the van. True, I had been a long time climbing out of the van. The waves of defeated intoxication had swept in as soon as I'd put on the brakes. Not defeated after all. Just postponed.

I finally made it on the road. Put one foot in front of the other round the front of the van, and leaned against the nearside wing.

Tonio peered at me with absolute incredulity.

'You're drunk.'

'You're so right.'

'Elizabeth . . .' he said anxiously.

I nodded my head towards the van and wished I hadn't. Hung on to the wing mirror. Still liable for drunk in charge, even on his pavement.

'Ty,' he said, 'for God's sake, man. Pull yourself together.'

'You try,' I said. 'I can't.'

He gave me a withering look and went round to the

back of the van to open the doors. I heard him inside, talking to Elizabeth. Tried hard not to slither down the wing and fold up into the gutter. Remotely watched a man in a raincoat get out of a taxi away down the street and cross into a telephone box. The taxi waited for him. Knew I couldn't drive any farther, would have to persuade Tonio to do it, or get someone else. No use thinking any more that one could remain sober by will power. One couldn't. Old bloody man alcohol sneaked up on you just when you thought you had him licked.

Tonio reappeared at my elbow.

'Get in the passenger seat,' he said. 'And give me the keys, so that you can't be held to be in charge. I'll drive you to the nursing home. But I'm afraid you'll have to wait ten minutes or so, because I still have that patient with me and there's a prescription to write . . . Are you taking in a word I say?'

'The lot.'

'Get in, then.' He opened the door for me, and put his hand on my arm when I rocked. 'If Elizabeth needs me, blow the horn.'

'Right.'

I sat in the seat, slid down, and put my head back. Sleep began to creep in round the edges.

'You all right?' I said to Elizabeth.

Her head was behind me. I heard her murmur quietly, 'Yes.'

The pump hummed rhythmically, aiding and

abetting the whisky. The sense of urgency drifted away. Tonio would drive us . . . Elizabeth was safe. My eyelids gave up the struggle. I sank into a pit, whirling and disorientated. Not an unpleasant feeling if one didn't fight it.

Tonio opened the door and shook me awake.

'Drink this,' he said. A mug of coffee, black and sweet. 'I'll be with you in a minute.'

He went back into the house, propping the door open with a heavy wrought-iron facsimile of the Tower of Pisa. The coffee was too hot. With exaggerated care I put the mug down on the floor. Straightened up wishing the load of ache across my shoulders would let up and go away, but was much too full of the world's oldest anaesthetic to feel it very clearly.

I had been as drunk as that only once before, and it wasn't the night they told me Elizabeth would die, but four days later when they said she would live. I'd downed uncountable double whiskies and I'd eaten almost nothing for a week. It was odd to remember the delirious happiness of that night because of course it hadn't after all been the end of an agony but only the beginning of the years of pain and struggle and waste . . .

I found myself staring vacantly at the off-side wing mirror. If I conshen . . . well, concentrated . . . very hard, I thought bemusedly, I would be able to see what it reflected. A pointless game. It simply irritated me that I couldn't see clearly if I wanted to. Looked obstinately at the mirror and waited for the slowed-down focusing process to come right. Finally, with a ridiculous smile of triumph, I saw what it saw down the street. Nothing much. Nothing worth the trouble. Only a silly old taxi parked by the kerb. Only a silly man in a raincoat getting into it.

Raincoat.

Raincoat.

The alarm bells rang fuzzily in my sluggish head. I opened the door and fumbled my way on to the pavement, kicking the coffee over in the process. Leaned against the side of the van and looked down towards the taxi. It was still parked. By the telephone box. Where the man in the raincoat had been ringing someone up.

They say sudden overwhelming disaster sobers you, but it isn't true. I reeled across the pavement and up the step to Tonio's door. Forget all about blowing the car horn. Banged the solid knocker on his door, and called him loudly. He appeared at the top of the stairs, which led to his consulting-room on the first floor and his flat above that.

'Shut up, Ty,' he said. 'I won't be long.'

'Shome . . . someone's followed us,' I said. 'It's dangerous.' He wouldn't understand, I thought confusedly. He wouldn't know what I was talking about. I didn't know where to start explaining.

Elizabeth, however, must have told him enough.

'Oh. All right, I'll be down in one minute.' His head

withdrew round the bend in the stairs and I swivelled unsteadily to take another look down the street. Taxi still there in the same place. Light out, not for hire. Just waiting. Waiting to follow us again if we moved. Waiting to tell Vjoersterod where we'd gone.

I shook with futile rage. Vjoersterod hadn't after all been satisfied that Ross's truncheon and the threats against Elizabeth had been enough to ensure a permanent state of docility. He'd left Raincoat outside to watch. Just in case. I hadn't spotted him. Had been much too drunk to spot anything. But there he was. Right on our tail.

I'll fix him, I thought furiously. I'll fix him properly.

Tonio started to come down the stairs, escorting a thin, bent, elderly man whose breath rasped audibly through his open mouth. Slowly they made it to the bottom. Tonio held his arm as they came past me, and helped him over the threshold and down the step to the pavement. An almost equally elderly woman emerged from the Rover parked directly behind my van. Tonio handed him over, helped him into the car, came back to me.

'He likes to come at night,' he explained. 'Not so many fumes from the traffic, and easier parking.'

'Lord Fore . . . Fore something,' I said.

'Forlingham,' Tonio nodded. 'Do you know him?'

'Used to go racing. Poor old thing.' I looked wuzzily up the street. 'See that taxi?'

'Yes.'

'Following us.'

'Oh.'

'So you take 'Lizabeth on to the nursing home. I'll stop the taxi.' A giggle got as far as the first ridiculous note. 'What's worse than raining cats and dogs? I'll tell you . . . hailing taxis.'

'You're drunk,' Tonio said. 'Wait while I change my coat.' He was wearing formal consultant's dress and looked young and glamorous enough to be a pop singer. 'Can we wait?'

I swung out a generous arm in a wide gesture. 'The taxi,' I said owlishly, 'is waiting for *us*.'

He went to change his coat. I could hear Elizabeth's pump thudding safely away; wondered if I ought to go and reassure her; thought that in my state I probably couldn't. The Forlinghams started up and drove away. The taxi went on waiting.

At first I thought what I saw next was on the pink elephant level. Not really there. Couldn't be there. But this time, no hallucination. Edging smoothly round the corner, pulling gently into the kerb, stopping behind the taxi, one Silver Wraith, property of Hire Cars Lucullus.

Raincoat emerged from the taxi and reported to the Rolls. Two minutes later he returned to the taxi, climbed in, and was driven away.

Tonio ran lightly down the stairs and came to a halt beside me in a black sweater instead of a coat.

'Let's get going,' he said.

I put my hand clumsily on his arm.

'Shee . . . I mean, see that Rolls down there, where the taxi was.'

'Yes.'

'In that,' I said carefully, 'is the man who . . . oh God, why can't I think . . . who said he would . . . kill . . .'Lizabeth if I didn't do what he wanted . . . well . . . he might . . . he might not . . . but can't rish . . . risk it. Take her . . . Take her. I'll stop . . . him following you.'

'How?' Tonio said unemotionally.

I looked at the Tower of Pisa holding the door open.

'With that.'

'It's heavy,' he objected, assessing my physical state.

'Oh for God's sake stop arguing.' I said weakly. 'I want her to go where they can't find her. Please . . . please get going . . . go on, Tonio. And drive away slowly.'

He hesitated, but finally showed signs of moving. 'Don't forget,' he said seriously, 'that you are no use to Elizabeth dead.'

''Spose not.'

'Give me your coat,' he said suddenly. 'Then they'll think it's still you in the van.'

I took off my coat obediently, and he put it on. He was shorter than me. It hung on him. Same dark head, though. They might mistake us from a distance.

Tonio gave a rip-roaring impression of my drunken

walk, reeling right round the back of the van on his way to the driving seat. I laughed. I was that drunk.

He started the van and drove slowly away. I watched him give one artistic weave across the road and back. Highly intelligent fellow, Tonio Perelli.

Down the road, the Silver Wraith began to move. Got to stop him, I thought fuzzily. Got to stop him smashing up our lives, smashing up other people's lives. Someone, somewhere, had to stop him. In Welbeck Street, with a doorstop. Couldn't think clearly beyond that one fact. Had to stop him.

I bent down and picked up the Leaning Tower by its top two storeys. As Tonio had said, it was heavy. Bruised-muscle-tearingly heavy. Tomorrow its effects would be awful. Fair enough. Tomorrow would be much more awful if I put it down again . . . or if I missed.

The Rolls came towards me as slowly as Tonio had driven away. If I'd been sober I'd have had all the time in the world. As it was, I misjudged the pace and all but let him go cruising by.

Down one step. Don't trip. Across the pavement. Hurry. Swung the wrought-iron Tower round with both hands as if I was throwing the hammer and forgot to leave go. Its weight and momentum pulled me after it; but although at the last moment Ross saw me and tried to swerve, the heavy metal base crashed exactly where I wanted it. Drunks' luck. Dead centre of the windscreen.

Scrunch went the laminated glass in a radiating star. Silver cracks streaked across Ross's vision. The huge car swerved violently out into the centre of the road and then in towards the kerb as Ross stamped on the brakes. A screech of tyres, a scraping jolt. The Rolls stopped abruptly at a sharp angle to the pavement with its rear end inviting attention from the police. No police appeared to pay attention. A great pity. I wouldn't have minded being scooped in for being drunk and disorderly and disturbing the peace . . .

I had rebounded off the smooth side of the big car and fallen in a heap in the road. The Rolls had stopped, and that was that. Job done. No clear thought of self-preservation spearheaded its way through the mist in my head. I didn't remember that Tonio's solid front door stood open only a few yards away. Jelly had taken over from bone in my legs. Welbeck Street had started revolving around me and was taking its time over straightening out.

It was Ross who picked me up. Ross with his truncheon. I was past caring much what he did with it: and what he intended, I don't know, because this time I was saved by the bell in the shape of a party of people in evening dress who came out into the street from a neighbouring house. They had cheerful, gay voices full of a happy evening, and they exclaimed in instant sympathy over the plight of the Rolls.

'I say, do you need any help . . .?'

'Shall we call anyone . . . the police, or anything?'

'Can we give you a lift . . .?'

'Or call a garage?'

'No, thank you,' said Vjoersterod in his most charming voice. 'So kind of you . . . but we can manage.'

Ross picked me to my feet and held on grimly to my arm. Vjoersterod was saying, 'We've been having a little trouble with my nephew. I'm afraid he's very drunk . . . still, once we get him home everything will be all right.'

They murmured sympathetically. Began to move away.

'S'not true,' I shouted. 'They'll prob'ly kill me.' My voice sounded slurred and much too melodramatic. They paused, gave Vjoersterod a group of sympathetic, half-embarrassed smiles, and moved off up the street.

'Hey,' I called. 'Take me with you.'

Useless. They didn't even look back.

'What now?' Ross said to Vjoersterod.

'We can't leave him here. These people would remember.'

'In the car?'

While Vjoersterod nodded he shoved me towards the Rolls, levering with his grasp on my right arm. I swung at him with the left, and missed completely. I could see two of him, which made it difficult. Between them they more or less swung me into the back of the car and I sprawled there face down, half on and half off the seat, absolutely furious that I still could not climb out of that crippling alcoholic stupor. There was a ringing in my head like the noise of the livid green corridors of gas at the dentist's. But no stepped-up awakening to daylight and the taste of blood. Just a continuing extraordinary sensation of being conscious and unconscious, not alternately, but both at once.

Ross knocked out a few of the worst-cracked pieces of the windscreen and started the car.

Vjoersterod, sitting beside him, leaned over the back of his seat and said casually, 'Where to, Mr Tyrone? Which way to your wife?'

'Round and round the mulberry bush,' I mumbled indistinctly. 'And goodnight to you too.'

He let go with four-letter words which were much more in keeping with his character than his usual elevated chat.

'It's no good,' Ross said disgustedly. 'He won't tell us unless we take him to pieces and even then . . . if we did get it out of him . . . what good would it do? He'll never write for you. Never.'

'Why not?' said Vjoersterod obstinately.

'Well, look at it this way. We threatened to kill his wife. Does he knuckle under? Yes, as long as we're there. The moment our backs are turned, first thing he does is to move her out. We follow, find her, he shifts her off again . . . That could go on and on. All we can do more is actually kill her, and if we do that we've no hold on him anyway. So he'll never write for you, whatever we do.'

Full marks, I said to myself fatuously. Masterly summing up of the situation. Top of the class.

'You didn't hit him hard enough,' Vjoersterod said accusingly, sliding out of the argument.

'I did.'

'You can't have.'

'If you remember,' Ross said patiently, 'Charlie Boston's boys made no impression either. They either do or don't respond to the treatment. This one doesn't. Same with the threats. Same with the drink. Usually one method is enough. This time we use all three, just to make sure. And where do we get? We get nowhere at all. Just like Gunther Braunthal last year.'

Vjoersterod grunted. I wondered remotely what had become of Gunther Braunthal. Decided I didn't really want to know.

'I can't afford for him to get away with it,' Vjoersterod said.

'No,' Ross agreed.

'I don't like disposals in England,' Vjoersterod went on in irritation. 'Too much risk. Too many people everywhere.'

'Leave it to me,' Ross said calmly.

I struggled up into a sitting position, propping myself up on my hands. Looked out of the side window. Lights flashing past, all one big whirl. We weren't going very fast, on account of the broken windscreen, but the December night air swept into the car in gusts, freezing me in my cotton shirt. In a minute, when my head cleared a fraction, I would open the door and roll out. We weren't going very fast . . . If I waited for a bit of main street, with people . . . couldn't wait too long. Didn't want Ross attending to my disposal.

Vjoersterod's head turned round my way. 'You've only yourself to thank, Mr Tyrone. You shouldn't have crossed me. You should have done what I said. I gave you your chance. You've been very stupid, Mr Tyrone. Very stupid indeed. And now, of course, you'll be paying for it.'

'Huh?' I said.

'He's still drunk,' Ross said. 'He doesn't understand.'

'I'm not so sure. Look what he's done in the past hour. He's got a head like a bullet.'

My eyes suddenly focused on something outside. Something I knew, that everyone knew. The Aviary in Regent's Park, pointed angular wire opposite the main entrance to the Zoo. Been there before with Vjoersterod. He must be staying somewhere near there. I thought. Must be taking me to where he lived. It didn't matter that it was near the Zoo. What did matter was that this was also the way to the nursing home where Tonio had taken Elizabeth. It was less than a mile ahead.

I thought for one wild horror-stricken moment that I must have told Vjoersterod where to go; then remembered and knew I hadn't. But he was much too close. Much too close. Supposing his way home took him actually past the nursing home, and he saw the van . . . saw them unloading Elizabeth even . . . He might change his mind and kill her and leave me alive . . . which would be unbearable, totally and literally unbearable.

Distract his attention.

I said with as much clarity as my tongue would allow: 'Vjoersterod and Ross. Vjoersterod and Ross.'

'*What?*' said Vjoersterod.

The shock to Ross resulted in a swerve across the road and a jolt on the brakes.

'Go back to South Africa before the bogies get you.'

Vjoersterod had twisted round and was staring at me. Ross had his eyes too much on the mirror and not enough on the road. All the same, he started his indicator flashing for the right turn which led over the bridge across Regent's Canal and then out of the Park. Which led straight past the nursing home, half a mile ahead.

'I told the stewards,' I said desperately. 'I told the stewards . . . all about you. Last Wednesday. I told my paper . . . it'll be there on Sunday. So you'll remember me too, you'll remember . . .'

Ross turned the wheel erratically, sweeping wide to the turn. I brought my hands round with a wholly uncoordinated swing and clamped them hard over his eyes. He took both of his own hands off the wheel to try to detach them and the car rocked straight halfway through the turn and headed across the road at a tangent, taking the shortest distance to the bank of the canal.

Vjoersterod shouted frantically and pulled with all his strength at my arm, but my desperation was at least the equal of his. I hauled Ross's head back towards me harder still, and it was their own doing that I was too drunk to care where or how the car crashed.

'Brake,' Vjoersterod screamed. 'Brake, you stupid fool.'

Ross put his foot down. He couldn't see what he was doing. He put his foot down hard on the accelerator.

The Rolls leaped across the pavement and on to the grass. The bank sloped gently and then steeply down to the canal, with saplings and young trees growing here and there. The Rolls scrunched sideways into one trunk and ricocheted into a sapling which it mowed down like corn.

Vjoersterod grabbed the wheel, but the heavy car was now pointed downhill and going too fast for any change of steering. The wheel twisted and lurched out of his hand under the jolt of the front wheel hitting another tree and slewing sideways. Branches cracked around the car and scraped and stabbed at the glossy coachwork. Vjoersterod fumbled on the glove shelf and found the truncheon, and twisted round in his seat and began hitting my arm in panic-stricken fury.

I let go of Ross. It was far too late for him both to assess the situation and do anything useful about it. He was just beginning to reach for the hand brake when the Rolls crashed down over the last sapling and fell into the canal.

The car slewed convulsively on impact, throwing me around like a rag doll in the back and tumbling Vjoersterod and Ross together in the front. Black water immediately poured through the broken windscreen and began filling the car with lethal speed.

How to get out . . . I fumbled for a door handle in the sudden dark, couldn't find one, and didn't know what I had my feet on, didn't know which way up I was. Didn't know if the car was on its back or its nose . . . Didn't know anything except that it was sinking.

Vjoersterod began screaming as the water rose up his body. His arm was still flailing about and knocking into me. I felt the truncheon still in his hand. Snatched it from him and hit it hard against where I thought the rear window must be. Connected only with material. Felt around wildly with my hand, found glass above my head, and hit at that.

It cracked. Laminated and tough. Cursed Rolls-Royce for their standards. Hit again. Couldn't get a decent swing. Tried again. Crunched a hole. Water came through it. Not a torrent, but too much. The window was under the surface. Not far under. Tried again. Bash, bash. Made a bigger hole but still not enough . . . and water fell through it and over me and from the front of the car the icy level was rising past my waist.

Great to die when you're dead drunk, I thought. And when I die don't bury me at all, just pickle my bones in alcohol . . . Crashed the truncheon against the hole. Missed. My arm went right through it. Felt it up there in the air, out of the water. Stupid. Silly. Drowning in less than an inch of Regent's Canal.

Pulled my arm back and tried again. Absolutely no good. Too much water, too much whisky. One outside, one in. No push in my battered muscles and not much compression in my mind. Floating off on the river of death . . . sorry, Elizabeth.

Suddenly there were lights shining down over me. Hallucinations, I thought. Hallelujah hallucinations. Death was a blinding white light and a crashing noise in the head and a shower of water and glass and voices calling and arms grasping and pulling and raising one up . . . up . . . into a free cold wind . . .

'Is there anyone else in the car?' a voice said. A loud urgent voice, speaking to me. The voice of earth. Telling me I was alive. Telling me to wake up and do something. I couldn't adjust. Blinked at him stupidly.

'Tell us,' he said. 'Is there anyone else in the car?' He shook my shoulder. It hurt. Brought me back a little. He said again, 'Is there anyone else?'

I nodded weakly. 'Two.'

'Christ,' he muttered. 'What a hope.'

I was sitting on the grass on the canal bank, shivering. Someone put a coat around my shoulders. There were a lot of people and more coming, black figures against the reflection on the dark water, figures lit on one side only by the headlights of the car which had come down the path ploughed by the Rolls. It was parked there on the edge, with its lights on the place where the Rolls had gone. You could see the silver rim of the rear window shimmering just below the surface, close to the bank. You could see the water sliding shallowly through the gaping hole my rescuers had pulled me through. You could see nothing inside the car except darkness and water.

A youngish man had stripped to his underpants and was proposing to go through the rear window to try to rescue the others. People tried to dissuade him, but he went. I watched in a daze, scarcely feeling. His head came back through the window into the air, and several hands bent over to help him.

They pulled Vjoersterod out and laid him on the bank.

'Artificial respiration,' one said. 'Kiss of life.'

Kiss Vjoersterod . . . if they wanted to, they were welcome.

The diver went back for Ross. He had to go down twice. A very brave man. The Rolls could have toppled over on to its side at any moment and trapped him inside. People, I thought groggily, were amazing.

They put Ross beside Vjoersterod, and kissed him too. Neither of them responded.

Cold was seeping into every cell of my body. From the ground I sat on it rose, from the wind it pierced, from my wet clothes it clung clammily to my skin. Bruises stiffen fast in those conditions. Everything started hurting at once, climbing from piano to fortissimo. The noises in my head were deafening. A fine time for the drink to begin dying out on me, I thought. Just when I needed it most.

I lay back on the grass, and someone put something soft under my head. Their voices sprayed over me, questioning and solicitous.

'How did it happen?'

'We've sent for an ambulance . . .'

'What he needs is some good hot tea . . .'

'We're so sorry about your friends . . .'

'Can you tell us your name?'

I didn't answer them. Didn't have enough strength. Could let it all go, now. Didn't have to struggle any more. Old man alcohol could have what was left.

I shut my eyes. The world receded rapidly.

'He's out cold,' a tiny faraway voice said.

It wasn't true at that moment. But a second later, it was.

CHAPTER SIXTEEN

I was in a dim long room with a lot of bodies laid out in white. I, too, was in white, being painfully crushed in a cement sandwich. My head, sticking out of it, pulsed and thumped like a steam hammer.

The components of this nightmare gradually sorted themselves out into depressing reality. Respectively, a hospital ward, a savage load of bruises, and an emperor-sized hangover.

I dragged my arm up and squinted at my watch. Four-fifty. Even that small movement had out-of-proportion repercussions. I put my hand down gently on top of the sheets and tried to duck out by going to sleep again.

Didn't manage it. Too many problems. Too many people would want too many explanations. I'd have to edit the truth here and there, juggle the facts a little. Needed a clear head for it, not a throbbing dehydrated morass.

I tried to sort out into order exactly what had happened the evening before, and wondered profitlessly what I would have done if I hadn't been drunk. Thought numbly about Vjoersterod and Ross being pulled from the wreck. If they were dead, which I was sure they were, I had certainly killed them. The worst thing about that was that I didn't care.

If I shut my eyes the world still revolved and the ringing noise in my head grew more persistent. I thought wearily that people who poisoned themselves with alcohol for pleasure had to be crazy.

At six they woke up all the patients, who shook my tender brain with shattering decibels of coughing, spitting, and brushing of teeth. Breakfast was steamed haddock and weak tea. I asked for water and something for a headache, and thought sympathetically about the man who said he didn't like Alka-seltzers because they were so noisy.

The hospital was equipped with telephone trolleys, but for all my urging I couldn't get hold of one until nine-thirty. I fed it with coins salvaged from my now drying trousers and rang Tonio. Caught him luckily in his consulting room having insisted his receptionist tell him I was calling.

'Ty! *Deo gratias* . . . where the hell have you been?'

'Swimming,' I said. 'I'll tell you later. Is Elizabeth OK?'

'She's fine. But she was extremely anxious when you didn't turn up again last night . . . Where are you now? Why haven't you been to find out for yourself how she is?'

'I'm in University College Hospital. At least, I'm here for another few hours. I got scooped in here last night, but there's not much damage.'

'How's the head?'

'Lousy.'

He laughed. Charming fellow.

I rang the nursing home and talked to Elizabeth. There was no doubt she was relieved to hear from me, though from the unusual languor in her voice it was clear they had given her some sort of tranquillizer. She was almost too calm. She didn't ask me what happened when Tonio had driven her away; she didn't want to know where I was at that moment.

'Would you mind staying in the nursing home for a couple of days?' I asked. 'Just till I get things straight.'

'Sure,' she said. 'Couple of days. Fine.'

'See you soon, honey.'

'Sure,' she said again, vaguely. 'Fine.'

After a while I disconnected and got through instead to Luke-John. His brisk voice vibrated loudly through the receiver and sent javelins through my head. I told him I hadn't written my Sunday column yet because I'd been involved in a car crash the night before, and held the receiver six inches away while he replied.

'The car crash was yesterday afternoon.'

'This was another one.'

'For God's sake, do you make a habit of it?'

'I'll write my piece this evening and come in with

it in the morning before I go to Heathbury for the Lamplighter. Will that do?'

'It'll have to, I suppose,' he grumbled. 'You weren't hurt in the second crash, were you?' He sounded as if an affirmative answer would be highly unpopular.

'Only bruised,' I said, and got a noncommittal unsympathetic grunt.

'Make that piece good,' he said. 'Blow the roof off.'

I put down the receiver before he could blow the roof off my head. It went on thrumming mercilessly. Ross's target area also alternately burned and ached and made lying in bed draggingly uncomfortable. The grim morning continued. People came and asked me who I was. And who were the two men with me, who had both drowned in the car? Did I know their address?

No, I didn't.

And how had the accident happened?

'The chauffeur had a blackout,' I said.

A police sergeant came with a notebook and wrote down the uninformative truth I told him about the accident. I didn't know Mr Vjoersterod well: he was just an acquaintance. He had insisted on taking me in his car to the nursing home where my wife was at present a patient. The chauffeur had had a blackout and the car had run off the road. It had all happened very quickly. I couldn't remember clearly, because I was afraid I had had a little too much to drink. Mr Vjoersterod had handed me something to smash our way out of the car with, and I had done my best. It was very sad about Mr Vjoersterod and the chauffeur. The man who had fetched them out ought to have a medal. The sergeant said I would be needed for the inquest and went away.

The doctor who came to examine me at midday sympathized with my various discomforts and said it was extraordinary sometimes how much bruising one could sustain through being thrown about in a somersaulting car. I gravely agreed with him and suggested I went home as soon as possible.

'Why not?' he said. 'If you feel like it.'

I felt like oblivion. I creaked into my rough-dried crumpled shirt and trousers and left my face unshaven, my hair unbrushed and my tie untied, because lifting my arms up for those jobs was too much trouble. Tottered downstairs and got the porter to ring for a taxi, which took me the short distance to Welbeck Street and decanted me on Tonio's doorstep. Someone had picked up the Leaning Tower and put it back in place. There wasn't a mark on it. More than could be said for the Rolls. More than could be said for me.

Tonio gave me one penetrating look, an armchair, and a medicine glass of disprin and nepenthe.

'What's this made of?' I asked, when I'd drunk it.

'Nepenthe? A mixture of opium and sherry wine. Very useful stuff. How often do you intend to turn up here in dire need of it?'

'No more,' I said. 'It's finished.'

He wanted to know what had happened after he had driven Elizabeth away, and I told him, save for the one detail of my having blacked out the chauffeur myself. He was no fool, however. He gave me a twisted smile of comprehension and remarked that I had behaved like a drunken idiot.

After that he fetched my jacket from his bedroom and insisted on driving me and the van back to the flat on the basis that Elizabeth needed me safe and sound, not wrapped round one of the lamp posts I had miraculously missed the night before. I didn't argue. Hadn't the energy. He put the van in the garage for me and walked away up the mews to look for a taxi, and I slowly went up the stairs to the flat feeling like a wet dishcloth attempting the Matterhorn.

The flat was stifling hot. I had left all the heaters on the night before and Mrs Woodward hadn't turned them off. There was a note from her on the table. 'Is everything all right? Have put milk in fridge. Am very anxious. Mrs W.'

I looked at my bed. Nothing on it but sheets. Remembered all the blankets and pillows were still downstairs on the stretcher in the van. Going down for them was impossible. Pinched Elizabeth's. Spread one pink blanket roughly on the divan, lay down on it still dressed, pulled another over me, put my head down gingerly on the soft, cool pillow.

Bliss.

The world still spun. And otherwise, far too little to

put out flags for. My head still manufactured its own sound track. And in spite of the nepenthe the rest of me still felt fresh from a cement mixer. But now there was luxuriously nothing more to do except drift over the edge of a precipice into a deep black heavenly sleep . . .

The telephone bell rang sharply, sawing the dream in half. It was Mrs Woodward, Lancashire accent very strong under stress, sounding touchingly relieved that no unbearable disaster had happened to Elizabeth.

'It's me that's not well,' I said. 'My wife's spending a couple of days in the nursing home. If you'll ring again I'll let you know when she'll be back . . .'

I put the receiver down in its cradle and started across to my bed. Took two steps, yawned, and wondered if I should tell Victor Roncey to go fetch Madge and the boys. Wondered if I should tell Willy Ondroy to slacken the ultra-tight security. Decided to leave things as they were. Only twenty-four hours to the race. Might as well be safe. Even with Vjoersterod dead, there was always Charlie Boston.

Not that Tiddely Pom would win. After all the trouble to get him there his chances were slender, because the bout of colic would have taken too much out of him. Charlie Boston would make his profit, just as if they'd nobbled him as planned.

I retraced the two steps back to the telephone and after a chat with Enquiries put through a personal call to Birmingham.

'Mr Boston?'

'Yes.'

'This is James Tyrone.'

There was a goggling silence at the other end punctuated only by some heavy breathing.

I asked, 'What price are you offering on Tiddely Pom?'

No answer except a noise halfway between a grunt and a growl.

'The horse will run,' I commented.

'That's all you know,' he said. A rough, bad-tempered voice. A rough, bad-tempered man.

'Don't rely on Ross or Vjoersterod,' I said patiently. 'You won't be hearing from them again. The poor dear fellows are both dead.'

I put down the receiver without waiting for the Boston reactions. Felt strong enough to take off my jacket. Made it back to bed and found the friendly precipice still there, waiting. Didn't keep it waiting any longer.

A long while later I woke up thirsty and with a tongue which felt woolly and grass-green. The nepenthe had worn off. My shoulders were heavy, stiffly sore, and insistent. A bore. All pain was a bore. It was dark. I consulted my luminous watch. Four o'clock, give or take a minute. I'd slept twelve hours.

I yawned. Found my brain no longer felt as if it

was sitting on a bruise and remembered with a wide-awakening shock that I hadn't written my column for the *Blaze*. I switched on the light and took a swig of Tonio's mixture, and after it had worked went to fetch a notebook and pencil and a cup of coffee. Propped up the pillows, climbed back between the blankets, and blew the roof off for Luke-John.

'The lawyers will have a fit,' he said.

'As I've pointed out, the man who ran the racket died this week, and the libel laws only cover the living. The dead can't sue. And no one can sue for them. Also you can't accuse or try the dead. Not in this world, anyway. So nothing they've done can be *sub judice*. Right?'

'Don't quote *Blaze* dictums to me, laddie. I was living by them before you were weaned.' He picked up my typed sheets as if they would burn him.

'Petrified owners can come out of their caves,' he read aloud. 'The reign of intimidation is over and the scandal of the non-starting favourites can be fully exposed.'

Derry lifted his head to listen, gave me a grin, and said, 'Our troubleshooter loosing the big guns again?'

'Life gets tedious otherwise,' I said.

'Only for some.'

Luke-John eyed me appraisingly. 'You look more as if you'd been the target. I suppose all this haggard-eyed stuff is the result of a day spent crashing about in cars.' He flicked his thumb against my article. 'Did you invent this unnamed villain, or did he really exist? And if so who was he?'

If I didn't tell, Mike de Jong in his rival newspaper might put two and two together and come up with a filling-in-the-gaps story that Luke-John would never forgive me for. And there was no longer an urgent reason for secrecy.

I said, 'He was a South African called Vjoersterod, and he died the night before last in the second of those car crashes.'

Their mouths literally fell open.

'Dyna . . . *mite*,' Derry said.

I told them most of what had happened. I left Gail and Ross's trucheon out altogether but put in the threat to Elizabeth. Left out the drunken driving and the hands over Ross's eyes. Made it bald and factual. Left out the sweat.

Luke-John thought through the problem and then read my article again.

'When you know what you've omitted, what you've included seems pale. But I think this is enough. It'll do the trick, tell everyone the pressure's off and that they can safely bet ante-post again, thanks entirely to investigations conducted by the *Blaze*.'

'That's after all what we wanted.'

'Buy the avenging *Blaze*,' said Derry only half-sardonically. 'Racket-smashing a speciality.'

Luke-John gave him a sour look for a joke in bad taste, as usual taking the *Blaze*'s role with unrelieved seriousness. I asked him if he would ring up a powerful bookmaking friend of his and ask him the present state of the Lamplighter market, and with raised eyebrows but no other comment he got through. He asked the question, listened with sharpening attention to the answer, and scribbled down some figures. When he had finished he gave a soundless whistle and massaged his larynx.

'He says Charlie Boston has been trying to lay off about fifty thousand on Tiddely Pom since yesterday afternoon. Everyone smells a sewer full of rats because of your articles and the *Blaze*'s undertaking to keep the horse safe and they're in a tizzy whether to take the bets or not. Only one or two of the biggest firms have done so.'

I said, 'If Boston can't lay off and Tiddely Pom wins, he's sunk without trace, but if Tiddely Pom loses he'll pocket all Vjoersterod's share of the loot as well as his own and be better off than if we'd done nothing at all. If he manages to lay off and Tiddely Pom wins, he'll be smiling, and if he lays off and Tiddely Pom loses he'll have thrown away everything the crimes were committed for.'

'A delicate problem,' said Derry judicially. 'Or what you might call the antlers of a dilemma.'

'Could he know about the colic?' Luke-John asked.

We decided after picking it over that as he was

trying to lay off he probably couldn't. Luke-John rang back to his bookmaker friend and advised him to take as much of the Boston money as he could.

'And after that,' he said gloomily, as he put down the receiver, 'every other bloody horse will fall, and Tiddely Pom will win.'

Derry and I went down to Heathbury Park together on the race train. The racecourse and the sponsors of the Lamplighter had been smiled on by the day. Clear, sunny, still, frosty: a perfect December morning. Derry said that fine weather was sure to bring out a big crowd, and that he thought Zig Zag would win. He said he thought I looked ill. I said he should have seen me yesterday. We completed the journey in our usual relationship of tolerant acceptance and I wondered inconsequentially why it had never solidified into friendship.

He was right on the first count. Heathbury Park was bursting at the seams. I went first to Willy Ondroy's office beside the weighing-room and found a scattered queue of people wanting a word with him, but he caught my eye across the throng and waved a beckoning hand.

'Hey,' he said, swinging round in his chair to talk to me behind his shoulder. 'Your wretched horse has caused me more bother . . . that Victor Roncey, he's a bloody pain in the neck.'

'What's he been doing?'

'He arrived at ten this morning all set to blow his top if the horse arrived a minute after twelve and when he found he was there already he blew his top anyway and said he should have been told.'

'Not the easiest of characters,' I agreed.

'Anyway, that's only the half of it. The gateman rang me at about eight this morning to say there was a man persistently trying to get in. He'd offered him a bribe and then increased it and had tried to slip in unnoticed while he, the gateman, was having an argument with one of the stable lads. So I nipped over from my house for a reccy, and there was this short stout individual walking along the back of the stable block looking for an unguarded way in. I marched him round to the front and the gateman said that was the same merchant, so I asked him who he was and what he wanted. He wouldn't answer. Said he hadn't committed any crime. I let him go. Nothing else to do.'

'Pity.'

'Wait a minute. My racecourse manager came towards us as the man walked away, and the first thing he said to me was, "What's Charlie Boston doing here?" '

'What?'

'Ah. I thought he might mean something to you. But he was extraordinarily clumsy, if he was after Tiddely Pom.'

'No brains and no brawn,' I agreed.

He looked at me accusingly. 'If Charlie Boston was the sum total of the threat to Tiddely Pom, haven't you been overdoing the melodrama a bit?'

I said dryly, 'Read the next thrilling instalment in the *Blaze*.'

He laughed and turned back decisively to his impatient queue. I wandered out into the paddock, thinking of Charlie Boston and his futile attempt to reach the horse. Charlie Boston who thought with his muscles. With other people's muscles, come to that. Having his boys on the sick list and Vjoersterod and Ross on the dead, he was as naked and vulnerable as an opened oyster.

He might also be desperate. If he was trying to lay off fifty thousand pounds, he had stood to lose at least ten times that – upwards of half a million – if Tiddely Pom won. A nosedive of epic proportions. A prospect to induce panic and recklessness in ever-increasing intensity as the time of the race drew near.

I decided that Roncey should share the care of his horse's safety, and began looking out for him in the throng. I walked round the corner with my eyes scanning sideways and nearly bumped into someone standing at the Results-at-other-Meetings notice board. The apology was halfway to my tongue before I realized who it was.

Gail.

I saw the pleasure which came first into her eyes, and the uncertainty afterwards. Very likely I was showing her exactly the same feeling. Very likely she, like me, felt a thudding shock at meeting. Yet if I'd considered it at all, it was perfectly reasonable that she should come to see her uncle's horse run in the Lamplighter.

'Ty?' she said tentatively, with a ton less than her usual poise.

'Surprise, surprise.' It sounded more flippant than I felt.

'I thought I might see you,' she said. Her smooth black hair shone in the sun and the light lay along the bronze lines of her face, touching them with gold. The mouth I had kissed was a rosy pink. The body I had liked naked was covered with a turquoise coat. A week today, I thought numbly. A week today I left her in bed.

'Are Harry and Sarah here?' I said. Social chat. Hide the wound which hadn't even begun to form a scar tissue. I'd no right to be wounded in the first place. My own fault. Couldn't complain.

'They're in the bar,' she said. 'Where else?'

'Would you like a drink?'

She shook her head. 'I want to . . . to explain. I see that you know . . . I have to explain.'

'No need. A cup of coffee, perhaps?'

'Just listen.'

I could feel the rigidity in all my muscles and realized it extended even into my mouth and jaw. With a conscious effort I loosened them and relaxed.

'All right.'

'Did she . . . I mean, is she going to divorce you?'

'No.'

'Ohhhh.' It was a long sigh. 'Then I'm sorry if I got you into trouble with her. But why did she have you followed if she didn't want to divorce you?'

I stared at her. The wound half healed in an instant.

'What's the matter?' she said.

I took a deep breath. 'Tell me what happened after I left you. Tell me about the man who followed me.'

'He came up and spoke to me in the street just outside the hotel.'

'What did he look like?'

'He puzzled me a bit. I mean, he seemed too . . . I don't know . . . civilized, I suppose is the word, to be a private detective. His clothes were made for him, for instance. He had an accent of some sort and a yellowish skin. Tall. About forty, I should think.'

'What did he say?'

'He said your wife wanted a divorce and he was working on it. He asked me for . . . concrete evidence.'

'A bill from the hotel?'

She nodded, not meeting my eyes. 'I agreed to go in again and ask for one.'

'Why, Gail?'

She didn't answer.

'Did he pay you for it?'

'God, Ty,' she said explosively. 'Why not? I needed

the money. I'd only met you three times and you were just as bad as me, living with your wife just because she was rich.'

'Yes,' I said. 'Well, how much?'

'He offered me fifty pounds and when I got used to the idea that he was ready to pay I told him to think again, with all your wife's money she could afford more than that for her freedom.'

'And then what?'

'He said . . . if I could give him full and substantial facts, he could raise the payment considerably.' After a pause, in a mixture of defiance and shame, she added, 'He agreed to a thousand pounds, in the end.'

I gave a gasp which was half a laugh.

'Didn't your wife tell you?' she asked.

I shook my head. 'He surely didn't have that much money on him? Did he give you a cheque?'

'No. He met me later, outside the art school, and gave me a brown carrier bag . . . Beautiful new notes, in bundles. I gave him the bill I'd got, and told him . . . everything I could.'

'I know,' I said.

'Why did he pay so much, if she doesn't want a divorce?' When I didn't answer at once she went on, 'It wasn't really only the money . . . I thought if she wanted to divorce you, why the hell should I stop her. You said you wouldn't leave her, but if she sort of left *you*, then you would be free, and maybe we could have more than a few Sundays . . .'

I thought that one day I might appreciate the irony of it.

I said, ‘It wasn’t my wife who paid you that money. It was the man himself. He wasn’t collecting evidence for a divorce, but evidence to blackmail me with.’

‘Ohh.’ It was a moan. ‘Oh no, Ty. Oh God, I’m so sorry.’ Her eyes widened suddenly. ‘You must have thought . . . I suppose you thought . . . that I sold you out for *that*.’

‘I’m afraid so,’ I apologized. ‘I should have known better.’

‘That makes us quits, then.’ All her poise came back at one bound. She said, with some concern but less emotional disturbance, ‘How much did he take you for?’

‘He didn’t want money. He wanted me to write my column in the *Blaze* every week according to his instructions.’

‘How extraordinary. Well, that’s easy enough.’

‘Would you design dresses to dictation by threat?’

‘Oh.’

‘Exactly. Oh. So I told my wife about you myself. I had to.’

‘What . . . what did she say?’

‘She was upset,’ I said briefly. ‘I said I wouldn’t be seeing you again. There’ll be no divorce.’

She slowly shrugged her shoulders. ‘So that’s that.’

I looked away from her, trying not to mind so appallingly much that that was that. Tomorrow was Sunday.

Tomorrow was Sunday and I could be on my own, and there was nothing on earth that I wanted so much as to see her again in her smooth warm skin and hold her close and tight in the half dark . . .

She said thoughtfully, 'I suppose if that man was a blackmailer it explains why I thought he was so nasty.'

'Nasty? He was usually fantastically polite.'

'He spoke to me as if I'd crawled out of the cracks. I wouldn't have put up with it . . . except for thc money.'

'Poor Gail,' I said sympathetically. 'He was South African.'

She took in the implication and her eyes were furious. 'That explains it. A beastly Afrikaner. I wish I'd never agreed.'

'Don't be silly,' I interrupted. 'Be glad you cost him so much.'

She calmed down and laughed. 'I've never even been to Africa. I didn't recognize his accent or give it a thought. Stupid, isn't it?'

A man in a check tweed suit came and asked us to move as he wanted to read the notices on the board behind us. We walked three or four steps away, and paused again.

'I suppose I'll see you sometimes at the races,' she said.

'I suppose so.'

She looked closely at my face and said, 'If you really feel like that, why . . . *why* don't you leave her?'

'I can't.'

'But we could . . . you want to be with me. I know you do. Money isn't everything.'

I smiled twistedly. I did after all mean something to her, if she could ever say that.

'I'll see you sometimes,' I repeated emptily. 'At the races.'

CHAPTER SEVENTEEN

I caught Victor Roncey coming out of the luncheon room and told him that the danger to Tiddely Pom was by no means over.

'He's here, isn't he?' he said squashingly.

'He's here thanks to us,' I reminded him. 'And there are still two hours to the race.'

'What do you expect me to do? Hold his hand?'

'It wouldn't hurt,' I said flatly.

There was the usual struggle between aggressive independence and reasonable agreement. He said grudgingly, 'Peter can sit outside his box over in the stables.'

'Where is Peter now?'

He waved a hand behind him. 'Finishing lunch.'

'You'll have to take him in yourself, if he hasn't got a stable lad's pass.'

He grumbled and agreed, and went back to fetch his son. I walked over to the stables with them and checked with the man on the gate who said he'd had the usual number of people trying to get in, but not the man he'd turned away in the morning. Wing Commander Ondroy had told him to sling that man in the storeroom and lock him in, if he came sniffing round again.

I smiled appreciatively and went in with Roncey to look at the horse. He stood patiently in his box, propped on one hip, resting a rear leg. When we opened the door he turned his head lazily and directed on us an unexcited eye. A picture of a racehorse not on his toes, not strung up by the occasion, not looking ready to win Lamplighter Gold Cups.

'Is he always like this before a race?' I said. 'He looks doped.'

Roncey gave me a horrified glance and hurried to his horse's head. He looked in his mouth and eyes, felt his neck and legs, and kicked open and studied a small pile of droppings. Finally he shook his head.

'No dope that I can see. No signs of it.'

'He never has nerves,' Peter observed. 'He isn't bred for it.'

He looked bred for a milk cart. I refrained from saying so. I walked back into the paddock with Roncey and got him to agree to saddle up his horse in the stables, not in the saddling boxes, if the stewards would allow it.

The stewards, who included Eric Youll, didn't hesitate. They said only that Tiddely Pom would have to walk the three stipulated times round the parade ring for the public to see him before the jockey mounted, but were willing for him to walk six feet in from the rails and be led and guarded by Peter and myself.

'All a waste of time,' Roncey muttered. 'No one will try anything here.'

'Don't you believe it,' I said. 'You'd try anything if you stood to lose half a million you hadn't got.'

I watched the first two races from the press box and spent the time in between aimlessly wandering about in the crowd trying to convince myself that I wasn't really looking for another glimpse of Gail.

I didn't see her. I did see Dermot Finnegan. The little Irish jockey walked in front of me and gave me a huge gap-toothed grin. I took in, as I was supposed to, that he was dressed in colours, ready to ride in a race. The front of his jacket was carefully unbuttoned. I added up the purple star on the pink and white horizontal stripes and he laughed when he saw my astonishment.

'Be Jasus, and I'm almost as staggered as yourself,' he said. 'But there it is, I've got my big chance on the Guvnor's first string and if I make a mess of it may God have mercy on my soul because I won't.'

'You won't make a mess of it.'

'We'll see,' he said cheerfully. 'That was a grand job you made of me in *Tally*, now. Thank you for that. I took that when it came and showed it to the Guvnor but he'd already seen it, he told me. And you know I wouldn't be certain that it wasn't the magazine that put him in mind of putting me up on Rockville, when the other two fellows got hurt on Thursday. So thank you for that, too.'

When I told Derry about it in the press box during the second race he merely shrugged. 'Of course he's riding Rockville. Don't you read the papers?'

'Not yesterday.'

'Oh. Well yes, he's got as much as he can chew this time. Rockville's a difficult customer, even with the best of jockeys and our Dermot isn't that.' He was busy polishing the lenses of his race glasses. 'Luke-John's bookmaker friend must have accepted a good deal of Boston's fifty thousand, because the price on Tiddely Pom has come crashing down like an express lift from 100 to 8 to only 4 to 1. That's a stupid price for a horse like Tiddely Pom, but there you are.'

I did a small sum. If Boston had taken bets at 10 or 12 to 1 and had only been able to lay them off at 4 to 1, that left him a large gap of 6 or 8 to 1. If Tiddely Pom won, that would be the rate at which he would have to pay: which added up still to more than a quarter of a million pounds and meant that he would have to sell off the string of betting shops to pay his debts. Dumb Charlie Boston, trying to play with the big boys and getting squeezed like a toothpaste tube.

There was no sign of him in the paddock. Roncey saddled his horse in the stables and brought him straight into the parade ring very shortly before the time for the jockeys to mount. Peter led him round and I walked along by his quarters; but no one leaned over the rails to squirt him with acid. No one tried anything at all.

'Told you so,' Roncey muttered. 'All this fuss.' He put up his jockey, slapped Tiddely Pom's rump, and hurried off to get a good position on the trainer's stand. Peter led the horse out on to the course and let him go, and Tiddely Pom cantered off unconcernedly with the long lolloping stride so at variance with his looks. I sighed with relief and went up to join Derry in the press box to watch the race.

'Tiddely Pom's favourite,' he said. 'Then Zig Zag, then Rockville. Zig Zag should have it in his pocket.' He put his race glasses to his eyes and studied the horses milling round at the start. I hadn't taken my own glasses as I'd found the carrying strap pressed too heavily on tender spots. I felt lost without them, like a snail without antennae. The start for the Lamplighter was a quarter of a mile down the course from the stands. I concentrated on sorting out the colours with only force four success.

Derry exclaimed suddenly, 'What the devil . . .'

'Tiddely Pom,' I said fearfully. Not now. Not at the very post. I should have foreseen . . . should have stationed someone down there . . . But it was so public. So many people walked down there to watch the start. Anyone who tried to harm a horse there would have a hundred witnesses.

'There's someone hanging on to his reins. No, he's been pulled off. Great God . . .' Derry started laughing incredulously. 'I can't believe it. I simply can't believe it.'

'What's happening?' I said urgently. All I could see was a row of peacefully lining up horses, which miraculously included Tiddely Pom, and some sort of commotion going on in the crowd on the far side of the rails.

'It's Madge . . . Madge Roncey. It must be. No one else looks like that . . . She's rolling about on the grass with a fat little man . . . struggling. She pulled him away from Tiddely Pom . . . Arms and legs are flying all over the place . . .' He stopped, laughing too much. 'The boys are with her . . . they're all piling on to the poor little man in a sort of rugger scrum . . .'

'It's a pound to a penny the poor little man is Charlie Boston,' I said grimly. 'And if it's Madge and not the *Blaze* who's saved the day, we'll never hear the end of it from Victor Roncey.'

'Damn Victor Roncey,' Derry said. 'They're off.'

The line of horses bounded forward, heading for the first jump. Seventeen runners, three and a half miles, and a gold trophy and a fat cheque to the winner.

One of them crumpled up over the first. Not Tiddely Pom, whose scarlet and white chevrons bobbed in a bunch at the rear. Not Zig Zag, already positioned in the fourth place, from where he usually won. Not Egocentric, leading the field up past the stands to give the Huntersons their moment of glory. Not Rockville, with Dermot Finnegan fighting for his career in a battle not to let the horse run away with him.

They jumped the water jump in front of the stands. A gasp from the crowd as one of them splashed his hind legs right into it. The jockey in orange and green was dislodged and rolled.

'That horse always makes a balls of the water,' Derry said dispassionately. 'They should keep it for hurdles.' No tremor of excitement in his voice or hands. It had cost him nothing to get Tiddely Pom on to the track. It had cost me too much.

They swept round the top bend and started out round the circuit. Twice round the course to go. I watched Tiddely Pom all the way, expecting him to fall, expecting him to drop out at the back and be pulled up, expecting him to be too weak from colic to finish the trip.

They came round the bottom bend and up over the three fences in the straight towards the stands. Egocentric was still in front. Zig Zag still fourth. Dermot Finnegan had Rockville in decent control somewhere in the middle, and Tiddely Pom was still there and not quite last.

Over the water. Zig Zag stumbled, recovered, raced on. Not fourth any more, though. Sixth or seventh. Tiddely Pom scampered over it with none of the grace of Egocentric but twice the speed. Moved up two places.

Out they went again into the country. Derry remarked calmly, 'Tiddely Pom has dropped his bit.'

'Damn,' I said. The jockey was working with his arms, urging the horse on. Hopeless. And half the race still to run.

I shut my eyes. Felt the fatigue and illness come swamping back. Wanted to lie down somewhere soft and sleep for a week and escape from all the problems and torments and disillusionments of weary life. A week alone, to heal in. A week to give a chance for some energy for living to come creeping back. I needed a week at least. If I were lucky, I'd have a day.

'There's a faller at that fence.' The race commentator's amplified voice jerked my eyes open. 'A faller among the leaders. I think it was Egocentric . . . yes, Egocentric is down . . .'

Poor Huntersons. Poor Harry, poor Sarah.

Gail.

I didn't want to think about her. Couldn't bear to, and couldn't help it.

'He's still going,' Derry said. 'Tiddely Pom.'

The red and white chevrons were too far away to be clear. 'He's made up a bit,' Derry said. 'He's taken a hold again.'

They jumped the last fence on the far side and began the sweeping bend round into the straight, very strung out now, with great gaps between little bunches. One or two staggered fifty yards in the rear. There was a roar from the crowd and the commentator's voice rose above it . . . 'And here is Zig Zag coming to the front . . . opening up a commanding lead . . .'

'Zig Zag's slipped them,' Derry said calmly. 'Caught all the others napping.'

'Tiddely Pom . . .?' I asked.

'He's well back. Still plodding on, though. Most we could expect.'

Zig Zag jumped the first fence in the straight five seconds clear of the rest of the field.

'Nothing will catch him,' Derry said. I forgave him the satisfaction in his voice. He had tipped Zig Zag in his column. It was nice to be right. 'Tiddely Pom's in the second bunch. Can you see him? Even if he hasn't won, he's not disgraced.'

Zig Zag jumped the second last fence well ahead, chased after an interval by four horses more or less abreast. After these came Tiddely Pom, and behind him the other half-dozen still standing. If we had to settle for that, at least the ante-post punters had had some sort of run for their money.

It was clear twenty yards from the last fence that Zig Zag was meeting it wrong. The jockey hesitated fatally between pushing him on to lengthen his stride and take off sooner or shortening the reins to get him to put in an extra one before he jumped. In the end he did neither. Simply left it to the horse to sort himself out. Some horses like to do that. Some horses like to be told what to do. Zig Zag went into the fence like a rudderless ship, took off too late and too close, hit the fence hard with his forelegs, slewed round in mid air, crashed down in a tangle of hooves, and treated his rider to a well-deserved thump on the turf.

'Stupid *bastard*,' Derry said, infuriatedly lowering his glasses. 'An apprentice could have done better.'

I was watching Tiddely Pom. The four horses ahead of him jumped the last fence. One of them swerved to avoid Zig Zag and his supine jockey and bumped heavily into the horse next to him. Both of them were thoroughly unbalanced and the jockey of one fell off. When Tiddely Pom came away from the fence to tackle the straight he was lying third.

The crowd roared. 'He's got a chance,' Derry yelled. 'Even now.'

He couldn't quicken. The low lolloping stride went on at the same steady pace and all the jockey's urging was having no constructive effect. But one of the two in front of him was tiring and rolling about under pressure. Tiddely Pom crept up on him yard by yard but the winning post was coming nearer and there was still one more in front . . .

I looked at the leader, taking him in for the first time. A jockey in pink and white stripes, riding like a demon on a streak of brown, straining, hard-trained muscle. Dermot Finnegan on Rockville, with all his future in his hands.

While I watched he swept conclusively past the post, and even from the stands one could see that Irish grin bursting out like the sun.

Three lengths behind, Tiddely Pom's racing heart defeated the colic and put him second. A genuine horse, I thought thankfully. Worth all the trouble. Or at least, worth some of it.

'All we need now,' said Derry, 'is an objection.'

He wrapped the strap round his race glasses, put them in their case, and hurriedly made for the stairs. I followed him more slowly down and edged gingerly through the crowd milling round the unsaddling enclosure until I reached the clump of other press men waiting to pick up something to print. There was a cheer as Rockville was led through into the winner's place. Another cheer for Tiddely Pom. I didn't join in. Had nothing to contribute but a dead feeling of anti-climax.

All over. Tiddely Pom hadn't won. What did I expect?

The crowd parted suddenly like the Red Sea and through the gap struggled a large, untidy earth mother surrounded by planets. Madge Roncey and her sons.

She walked purposefully across the comparatively empty unsaddling enclosure and greeted her husband with a gentle pat on the arm. He was astounded to see her and stood stock still with his mouth open and Tiddely Pom's girth buckles half undone. I went across to join them.

'Hullo,' Madge said. 'Wasn't that splendid?' The faraway look in her eyes had come a few kilometres nearer since fact had begun to catch up on fantasy. She wore a scarlet coat a shade too small. Her hair floated in its usual amorphous mass. She had stockings on. Laddered.

'Splendid,' I agreed.

Roncey gave me a sharp look. 'Still fussing?'

I said to Madge, 'What happened down at the start?'

She laughed. 'There was a fat little man there going absolutely berserk and screaming that he would stop Tiddely Pom if it was the last thing he did.'

Roncey swung round and stared at her. 'He started hanging on to Tiddely Pom's reins,' she went on, 'and he wouldn't let go when the starter told him to. It was absolutely crazy. He was trying to kick Tiddely Pom's legs. So I just ducked under the rails and walked across and told him it was our horse and would he please stop it, and he was frightfully rude . . .' A speculative look came into her eye. 'He used some words I didn't know.'

'For God's sake,' said Roncey irritably. 'Get on with it.'

She went on without resentment, 'He still wouldn't let go so I put my arms round him and lifted him up and carried him off and he was so surprised he dropped the reins, and then he struggled to get free and I let him fall down on the ground and rolled him under the rails, and then the boys and I sat on him.'

I said, trying to keep a straight face, 'Did he say anything after that?'

'Well, he hadn't much breath,' she admitted judiciously. 'But he did say something about killing you, as a matter of fact. He didn't seem to like you very much. He said you'd smashed everything and stopped him getting to Tiddely Pom, and as a matter of fact he was so hysterical he was jolly nearly in tears.'

'Where is he now?' I asked.

'I don't know exactly. When I let him get up, he ran away.'

Roncey gave me a mean look. 'So it took my wife to save my horse, not the *Blaze*.'

'Oh no, dear,' she said placidly. 'If Mr Tyrone hadn't been looking after him, the little man would have been able to reach him sooner, and if I hadn't come back from the Isle of Wight because I thought it would be quite safe if no one knew, and we all wanted to see the race, if I hadn't been there at the starting gate, someone else would have taken the little man away. Lots of people were going to. It was just that I got to him first.' She gave me a sweet smile. 'I haven't had so much fun for years.'

The day fragmented after that into a lot of people saying things to me that I didn't really hear. Pieces still stick out: Dermot Finnegan being presented with a small replica of the Lamplighter Gold Cup and looking as if he'd been handed the Holy Grail. Willy Ondroy telling me that Charlie Boston had been slung off the racecourse, and Eric Youll outlining the stewards' plan for warning him off permanently, which would mean the withdrawal of his betting licence and the closing of all his shops.

Derry telling me he had been through to Luke-John, whose bookmaker friend had taken all of Charlie Boston's fifty thousand and was profoundly thankful Tiddely Pom hadn't won.

Colly Gibbons asking me to go for a drink. I declined. I was off drink. He had his wife with him, and not an American colonel in sight.

Pat Roncey staring at me sullenly, hands in pockets. I asked if he'd passed on my own telephone number along with the whereabouts of Tiddely Pom. Belligerently he tried to justify himself: the man had been even more keen to know where I lived than where the horse was. What man? The tall yellowish man with some sort of accent. From the *New Statesman*, he'd said. Didn't Pat know that the *New Statesman* was the one paper with no racing page? Pat did not.

Sandy Willis walking past leading Zig Zag, giving me a worried smile. Was the horse all right, I asked. She thought so, poor old boy. She muttered a few unfeminine comments on the jockey who had thrown the race away. She said she'd grown quite fond of Tiddely Pom, she was glad he'd done well. She'd won a bit on him, as he'd come in second. Got to get on, she said, Zig Zag needed sponging down.

The Huntersons standing glumly beside Egocentric while their trainer told them their raffle horse had broken down badly and wouldn't run again for a year, if ever.

That message got through to me razor sharp and clear. No Egocentric racing, no Huntersons at the races. No Gail at the races. Not even that.

I'd had enough. My body hurt. I understood the full meaning of the phrase sick at heart. I'd been through too many mangles, and I wasn't sure it was worth it. Vjoersterod was dead, Bert Checkov was dead, the non-starter racket was dead . . . until someone else tried it, until the next wide boy came along with his threats and his heavies. Someone else could bust it next time. Not me. I'd had far, far more than enough.

I wandered slowly out on to the course and stood beside the water jump, looking down into the water. Couldn't go home until the race train went, after the last race. Couldn't go home until I'd phoned in to Luke-John for a final check on what my column would look like the next day. Nothing to go home to, anyway, except an empty flat and the prospect of an empty future.

Footsteps swished towards me through the grass. I didn't look up. Didn't want to talk.

'Ty,' she said.

I did look then. There was a difference in her face. She was softer; less cool, less poised. Still extraordinarily beautiful. I badly wanted what I couldn't have.

'Ty, why didn't you tell me about your wife?'

I shook my head. Didn't answer.

She said, 'I was in the bar with Harry and Sarah, and someone introduced us to a Major Gibbons and his wife, because he had been in your *Tally* article too, like Harry and Sarah. They were talking about you . . . Major Gibbons said it was such a tragedy about your wife . . . I said, what tragedy . . . and he told us . . .'

She paused. I took a deep difficult breath: said nothing.

'I said it must be some help that she was rich, and he said what do you mean rich, as far as I know she hasn't a bean because Ty is always hard-up with looking after her, and he'd be reasonably well off if he put her in hospital and let the country pay for her keep instead of struggling to do it himself . . .'

She turned half away from me and looked out across the course. 'Why didn't you tell me?'

I swallowed and loosened my mouth. 'I don't like . . . I didn't want . . . consolation prizes.'

After a while she said, 'I see.' It sounded as if she actually did.

There was a crack in her cool voice. She said, 'If it was me you'd married, and I'd got polio . . . I can see that you must stay with her. I see how much she needs you. If it had been me . . . and you left me . . .' She gave a small laugh which was half a sob. 'Life sure kicks you in the teeth. I find a man I don't want to part with . . . a man I'd live on crumbs with . . . and I can't have him . . . even a little while, now and then.'

CHAPTER EIGHTEEN

I spent Sunday alone in the flat, mostly asleep. Part of the time I pottered around tidying things up, trying to put my mind and life into order along with my house. Didn't have much success.

On Monday morning I went to fetch Elizabeth. She came home in an ambulance, with two fit uniformed men to carry her and the pump upstairs. They laid her on the bed I had made up freshly for her, checked that the pump was working properly, helped replace the Spirashell on her chest, accepted cups of coffee, agreed that the weather was raw and cold but what could you expect in December, and eventually went away.

I unpacked Elizabeth's case and made some scrambled eggs for lunch, and fed her when her wrist packed up, and fixed another mug of coffee into the holder.

She smiled and thanked me. She looked tired, but very calm. There was a deep difference in her, but for some time I couldn't work out what it was. When I finally identified it, I was surprised. She wasn't anxious any more. The long-established, deep-rooted insecurity no longer looked out of her eyes.

'Leave the dishes, Ty,' she said. 'I want to talk to you.'

I sat in the armchair. She watched me. 'It still hurts . . . what that man did.'

'A bit,' I agreed.

'Tonio told me they were both killed that night . . . trying to find me again.'

'He did, did he?'

She nodded. 'He came to see me yesterday. We had a long talk. A long, long talk. He told me a lot of things . . .'

'Honey,' I said, 'I . . .'

'Shut up, Ty. I want to tell you . . . what he said.'

'Don't tire yourself.'

'I won't. I am tired, but it feels different from usual. I feel just ordinary tired, not . . . not *worried* tired. Tonio did that. And you. I mean, he made me understand what I saw on Thursday, that you would let yourself be smashed up . . . that you would drive when you were drunk and risk going to prison . . . that you would do anything, however dangerous . . . to keep me safe . . . He said, if I'd seen that with my own eyes, why did I doubt . . . why did I ever doubt that you would stay with me . . . It was such a relief . . . I felt as if the whole world were lighter . . . I know you've always told me . . . but now I do believe it, through and through.'

'I'm glad,' I said truthfully. 'I'm very glad.'

She said, 'I talked to Tonio about . . . that girl.'

'Honey . . .'

'Hush,' she said. 'I told him about the blackmail. We talked for ages . . . He was so understanding. He said of course I would be upset, anyone would, but that I shouldn't worry too much . . . He said you were a normal, healthy man and if I had any sense I would see that the time to start worrying would be if you *didn't* want to sleep with someone.' She smiled. 'He said if I could face it, we would both be happier if I didn't mind if sometimes . . . He said you would always come home.'

'Tonio said a great deal.'

She nodded. 'It made such sense. I haven't been fair to you.'

'Elizabeth,' I protested.

'No. I really haven't. I was so afraid of losing you, I couldn't see how much I was asking of you. But I understand now that the more I can let you go, the easier you will find it to live with me . . . and the more you will want to.'

'Tonio said that?'

'Yes, he did.'

'He's very fond of you,' I said.

She grinned. 'He said so. He also said some pretty ear-burning things about you, if you want to know.' She told me some of them, her mouth curving up at the corners and the new security gleaming in her eyes.

'Exaggeration,' I said modestly.

She laughed. A breathy giggle. Happy.

I got up and kissed her on the forehead and on the cheek. She was the girl I'd married. I loved her very much.

On Tuesday morning, when Mrs Woodward came back, I went out along the mews, round the corner and into the telephone box, and dialled the number of the Western School of Art.

BLOOD SPORT

CHAPTER ONE

I awoke with foreboding. My hand closed in a reflex on the Luger under the pillow. I listened, acutely attentive. No sound. No quick surreptitious slither, no rub of cloth on cloth, no half-controlled pulse-driven breath. No enemy hovering. Slowly, relaxing, I turned half over and squinted at the room. A quiet, empty, ugly room. One-third of what for want of a less cosy word I called home.

Bright sunshine by-passed the thin pink curtains, spilling a gold slash on the faded brown Wilton. I didn't like pink. Also I didn't have the energy it would take to argue the landlord into changing to blue. After eight months I knew he never renewed anything until it had fallen to bits.

In spite of the prevailing calm the feeling of foreboding deepened and then identified itself and dissolved into a less threatening, more general state of gloom. Sunday morning, June 20th. The beginning of three weeks' leave.

I rolled back on to my stomach and shut my eyes

against the sun, and took my hand six inches from the Luger, which was far enough, and wondered how long a man could sleep if he really put his mind to it. Even a man who never slept soundly to start with. Three weeks, the three obligatory overdue weeks could be got through more easily asleep.

Three millenniums of sleep lay under the pillow. The nine-millimetre equalizer, my inseparable friend. It went with me everywhere, to beaches, to bathrooms, to beds other than my own. It was there to save my life. Not to take it. I had lived through a lot of temptations, and I lived with that too.

The telephone bell put paid to the three weeks before they had gone half an hour.

''Lo,' I said blearily, balancing the receiver on the pillow.

'Gene?'

'Uh huh.'

'You haven't gone away then.' There was relief in the voice, the voice of my boss. I looked at my watch. Ten o'clock.

'No,' I said unnecessarily. He knew I wasn't going away. I didn't understand his relief. It was missing when he spoke again.

'How about a day on the river?'

He had a motor cruiser somewhere on the upper Thames. I'd never seen it. Hadn't been asked before.

'Invitation or order?' I said, yawning.

He hesitated. 'Whichever you'll accept.'

What a man. You did more for him than you believed you would, every time.

'Where do I go, and when?'

'My daughter will fetch you,' he said. 'She'll be there in about half an hour. Family party. Boating clothes. Come as you are.'

'Sure,' I said. Complete with stubble, Luger, and shorts. A riot. I never wore pyjamas. They slowed you up too much.

Boating clothes, I decided, were greyish brown cotton trousers and an olive green nylon jersey shirt. I carried the Luger with me in the left hand pocket when the doorbell rang. One never really knew. But a look through the wide-angled spyhole showed it was only Keeble's daughter, as arranged. I opened up.

'Mr Hawkins?' she said hesitantly, looking from me to the dingy brass six screwed on to the solid dark stained wood.

'That's right,' I smiled. 'Come in.'

She walked past me and I shut the door, interested to notice that four flights of stairs hadn't left her breathless, as they did most visitors. I lived high up for that purpose.

'I was just finishing my coffee,' I said. 'Would you like some?'

'It's very kind of you, but Daddy said not to waste time, he wants to be off up river as soon as possible.'

Keeble's daughter was just like her photograph on Daddy's desk. Half woman, still at school. Short bouncy dark hair, and watchful dark eyes, a rounded body slimming down, a self-possessed touch-me-not expression, and an endearing gaucheness in her present situation.

She looked cautiously round the sitting room, which neither she nor I nor anyone else would have classed as elegant living. The landlord's furniture was junk-shop stuff and I had made no effort to improve it. My total contributions to the scene were two rows of books on the shelves and in one corner a tin trunk of oddments which I had never bothered to unpack. A drawn back curtain revealed the kitchen alcove and its entire contents: cupboard, refrigerator, sink, and cooker, all of them showing their age.

One went through the sitting room to the bedroom, through the bedroom to the bathroom, and through the bathroom to the fire escape. The flat had everything but a drawbridge and a moat, and it had taken me weeks to find it. Only the tiny spyglass had been lacking, and the landlord had been furious when he finally noticed I had installed it. It had cost me three months' rent in advance to convince him it wasn't there for the sole purpose of being out when he came.

I watched Keeble's daughter search for something nice to say about my living quarters and give up the struggle with a defeated shake of her young head. I could have told her that I had once had a better flat, a spacious comfortable first-floor front with a balcony overlooking a tree-dotted square. It had proved too accessible to unwanted guests. I had vacated it on a stretcher.

'I'll fetch my jacket,' I said, finishing the coffee. 'And then we'll go.'

She nodded, looking relieved, oppressed already by the emptiness of my home life. Five minutes of it had been enough, for her.

I went into the bedroom, picked the jacket off the bed, and transferred the Luger from my trousers into its built-in under-arm holster, fastening it there with a press stud on a strap. Then, coat over arm, I dumped the dirty coffee cup in the sink, pulled the curtain across the kitchen, opened the front door, and let myself and Miss Keeble out.

Four uneventful storeys down we emerged into the quiet sunlit Putney street, and she looked back and up at the solid old converted house. It needed paint and oozed respectability, exactly like its row of neighbours.

'I wasn't sure I'd come to the right place. Daddy just said the fourth house along.'

'He gives me a lift home, sometimes.'

'Yes, he said so.' She turned to the white Austin standing at the kerb and paused with the key in her hand. 'Do you mind if I drive?'

'Of course not.'

She smiled for the first time since she'd arrived, a quick flashing affair which verged on friendliness. She unlocked her door, climbed in, and reached over to unlatch the opposite one for me. The first thing I noticed as I bent to get in were the L plates lying on the back seat.

'When did you pass the test?' I said mildly.

'Well . . .' the smile lingered, 'as a matter of fact, yesterday.'

For all that, she drove very well, careful but confident, quiet with the gears though a bit heavy with the hand signals. She crept somewhat tentatively around the Chiswick roundabout and up the slope to the M4. The big blue motorway sign said no L drivers, and her nose twitched mischievously as we passed it.

'Did you come this way to fetch me?' I asked idly.

She edged into the slow lane and hit forty.

'Er, no. I live in a hostel with about sixty other girls in South Ken. Daddy just rang me and said as I'd got the car up in London this weekend I could collect you and meet him in Henley. Sort of spur of the moment thing.'

'I see.'

We came to the end of the fifty mile an hour limit and her foot went down with determination.

'Do I scare you?' The needle quivered on sixty-five.

I smiled wryly. 'No.'

'Actually . . .' Her hands gripped the wheel with the tension of inexperience. 'Actually, you don't look as if you'd scare easily.'

I glanced at her in surprise. I look ordinary. Quiet and ordinary. And very useful it is, too.

'Anyway,' she went on frankly, 'I asked Daddy about coming this way, and he said he guessed your nerves would stand it. He seemed to find it very funny, for some reason or other.'

'He has his own brand of humour.'

'Mm.' She drove on for several miles in silence, concentrating on the road. The speed dropped slowly down to fifty again, and I guessed she was finding the motorway not such pure fun as she'd imagined. The usual number of Sunday Jim Clarks were showing off in the fast lane and family outings with Grandma driving from the back seat were bumbling about in the slow. We went down the centre and pulled out bravely now and then to pass an airport bus.

Eventually, in thinner traffic after Windsor, she said, doubtfully, 'You do . . . er . . . work for Daddy?'

'Yes. Why not?'

'Well, no reason why not. I mean,' she looked embarrassed, 'I mean, I can't remember him ever asking anyone from work . . . well, he just doesn't usually, that's all.' She looked as if she wished she hadn't started.

'A kind thought,' I suggested; and wondered what he wanted. Not just to give me a sunny day out. As his daughter said, he didn't do that sort of thing.

We made it to Henley with the paint intact, and she parked neatly in a large gravelled enclosure by the railway station. Her hands trembled slightly as she locked the doors, and I realized that it must have been her longest drive, as well as her fastest.

'You drove beautifully,' I said sincerely. 'Like a veteran.'

'Oh.' She gave a laugh which was half a cough, and looked relieved and pleased. 'Well, thank you.' She would be more relaxed, I knew, on the way back, and less strung up when she got there. To give and to remove confidence were tools of my trade, and there was no union to say I couldn't use them on Sundays.

'*Flying Linnet* . . . that's our boat . . . will be somewhere along the bank,' she said. 'It isn't far.' She smiled again and gestured, 'That way.'

We walked down to the river and along the neatly built broad tarmac towpath, where half the town seemed to be out feeding the ducks. The sun sparkled on the dark green water and there was a queue at the boatyard for rowing boats and punts. There were gardens and lawns and seats, and a bowling green, and a playground with a slide and swings, all of them sprinkled with sunny Sunday faces and murmuring summer voices. Families and couples and groups: few alone. Three weeks alone, I thought bleakly. I could spend them beside the deep green river feeding ducks, and just jump in when I couldn't stand any more of it.

'There's Daddy,' said Keeble's daughter, pointing. The sun lay along her light brown arm and shifted in burnt toffee shadows on the curves of her orange tan dress. Too young for me, I thought inconsequentially.

Or rather, I was too old. Aeons too old. Forty still lay a couple of years ahead, but I could have told Methuselah a thing or two.

Keeble had stepped ashore from one of the boats moored top to tail along the towpath and was walking towards us, hand outstretched, welcoming smile in face. My boss, except for an open-necked shirt, looked his usual weekday self, a short slightly chubby man with a mild manner and a faintly anxious expression. The light blue-grey eyes blinked freely as usual behind the unimpressive spectacles and as usual he had missed a patch while shaving. Premature baldness had made him look fifty at thirty-five, but far from regretting this, he believed it was the cause of his rapid promotion over well-thatched contemporaries. He may have been right. He looked harmless, cautious, unambitious, one of nature's safest plodders. It was eight years since he had inherited me along with the rest of the setup, and to discern the cutting brain behind the waffle had taken me two minutes flat.

'Gene,' he said. 'Glad you could come.' He pumped my hand up and down perfunctorily, the social gesture as meaningless to him as to me, and we exchanged smiles to match. For his daughter the warmth came from the heart. She kissed him affectionately on the cheek and his eyes held a glimmering pride I had never seen in him before.

'Well, Lynnie my love, you got here safely. Or did you let Gene do the driving?'

'Do me a favour,' she said. 'He didn't even flinch.'

Keeble flicked me an amused glance, and I repeated the compliment to her skill, with her father nodding his thanks to me over her head, knowing exactly why I said it.

They turned and began to walk back along the path, gesturing to me to come. Keeble's boat, the one they stopped at, was a graceful neat-looking fibre-glass cruiser with a cabin forward and a large open cockpit at the back, the decks spotless and the chromium shining. Sitting casually side by side on the pale blue plastic upholstery were a man and a woman, both of whom raised smiling faces at our approach and neither of whom got up.

Lynnie jumped down into the boat and kissed the woman, and Keeble stepped carefully after.

'Come aboard,' he said to me, and again in his tone there was a choice. An invitation or an order, whichever I would accept. I opted for the invitation, and embarked on more than the *Flying Linnet*.

'My wife Joan,' said Keeble, stretching a hand to the seated woman. 'Gene Hawkins, honey.'

Joan Keeble was a frail birdlike woman with a coyness of manner left over from the time when she was pretty. She twinkled her eyes at me, inviting admiration. I scraped some up, and exchanged the necessary platitudes about weather, boating and driving daughters. Keeble waded into this with a wave towards the man sitting beside her.

'You two haven't met . . .' he hesitated a fraction. 'Dave . . . Gene, this is Dave Teller.'

Teller stood up, shook hands economically, and said he was glad to know me. He wore a sloppy wrinkled pale blue shirt hanging out over patched cotton trousers, battered plimsolls on his feet, and a dirty old baseball cap on his head. American, well educated, prosperous, assured: the categories clicked over from habit in my assessing mind. Also he was a lean man nearing fifty, with a strong beaky nose, straightforward eyes, and a marvellous dentist.

Keeble offered no information beyond that bald introduction, but bustled about getting his ship ready to put to sea. His yell into the cabin for a certain Peter to come and help produced no results. I stuck my head through the door and saw a boy of about twelve engrossed in fitting a new roll of film into a small simple camera.

'Peter,' his father yelled.

Peter heaved a martyred sigh, scrambled the back of the camera shut, and went out past me with his eyes down and his fingers winding the knob. Sure-footed, he stepped without looking on to the narrow side of the boat and from there to the towpath.

'He'll fall in one day,' Lynnie said to the world in general. Her brother didn't even hear. Still concentrating on his camera with one hand he was slowly untying the rope from the mooring ring with the other, crouching down on the tarmac in his clean black jeans and getting up with two large dusty patches on the knees. Pointing his viewfinder at a passing formation of ducks he clicked the shutter and with a serious, absorbed expression wound on the film.

Farther up the path Keeble and Teller were undoing the bow rope, talking amicably in the sun. Lynnie and her mother straightened the cushions and coiled the ropes and fussed around over a lot of nothing, chatting trivialities. I wondered what the hell I was doing there and felt out of contact with everything around me. Not a new feeling, but recurring more often. The two levels of living were growing farther apart. The day-to-day social level had lost all meaning, and underneath, where there should have been rock, had opened a void of shrivelling loneliness. It was getting worse. The present was bad enough: the future an abyss. Only work brought my splintering self into any sort of whole, and I knew well enough that it was the work itself which had started the process. That and Caroline. Or, to be more accurate, Caroline's husband.

'I say, hold this rope, will you?' Peter said. I took the wet snake he offered. 'Hi,' he added, seeing me properly for the first time, 'Who are you?'

'Anybody's guess,' I said with more truth than sense, and his mother stared at me with astonishment and told him my name.

Keeble came back on board and started the engine. Teller stood up on the small forward deck and cast off the bow rope when Keeble told him, and Peter left it until almost too late to leap on board with the stern. The camera bounced on the cord round his neck. 'Birthday present from Gran,' he said to Lynnie with pride. 'Super, isn't it.'

'You'll drop it in the river, if you aren't careful.'

'This is only my second film. I used the first one up on the boys at school. Do you think those ducks will come out all right?'

'I expect you had your finger over the shutter.'

'I've got a book in there.' He nodded to the cabin, expertly sifting out the affection behind her sarcasm and showing no resentment. 'It tells you about exposures and focuses. I think I'll just check what it says about sunny days. It was cloudy dull all week at school.'

I don't belong here, I thought. I wished I were asleep.

The *Flying Linnet* nosed upstream through a scatter of row-boats, Keeble at the wheel, Teller sitting forward still on the cabin roof, and Peter trying to get past Lynnie teasing him in the cabin doorway. Joan Keeble sat down on the wide seat across the back and patted the place next to her for me to join her. With an effort I did so, but after a minute or two, in the middle of apparently idle hostessy chat, she pulled me back to attention by trying delicately to find out who I was and why I had been invited, while not wanting to have me realize that she didn't know.

I could play that sort of game for ever. Inference

on inference. I didn't know the answer to why was I there, but that she needed to ask it, that indeed she had asked it, told me a great deal about non-contact between Keeble and his wife, and opened new doors on to Keeble himself. I knew then why he'd never before asked me home. It was one thing to employ a microscope, but another to put oneself under the lens. I thought it all the odder that he'd done it now.

As if he could feel my mind on the back of his neck he turned round and said, 'The lock's just ahead.' I stood up and joined him, and Peter gave up his struggle and went back to his duty with the stern rope.

'Marsh Lock,' Lynnie said, standing beside me and looking forward through the windscreen. 'Not an easy one, from this side, going upstream.'

When we got nearer I saw what she meant. The broad stretch of river narrowed abruptly to the lock gates on the left and the weir on the right, alongside. Baby whirlpools and trails of bubbles met us fifty yards away, with larger eddies and convolutions bubbling up as we went on. The boat tended to swing sideways under their power, and Keeble spun the wheel rapidly to keep her straight. Ahead of us water in tons tumbled over the weir, green and brown and splashing white, thundering down in great curving leaps, smelling of mustiness and mud.

A low wooden wall divided the lock approach from the turbulent weir water, and to the calm side of the barrier Keeble neatly steered his boat. Teller standing at the bow threw his rope over the hook on a mooring post there, and Peter slung a loop over a bollard at the stern.

I looked idly over the side of the boat, over the wall, up to the weir. Bouncing, tumbling, foaming, sweeping away back into the width of the river, the rough water looked superb in the sun. I felt the warmth and the fine spray mixed on my face and wondered whether if someone fell in there, he would ever come up.

The lock gates opened, the downcoming boats chugged out, and the *Flying Linnet* went in. Teller and Peter did their stuff mooring us to the side and Peter took a photograph of the boat in the lock. Water surged through the sluices in the upper gates, lifting us up, and in ten minutes we were going out of the lock on to another broad calm stretch of river, six feet higher than the one below.

'There are fifty locks on the Thames,' Keeble said. 'Lechlade is as far up as you can go except in a rowing boat, and that's about 300 feet above sea level.'

'Quite a staircase,' I commented.

'The Victorians,' he nodded, 'were a brilliant lot. They built them.'

Teller stood up on the foredeck holding the coil of rope, the peak of his baseball cap pointing forward like an attentive bird. I watched him, speculating, and Keeble followed the direction of my eyes and gave me only silence to work on.

Less than half a mile upstream from the lock we made an obviously pre-arranged stop at a riverside pub, Teller jumping ashore with his rope and fending the boat off the concrete edges as we drifted towards it. He and Peter tied expert knots, and everyone followed them ashore.

We drank sitting on a ring of uncomfortable metal chairs round a table with a sun umbrella spiked through its centre. Lynnie and Peter had Cokes and without consultation Keeble bought Scotch for the rest of us. Joan sipped hers with a pursed mouth and screwed eyes, as if it were a mite too strong for fragile little her, but I noticed she finished a long way first. Teller left his untouched for several minutes and then tossed it back in kingsized gulps. Keeble drank in pauses, revolving his glass in his hands and squinting through it at the sun. They were talking about the river, and other days on it, and other weather. On either side of us, round more umbrellas, sat more family parties much the same; Sunday morning drinks, Sunday lunch, Sunday snooze, *Sunday Express*, Sunday supper, *Sunday Night at the London Palladium* . . . safe little families in a sheltered routine, well-intentioned and more or less content. Even Keeble fitted in. Whereas I . . . was apart.

'Drink,' Keeble said. 'You're on holiday.'

Faced with instant sharp curiosity from the rest of his family I meekly picked up my glass, still full when theirs were empty. It felt wrong to drink in the morning; it raised sub-conscious bells of alarm. I liked the taste of alcohol all right, but couldn't afford its effects. Alcohol encouraged you to put your trust in luck, and I was better off trusting a clear head. Consequently I sometimes didn't touch the stuff for weeks on end, and on that morning had had none for nearly a month.

Keeble watched me swallow the whisky, as vivid and familiar as a long-lost friend. The extent to which I was ever on holiday lay in the jacket across my knees, a pound of deadly mechanism in an under-arm holster; but it did seem most unlikely that I would need it on the Thames. When Teller ordered a refill, I drank that too. And then, since it was my turn, a third.

Peter lasted the course to three Cokes, and then wandered away with his camera poised, looking for excuses to use it. Next door a boatyard, like the one at Henley, was doing a roaring trade in punts. Four of the pub's more enthusiastic customers were having trouble stepping aboard, and Teller said chuckling, 'What's the fine for punting under the influence . . .?'

'A soaking,' Lynnie said. 'Silly nits.'

The punt pole waved recklessly as they set off, but the four men didn't fall in. The punt skidded ten feet up the river and hit the pub's landing stage with a thump that tumbled them into a leg-waving heap. I tried to laugh with everyone else and only succeeded in feeling more remote than ever.

We finished the drinks, re-embarked, and went up through the next lock, Harbour, to an unpopulated green-pasture stretch of river, where we moored for lunch. Peter swam, jumping off the boat repeatedly in glittering splashes, and Lynnie helped her mother in the cabin, preparing the food. Teller sprawled lazily on the back seat, and Keeble sat down with a Sunday newspaper and unfolded it, and I wearily began to wonder just when he would come to the point.

The point, however, was the newspaper. We had arrived.

'Read that,' he said, tapping a small paragraph on an inside page.

I read it.

'There is still no sign of Chrysalis, free in Kentucky, US, since Tuesday. Anxiety mounts for the safety of the £500,000 stallion, sire of this year's Derby winner, Moth.'

'Is this what you mean?' I asked, puzzled, making sure I'd read the right section. I had. He nodded vigorously.

'Didn't you know about it?' he asked.

'That Chrysalis had got lost? Yes, I suppose so. It was on all the news bulletins on Wednesday.'

'And it didn't mean a damn thing to you,' Teller said, with a trace of controlled and civilized bitterness under his smile.

'Well . . .'

'I have a share in that horse,' Teller said. 'A one-eighth share, 200,000 dollars worth.'

'Wow,' I said blankly. It seemed a lot of money to invest in one-eighth of a horse.

'What is more,' he said, sighing, 'I have spent all of last month negotiating the sale, and was lucky to beat out another syndicate that was bidding for him. And now as soon as he gets over there, this has to happen.'

'I'm sorry,' I said, conventionally polite.

'I can't expect you to understand.' He shook his head, excusingly. 'It isn't the money which matters, it's the horse. He's irreplaceable.'

'They'll find him.' I had no doubts of it, and I didn't care one way or the other.

'I am not so sure,' he said. 'And I would like you to get out there and look for him.'

For five seconds no one twitched a muscle, least of all me. Then Teller turned his head to Keeble and smiled his glossy smile. 'I wouldn't play poker with him,' he said. 'OK, I'll buy what you say about him being all that good.'

I glanced at Keeble and he gave me raised eyebrows, a tiny shrug, and a slightly embarrassed expression. I wondered just how complete his testimonial had been.

Teller turned back to me. 'Sim here and I, we were in the same business, way back in World War II.'

'I see,' I said. And I did see. Quite a lot.

'It was just a war job for me, though,' he said. 'I got out of the Army in '47 and went back home to Pappy, and a couple of years later he died and left me his racehorses and a few bucks on the side.' The beautiful teeth flashed.

I waited. The story had hardly begun.

After a pause he said, 'I'll pay your fare and expenses, of course, and a fee.'

'I don't hunt horses,' I protested mildly.

'I can guess what you hunt.' He glanced again at Keeble. 'Sim says you're on vacation.'

I didn't need reminding.

'Chrysalis', he said, 'is the third stallion of international status to have disappeared in the last ten years.'

CHAPTER TWO

They tried pretty hard in their subtle way, but it seemed ridiculous to me.

'You know about horses,' Keeble said. 'Your father trained them for racing.'

'There's the police,' I pointed out. 'Also the insurance company. Also every man, woman, and child with an eye for a horse in the state of Kentucky. And I presume there's a reward?'

Teller nodded.

'So why me?'

'No one found the other two.'

'There's a lot of land in America,' I said. 'They're both probably free on a prairie somewhere having a high old time siring herds of wild horses.'

Teller said grudgingly, 'The first one was found dead in a gully two years after he disappeared.'

'That's it, then.'

'But the second one . . . I bought that one too. I had a one tenth share. This is second time around for me.'

I stared at him. 'Were any of the circumstances the same?'

Reluctantly he shook his head. 'No . . . except that they both got free. Allyx was never found. That's why I want something special done about Chrysalis.'

I was silent.

Keeble stirred. 'You've got nothing else to do, Gene. Why not take your holiday in the States? What will you do with yourself, if you stay in Putney?'

His eyes had stopped blinking, as they always did when he was intent. It was the surest guide I had to the complex calculations which sometimes lay beneath his most casual remarks. He couldn't have guessed, I thought in alarm. He was a manipulator but not clairvoyant. I shrugged and answered him on the surface.

'Walk round Kew Gardens and smell the orchids.'

'They have no scent,' said Teller, pointing out the obvious.

'He knows that.' Keeble nodded, still unblinking. 'Any fruitless way of passing the time, is what he meant.'

'I guess you two operate on your own private wavelength,' Teller said with a sigh. 'But I'd like you to come back with me, Gene, and at least take a look. What's the harm in that?'

'And what's the good in it? It's not my sort of job.' I looked away, down into the green water. 'And . . . I'm tired.'

They hadn't a quick answer to that. I thought it would have been simple if all that was the matter with me was the straightforward tiredness of overwork, not the deadly fatigue of a struggle I wasn't sure I could win. Chasing some crazy colt over a thousand square miles didn't look like any sort of a cure.

Joan came out of the cabin into their defeated silence with a bowl of salad and a string of bright fussing chatter. A folding table was erected and the dishes put on to it, and we sat around in the sun eating cold chicken and hot french bread. There was a pleasant pink wine to drink and strawberries and cream afterwards, and Peter, still in wet bathing trunks despite orders from his mother, took mouthfuls and photographs by turn. Lynnie, sitting beside me, told Dave Teller an amusing story about the finishing school she attended, her warm bare arm brushing unselfconsciously against mine. I should have enjoyed that placid Sunday picnic on the river. I tried to. I smiled and answered when I was spoken to and concentrated carefully on the taste and texture of what I was eating, and all that happened was that the fat black slug of depression flexed its muscles and swelled another notch.

At four o'clock, after dishwashing and dozing, we started back towards Henley. My refusal to go to America hadn't basically disturbed Teller or Keeble an ounce. I concluded that whatever had prompted the suggestion it wasn't a burning conviction that I and only I could find the missing horse. I put the whole thing out of my mind. It wasn't hard.

There was a punt in difficulties at the approach to Harbour Lock. Teller, again standing up on the bow with rope at the ready, shouted back to Keeble and pointed ahead. We looked, all of us, following his finger.

Where the river divided, going slowly into the left fork round the bend to the lock and fast on the right straight to the weir, a sturdy post in mid-stream bore a large notice, a single word: DANGER.

A girl, lying flat half in and half out of the punt with her arms round the post, was trying to tie up to it by passing a rope from one hand to the other, and making a poor job of it. On the stern, watching anxiously, punt pole in hand, stood a young man in a red-and-yellow shirt. He waved his arms when he saw us coming, and as Keeble throttled back and drifted near, he shouted across the water.

'Could you help us, sir?'

Since the punt was full in the weir stream with only the girl's slender arms keeping it from floating straight to destruction, he seemed remarkably cool. Keeble cursed about ignorant nitwits and edged nearer with his engine in slow reverse. The *Flying Linnet*, unlike the punt, was too big to go through this particular weir, a long row of separately openable gates; but the summer current was quite strong enough to crash her nastily against the thick concrete supports and pin her there for someone else humiliatingly to rescue.

Keeble shouted to the girl that we would tow them away, and to hand the mooring rope to me or Lynnie, whichever she could reach, as soon as we were nearer. The girl nodded, her arms still stretched forward round the big post, her long fair hair nearly brushing the water, her body quivering with the strain.

'Hold on,' Lynnie shouted urgently. 'Oh do hold on. Just a little longer, that's all.' She leaned over the side as if trying to shorten the few yards of water which still lay between, her worry and fright growing as we drew nearer. With the engine doing little more than tick over, the noise of the water on the far side of the weir began to fill our ears with its threat, but Keeble at any rate remained calm and sure of himself, an easy master of his boat and the situation. With six feet still to go the girl took one arm off the post and held out the rope towards Lynnie's groping hand. Then, disastrously she dropped it. Crying out, beating in big splashes on the water, she struggled to get her arm back round the post. Lynnie yelled to her to get hold of the rope again, it was fastened to the punt under her chest, to get hold of it again and hand it over. But the girl was now far too frightened either to listen or to let go of the post again, and the panic was rising to screams in her voice.

Out of the side of my vision I saw the young man start forward to help her, apparently at last realizing that their position was serious. The punt pole swung awkwardly in his hands, curved through the air in a clumsy arc, and hit Dave Teller on the head. With buckling knees the American fell forward off the bows and straight into the water.

I was up on the cabin roof, out of my shoes and into the river after him almost before any of the others realized what had happened. I heard Keeble's despairing voice shouting 'Gene' in the second before I went under, but I was thinking simply that speed was the only chance of finding Teller, since anything that sank in a river the size of the Thames was instantly out of sight. Algae made the water opaque.

Diving in as near to where he had gone as I could judge, I kicked downwards, arms wide. I was going faster than Teller, I had to be. I had a strong impression that the punt pole had knocked him out, that he was on a slow one-way trip to the bottom.

About eight feet down my fingers hooked almost immediately into cloth. Even with my eyes open I could see nothing and with my right hand I felt for his face while I tried to kick us both to the surface. I found his face, clamped his nose between my fingers and the heel of my hand on his mouth, and turned him so that I held his head against my chest. He didn't struggle; couldn't feel.

From that point on the rescue operation failed to go as per scheduled. I couldn't get back to the surface. The current underneath was much stronger, very cold, sweeping us downwards, clinging round our bodies with irresistible force. I thought; we'll hit the weir and be pinned there down deep, and that will be that. For a treacherous instant I didn't even care. It would solve all my problems. It was what I wanted. But not really with another life in my arms, for which I was literally the only hope.

My chest began hurting with the lack of air. When we hit the weir, I thought, I would climb my way up it. Its face might not be slippery smooth. It had to be possible . . .

There was a sudden tug as if some fisherman had us hooked. I felt us change direction slightly and then a tug again, stronger and continuing and stronger still. No miraculous rescue. It was the water had us, gripping tighter, sucking us fast, inexorably, into the weir. The sheer overwhelming weight and power of it made nonsense of human strength, reduced my efforts to the fluttering of a moth in a whirlwind. The seizing speed suddenly accelerated further still, and we hit. Or rather, Teller hit, with a jar which nearly wrenched him away from me. We spun in the current and my shoulder crashed into concrete and we spun again and crashed, and I couldn't get hold of any surface with my free hand. The tumbling and crashing went on, and the pain in my chest went deeper, and I knew I wasn't going to be climbing up any weir, I could only find it when it hit me, and when I reached for it it hit me somewhere else.

The crashing stopped, but the tumbling went on. My ears were roaring to bursting point. There was a sword embedded in my chest. The searing temptation came back more strongly just to open my mouth and be finished with it. But by my own peculiar rules I couldn't do that, not with someone else involved, not when what I was doing was in a way what I'd been trained for. Some other time, I thought lightheadedly, some other time I'd drown myself. This time I'll just wait until my brain packs up from lack of oxygen, which won't be long now, and if I haven't any choice in the matter, then I haven't any guilt either.

The tumbling suddenly died away and the clutching current relaxed and loosened and finally unlocked itself. I was only seconds this side of blackout and at first it didn't register: then I gave a feeble kick with legs half entwined round Teller and we shot upward as if on springs. My head broke the surface into the sun and air went down into the cramp of my lungs like silver fire.

The weir, the killing weir, was fifty yards away. Fifty yards *upstream*. We had come right through it under the water.

I took my freezing, stiffened fingers off Teller's face, and held his head up to mine, and blew into his flaccid mouth. The current, gentle again and comparatively warm, carried us slowly along, frothy bubbles bursting with little winks against our necks. I trod water with my legs, and held Teller up, and went on pushing into him all my used-up breath. He showed no response. It would be exceedingly inconsiderate of him, I thought resignedly, if he had died right at the beginning and I had gone to all that trouble for nothing.

There were shouts from the banks suddenly and people pointing, and someone came after us in a dinghy with an outboard motor. It puttered noisily by my ear and hands stretched over the side to grasp.

I shook my head. 'A rope,' I said, and breathed into Teller. 'Give me a rope. And pull slowly.'

One of the two men argued, but the other did as I asked. I wound the rope round my arm twice and held it, and when I nodded they let the boat drift away until we were a safe distance from its propeller and slowly began to pull us towards the bank. Teller got ten more of my ex-breaths on the way. They didn't seem to be doing him a bit of good.

The dinghy towed us out of the weir stream side of the river and landed on the same side as the lock. People appeared in a cluster to help, and there was little doubt it was needed, but even so I was loth to part with Teller until one large calm man lay on his stomach on the grass and stretched his arms down under the American's armpits.

'Don't worry,' he said. 'We'll go straight on with the breathing.'

I nodded, took my mouth away from Teller's and transferred his weight into the stranger's arms. He began to pull him out of the water as fast as he could.

I put a steadying hand on Teller's chest and felt it heave suddenly under the clinging blue shirt. I hadn't enough breath left myself to tell the man who was lifting him, and while I was still trying to, Teller, half out, gave a choking cough and opened his eyes. There was some water in his lungs, racking him. The stranger pulled him even more quickly out on to the grass, and as his ankles bumped over the edge his returning consciousness flooded into a stark sort of awareness which had nothing to do with a release from drowning. Somewhere between a cough and a groan he said 'Jesus,' and again went completely limp.

Another couple of strong wrists hauled me up on to the bank in his wake, and I knelt there beside him feeling the reassuringly small swelling on the side of his head but anxiously listening to the dragging breath bubbling in his throat.

'Roll him over,' I said. 'Carefully . . . just so his tongue isn't choking him.'

We put him on his side and his breathing eased immediately, but I wouldn't let them pick him up and carry him up to the lock. Almost any injury was bound to be made worse by moving, and he'd been moved too much already. The calm man agreed and went briskly off to fetch a doctor.

The lock-keeper arrived along the towpath, followed at a rush by Keeble and all his family. Their faces were all strained with shock, and Lynnie had been crying.

'Thank God,' Keeble said, crouching beside me. 'You're both all right.' His voice held almost more incredulity than relief.

I shook my head. 'He's hurt, somewhere.'

'Badly?'

'Don't know . . . He crashed into the weir.'

'We didn't see you go over. We were watching . . .'

'They must have gone under,' said the lock-keeper. 'Through one of the gates. Those gates wind upwards, same as a sash window. We've got two of them a couple of feet open at the bottom today, with the river a bit full after all that rain.'

I nodded. 'Under.'

Dave Teller choked and woke up again, coughing uncontrollably through the puddle in his lungs, every cough jerking him visibly into agony. From his fluttering gesture it was clear where the trouble lay.

'His leg,' Keeble said. 'He's not bleeding . . . could he have broken it?'

The jar when he had hit the weir had been enough. I said so. 'We can't do anything for him,' said Keeble, watching him helplessly.

The crowd around us waited, murmuring in sympathy but enjoying the disaster, listening to Teller coughing, watching him clutch handfuls of grass in rigid fingers. Not a scrap of use begging them to go away.

'What happened to the punt?' I asked Keeble.

'We towed it ashore. Lynnie got hold of the rope.

Those kids were terribly shocked.' He looked round for them vaguely, but they weren't in the crowd. 'I suppose they've stayed back at the lock. The girl was nearly hysterical when you and Dave didn't come up.' A remembering bleakness came into his face. 'We towed them into the lock cut and moored there. Then we ran along to the lock to get the lock-keeper . . . and he was already down here.' He looked up across the river to the pretty weir. 'How long were you under the water?'

'A couple of centuries.'

'Seriously.'

'Can't tell. Maybe three minutes.'

'Long enough.'

'Mm.'

He looked me over objectively, boss to employee. One shoulder of my green jersey shirt was ripped in a jagged tear.

'Bruised,' he said matter-of-factly.

'The weir,' I agreed, 'has knobs on.'

'It's like a flight of steps under there,' said the lock-keeper solemnly. 'Going down from the top level to this one, you see. The current would have rolled you right down those steps, I reckon. In fact, it's a bleeding miracle you ever came up, if you ask me. There's some every year fall in this river and never get seen again. Current takes them along the bottom all the way to the sea.'

'Charming,' Keeble said under his breath.

Dave Teller stopped coughing, rolled slightly on to his back, and put his wrist to his mouth. His strong beaky nose stuck uncompromisingly up to the sky, and the wetness on his face wasn't from the Thames. After a while he moved his hand and asked Keeble what had happened. Keeble briefly explained, and the screwed-up eyes slid round to me.

'Lucky you were with us,' he said weakly, the smile in his voice making no progress on his face. He moved his hand apprehensively behind his ear, and winced when it reached the bump. 'I don't remember a thing.'

'Do you remember asking me to look for your horse?'

He nodded a fraction, slowly. 'Yuh. You said no.'

'I've changed my mind,' I said. 'I'll go.'

In the cabin of the *Flying Linnet* Keeble watched me slowly strip off my sodden clothes. I had never, as far as I remembered, felt so weak. I'd left half my muscles under the weir. Buttons would no longer come out of their holes.

'You heard what the man said,' Keeble remarked. 'It was lucky you were with us.'

I didn't answer.

'Make a note of it,' Keeble said. 'Stick around. You never know when you'll be needed.'

'Sure,' I said, refusing to acknowledge that I understood what he was talking about.

He wouldn't be deterred. 'You're like Dave's horse. Irreplaceable.'

My lips twitched. That was the crunch, all right. His job would be a little harder if he lost his head cook and bottle-washer. Personal regard didn't come into it.

I struggled out of my jersey. He handed me a towel, glancing non-committally at the marks of this and previous campaigns.

'I'm serious, Gene.'

'Yeah,' I sighed. 'Well . . . I'm still here.'

It was too much of an admission, but at least it seemed to reassure him enough to change the subject.

'Why are you going to the States?'

'Maybe I owe it to him.'

'Who? Dave?'

I nodded.

'I don't follow,' he said, frowning. 'Surely he owes you? If anyone owes anything.'

'No. If I'd been quicker, he wouldn't have gone in, wouldn't now have a smashed thigh. Too much whisky and wine and sleeping in the sun. I was much too slow. Abysmally, shamefully slow.'

He made a gesture of impatience. 'Don't be ridiculous, Gene. No speed on earth could have prevented an accident like that.'

I put the towel round my neck and started to take off my trousers.

'That accident', I said briefly, 'was attempted murder.'

He gazed at me, eyes blinking slowly behind the mild spectacles. Then he turned, opened the cabin door, and stepped up into the cockpit. I heard him shouting to Peter.

'Get out of that punt at once, there's a good chap. And don't let anyone else get in it. It's important.'

'Not even Lynnie?'

'Not even Lynnie.'

'I don't want to,' said Lynnie's voice in a wail from the cockpit. 'I never want to go in a punt again.'

She wasn't much her father's daughter. His mind was as tough as old boots. The chubby body which contained it came back into the cabin and shut the door.

'Convince me,' he said.

'The boy and girl have scarpered.'

He raised his eyebrows and protested. 'They were frightened.'

'They didn't stop to answer questions. They may quite possibly think Dave and I are dead, because they didn't even wait to make sure. I should say they never even intended to appear at any inquest.'

He was silent, thinking about it. The boy and girl had gone from the lock when we had eventually returned to it: gone unnoticed, leaving the punt behind. No one had given them a thought until after the doctor had splinted Teller's leg and seen him carried on a stretcher a hundred yards to an ambulance.

When the doctor asked how the accident happened, the causes of it weren't around.

'We don't know,' Keeble said. 'They may very likely have come down the towpath and seen you were all right, and they might have dozens of personal reasons for not wanting to stay.'

I finished kicking my legs out of the clammy cotton trousers and peeled off my socks.

'The boy stood on the stern too long. He should have been helping with the rope.'

Keeble frowned. 'Certainly he seemed unconcerned, but I don't think he realized quite what a jam they were in. Not like the girl did.'

'The first time he moved, he hit Dave straight on the head.'

'Punt poles are clumsy if you aren't careful . . . and he couldn't have counted on Dave standing in so vulnerable a spot.'

'He'd been standing there most of the way, seeing to the bow rope.'

'The boy and girl couldn't know that.'

'He was certainly standing there when we approached the punt.'

'And,' Keeble said in a demolishing voice, 'no one would deliberately put themselves into so much danger just to bait a trap.'

I dried my legs and wondered what to do about my underpants.

Keeble sighed down his nose and fluttered his fingers. 'No one except you.'

He reached into a locker and produced a bundle of clothes.

'Emergency falling-in kit,' he explained, giving them to me. 'I don't suppose anything will fit.'

As there was a mixture of his own cast-offs, which were too wide, and Lynnie's, which were too narrow, he was right. Everything, besides, was too short.

'In addition,' he went on, 'how did the boy and girl know we were on the river at all and would be coming down through Harbour Lock? How long did you expect them to wait there clinging to the post? How did they know exactly which boat to hail, and how did they avoid being rescued by any other boat?'

'The best accidents always look as if they couldn't possibly be anything else.'

'I grant you that,' he said, nodding. 'I just think that this one literally couldn't be set up.'

'Yes, it could. With a safe getout, in that if it didn't work according to plan, if for instance Peter had been on the bows instead of Dave, they had no need to go into the act of yelling for help, because of course they wanted to make sure it was us before they started.'

'They were in danger,' Keeble protested.

'Maybe. I'd like to take a closer look at that post.'

'And there might have been other boats around, helping. Or watching.'

'If Dave never came within range of the punt pole

they lost nothing but an opportunity. If other boats had been watching there would simply have been more people to cry accident. The girl was screaming and splashing and dramatically dropping her rope when the boy hit Dave. We were all watching her, not him. Any sized audience would have been doing the same.'

'And how could the boy and girl have known where Dave would be this Sunday, in the first place? And why on God's earth should anyone want to kill him?'

I stepped into some aged grey trousers of Keeble's and found them a foot too generous round the waist. My boss wordlessly held out a short striped elastic schoolboy belt, which took care of the problem by gripping like a tourniquet.

'It was a simple accident, Gene. It had to be.'

The trousers ended four inches above my ankles, and the socks I slowly fumbled my way into made no effort to bridge the gap.

'Gene!' said Keeble, exasperated.

I sighed. 'You'll agree I'm a sort of specialist in arranging accidents?'

'Not usually fatal ones,' he protested.

'Not often.' And no more, if I could wriggle out of it. 'Just a general stage managing of events, so the victim believes that what has happened to him is the merest mischance.'

Keeble smiled. 'You've sprung more hares that way . . .'

'So,' I said reasonably, 'I'm apt to spot a rig-up when I see one.'

The smile half faded and changed into speculation.

'And no,' I said, 'I was not concussed in the recent boating party and I haven't got water on the brain.'

'Keep your telepathy to yourself,' he said uncomfortably. 'I just think you are mistaken.'

'OK, then I'll spend my holiday in Putney.'

He said 'No,' so vehemently, so explosively, that there was no subtlety left in the situation. From his naked alarm I saw unmistakably how much he understood of my depressed mental state and how convinced he was that I wouldn't survive three weeks of my own company. Shocked, I realized that his relief when I answered his telephone call had not been at finding me at home, but at finding me alive. He had dug me out on to the river to keep an eye on me and was prepared to send me off on any old wild goose chase so long as it kept me occupied. Then maybe, I supposed, he thought I would snap out of it.

'The blues', I said gently, 'have been with me for a long time.'

'Not like this.'

I had no answer.

After a pause he said persuasively, 'Three world class stallions disappearing . . . isn't that also the sort of accident you don't believe in?'

'Yes, it is. Especially when someone tries to get rid of the man who bought two of them.'

He opened his mouth and shut it again. I almost smiled.

'It was a craftsman's accident,' I said. 'It could hardly have been done better. All they didn't bargain for was interference from someone like me.'

He still didn't believe it, but as he was now happy that I should, since it meant that I would go to the States, he raised no more objections. With a shrug and a rueful smile he tossed me a darned brown sweater, which hung round me like a tent; and I picked up my own wet clothes and followed him out into the sunshine.

Peter and Lynnie both giggled at my baggy appearance, the nervous shock still sharp in their voices, especially Lynnie's. I grinned at her and ruffled her hair, and made as if to kick Peter overboard, and some of the tension loosened in their eyes. In another half hour they would have reached the compulsive talking stage and an hour after that they would be back to normal. Nice, ordinary kids, with nice, ordinary reactions.

I climbed wearily up on to the cabin roof and spread out my clothes to dry. My shoes were still there where I had stepped out of them, and absentmindedly I put them on. Then, standing up, I looked across to the weir, and back to the hefty post with its notice; DANGER, and at the innocent empty punt tied up behind the *Flying Linnet*: and I found myself thinking about the legend of the Sirens, the sea nymphs who sat on a rock near a whirlpool and with their pretty voices drew passing sailors towards them, to lure them to their death.

CHAPTER THREE

The punt had the name of the owner screwed on to the stern on a small metal plate. The lock-keeper, consulted, said that it came from a boatyard about a mile down the river, next to a pub; you couldn't miss it.

'That,' I murmured to Keeble, 'is where we had our drinks this morning.'

His eyelids flickered. He said to the lock-keeper, 'I suppose a lot of punts from there come up through your lock?'

'They sure do, on a fine Sunday like this,' he agreed.

'Did you happen to notice this one, with a girl and a young man in it? The girl had long fair hair, white trousers, and a pink shirt, and the boy was wearing tight pale blue jeans and a red-and-yellow check shirt.'

'I should say they came up before my dinner break. I can't remember anyone like that this afternoon.'

The lock-keeper eased the white-topped hat back on his head and eyed the boats lining up to go into the lock. He was a youngish man with an air of long-suffering patience, the occupational result, no doubt, of a life spent watching an endless procession of incompetence. People, he had said matter-of-factly, fell into his lock every day of the week. Near-drownings, however, were of no special interest to him: he too often had to deal with the unsaved.

'Would you know them again?' Keeble asked.

The lock-keeper shook his head decisively. 'Not a chance. And if I don't get back to my lock there'll be a lot of bad tempers coming through the gates and as like as not we'll be fishing out another one . . .'

He gave me a sketchy farewell salute as one of the few who had gone down his weir and walked away, and strolled unhurriedly back to deal with his Sunday going home traffic problem.

'We may as well tow the punt back to the boatyard,' Keeble said thoughtfully. 'We've got to go down past there anyway, and they won't be able to spare anyone to come and fetch it on a busy day like this. And maybe they'll know where the boy and girl came from . . .'

And maybe they wouldn't, I thought: but even the most hopeless questions have to be asked.

'I'd like to look at the post,' I said.

Keeble was agreeable, but Lynnie and Peter and their mother were horrified when they found where we were proposing to go, and said they would wait on the bank. In a row, with anxious faces, they stood guard over the punt, while Keeble neatly manoeuvred the *Flying Linnet* upstream a little way through the downcoming cruisers, and then drifted gently across towards the post. I, standing on the stern seat, caught hold of the crossbar with its emphatic warning and clung on to it while Keeble put the boat into reverse against the drag of the weir stream.

Once the engine was thrusting hard enough to hold its own, so that the tension on my arms slackened, I knelt down on the seat and tried to do what the girl had been doing, to pass a rope round the post from one hand to the other. The tendency of the two-ton *Flying Linnet* to drift away couldn't have been much less to deal with than the weight of the punt, but even allowing also for the fact that my arms were longer and stronger, it was easy. I secured the rope and gave a thumbs up to Keeble, who stopped the engine. Then with one toe wedged and the narrow side of the boat under my pelvis, I shoved up the sleeves of the brown sweater and leaned down and over to inspect the scenery.

'For God's sake be careful,' Keeble said, his voice sharp over the noise of the weir.

I turned my head and laughed at him.

'We haven't any more dry clothes,' he pointed out, scowling. 'None that you can get into. If you fall in again you'll have to go home wet.'

Smiling, I turned back to the post. But feel and look how I might, there was nothing out of the ordinary about the square sturdy white-painted baulk of timber set rock-like up on end in the Thames' bed.

Keeble shrugged and said, 'I told you so,' and steered his boat back to the bank.

'How about fingerprinting the punt?' I said.

'You never let up.'

'You should be glad of it.'

The long line of past occasions when not letting up had led to a useful harvest rose up between us, and I saw his conviction waver.

'All right, Gene, if you're sure.'

'Get Raben to do it. He's the best.'

'All right. Tomorrow.'

'How about the police?'

He pursed his lips. 'It's not our usual territory. More theirs I agree. But they're not likely to take your theory seriously, or to act on it, unless we tell them what your job is . . . and impress them with it. No, I'm not in favour of that. We could just go along with this quietly on our own for a little while, I think.'

'So that if nothing turns up, we won't have made bloody fools of ourselves?'

All his facial muscles contracted for a second. 'You are not paid to turn your perceptions on your boss.'

'I probably am.'

'That's a point.'

The boat grounded gently against the bank, and I helped Joan and Lynnie back on board. Peter, on his father's directions, stepped into the punt and handed him up the mooring rope, which Keeble fastened to the cleat on the *Flying Linnet*'s stern. Then, towing the punt, we took our turn into the lock, explained what we were doing to the lock-keeper, and cruised downstream to the pub and its next door boatyard.

A flustered middle-aged boatman there was trying to cope with returning family picnic parties and a bunch of youths and girls who wanted to fill in the half hour before the pub opened at seven o'clock. The late afternoon shone redly on his big sweating face and his freckled bald head, and we had to wait while he juggled his customers precariously in and out of skiffs and punts and took their money and warned the young couples that it was an offence to be on the river without lights after dark and that the boatyard closed at nine-thirty anyway.

When Keeble at last had a chance he asked the boatman if he had seen the girl with fair hair and the boy in a red-and-yellow check shirt who had hired a punt that morning.

'Seen 'em? I suppose so, I've been here all day.'

'I mean, do you remember them?' Keeble said patiently.

'Where are they then?' The boatman looked round suspiciously.

'They've gone,' Keeble began.

'Then who's going to settle up?' said the boatman belligerently, this last problem looking to be just one too many for his temper.

'Oh, I will,' said Keeble soothingly. He took his wallet out of his back pocket and unfolded it to show the usual thickish wad. Keeble didn't have to live on Her Majesty's pay and worked from conviction, not need; his beer money represented a week's wage to me, and his boat a year's.

'How much do they owe you?' He handed over what the boatman asked and offered a fiver on top. 'I'd like to hire this punt for this evening and tomorrow,' he said. 'Is that all right?'

The boatman took the money without hesitation and made a few half-hearted efforts to appear cautious.

'Where'll you be taking it?'

'Henley,' Keeble said.

'You won't leave the cushions out if it rains?'

Keeble shook his head.

'All right then.' The boatman had already tucked the notes away. 'And you'll bring it back tomorrow?'

'Tomorrow afternoon,' Keeble agreed. 'Now, about those young people who took it this morning . . .'

Unexpectedly the boatman suddenly leered. 'I remember 'em,' he said, 'come to think of it, they was the two who had no business to be out together.'

'What do you mean?' Keeble asked.

'Well, see, this girl, she said like, what if her old man had put detectives on her, what would they say if she went off all day with him in a punt, and how she'd said she'd only come out as long as it was nothing anyone could use in a divorce. And the fellow in the check shirt turned round and said old money bags, meaning her old man, see, would never find out where they'd been, he was in France on business wasn't he, or somesuch, and then they took note that I was standing there hearing and they sort of nudged each other and shut up. But I reckon as they were off for a bit on the side see, and didn't want no one to catch 'em.'

'Exactly,' said Keeble to me with another touch of I-told-you-so.

'And very nicely done,' I agreed. 'Artistic.'

'You haven't seen them since this morning, I suppose?' Keeble said to the boatman. 'Do you happen to know how they got here?'

'Car,' said the boatman, waving an arm. 'They came from the car park back there.'

'Which car, do you know?'

He gave Keeble a pitying stare. 'Look, there's cars in and out all day, what with the pub and us. And I'm looking at the river, see, with my hands full an' all, and I couldn't tell you no one who's come and gone nor what they came in, but they must have come in a car, because they come in the morning, and there's no buses along here on Sundays before half-two in the afternoon.'

'Thank you anyway,' said Keeble, sighing. 'You've been very helpful.' He added another pound to his overpayment and the boatman's eyes swivelled rapidly from the pub to the clock over the boathouse door.

Still ten minutes until the bar opened. I proceeded to fill them.

'Did the young man, or the girl, or both of them, speak with any special type of accent?' I asked.

Since he spoke broad Berkshire himself, the boatman's hesitation was understandable. 'They talked', he said, considering, 'like they do on the telly.'

'Not much help,' Keeble commented.

'How do you lash the end of your punts' mooring ropes?' I asked.

'Eh?' said the boatman, puzzled.

'Do you lash the end of the ropes to stop them unravelling?'

'Oh, I get you. No, we splice 'em. Turn the ends back and sort of weave them in. Lashing's no good as it comes undone too easily.'

I unwound the punt's mooring rope from the *Flying Linnet*'s stern cleat. 'This one is coming undone, though.'

'Let's see that,' he said suspiciously, and I gave it to him. He twisted the frayed unravelling strands in his strong dirty fingers and hovered in what I guessed to be a fairly usual mixture of fury and resignation.

'These bleeding vandals . . . excuse me, ma'am,' he apologized to Joan. 'These so and sos, they tie up to a tree, see, or something, and come they want to push on, they can't undo the knots if the rope's wet, and they just don't bother, they cut through the rope and off they go.'

'Does that often happen?'

'Every summer, we has this trouble now and then.' He pulled the rope up straight, measuring its length with his eye. 'There's a good four or five feet gone off this one, I shouldn't wonder. We've been talking of switching to chains, but they can get into holy terrors of knots, chains can. Here,' he added to Keeble, 'you'd better have another punt, one with a better rope.'

'This one will be fine,' Keeble said, fastening it on again. 'We'll see you tomorrow.'

He towed the punt down to Henley and right into the garage-like boathouse which kept the English summer off the *Flying Linnet*. The punt was secured alongside by Peter and his father and everyone disembarked along a narrow boardwalk carrying things like the remains from lunch, newspapers, bathing towels, and in my case, wet clothes and a loaded jacket, out through the boathouse and into Keeble's Rover, which was parked on a neat square of grass at the back.

Peter's main care was for his precious camera, again hanging round his neck on its cord.

'I suppose,' I said idly, 'you didn't happen to take a photograph up there by the weir? You didn't happen to get a shot of those people in the punt?'

He shook his head, blinking like his father.

'Gosh, no, I didn't. I don't suppose actually I would have thought of taking one, not when everything was happening, do you think? I mean, it would have looked a bit off if you and Mr Teller had been drowning and I was just standing there taking pictures and so on.'

'You'll never be a newspaperman,' I said, grinning at him.

'Wouldn't you have minded, then?'

'I don't think so.'

'But, anyway,' he said mournfully, 'I couldn't, you see, because I finished the film at lunch-time and I didn't have another one, so even if there had been a fire or something I couldn't have taken it.' He looked at his camera thoughtfully. 'I won't finish up any more films in the middle of the day, just in case.'

'A fire,' I agreed seriously, 'would anyway make a much better picture than just people drowning, which they mostly do out of sight.'

Peter nodded, considering me. 'You know, you're quite sensible, aren't you?'

'Peter!' exclaimed his mother in unnecessary apology. 'That's not the way to talk.' And she wasn't much pleased when I said as far as I was concerned he could say what he liked.

Keeble drove round to the station car park, where Lynnie and I transferred to the Austin.

'I'll ring in the morning,' Keeble said, standing half out of his respectable car.

'Right.'

'Take care of Lynnie.'

'I'll do that.'

Lynnie kissed her parents goodbye, but her father

more warmly, and made a face at Peter as the Rover rolled away out of the gate. Then she climbed into the Austin, waited until I was sitting beside her, and stretched out her hand to the ignition.

She was trembling again.

'Shall I drive?' I said mildly, making it absolutely her own choice.

She put both her hands in her lap and looked straight out through the windscreen. Her face was pale above the orange dress.

'I thought you were both dead.'

'I know.'

'I still feel churned up. It's silly.'

'It's not silly. And I expect you're fond of Dave Teller.'

'He's sent us presents and things, since we were little.'

'A nice man.'

'Yes.' She sighed deeply and after a pause said calmly, 'I think it would be better, if you really don't mind, if you drive back.'

'Of course I will.'

We changed places, and went back to London with more cars passing us than we passed. At Chiswick roundabout I said I would drive her to her flat and go home by taxi, but with a sideways laughing glance she said no taxi would stop for me in her father's clothes, and that she was feeling better and could quite easily do the last lap herself: so I rolled round the few corners to Putney and stopped outside my own front door.

Summer dusk filled the quiet streets. No one about. Lynnie looked out of her window upwards at the tall house, and shivered.

'You're cold,' I said, concerned for her bare arms.

'No . . . I have a cardigan in the back . . . I was just thinking about your flat.'

'What about it?'

'It's so . . . empty.' She gave a half laugh, shrugging it off. 'Well, I hope you won't have nightmares, after today.'

'No . . .' I collected my things and got out of the car, and she moved over into the driver's seat.

'Will they have saved any dinner for you at the hostel?' I asked.

'Not a hope,' she said cheerfully. 'But I expect there'll be some cake and milk about, there usually is.'

'Would you care to eat with me? Not up there,' I added hastily, seeing the beginnings of well-brought-up suspicion. 'In a restaurant, I mean.'

'I've my mother to thank for my beastly mind,' she said unexpectedly. 'I really am rather hungry, and I don't see at all why I shouldn't have supper in your flat, if you've got any food.' And without more ado she got out of the car and locked it, and stood expectantly beside me on the pavement.

'There are some tins,' I said, reflecting. 'Wait here

just a second, would you. I just want to have a look round the back.'

'Round the back?'

'For burglars,' I said sardonically. But I went to look, as usual, at the powder-coated bottom flight of the fire escape. No one had been up or down all day.

Lynnie climbed the stairs to the fourth floor as easily as before, and having checked via a well-placed paper clip that my door hadn't been opened since I had shut it that morning, I put the key in the lock and let us in.

The green plastic lampshade in my sitting room scattered its uncosy glare over the tidy room, switching the soft grey light outside into sudden black, and evoking the forlornness of institution buildings on winter afternoons. It wouldn't be much trouble, I thought, to go out and buy myself a red shade in the morning, and see if it propagated rosy thoughts instead.

'Sit down,' I suggested. 'Are you warm enough? Switch the electric fire on if you'd like it. I think I'll go and change, and then we can decide about going out.'

Lynnie nodded, but took things into her own hands. When I came out of the bedroom she had already investigated my meagre store cupboard and had lined up a packet of soup, some eggs, and a tin of anchovies.

'Soup, and anchovies on scrambled eggs,' she said.

'If you'd really like that,' I said doubtfully.

'I can't cook much else.'

I laughed. 'All right. I'll do the coffee.'

There were burnt specks in the eggs when she had finished, which harmonized nicely with the scraped off over-done toast and the brown anchovy strips, and there had been a slight over-emphasis on pepper.

'No one', she sighed, 'is going to marry me for my cordon bleu.'

There were plenty of other reasons why she'd be fending off suitors knee-deep in a year or two: a curvy figure, delicate neck, baby skin; the touch-me-not expression, the awakening social courage, the quick compassion. No one was going to care if she couldn't cook. But she wasn't secure enough to be told so at that moment.

'When were you seventeen?' I asked.

'The week before last.'

'You didn't waste much time passing the driving test.'

'I've been able to drive since I was eight. Peter can, too.' She finished her eggs and stirred two heaped teaspoonfuls of sugar into her coffee. 'I was hungry. Funny, that.'

'It's a long time since lunch.'

'A terribly long time . . .' She suddenly looked me straight in the face, which she had mostly been avoiding, and with devastating innocence said, 'I'm so glad you're alive.'

I turned a hopeless wince into a laugh. 'I'm so glad Dave Teller is.'

'Both of you,' she said. 'It was the worst thing in my whole life when you didn't come up.'

A child untouched by tragedy, I thought. A pity the world was such a rough place, would catch her by her pretty neck one day and tear her guts apart. No one ever escaped. To have got to seventeen unlacerated was merely a matter of luck.

When we had finished the coffee she insisted on doing the dishes, but when she hung up the tea towel I saw all her mother's warnings pour back, and she glanced at me and quickly away, and stood stiffly in the centre of the room, looking nervous and embarrassed.

'Why don't you have any pictures on your walls?' she said jerkily.

I gestured to the trunk in the corner. 'There are some in there, but I don't like them very much. Not enough to bother with hanging them up . . . Do you know it's after ten? I'd better take you home or the hostel will shut you out.'

'Oh yes,' she said in great relief, and then hearing her own voice, added in confusion, 'I mean . . . I didn't know if you would think me very rude, dashing off as soon as we'd finished eating.'

'Your mother is quite right to tell you to be cautious,' I said lightly. 'Little Red Riding Hood couldn't tell a wolf from her grandmother . . . and you can never rely on a woodcutter turning up in the nick of time.'

The rigidity dissolved like mist. 'You do say some

extraordinary things,' she said. 'As if you could read my mind.'

'I could,' I smiled. 'You'd better put that cardigan on. It will be cold outside.'

'OK.' She pulled a dark brown jersey out of her bucket-shaped holdall and put it on. I bent to pick up a clean folded handkerchief which had fallen out with it, and when she was ready, handed it to her.

'Thanks,' she said, looking at it casually. 'That's the one Peter found in the punt.'

'In the punt?'

'Yes, down a crack between two of the cushions. He gave it to me because it was too small for him, he said. Too cissy.'

'Did he find anything else?'

'I don't think so . . . I mean it isn't stealing or anything, is it, to keep her handkerchief? I'll give it to her of course if she comes back, but by the time Peter was sitting in the punt, they had been gone already for ages.'

'No, it's not stealing,' I reassured her, though technically it was doubtful. 'But may I have a look at it?'

'Of course.'

She gave it back and I unfolded it: a white square of thin gauzy material. In one corner, a stylized bear in a flat straw hat.

'Is that out of Walt Disney?' I asked.

She shook her head and said with surprise at my ignorance, 'Yogi Bear.'

'Who is Yogi Bear?'

'I can't believe it! Well, he's a character in a lot of cartoon films. Like Top Cat and Atom Ant and the Flintstones.'

'I've seen the Flintstones,' I agreed.

'Like them, then. The same people make Yogi Bear.'

'Do you mind if I keep it for a day or two?'

'Of course, if you really want to,' she said, puzzled. 'But it surely hasn't any value.'

Down in the street I said I might as well finish the job and drive her to her hostel.

'I'm really all right now,' she protested. 'You don't need to come.'

'Yes I do. Your father said to look after you, and I'm seeing you safe to your door.'

She raised her eyebrows and gave me a comical look, but compliantly went round to the passenger's seat. I started the car, switched on the lights, and started towards Kensington.

'Do you always do what Daddy tells you?' she asked, smiling.

She was feeling much surer of herself, I thought.

'Yes, when I want to.'

'That's a contradiction in terms.'

'So it is.'

'Well, what do you actually *do*? What does *anyone* do in the Civil Service?'

'I interview people.'

'What sort of people?'

'People who want jobs in Government departments.'

'Oh!' She laughed. 'A sort of Personnel Officer?'

'Sort of.'

'It sounds a bit drizz.'

'The sun shines occasionally.'

'You're pretty quick. We only made up drizz yesterday.'

'A very useful word.'

'Yes, we thought so, too. Covers a lot of things nicely.'

'Like wet boyfriends?'

She laughed. 'Actually, it's pretty drizz to *have* a wet boyfriend.' She pointed. 'The hostel's down there, but we have to drive around and find somewhere to park the car all night. One or two squares down here don't have meters yet.'

The nearest empty space was a good quarter of a mile from the hostel, so I walked her back.

'You don't need to . . .' she began. 'Well . . . don't say it. Daddy said.'

'Right,' I agreed.

She sniffed resignedly and walked beside me out of step, the leather bucket bag swinging and her flat shoes silent on the pavement. At the hostel's glossy black well-lit front door she came to a stop and hovered on one foot, her half anxious uncertain expression saying clearer than words that she wasn't sure how to part from me. I wasn't old enough for uncle terms or young enough for a casual contemporary brush-off. I worked for her father, but wasn't his servant. Lived alone, looked respectable, asked nothing: I didn't fit into any of the categories she had yet learnt how to deal with. I put out my hand and smiled.

'Goodnight, Lynnie.'

Her clasp was brief, warm, relieved.

'Goodnight . . .' There was a pause while she made up her mind to it; and even then it was little more than a breath. '. . . Gene.'

'I wish you,' I said, 'blind traffic wardens and foam rubber bumpers.'

'Goodnight.' The chuckle rolled spontaneously in her throat. 'Goodnight.' She turned on one toe and jumped the two steps up to the door, then looked over her shoulder and waved as she went inside.

Little Lynnie, I thought, whistling to a passing taxi, little Lynnie, right at the beginning of it. Flying half consciously, half unconsciously, the notice-me flags of the pretty young female; and it was no use pretending that she didn't make me hungry; that she wasn't absolutely what I would have liked as an oasis in my too continent life. But if I had learnt anything in thirty-eight years it was who not to go to bed with.

And, more drearily, how not to.

CHAPTER FOUR

The Buttress Life Offices on Thirty-Third Street were high on customer appeal on the sixth floor. On the fifth and seventh they tucked the computers and electric typewriters into functional plasterboard cubicles. I sat three inches deep in black leather and considered that of all American craftsmen, I admired their chair designers most: in no other country in the world could one sit on the same seat for several hours without protest from the sacro-iliac.

I had waited forty pleasantly cool minutes already. Long enough to discover that the rows of pot plants along the low wall dividing the forty-foot-square hall into five smaller bays were made of plastic. Long enough to admire the pinewood walls, the ankle-deep carpet, the carefully lowered ceiling with its inset lights. In each bay there was a large desk, with one large chair behind it, one at the side, one in front. Nearly all occupied. Dividing each bay neatly in two stood a second, smaller desk; for the secretary-receptionist with his back discreetly to his boss. In front of him, in each bay, the long black leather bench for waiting on.

I waited. There was still someone for the big man to see before me. Very sorry, said the secretary apologetically, but the schedule had been crowded even before Mr Teller's cable arrived. Could I possibly wait?

So why not? I had three weeks to spare.

The light was dim, and piped music poured over everything like syrup. That and the built-in deadness of the acoustics made the earnest consultations going on at the five big desks completely inaudible to the waiting benches, while at the same time giving the customers a comforting illusion that they weren't alone in their troubles. Everyone, at the core of things, was alone. Just some more than others.

I hadn't slept all night after leaving Lynnie; but not her fault. It had been one long stupid struggle between a craving for oblivion and conviction that appeasing it wasn't so much morally wrong as a thoroughgoing defeat. I had never learnt to accept defeat. Obstinacy had given me what success I had had in my job, and it alone seemed to be keeping me alive, since all other props were as much use as toothpicks in an avalanche. Enthusiasm for finding Dave Teller's horse burned in me as brightly as wet coal dust: and the nation would hardly collapse if I left its employ.

Caroline had crowded like a flood-tide through my head and down my body. Caroline . . . whom I would have married, had it not been for the husband who would not divorce her.

Caroline had left him to live with me, and had felt guilty about it. A mess. An ordinary, everyday mess. Her fine passion had fretted away over six frustrating years of will-he won't-he; and to the end he wouldn't. Not that he'd ever got her back. In the year since she had left me she had returned to nursing and was working as a sister in a Nairobi hospital, impervious to come-back letters from either of us.

The sharp pain of her departure had dulled to the extent that I no longer felt it through every waking minute: it came stabbing back at longer and longer intervals. But when it did, I remembered her as she'd been at the beginning, and the hunger was pretty well unbearable. It was easy enough to find different girls to talk to, to work with, to take to bed: hard to find a match on all levels: and Caroline had been a match. In the past year, instead of receding, the loneliness had closed in. My work, of its nature, set me apart. And I had no one to go home to, to share with, to care for. The futility and emptiness had gone down to my roots, and nothing seemed to lie ahead but years and years more of what I was already finding intolerable.

The clients at the big desk stood up, shook hands, and left. The secretary ushered the man with the earlier appointment round into the presence. I went on waiting, without impatience. I was accustomed to it.

The punt, investigated in Henley that morning, had produced nothing but ten different sets of smudged fingerprints, of which the topmost and stickiest were Peter's. The Yogi Bear handkerchief was on its way round the manufacturers, in the distant hope that someone could tell where it had been sold. Dave Teller, briefly visited, had said wanly to charge everything to him. The Super VC 10 which lifted off at 3 PM British Summertime from Heathrow had landed at Kennedy at 3.10. Buttress Life closed its doors at 6, which gave it still a half hour to go. And outside in the canyon streets the hundred degree heatwave crept up a notch to a hundred and one.

My turn came round for the big desk. The big man, on his feet behind it, held out a large dry flabby hand and produced the sincere smile of the professional insurance man. Having settled me into the large comfortable chair alongside he sat down himself and picked up the cable discreetly placed to hand by the secretary. A polished chunk of wood sat on the desk between us. On it, neat gold letters facing me said helpfully: Paul M. Zeissen.

'We received this cable from Mr Teller,' he said. A slight, very slight undertone of disapproval.

I nodded. I had sent it myself.

'Our own investigators are experts.' He didn't like me coming: but he wouldn't want to lose the Teller policies. His politeness had effort behind it.

I smoothed him down, more from habit than anything else.

'Of course. Please think of me simply as an auxiliary. Mr Teller persuaded me to come over because he has unfortunately broken a leg in England, and will be immobilized in hospital for a few weeks. He sent me very much on impulse, as a personal friend, to . . . kind of represent him. To see if there was anything I could do. There was no suggestion that he wasn't satisfied with your firm.' I paused delicately. 'If he criticized anyone, it was the police.'

Paul M. Zeissen's smile warmed up a fraction from within: but he hadn't risen to high executive status in his tough profession without disbelieving half that everyone said. That was all right with me. Half of what I'd said was true. Or half true, anyway.

'Mr Teller understands of course,' he said, 'that it is for our own sakes that we are looking for the horse?'

'Naturally,' I agreed. 'Mr Teller is also most anxious that you should succeed, as the horse is irreplaceable. He would infinitely prefer his return to any amount of insurance money.'

'A million and a half,' said Zeissen reverently.

'Worth more on the hoof,' I said.

He glanced at me with a first gleam of real welcome. Once he'd swallowed the firm's affronted pride, it was quite clear that they'd nothing to lose by letting me in.

'One of our best men, Walt Prensela, is in charge of the Chrysalis case,' he said. 'He'll give you the picture. He knows you're coming, I sent him a memo with a copy of the cable.' He pressed the switch on his desk intercom.

'Walt? We have Mr Hawkins from England here. Shall I have him come up to you now?'

The polite question was, as so often in American affairs, an equally polite order. The affirmative duly came. Zeissen flipped the switch and stood up.

'Walt's office is one floor up, number four seven. Anyone will direct you. Would you like to go up now?'

I would; and I went.

I'd expected to have to deal with the same ruffled feathers in four seven, but I didn't, because Walt had done his homework, though I wasn't sure of that at first. He greeted me with business-like casualness, shook hands, waved me to the spare chair, and sat down himself, all in five smooth seconds. Much my age, I judged, but shorter and a good deal thicker. His hands were square and powerful with nails so brief that the fingertips' pads seemed to be boiling over backwards. There were middle European origins in the bone structure of the skull, topped by roughly cropped wiry grey-brown hair, and his deep-socketed brown eyes were set permanently into the I-don't-believe-a-word-of-it expression of his boss downstairs, only more so.

'So, Gene,' he said, neither with nor without much friendliness, 'you've come a long way.'

'Dave Teller's idea, Walt,' I said mildly.

'Looking for horses... do you do much of that?' His voice was flat; uninformative.

'Practically none. How about you?'

His nostrils twisted. 'If you mean, was it I who didn't find the other two, then no, it wasn't.'

I tried a smile: didn't get one back.

He said: 'Buttress Life had to pay up for Allyx three years ago. One million six hundred and forty-three thousand seven hundred and twenty-nine dollars, give or take a nickel. Showman, the first one, was insured with another company.'

'Accident?' I murmured. 'Or design.'

He rubbed his left thumb over the top of the round-ended fingers, the first of a hundred times I saw that gesture.

'Now that you've come, design. Before, I wasn't sure.'

'I'm officially on holiday,' I protested. 'I came only because Teller asked me. You should read no meaning into it.'

He gave me a level, half sardonic stare.

'I checked you out,' he said, flicking at the copy of the cable, which lay on his desk. 'I wanted to know just what sort of limey busybody was being wished on to me.'

I didn't say anything, and he made a clicking noise at the side of his mouth, expressive of understanding, resignation and acceptance, all in one.

'A screener,' he said. 'How come Teller found you?'

'How come you found me?' I asked instead.

'I mentioned your name in two places,' he said complacently. 'The FBI, and the CIA. And got a positive reaction from both. A couple of useful pals there filled me in. It seems you're a major stumbling block in the way of the planting of spies in certain Government departments and places like biological warfare research laboratories; and you've passed on some useful warnings on that subject to our people at Fort Detrick. They say the other side have tried to deter you, a little roughly, once or twice.' He sighed. 'You have a clean bill with our boys. And how.'

'And with you?'

'They said you didn't like limelight.'

'It's all yours.'

'Just so as I stand in right with Buttress.'

My decisive nod satisfied him. If we found the horse, he was welcome to the handshakes.

'Fill me in, then,' I said. 'How did Chrysalis get lost?'

Walt glanced at his watch and checked it against the electric clock on the wall. The little box-like office had no windows, as the single glass panel faced out on to the corridor; and although it was cool and comfortable enough, it was no place to talk if one didn't have to.

'Five after six,' Walt said. 'Do you have any other engagements?'

'Know any good bars?' I suggested.

'A mind reader.' He raised eyes to heaven. 'There's Dalaney's a block up Broadway.'

We stepped out of the air-conditioning into the sweltering street, up 30 degrees in two paces. With the humidity running also at 98 per cent, walking as little as a hundred yards left one damp to the skin. I never minded it: New York in a heatwave was always preferable to New York in a snowstorm, or anywhere hot to anywhere cold, for that matter. Cold seeped farther than into the bones; numbed the mind, drained the will. If the depression deepened towards winter, defeat would come with the snow.

Dalaney's was spilling out on to the pavement with a business convention let out of school. An oblong name tab sat on each neat Terylene lapel, a confident smile hid the anxiety behind every face; they stretched from the substantial group outside into the deep cool gloom of the bar. Pushing through them looked a problem; conversation in their company an impossibility.

'How about your hotel? Where are you staying?' Walt said.

'The Biltmore.'

Walt's eyebrows rose two clear inches.

'Teller's paying,' I said. 'He has an account there.'

'What did you do then? Save his life?'

'Six times,' I agreed, matching his sarcasm.

'He must really think,' Walt said reflectively, 'that you might get his horse back.'

'We,' I said.

'Nope. You. There's no trail. I've looked.'

A coloured cab driver in rolled-up shirt sleeves took us to the hotel, hot air blowing in gusts through the open window each time he accelerated. The city moved sluggishly under the brazen sun, and there was more rubbish than usual littering the streets.

'This is a filthy town,' said Walt, seeing it through my eyes. 'Give me Chicago.'

'Too cold,' I said automatically. 'Beautiful, but too cold. That freezing wind off the lake . . .'

'Are you guys from Chicago?' said the cab driver. 'I was born there, in the Loop.'

We talked to him about that. I drifted away into the disorientated state of not caring a jot about the cab driver, or Walt, or Dave Teller, or Caroline, or anyone on earth. We went up to my room in the Biltmore and I dragged through the host motions of ringing down for a bottle of Scotch and ice and seeing to heat, light and ashtrays. Walt loosened his tie and took a first appreciative swallow.

'You look pooped,' he said.

'Natural state.'

'I guess it's midnight already, to you.'

'I guess.'

There was a considerable drinking pause. Then he said, shifting his sturdy body in the white leather chair, 'Well, do you want to know about this horse, or don't you?'

'Sure.' The boredom in my answer came over shockingly strong, even to me. He looked faintly startled and then speculative, but when he spoke it was strictly business.

'They were taking him in a horse van from Kennedy Airport to Lexington, Kentucky. He'd spent the compulsory twenty-four hours immigration quarantine in the airport stable, along with six other horses which came over on the same flight. All normal at that time. They loaded Chrysalis and four others into the van, and drove westwards from New York on the Pennsylvania turnpike.'

'Time?' I asked.

'Left Kennedy 4 PM Monday. Last Monday, that is. A week today. Estimated Lexington midday Tuesday. Seven hundred miles.'

'Stops?'

'Yeah,' Walt said. 'Stops. That's where the trouble started.' He swirled the clinking ice round in his glass. 'They took their first meal stop at a diner near Allentown, about eighty-five miles from New York. There were four men in the van, two drivers and two grooms. Drivers in the cab, grooms in back with the cargo. At the first stop they took turns to eat, drivers first, grooms after. The drivers chivvied the grooms, and gave them too short a time to eat a good meal. There was an unfriendly argument.'

'They all say so?'

'Yeah. I've talked to all four, one at a time. They're

all trying their hardest to pin the blame on the others. They left the diner and went about two hundred miles to their night stop at Bedford. That was no better. Far from cooling off, they had begun to scuffle.

'They turned off the turnpike on to the interstate highway – seventy – south of Pittsburg, and left that again at Zanesville, taking the south-west fork to Cincinatti. About fifty miles farther on they turned due south to cross the Ohio River into Kentucky, and go on through Paris and down the Paris Pike to Lexington.'

'I'll need to see it on a map,' I said.

He nodded. 'From Zanesville to Paris they took secondary routes, though all paved roads, of course. Right? Now it was in Ohio that the van was hi-jacked, and it was over the state border in Kentucky when it was found, which has caused a couple of arguments here and there.'

'Hi-jacked! That's the first I've heard of that.'

'It was hi-jacked by mistake for a truckful of liquor which was about twenty miles behind it along the road. The vans looked alike, same colour, same size, and neither of them had any large identifying signs.'

'How did it happen?'

'By that time, Tuesday morning, the drivers and grooms were all eating at the same time, though at each end of the lunch counter. They left the horses unguarded for a full quarter hour, and during that time someone simply drove off with the whole works.'

'Surely the drivers locked up, and took the keys, at least?'

'Oh sure. It was an expert job though. A direct wire contact from the battery terminals to the starter motor.'

'So then what?'

'When they found the van gone the drivers called the police but it wasn't until Wednesday morning that the van was found off the road and out of sight around a hill in Kentucky. But – no horses. The ramps were down, and all the horses had been let loose.'

'Deliberately.'

'Sure. Untied. All the halters were still in the van. Those racehorses were all free with no bridle or anything to catch them by. The Kentucky boys reckon the horses were let out to create a diversion, to get the cops off the tails of the hi-jackers by making them chase horses all over.'

'And it worked.'

'Yeah,' said Walt gloomily. 'The owner kicked up stink. All the horses were valuable, not only Chrysalis. But only Chrysalis was insured with Buttress.'

'Did they get all the others back?'

'Yeah. But Chrysalis has as good as disappeared off the face of the earth.'

'How do you know the hi-jackers meant to take the liquor truck?'

'The only thing they left in the cab of the horse van was a screwed-up scrap of paper. It was a note of the time the liquor company's truck made its daily run along that route.'

'Fingerprints?'

'Gloves. Even for writing the note.'

Walt had talked himself dry. I refuelled his glass and felt like sleep.

'What do you think?' he said.

I shrugged. 'It was Chrysalis they really wanted. The timetable note was the blind.'

'But why? Why should anyone want to steal a stallion? That's what's got us all floored. I don't know much about horses, I'm a false claims man really. I just got pitched into this between cripple cases, if you get me. But even I know that it's the stallion's name that brings in the stud fee. Say someone's stolen Chrysalis, what's the point? They can't advertise him for stud, so he isn't worth a dime. We figured someone might be nutty enough to want him all to themselves, like some world famous painting, but you can hide a painting quietly in a cellar, which you can't do with a horse. The whole thing don't make sense.'

I had my own views on that, but I said only, 'What happened to Allyx?'

'I only know about that from the files. I got the case out and looked it up this morning. Allyx was a French horse, apparently one of the best young sires in Europe. He was nine when he came over here, and already his get had won a list of races as long as your arm. Dave Teller was head of the syndicate which bought him; that's why he was insured with us, as we do all the Teller estate work. Allyx was delivered safely to the Teller stud farm. No trouble in transit that time. But he was there only four days. Then there was a fire in the stables one night and they took all the horses out of the barn and turned them loose into a small corral.'

'And when they came to fetch them – no horses?'

He nodded. 'There was a broken rail over the far side, which no one knew about. All the horses had got through it, including Allyx. They caught all the others, though some were free for days. No sign ever of Allyx. The company had to face that he probably got into the foothills of the Appalachian Mountains and maybe broke his neck, and in the end they had to pay up.'

'What about that fire?'

'There was apparently nothing suspicious about it at the time. One of our very best men found no evidence of a fire being set. Still, stable fires can be started so easily . . . a cigarette butt in a pile of straw leaves no trace. This one didn't do much damage before they put it out. No question of kerosene, for instance. The whole chain of events was agreed to be accidental.'

I smiled thinly.

'What about Showman?'

Walt shook his head. 'I don't know how he got loose. But they found *him*. Dead, of course. He'd been dead some time, I think.'

'Where?'

'Oh, in the Appalachians. He came from that area, same as the others. But then Lexington has more stud farms than anywhere else in the States, so there's no significance in that really.'

'You went down to Lexington last week?'

He nodded. 'Flew there Wednesday, when Mrs Teller called us.'

'Mrs Dave Teller?'

'Uh huh.' Something moved obscurely in Walt's face. Dave's wife had made an impression. 'She's English, like you.'

'I'll go down there tomorrow,' I said. I watched him waver and decide not to tell me about her. Instead, he looked at his watch, put down his glass firmly, and stood up.

'Must be off,' he said. 'It's our anniversary, and my wife's fixed something special.'

'Give her my apologies for keeping you.'

'That's all right. It fitted in fine. I go home from Grand Central, right downstairs. A quarter of an hour to train time.'

I walked with him to the door.

'Walt . . . would you be free to come down to Lexington in the morning?' As he hesitated, I added, 'There's no point in my covering all the ground twice. I'd appreciate having you along.'

'Be glad to, Gene,' he said too politely, and I thought to hell with you Walt, to hell with everything on earth, including me, but I'm stuck with this horse nonsense for the next three weeks, and if I say go to Lexington, you go. I hid the violent moment of irritation in turning from him to open the door, and I understood his reluctance anyway, as who likes to be dragged down to do the same piece of work twice, especially under the critical eye of an imported limey busybody? He shook my hand. 'I'll call you in the morning,' he said, his feelings under better control than mine.

'Seven-thirty?'

'All right.' He loosened his jaw muscles into what looked like going to be a smile but didn't quite make it, sketched a salute with the thick-topped fingers, and ambled unhurriedly away down the passage.

I had dinner in the hotel restaurant. A steak. Never eat steak west of Nebraska, they used to say. The beef was bred on the prairie and walked eastwards to the markets: when it got to Nebraska it hit the corn belt and only after that was it fat enough to kill. New York steaks were mostly superb, but I didn't suppose they'd walked in through the New Jersey Tunnel. Long distance haulage took care of that . . . and whoever had removed Allyx and Chrysalis had had a haulage problem too. You couldn't ride a stallion along state highways. For one thing, they no longer took kindly to a saddle after years at stud, even if they had been reasonable to handle in the first place.

Nightclubs attract me like wet Mondays in

Manchester, and apathy kept me from even reading the list of shows. I went straight upstairs after dinner to catch up on a lot of lost sleep and woke again infuriatingly at two, dead tired and with a restless brain.

From habit, the Luger lay under my pillow.

It was another long night.

CHAPTER FIVE

We flew down in the morning, Walt's puffed eyes showing that the anniversary had been duly celebrated, and mine feeling as if they'd been rolled in grit.

The two drivers, reached by telephone, met us by appointment in the entrance hall of a motel near the centre of Lexington, where Walt had stayed on his previous trip. He booked rooms for us both, and we took the drivers up to his, which proved a mile short of Biltmore standards but hot on cleanliness and Kleenex.

Walt switched on the air-conditioning, shuffled chairs around, and promised beer later. The drivers, very much on the defensive, went sullenly through the disastrous tale again, aware beyond any doubt that they should never have left the horses unwatched and were more than likely to lose their jobs. Nothing they said added much to what Walt had already told me.

'Do you know each other well?' I asked.

The thin birdlike one said they did.

'And the grooms. Do you know them? And do they know each other?'

'Seen them around,' said the heavy one. 'The lazy so and sos.'

The thin one said, 'One of them came from the Midway Farm.'

That was Dave Teller's. 'He came specially for Chrysalis. It's him ought to be blamed for the whole thing.'

'Did the boys know each other, before the trip?'

'Sure,' said the heavy one. 'Way they talked they both been in the horse game all their lives.'

Walt sniffed and nodded. He'd checked all this, his resigned face said. Routine.

To the drivers I said, 'I want you to think back, and make a list of all the cars and trucks you can remember seeing on the road, all the way from Kennedy to the place you lost the horses.'

They looked aghast and as if I were crazy.

'Look,' I said, 'on those turnpikes you sometimes see the same cars over and over. The ones going your way, that is. You see them at the rest stops, and maybe you start off first, and then they pass you, and then you see them again maybe stopped at another diner while you go on to the next one, and then they come past you again. Right?'

They nodded.

'So maybe you still remember some of the cars and

trucks you saw on that trip? Especially any you saw on both days.'

They stared at me. The heavy one said, 'It's impossible. It was a week ago.'

'I know. Try, anyway. Think it over. See if you can remember any at all, between you. Then write them down and leave the list here for us, sometime this evening.'

I took out my wallet and tried twenty dollars each for size. It went down well enough. They said they would try.

'Don't invent anything,' I said. 'I'd rather pay for nothing than a lot of hogwash.'

They nodded and went, with the beer postponed to their return.

'What are you looking for?' Walt said curiously.

'Another horse van, I suppose.'

He thought it over. 'They could just have planned to rendezvous where the empty van was found. They didn't need to be seen on the road.'

'I don't think they can have been sure when they would be able to do the hi-jacking. They wouldn't know where the drivers would stop for meals. No good fixing a rendezvous in Kentucky if the opportunity came earlier, up near Wheeling.'

'They wouldn't want to drive too far with a hot truck,' Walt agreed. 'In fact, it was twenty-five miles, mostly back roads. They made straight for the hills, where it would take longest to round up loose horses.'

'Any tracks?'

'No tyre tracks of any use. The nearest road was gravel, dry and dusty this time of year. There were the tracks of the van going off the road round behind a hillock, but on the road itself they were just a jumble. Every car which passed raised a cloud of dust and wiped out all tracks which were there before.'

I grunted. 'Hoof prints?'

'Dozens of those. In all directions.'

'Back on to the gravel road?'

He shook his head resignedly. 'Impossible to tell. None on top of the van's tyre tracks, anyway. But we took a lot of soil samples, on the outside chance something would turn up later.'

'You did it pretty thoroughly.'

The smile almost came. 'A million and a half', he said briefly, 'is a lot of insurance.'

Midway Farm had prosperity printed on its gate posts, and I went through them alone, as Walt had said he felt the onset of a migraine headache.

A middle-aged Hungarian woman opened the door to me and in halting English asked me my business. Diagnosing her accent from long practice I replied in her own language, as it was simpler, and presently, having consulted in the drawing room, she showed me in there.

Dave's wife stood in the centre of a quarter acre of

deep green carpet, surrounded by deep green walls, white paint, and tomato red upholstery. She flicked my card with one thumb and said, 'You're the man who fished Dave out of the river.'

'Yes,' I said, surprised.

'He telephoned to me yesterday,' she explained. 'He says I am to trust you entirely.'

She was a slim small-boned creature with the rounded tight little bottom which comes from riding horses a great deal in early girlhood. Her jawline was delicately square, nose narrow, eyes wide and bright. Grey speckled the mouse-brown springy hair, and if she was wearing cosmetics one would have needed to be nearer than I was to be certain of it. Decisive assurance showed from every crisp gesture, and from her tone I gathered that taking her husband's word for things was not her habit.

'Sit down,' she said, pointing to a tomato chair. 'Drink?' It was two o'clock on a hot afternoon. 'Scotch,' she said without waiting for an answer, making it a statement, not a choice.

I watched her splash the pale golden liquid on to ice cubes in two tall glasses, and add a token drop of water. She came across and held out one of them with a graceful suntanned arm. A heavy gold chain bracelet loaded with fobs and charms clinked from her wrist, and into my nostrils floated a trace of 'Joy'.

I tasted the whisky. Hedges and Butler's Royal, I

thought. Too fine and light for anything else. The flavour from one sip lasted a long time on my tongue.

'Eva says you speak Hungarian,' she said, moving away, picking up her own glass, and taking an adult swallow.

'Mm, yes.'

'She was most impressed.'

'I came about Chrysalis,' I began.

'Do you speak any other languages?' Her voice veered more to American than English and had the abrupt, inconsequential lurch of two drinks too many; but it didn't show in her face.

'German,' I said, raising a dutiful social smile.

The way I'd been taught languages, it took a week for a smattering, three months for fluency, and two years to bring one to the point of recognizing typical speech and thought patterns when one heard them translated back into perfect English. In one period of seven years, in my twenties, I'd been crammed with German, Hungarian, and five Slavonic languages, from Russian and Czech to Serbo-Croat. None of them was likely to come in handy for finding stallions, and in any case they were almost out of date. The new boys were learning Swahili, Arabic, and Chinese.

'And French, I suppose?' she said.

'A little,' I agreed.

'Enough for the necessities of life, I expect.' Her expression and emphasis gave the word necessities a precise meaning, which wasn't food and drink.

'Absolutely,' I agreed, acknowledging her definition.

She laughed. Nothing frail or fine-boned about that.

'Chrysalis,' she said, 'is a right bloody nuisance. He wouldn't have been my choice in the first place; that Purple Emperor strain is as soft as an old man's pencil and he's passing it on, they always do. Moth won the Derby in a shockingly bad year and if anything had given him half a race he'd have folded like a wet sheet.' She took a deep swallow. 'Do you know the first bloody thing about horses?'

'What *is* the first bloody thing about horses?'

She gave me a startled stare which turned into an incredulous laugh. 'The first bloody thing about horses is that they make bloody fools of men.'

I smiled back spontaneously, amused by the contrast between her robustness of thought and language and her delicacy of frame.

'I'm going for a swim,' she said. 'Bring your drink.'

She mixed herself a new one in passing, and without looking back crossed the green carpet, pulled open a sliding glass door, pushed through the insect screen outside it, and walked with rock-like steadiness across a paved terrace and on to a deep green lawn. Sighing, I got to my feet and followed her. The grass was thick and resilient, a different species altogether from English turf, and a sprinkler on one side threw diamond sprays around like water.

She stopped on another paved area round a kidney-shaped pool and unfastened some clips on her yellow dress, which came off in one piece, and left two more in view underneath. Her body was slender and well cared for, but not at all a young girl's. Middle to late forties, I thought: and the sort of woman who would have been uninteresting under thirty.

She slipped into the water and floated, and I watched the sun make watered silk ripples over her brown stomach.

'Come on in,' she said. 'There are plenty of swim suits in the hut.'

I smiled and shook my head, and sat down on one of the soft plastic pool-side chairs. She took her time, humming and splashing gently with her hands. The sun was hot, but not like in the city. I took my jacket off and felt heat baking into my skin through the white cotton shirt. Peacefulness gradually seeped in too. I was in no hurry for her to rejoin me, which she presently did, the water drops shining singly on her oiled skin.

'You've hardly touched your drink,' she observed accusingly. 'Surely you're not one of those soft buggers who can't hold their liquor?' She picked up her own glass and went on proving that she, at any rate, wasn't.

'Chrysalis . . .' I began.

She interrupted immediately. 'Do you ride?'

'I can,' I said, 'but I don't.'

'Why not?'

'I haven't a horse. Nor a kingdom to give for one.'

'Drink your whisky,' she said, smiling.

'In a while.'

'Then strip off and get in the pool.'

I shook my head.

'Why not?'

'I like it as I am.' And I had too many bruises, from the weir.

She shrugged, half annoyed. 'Don't you do any bloody thing?'

'How many people knew at what hour Chrysalis would leave Kennedy Airport?'

'God,' she said, 'you're a bloody bore.'

'Don't you want the horse back?'

'No,' she said vehemently, 'as far as I'm concerned, we'd be far better off with the insurance.'

'Two hundred thousand dollars', I agreed, 'is a heck of a gamble. Supposing he never sired another like Moth?'

'There's no stopping Dave, when he's set his mind on something.' She sat on the edge of a full-length chair bed and smoothed cream on to her face from a dusky pink tube. 'And he had meant to sell off a bit of that, when he got back. God knows what will happen now he's strung up in those goddam pulleys.'

'He'll be home in about four weeks.'

'Yeah. So he said.' She lay down flat and closed her eyes. 'I told him to take his time. It's too bloody expensive being ill over here.'

Five quiet minutes passed. A single jet plane flew across, a silver streak so high up one couldn't hear it until it had gone. The air was still. The oiled brown body in the yellow bikini took in a hefty dose of ultra violet and the ice cubes melted in the drinks.

'Take your clothes off, for God's sake,' she said, without opening her eyes. 'Or are you ashamed of that pink-white slug of a body the English usually bring over here?'

'I'd better be going.'

'Do what you damn well like.' She fluttered a lax wrist in a double gesture which said, equally well, stay or goodbye.

I stood up and walked over to the hut, a large beautifully made pinewood structure with a protruding front roof, for shade. Inside were a bathroom and two changing rooms, and in the tiny lobby some shelves in a cupboard held bright coloured towels and swimsuits. I took a pair of blue shorts and put them on. The bruises on my legs very nearly matched. I left my shirt on, picked up a towel for a pillow, and went back and lay down on the next bed to hers.

She merely grunted with her eyes still shut, but after another minute she said, 'If you want to know about the timetable for Chrysalis, you'd better ask Sam Hengelman in Lexington. He fixed the van. He runs a private service from here. Dave called me and told me the date the horse was being shipped over, and I called Sam Hengelman. And he took it from there.'

'Who else did you tell the shipping date to?'

'It wasn't any goddam secret, for God's sake. I

called six or seven of the syndicate to let them know. Dave asked me to. Half Kentucky knew about it, I guess.'

She suddenly sat up straight and opened her eyes.

'Why the hell does it matter how many people knew when Chrysalis was coming? It wasn't him the hijackers wanted. They simply made a balls of it and took the wrong truck.'

'Supposing they got just what they wanted?'

'Were you born yesterday? The blood-line is what breeders pay stud fees for. Chrysalis isn't worth a sou to anyone, if they can't use his pedigree. No one's going to even send a decent mare to a stallion someone just happens to have handy, which has no name in the stud book, no history, and no papers; let alone pay fifteen thousand dollars for the privilege.'

'Buttress Life have been looking for an insurance swindle.'

'They can look till they're blue in the face.' She picked up her glass, swallowed, and grimaced. 'This drink's as warm as that pool and just as sodden. Mix me another, will you?' She held out the glass to me and I unwound myself from the bed and took it and my own back into the house. I mixed her the same size dose as before, concocted a different one for myself, and took them both back, the ice clinking coolly as I walked.

'Thanks.' She sank almost half. 'That's better.'

I stood beside the pool and put one toe in the water. It was blood warm, or more.

'What's the matter with your legs?' she said.

'The same as your husband's, only mine didn't break.'

'What's under the shirt?'

'The sun's too hot. I can do without a sunburn.'

'Yeah.' She lay flat again. 'Pink-white slug.'

Smiling, I sat down on the edge of the pool with my back towards her and dangled my feet in the water. I ought, I supposed, to go away and do something more useful, like interviewing Sam Hengelman. But Walt would no doubt have thought of that, and done it, since his threatening migraine would only have lasted until the car we had rented had taken me out of sight. Walt and Dave's wife hadn't exactly clicked.

'Mr Hawkins,' she said from behind me.

'Mm?'

'What do you do for a living?'

'I'm a civil servant.'

'With this?'

There was a sharp metallic click, the one sound guaranteed to raise the hairs on my neck as if I'd never left the jungle.

'Do you know what you're doing with that thing?' I asked, as conversationally as I could.

'Yes.'

'Then put the safety on.'

She didn't answer, and I stood up and turned round, and looked straight into the barrel of my own gun.

I deserve it, I thought. Slow, careless, and stupid. I was anything one cared to mention.

She was sitting with her legs curled underneath her, the Luger lodged unwaveringly in her fist. The gap between us, five yards at least, was too great for anything constructive in the way of action, so I simply stood still.

'You're a cool bastard, I'll say that for you.'

'You won't shoot me,' I said, smiling.

'Why not?'

'I'm not insured for a million and a half.'

Her eyes widened. 'Does that mean that you think that I . . . *I . . . shot Chrysalis*?'

'It's possible.'

She stared. 'You're a goddam fool.'

'So are you, if I may say so. That gun goes off very easily.'

She looked down at it vaguely and before I could stop her she threw it away from her on to the paving stones. The jar as it hit the ground inevitably fired it. Flame streaked out of the barrel, and the bullet smashed through the whisky glass which stood on the ground beside her long chair, nine inches from her body.

It took her a second to realize what had happened, then she shuddered heavily and put her hands over her face. I walked across to fetch the gun, and put the safety on, and then perched on the bed facing her.

'Games,' she said in a shattered voice. 'What do I have but games? Bridge and golf. All games.'

'This too?' I put the Luger back in the under-arm niche and buttoned the strap.

'I just thought I'd make you sweat.'

'Why?'

'That's a bloody good question. A bloody good question. All games. Life is all bloody games.'

'And we're all poor bloody losers,' I agreed sardonically.

She put her hands down and looked at me. Her eyes were dry, but half her assurance had drained away.

'It was only a game. I didn't mean you any harm.'

She thought she was telling the truth, but I'd met too many of the tricks the unconscious mind gets up to. Perhaps because I'd saved her husband, or was looking for his horse, or merely represented some obscure form of male challenge, she'd had an undoubted urge to destroy me. And she was a very troubled lady in far more obvious ways than that.

'Give me your drink,' she said abruptly.

'I'll get you some more whisky,' I said.

'Yours will do,' she insisted.

I gave her the glass, but one sip was enough. Dry ginger ale. On the rocks.

'Do you cheat all along the line?'

'Whenever it's kinder, or safer, or gets better results.'

I walked away across the lawn and brought her back another glass. She took a moderate pull and put it down amid the ruins of the first one.

'Stay to dinner,' she said. She made it a casual suggestion rather than a warm invitation, and I answered her need, not her tone.

'All right.'

She nodded briefly and flattened herself face down, to roast her back. I lay with one arm over my eyes to shield them from the direct sun, and thought about all the things she hadn't asked, like how was Dave when I saw him and how bad was the broken thigh.

After a while she went back to floating.

'Come on in,' she called.

I shook my head.

'Don't be so prissy,' she said. 'I'm not a swooning virgin. If your legs are like that, the rest of you must be the same. Take that bloody shirt off and give yourself a break.'

It was indeed very hot, and the clear blue water looked good. I sighed, stood up, took the shirt off, and slid down into the pool. Its lukewarm antigravitational gentleness unlocked knots and tensions in my nerves and muscles that I hadn't even realized were there, and I swam and floated tranquilly for nearly an hour. When finally I hauled myself out over the edge she was smoothing on another coating of oil. Her whisky glass was empty.

'Is Dave in that state too?' she asked, eyeing me.

'Pretty much.'

She grimaced slightly and said nothing when I put my shirt back on.

The sun had begun to lose its height in the sky and shadows were fanning out from the trees. A golden sheen lay on the big cream colonial type house across the green lawn. The pool water stilled, and the quietness of the place crept subtly into all the senses.

'It's so beautiful here,' I said. A banal enough phrase for the promise of peace.

She looked round casually. 'I suppose it is. But we're moving, of course.'

'Moving?'

'Yes. To California.'

'Moving the stud? Horses, and everything?'

'That's right. Dave's just bought a farm down near Santa Barbara, and we're moving over there in the fall.'

'I would have thought you were settled here for life. Wasn't this Dave's father's place?'

'Oh no. We moved here about ten years ago. The old farm was on the other side of Lexington, out on the Versailles Road.'

'California is a long way,' I commented. But she didn't respond with a reason for the move, and after a pause I said, 'If it wouldn't be much trouble to you,

I'd like very much to see the horses and stables you have here.'

She narrowed her eyes. 'Business or pleasure?'

'Both,' I smiled.

She shrugged. 'Help yourself. But get me another drink first.'

A pool-side icebox, I reflected, would save a lot of walking: but maybe she still needed the illusion that she didn't drink in the afternoon. I fetched her a refill, changed into my clothes, and found her still face down in the bikini.

'Say I sent you,' she said.

Before I could move, however, Dave rang from England, and Eva brought a portable telephone out and plugged the long cord into a socket in the hut. Dave's wife made three or four unanxious inquiries about her husband's condition, and then said, 'Yes, he's here right now.' She held out the receiver to me. 'He wants to talk to you.'

'Gene?' His voice was as clear as if he'd been in Lexington, and much stronger than it had been the previous morning.

'Hi,' I said.

'Look fella, Sim and I want you back here for a conference. Can you get a plane tomorrow?'

'But the fare . . .' I protested mildly.

'To hell with the fare. You've got a return ticket.'

'All right.'

'You haven't found the horse yet?'

'No.'

'Do you think you will?'

'I don't know yet.'

He sighed. 'See you Thursday, then,' and the line went dead.

The stables lay some distance away on the far side of the house. I walked round there and was shortly talking to the stud groom, Chub Lodovski, a large good-natured man with slow speech, a bird head, and great ham-like hands. He showed me round the whole setup with unlimited patience and an obvious pride in his job. The state of the place was his testimonial. The mares and foals ate peacefully in neatly railed paddocks reached by impeccable narrow drives with sharply cut grass edges. The stallions lived in a short row of six large airy box-stalls in a spacious barn, with a wooden railed exercise paddock in front, flanked by two high-walled mating compounds.

Only five of these stalls were occupied. The vacancy was for Chrysalis.

'Is this where you kept Allyx?' I asked.

'That's right. Second stall from the end. He was only in it four days.'

'And where was the fire?'

He frowned. 'It started in some straw one night, just about here.' We were fairly central. 'It wasn't much. Mostly smoke.'

'And you turned the horses out into the exercise paddock in front here?'

'That's right. Just as a precaution. But one of those doggone animals got scared and broke a rail on the far side, and the whole bunch got out across that stretch of grass on to that dirt road over there. We never did find Allyx. There hasn't been sight nor sound of him since.'

We talked for a while about the search they'd made next morning, but, Lodovski said, the whole of Kentucky was plastered with horses, and no one thought much about it if they saw one loose, and although a reward had been offered, and the insurance people had swarmed around like bloodhounds, they'd never found him.

'And now Chrysalis,' I sighed sympathetically.

'Sure. And they say lightning never strikes the same place twice!'

He was moderately upset that the stud looked like losing another major attraction, but it wasn't his money that was involved, and besides that he was proud enough of the stallions remaining in residence. I asked him if he'd ever been to California.

'The farm's moving out there, did you know?' he said.

'Are you going, yourself?'

'Mebbe, mebbe not. Depends on the missus, and she can't make up her mind.' He grinned comfortably and accepted the note I gave him with dignity.

When I got back to the pool Dave's wife had got her dress on again and Eva was brushing the splinters of whisky glass into a dustpan, which she carried carefully away across the lawn.

'Well, what did you think of the place?'

'The horses all looked very well. The stallions especially.'

'So would you, if all you had to do was . . .' she began, and then stopped and shrugged. 'So would you.'

Apart from an occasional 'bloody' which crept in from habit, that was the last of her verbal squibs for the day. But my lack of scandalized reaction didn't have the same effect on her drinking, and she kept up a slow but steady intake right through dusk and dinner. Her mental brakes remained half on, half off, as before.

Over thick slices of rare beef she said, 'Are you married?'

'No.' I shook my head.

'Divorced?'

'No,' I said. 'I've never been married at all.'

'Are you queer?' she asked, as simply as if she'd said, 'Are you comfortable?'

I smiled slightly. 'No.'

'Then why aren't you married?'

'I haven't found anyone who will marry me.'

'Don't be ridiculous. You must have women lying down for you in droves.'

'It's not the same thing.'

She looked at me broodingly over the rim of her glass. 'So you live all alone?'

'That's right.'

'No parents?'

'They're both dead,' I said. 'And I've no brothers, no sisters, no uncles, aunts, or cousins.' I smiled. 'Anything else?'

'Stay the night.'

She said it abruptly, as if it came from a deeper level than her fairly harmless interrogation, and there was an element of surprise and alarm on her face afterwards.

'I'm sorry,' I said matter-of-factly, 'but I can't.'

She looked at me without expression for about ten seconds.

'I have a mother,' she said. 'And sisters, and brothers, and dozens of relations. And a husband, and a son, and all this.' She waved a hand around the millionaire bracket walls. 'I have everything.' Her eyes filled with tears, but she went on looking straight across the table, without blinking.

'I have . . . bloody . . . everything.'

CHAPTER SIX

There was an envelope from Walt in my room at the motel containing a short note and a list.

Gene,
This is all the drivers came up with. I think it's safe to bet that they actually did see these vehicles. The top three, they both remembered. The others, only one of them remembered. No horse vans, though.

Walt

The list read:

'Impala, lilac, two years old, California number plates. Passengers included a fat child who made faces out of the rear window. Both days.

Grey station wagon trailing a load of furniture. Both days.

Dark green Ford Mustang, Nevada plates. Young couple, no description. The horse van drivers remember this one because they were discussing whether the Mustang was a good car or not. Second day only.

White convertible: young woman with blond hair wound on rollers. Second day only.

Army green pick-up truck with white lettering on the doors. Second day only.

The pick-up, one of the drivers thinks, was probably on Inter-state 70, after Zanesville and before they turned off south. He doesn't remember clearly.'

I read the list through three times while I dressed. The load of furniture looked the most promising, but none of it exactly inspired.

Walt, driving to the airport in the morning, damped even the furniture.

'It was only one of those Snail Express trailers.'

'Like the U-Haul,' I said.

'That's right. "Carry your house on your back, but let us take the weight",' he said, quoting the Snail Express advertising slogan. 'The drivers said it wasn't big enough to put a horse in.'

There were furniture trailers of all sizes all over the country: people moving house hired one at their old home, loaded up, and drove off to the new, maybe six states away. There they unloaded and simply left the trailer in a local depot, from where the haulage firm hired it to the next removing client. The bright orange U-Haul trailers and the aluminium and blue ones of the Snail Express were as frequent on the roads as the Greyhound buses.

'How about the pick-up?' I asked.

'Much too small for a horse,' Walt said gloomily.

He came back with me to New York and rubbed his thumb continuously over the finger pads while I went through the file we had made on the case.

There was a batch of photographs of the missing horse, mostly taken from stud book advertisements, by the look of them. Not a very remarkable creature on paper, I thought.

Sam Hengelman had sent his two most careful drivers to fetch Chrysalis. He had had a call from Mrs Teller informing him of the date fixed for the horse to fly over, and also a cable from England when he was on his way. Hengelman had telephoned Kennedy Airport and been told the horses would be through the twenty-four hour immigration regulations at noon, Tuesday. He had sent the van as soon as he got the cable, on Sunday. There was, he agreed, a system like the U-Haul in operation among horse vans, to avoid the need for long empty journeys, but some folks liked personal service, and Mr Teller was one of them.

The Buttress Life Insurance covered transport. Sam Hengelman had not had to take out a policy for the trip, and neither stood to lose nor gain from the hi-jacking.

Both drivers had clean records going way back.

Both grooms had been in their present jobs for more than three years. One of them came from Midway Farm; the other from another farm which had a horse coming in on the same trip.

An interview with Mrs Eunice Teller had produced no helpful information.

I shut the folder with a smile, and gave it back to Walt.

'How about checking with Snail Express, on the off-chance?'

He looked sceptical. 'The drivers said the trailer wasn't high enough.'

'They're used to thinking in terms of ordinary horse vans. And they were looking down, from their cab. You could squeeze a racehorse into a box about seven feet by four, by six feet high, if you were ruthless enough. Find out how many trailers that size or larger Snail Express had out last Monday or Tuesday, which might conceivably have been on the turnpike.'

'All right,' he said expressionlessly. 'If you say so.'

With the time lag working in reverse it was 3 AM Thursday morning when I landed at Heathrow, and 12 before I walked into Dave Teller's room in a Reading hospital. Flaming June had come and gone: it was raining again.

If one discounted the ropes, pulleys, slings, and plaster suspending his leg in mid air, the patient looked healthy enough. He greeted me without fuss, the direct eyes steady and bright.

'Tiring trip?'

'So so.'

'You've eaten?' He waved vaguely at a collection of chocolates and grapes.

'I had breakfast over Ireland, at two o'clock.'

He laughed, eased himself on the pillows, and stretched out a hand for a cigarette.

'How's my wife?'

'Very well.'

He lit his cigarette and flicked shut the lighter.

'What was she doing, when you called?' His apprehension was pretty well concealed.

'Sunbathing. Swimming. There's a heatwave coast to coast.'

A couple of muscles relaxed in his forearm and he inhaled deeply. 'She gave you a drink . . . I hope?'

'Sure. And a swim. And I stayed to dinner.'

He looked at me directly for some time without speaking. Then he said merely, 'A good one?'

'Very, thank you. And I saw your horses. Chub Lodovski showed me round.'

He talked much more naturally about the horses: no problems there.

'I hear you're moving to California,' I said, after a while.

The tenseness instantly came back; the small giveaway tightening of eye, neck, and respiratory muscles that I looked for every day in my job, and couldn't be blind to in my friends.

'Yes,' he said, tapping off ash. 'Eunice loves the ocean, and in Kentucky we're as far from it as can be . . . and of course, the horse breeding business in California is every bit as profitable. We will do very well out there, I've no doubt.'

Eunice would take her problems right along with her, I thought: though with a bit of luck they would recede for a year or two. Perhaps Teller considered the upheaval worth it.

'What's the new place like?' I asked.

'It's good land, pretty well irrigated. And the stable and general layout are as good as Midway. Better even, in some respects. It's Davis L. Davis's old place.'

I looked blank, and he explained. 'Made his money out of roadside hamburger stands. Well, he died early this year, and last month they held a dispersal sale of his brood mares and stallions, to divide up his estate for inheritance. I put in a bid for the farm to his executors before I came over here this time, and they wrote me a week or so back to say they're accepting it. The contracts are in hand right now, but I don't foresee any difficulties. I'm sure glad to have got it settled at last.'

'At last?'

'Been looking for a farm in southern California for over a year now, but there were too many snags to most of them. Eunice and I took a trip over in March of this year, and we saw the Davis farm then, and liked it. So . . .' He waggled his fingers to finish the sentence.

The door opened and Keeble came in, mild

spectacles reflecting the pallid light from the window, eyes blinking rapidly, and the usual patch of bristle growing grey where he had short-sightedly missed with the razor. He said hellos all round and settled himself comfortably into the spare armchair.

'Well, how's it with the States?' he said: and I told them everything Walt had told me. They thought it over for a while in silence.

'So what do you think now?' Keeble said.

I glanced doubtfully at Teller, but he tapped ash off his cigarette and remarked simply, 'Sim says you were convinced I was pushed into the river on purpose. I guess what he's asking you is, have you changed your mind?'

'No, I haven't.'

Keeble and Teller looked at each other. Then Teller said, sighing, 'We've come up with one or two things which makes it almost certain you are right.'

Keeble nodded. 'I went to Dave's hotel in London to collect his luggage and pay his bill, and explained where he was if anyone wanted him. The young man at the reception desk asked me if the lady journalist from *Stud and Stable* had found Dave all right on Saturday. She had, he said, been most insistent, owing to a deadline on the magazine, and he had given her my address and telephone number, which Dave had left with him in case he was wanted hurriedly in connection with Chrysalis.'

'And that', I remarked, 'is how boy and girl knew where to find you.'

'Quite,' Keeble agreed. 'From the house to the river was no doubt a simple piece of following. Incidentally, I checked with *Stud and Stable.* They didn't want Dave, and their deadline is the first day of each month.'

'Nice,' I said.

Keeble took an envelope from his pocket and fished out some three by three inch black-and-white photographs. 'There are Peter's snaps,' he said. 'Take a look.'

I took them from him and looked. The ducks had come out splendidly; better than one of Lynnie, who had been moving. The picnic lunch was there, and the *Flying Linnet* in Marsh Lock, and one of Dave Teller standing on the bows, and a rather grim one of myself staring down into the water. There was one of the four men fallen in a heap in the punt at the hotel where we'd had our morning drinks, and another, taken with the photographer's back to the river, of Keeble, Joan, Dave, Lynnie, and myself sitting round the little table under the sun umbrella, with glasses in our hands.

Keeble waited without blinking. With this in mind I started through the pile again, and found what he had seen. I looked up at him. He nodded, and from an inside pocket produced a magnifying lens, which he threw over to me. With the help of that, the two figures were clear. A girl with long hair and white trousers, a young man with pale trousers and a check shirt, standing side by side in the background of the photograph of us all drinking at the pub.

'It's them,' I nodded.

'Yes,' Keeble agreed. 'They were there in the morning. So I'll grant you they could have followed us by car from Henley . . . you can see the river from several places along that road . . . and also that they saw Dave standing on the bows when we left Henley and when we left the pub. And possibly also when we arrived at the pub, and at Marsh Lock. They would know there was a good chance of him being there again when we came back through Harbour.'

I smiled. 'And the five feet which was missing from the punt's mooring rope had been used to tie it securely to the Danger post while they waited for us.'

'I agree,' Keeble said. 'We took that punt right out of the water after you'd gone on Monday, and we found that the cleat for the stern rope had been unscrewed from the stern, and screwed on again under the water line at the bow end.'

'So both mooring points were at one end,' Teller said. 'The safe rope was under water all the time, hidden by the punt itself and the girl's body and arms. And, of course, we weren't looking for anything like that at the time, so we'd never have seen it.'

Keeble finished it. 'Once they'd got the visible rope safely in Joan's hands, and we were all looking anxiously for you and Dave to surface, the girl had only to pull some sort of quick release knot, and the punt was free. So I'll agree, Gene, that that was an accident which could be staged, and was staged, and you were right and I was wrong. Which, I seem to remember vaguely, has happened once or twice before.'

He smiled at me with irony, and I reflected that there were few superior officers who would say that sort of thing so utterly ungrudgingly.

A nurse clattered in with Teller's lunch, which proved to be chicken salad and tinned mandarin oranges. The patient poured the oranges on to the salad and ate the combined course with resignation.

'The food is lousy,' he said mildly. 'I've forgotten what a good steak looks like.'

We watched him eat without envy, and I asked Keeble if he'd had any results with the handkerchief.

'Only negative ones. None of the Yogi Bear concessionists in this country imported it. They say, from the material and the sort of paint used for the bear, that it was probably made in Japan. And some of them had doubts it was done by the Hanna-Barbera artists. Not well enough drawn, they said.'

'I'll take it back to the States and try there,' I said. 'After all, boy and girl were almost certainly American.'

Teller raised his eyebrows with his mouth full.

'The boy shouted "Can you help us, sir," and that "sir" comes a great deal more commonly from Americans, than from the English. Also, the boatman said their accent was "same as on the telly" and there's as much American as English on our television.'

'The same argument might apply to public schoolboys,' Keeble said casually. 'But they were Americans, I agree.'

'So all we need to know now, apart from who were they,' I said to Teller, 'is why they wanted you dead.'

No one had any constructive ideas on that point. Teller drank his coffee and a maid in a green overall came to take the tray.

'You're guarding against them having another go?' I said to Keeble, watching the maid's back disappear through the door.

Keeble followed my eyes. 'All precautions,' he nodded. 'The works. I got the Radnor-Halley Agency. Only the best for Dave!'

'They won't let me open any packages,' Teller complained. 'I think they take them outside, dunk them in a bucket, and wait for the ticking to start. And the only chocolates I have were bought by Sim personally. You'd never believe the half of what goes on in here.'

I laughed. 'It's when you get out of here you'll notice it.'

'He'll stay here till you've wrapped it up,' remarked Keeble; and he wasn't joking.

I stared. 'I'm in anti-infiltration, remember? Not the CID.'

'Oh sure. But the same motivation, I imagine. Just

let your hunter instincts loose . . . and tell us what you plan to do next.'

I stood up restlessly and went to the window, still raining. Two nurses ran from one building to another, clutching capes around them and skitting mud up the backs of their stockings. Useful people, nurses. Needed people. Constructive, compassionate, tough people . . .

'Well?' said Keeble, behind me.

I turned round and leaned against the wall. 'How's the exchequer?'

Teller answered, 'Look, Gene, I've enough to launch a minor space programme. And as I said before, if it weren't for you I wouldn't be here at all. So spend what you need to, and I'll pick up the chits.'

'Right . . . then I think it would be best to let the Radnor-Halley Agency deal with anything which crops up here . . . I suppose they did the handkerchief inquiry?'

Keeble nodded.

'And I'll go back to the States tomorrow. I can't believe the attempted murder isn't tied in with the horse theft, so the springboard for everything must be in America. Unless some Irish fanatic disapproves of you skimming off the cream of British bloodstock!'

'Is Chrysalis Irish, then?' Keeble asked seriously.

'Irish-bred dam,' I said. 'That's all. His sire was Purple Emperor, in the Read Stud at Newmarket.'

'How do you know?' Teller asked, surprised.

'I looked it up,' I said briefly. 'Also his markings.

And that is important.' I paused. 'Whoever took Allyx and Chrysalis knew a lot about horses. Allyx was one of six stallions loose in a paddock at night. Chrysalis was one of five horses in a horse box. Yet each time the right horse was singled out for removal. We have to believe it was the right horse, not just chance, because each time it was by far the most valuable one of the collection which disappeared. Well . . . Chrysalis is a dark bay with no distinguishing marks. No socks, no blaze, no star. One colour all over. And Allyx was exactly the same. There are literally thousands of horses like that.'

The two men didn't stir.

I went on, 'This means that if we ever do find Chrysalis, there will be an enormous problem of identification. English horses have no tattooed numbers, like American.'

'Christ,' Teller said.

'I wouldn't know him if he came up and ate sugar out of my hand. Would you?' He shook his head. I went on, 'The only people at all likely to be able to pick him out for us with any certainty are those who handled him in England. And that's where we hit a very big snag. The stud groom at Read's died of a heart attack two months ago and the new man couldn't be sure of knowing Chrysalis again. Read himself is too short sighted, apparently, to be of any help. This means we have to go back nearly five years, to the season when Chrysalis last raced. To his owner at that time, and his trainer. Though the only one I'd pin any faith on would be the lad who looked after him. And it's the lad, I think, who we'll need to take to the States, if we find a horse which might be Chrysalis.'

'We could easily find out who the lad is,' Keeble nodded, 'and shunt him over.'

'His name is Sam Kitchens, and he'll be at Ascot at this moment, as one of his horses is running in the four-thirty. It's Gold Cup day today.' I smiled faintly. 'I thought I might just drift along to the races when I leave here.'

'Just tell me,' Teller said in a small voice, 'how and when you found out all this?' He spread his fingers. 'I only ask.'

'I spent an hour this morning at the British Bloodstock Agency . . . I was practically camped on their doorstep at nine o'clock. And then I did some telephoning. That's all.'

'When do you sleep, fella?'

'Between meals. Very bad for the appetite.'

'He's mad,' Teller said to Keeble.

'You get used to it,' Keeble assured him. 'The first eight years are the worst.'

'And this is the guy you'd trust your daughter to?'

'Hm,' said Keeble. 'We haven't mentioned that.'

'What?' I said suspiciously.

'We'd . . . er . . . like you to take Lynnie back with you, to the States,' Teller said. 'She's going to visit with Eunice for a while.'

I glanced at Keeble and saw that he knew what I was inevitably thinking: that Eunice's special need for company was more compelling than the rest of Lynnie's finishing-school term.

'I'd be glad to,' I said to them both with formality. 'On a slow boat via New Zealand, if you like.'

'She's too young for you,' said Keeble, without anxiety.

'She is indeed.' I pushed myself away from the wall and stood upright. 'Where will I collect her?'

Keeble handed me an envelope. 'Air tickets for you both. She'll be at the Victoria Air Terminal at eight-thirty tomorrow morning. Is that all right?'

I took the tickets and nodded. 'Can I have the handkerchief?'

He obligingly produced it, in another envelope. I put that and the air tickets away, and picked up Peter's snaps. Holding the negatives up to the light I singled out the drinking group and put it in my wallet.

'I'll get it blown up tomorrow in New York,' I said. 'Then it'll only be a matter of sifting through two hundred million inhabitants.'

Drizzle was wilting the fluffy hats when I got to Ascot, but the turf looked greener for it, and the horses glossier. I spotted the trainer I wanted and walked across to where he was talking to a large woman in a creased pink dress under a dripping pink umbrella. He caught sight of me over her shoulder, and I watched the initial memory-jog pass through mind-search to recognition. He smiled warmly at his success.

'Gene Hawkins.'

The large woman turned round, saw she didn't know me, decided she didn't want to, and departed.

'Mr Arkwright.' We shook hands, and I thought how little age had changed him. Still the upright, brisk, grey-headed neighbour from my father's days in Yorkshire.

'Come and have a drink,' he said, 'and let's get out of this rain.' There were misty beads of water fuzzing his tall grey hat. 'Though it's much better than it was an hour ago, isn't it?'

'I've only just come.'

He led the way up the staircase into the balcony bar and ordered vodka and tonic. I asked if I could have the tonic without the vodka and he remarked that my father, an enthusiastic alcoholic, would have turned in his grave.

'What are you doing now then?' he said, sipping the clear fizzy mixture. 'Still in the Civil Service?'

'Yes,' I nodded. 'But I'm on leave at present.'

'It always seemed rum to me, you doing something so . . . so tame,' he said. 'Considering the sort of boy you were.' He shrugged. 'Never would have thought it. Your old father always thought you'd do something in racing, you know. You rode well enough, you knew your way around. Can't understand it.' He looked at me accusingly. 'Those two years in the Army did you no good.'

I smiled. 'It was while I was in the Army that they offered me this job.'

'Safe, I suppose,' he said, making allowances. 'Prospects, pension, and all that.'

'Mm,' I said non-committally. 'Actually, I really came here today to see you, to ask you about Chrysalis.'

'Have they found him, do you know?' he said.

'Not yet, no. The American who bought him is a friend of my boss, and they've asked me, as I know you, to see if you would do them a favour.'

'If I can,' he said promptly. 'If I can.'

'Their problem is', I explained, 'that if and when a loose horse is found, especially if he's some distance from where he was lost, how are they to be sure it is Chrysalis.'

He looked startled and then amused. 'That certainly is a problem. But Chrysalis hasn't been in my yard since . . . let's see . . . four years last October. I don't know whether I'd be certain of him, not absolutely certain, if I saw him, for instance, among twenty others rather like him. And you'd want it to be more positive than that.'

'Yes,' I agreed. 'Actually I rang your home this morning and your secretary said I'd find you here. And he also said Chrysalis's old lad would be here. Sam Kitchens. Would you mind if I had a word with him?'

'That's right, he came with Milkmaid for the four-thirty. No, I don't mind, you ask him what you like.'

'Mr Dave Teller, who bought Chrysalis, wonders whether you would let Sam Kitchens go over to the States for a few days, if and when the horse turns up, to identify him. Mr Teller will pay his fare and expenses.'

Arkwright laughed. 'Sam will like that. He's not a bad chap. Pretty reliable.'

'Then if he's needed, you'll get a cable saying which flight he's to go on, and so on. Will that be all right?'

He nodded. 'You tell the American I'll let him go.'

I thanked him. 'They'll be very grateful.' I bought him another vodka and tonic and we talked about horses.

Sam Kitchens walked his fair young Milkmaid around the parade ring and I risked ten bob on her, but she turned out to be a cow. I joined Arkwright while he ran his hand down the filly's legs and listened to the jockey explaining forcibly that it wasn't down there that the trouble lay, but up in her pea-sized brain.

Lads usually resent criticism of their charges, but from his expression Kitchens, a short stocky man of about thirty, held much the same view. I asked him, after introductions from Arkwright, whether he would know Chrysalis again with enough certainty to testify if necessary in a court of law.

'Sure,' he said without hesitation. 'I'd know the boy.

I had him three years. Sure, I'd know him. Maybe I couldn't pick him out of a herd, now, but I'd know him close to. The way his hide grows, and little nicks in his skin, I wouldn't have forgotten those.'

'That's fine,' I said, nodding. 'Was there . . . is there . . . anything special about him, which might help someone who'd never seen him before to recognize him?'

He thought it over for several minutes. 'It's four years. More, nearly five, see. The only thing I remember is, we had trouble with his off hind hoof. It was thin, used to crack at the same place every time. But the stud he went to might have cured it, as he wasn't racing any more. Or he might just have grown out of it, being older now.' He paused. 'Tell you something, he liked sardines. He's the only horse I know of who had a taste for sardines.'

I smiled. 'That's pretty odd. How did you find out?'

'Took my tea into his box once. Sardines on toast. I put it down for a minute on the window sill, and when I looked round he'd scoffed the lot. It tickled me, it did. I used to share a tinful with him sometimes, after that. He always liked them.'

I stayed for the last race and picked another loser. I would have made a lousy trainer, anyway.

CHAPTER SEVEN

I reached the Air Terminal at eight-fifteen, but Lynnie was there first.

'I couldn't sleep much,' she said. 'I've never been to America before.'

I'd been to America a dozen times. I hadn't slept much either.

Lynnie's clothes, a deep pink shiny PVC raincoat over the orange tan dress, were having an anti-soporific effect on everyone in sight. Resisting an urge to grope for dark glasses I felt an uncommon lift to the spirits, which lasted to mid Atlantic. There Lynnie went to sleep and a strong wave of non-enthusiasm for finding Chrysalis invaded my mind like one enormous yawn. I wouldn't mind, I thought idly, I really wouldn't mind lazing around that swimming pool with Eunice and Lynnie, doing nothing at all but drink in sunshine, peace, Scotch, and an uninterrupted view of two well-shaped females in bikinis. Peace most of all. Lie like a log, and not think, not feel. And sleep. Sleep for sixteen hours a day and mindlessly laze away the other eight: a programme as near to death as dammit. A very small step from there to eternity, to make the peace permanent . . .

'What are you thinking about?' Lynnie said.

She had opened her eyes and was watching my face.

'Heaven,' I said.

She shook her head slightly. 'Hell, more like.' She sat up briskly. 'How long before we land?'

'About an hour.'

'Will I like Mrs Teller?'

'Haven't you met her before?' I asked.

'Once, when I was little. I don't remember her.'

I smiled. 'She isn't easy to forget.'

'Exactly,' Lynnie said. 'There's something odd about me going to stay with her. Of course I said I'd love to, and who wouldn't go off on any trip to get away from school, let alone a super one like this, but I distinctly think that Daddy and Mr Teller have an ulterior motive and I want to know what it is.'

'They want her to have company, to stop her drinking too much alone.'

'Wow!' She looked surprised. 'You're not serious?'

'They didn't say so. I'm only guessing.'

'But I can't stop her drinking,' she protested.

'Don't try. She doesn't get drunk. And you'll like her all right, as long as your ears don't fall off.'

She laughed. 'My mother wouldn't approve of her?'

'Quite likely not.'

'I expect that's why I've only met her once.' She

grinned at me mischievously without a shred of self-consciousness, Joan's influence waning visibly with every hundred miles.

It was late morning, local time, when we checked in at the Biltmore. From there Lynnie departed on foot for a private tour of New York, and I cabbed down town to Buttress Life. The heatwave was still in position, the air still saturated. Lethargy and haze hung over the city, and buildings shivered like mirages through the blue exhausts of the cars. Once over the Buttress building's threshold the temperate zone took over: I rode up to the seventh floor with the humidity in my clothes condensing into water, and sagged damply into Walt's spare chair in four seven.

'Good trip?' he said. 'You look . . .' he hesitated.

'Yeah,' I said. 'Pooped.'

He smiled. It was worth waiting for. There's a load to be read in a smile, and Walt's was a good one.

'How's it with the Snail Express?' I asked.

He picked a list off his desk. 'They were very co-operative. Only trouble is, they had about thirty-five trailers out on those dates which just might have been going west on the turnpike.' He handed me the paper sympathetically. 'It was a pretty long shot, of course.'

'Hm.' I looked at the list of names and addresses, and at my watch. 'I think we'd better check them.'

'I had a feeling you'd say that.' A touch of gloom.

I smiled at him. 'I'll start it, if you like. Do you know where we can get good enlargements of a snapshot done quickly?' He nodded and mentioned a name, and I gave him the negative. 'The top left hand corner. A couple. Man and girl.' He nodded again. 'And there's this handkerchief.' I produced it. 'Would you mind making a tour of all the offices on this floor, and perhaps the fifth as well, and finding out what everyone associates with it?'

Walt took the small white square curiously.

'Yogi Bear,' he said. 'What's the point?'

'It belonged to a girl who may know more than she ought about Chrysalis. The girl on the negative.'

'Find her, find the horse?' He was half incredulous, a fraction excited.

'Maybe.'

'Right then,' he said at the door. 'See you.'

I studied the list. Snail Express had done their best. Most names had two addresses, the old and the new. All were followed by a place and a date, the depot where the trailer had been checked in after its trip. There were several telephone numbers for the eastern addresses, a few for the west.

Working stolidly down the list, with long pauses while new inhabitants went to find the new telephone numbers of the old, I said I was calling from Snail Express, wanting to know that the service had been satisfactory, or if the customers had any suggestions or complaints. I listened to more praise than criticism, and eventually checked off twenty-seven genuine hirings.

Walt came back while I was biting the end of one of his pencils and wondering what to do next. It was three o'clock. He'd added lunch to his itinerary but he carried a large white package, which he opened carefully. Six enlargements of the corner of Peter's negative. Various sizes, from postcard to nine by seven. The faces were clearest on the smallest print, too fuzzy on the largest.

'He says he'll run off as many as you want by this evening, if you let him know at once.'

'Ask him for six, then. Postcard size.'

'OK.' He picked up the receiver, pressed the buttons, and asked.

The boy and girl stood side by side, their heads turned slightly to the left, towards where we had sat under the sun umbrella. Their faces were calm, good-looking, and somewhat alike. The boy's hair was darker. They were of almost the same height. The checks of the boy's shirt stood out clearly, and one of its buttons was either undone or missing. The girl had a watch with an extra wide strap on her left wrist. She hadn't been wearing it while she hung on to the post.

'All-American kids,' Walt commented. 'So what?'

'So how did you get on with the handkerchief?'

Walt produced it. A little limper, a little grubbier than before.

'Fifteen Yogi Bears, ten don't-bother-me-nows, six lewd suggestions, and one Yellowstone Park.'

'One where?'

'Yellowstone Park?'

'Why Yellowstone Park?'

'That's where Yogi Bear lives. At least, it's called Jellystone in the cartoons, but it's Yellowstone really.'

'Real live bears still in Yellowstone?'

'Oh sure.'

'A natural beauty spot . . . holiday place, isn't it?' I remembered vaguely.

Walt nodded.

'With souvenirs?' I suggested.

'Great lot of help that would be to us.'

I agreed. It would only narrow the field down to one of the thousands who'd been to Yellowstone sometime, or one of the other thousands who knew someone who'd been to Yellowstone sometime. But I remembered a Jamaican would-be assistant to the Biological Warfare Defence Laboratory at Porton who'd been turned down because of a Russian-made bust of Castro in his bedroom. Souvenirs sometimes had their uses.

'The handkerchief probably came from Japan. Do you have a leg-man who can check who imported it, and where it was sold over here?'

'Leg-man?' Walt echoed dismally. 'That's me.' He put the handkerchief away in its envelope, chased up a few answers on the telephone, and heaved himself reluctantly to his feet. 'I may as well go see a man about a Yogi, then. How're the trailers?'

'Twenty-seven are OK. Of the other eight, five don't answer, and three have no telephone.'

I tried two of the non-answerers yet again. Still no reply. Walt looked through the shorter list I'd made of the unchecked.

'They sure went all over, didn't they?' He said, 'Nebraska, Kentucky, New Mexico, California, Wyoming, Colorado, Texas, and Montana. Just don't ask me to leg it around all those places!' He drifted out of the door and his solid footsteps diminuendoed down the passage.

I went on trying the numbers now and then. After two hours I had crossed Texas off the list, bitten the end right off Walt's pencil and started on it an inch farther down, decided I couldn't work many days in his rabbit hutch of an office, and wondered how Eunice was making out beside her pool.

The telephone buzzed.

'Are you staying at the Biltmore again?' Walt said.

'Yes.'

'Meet me in the bar there,' he suggested. 'I'm nearer there than to you.'

'Sure,' I said. 'I'm on my way.'

Lynnie wasn't back. I left a message at the desk for her and joined Walt. His pale blue suit looked as if it had just come out of a spin dryer and there was a damp translucent look to his skin. Repentant, I bought him a large Scotch on the rocks and waited until he had it where it would do most good. He sighed, rubbed the back of one wrist across his eyes, fished a crumpled piece of paper out of his pocket, and spread it open on the bar.

'To start with,' he said disgustedly, 'it's not Yogi Bear.'

I waited in sympathetic silence and beckoned to the barman for a refill. On the paper a list of about eight souvenir manufacturers and distributors had been crossed out, a single line through each. The top lines were neat and straight, the last three a great wild slash across the paper. Walt had had a very bad day.

'The handkerchief came from Japan, like you said.' He took a swallow of his second drink and began to revive. 'Several of the firms phoned their west coast offices for me. No dice. It seems as if at least half of the souvenirs sold in the west are made in Japan, but all these Yogi Bear concessionists say that this isn't Yogi Bear at all, it's the wrong shaped head.'

He pulled out of the by now battered envelope a very bedraggled looking handkerchief and looked at it with loathing.

'If it was sold at or near Yellowstone Park, it could have come from any two-bit import business. As it's not Yogi Bear, no one will have had to pay commission to use the picture, and there isn't any way that I know of finding who brought it into the country and who sold it to where.'

After ten seconds I suggested diffidently, 'We could start from the other end.'

He glared at me incredulously. 'Are you plumb nuts? You can't mean what I think you mean.'

The rocks in my drink had melted to pebbles. I tasted the drowned whisky and put the glass back on the bar.

I said, 'One of the Snail Express trailers was checked in at Rock Springs, Wyoming. It's still there: they haven't had another customer for it yet. I've asked them to hold it until I've had a look at it.'

'Why that one? Why that one particularly?' Walt asked. Irritation only half repressed sharpened his voice.

'Because it's one of the three with no phone number. Because it's in the same state as Yellowstone. And because it gives me an itch.'

'Yellowstone is clear across Wyoming from Rock Springs,' he said. 'Must be four hundred miles.'

'Three hundred. I looked at the map.'

He drank and rubbed his thumb over his fingers much faster than usual. Tired lines had appeared round his eyes.

'I think it's a futile waste of time,' he said abruptly.

'I've time to waste.'

'And I haven't.'

He put the glass down with a thump, reached into an inner pocket and brought out another white package which he tossed down in front of me.

'These are your photographs.'

'Thanks.'

The look he gave me was a long way from the smile of that morning. I wondered whether I would have let him go looking for answers if I'd known he was short on stamina, and decided I probably would. He hadn't given up half way: only at the end.

Lynnie appeared in the bar doorway in her orange dress and the tired looking men there straightened their spines in a hurry. She wouldn't come in. I eased Walt with me across the heavy carpet and introduced him to her in the hall outside. He made only a few perfunctory remarks and left in a short time with a glowering face and solid back.

'Whatever's bitten him?' said Lynnie, looking after him.

'He's had a tiring day and he's going home to his wife.'

She looked at me quickly, half laughing. 'Do you always know what you're saying?'

'Frequently.'

She chuckled. 'Anyway, you look a lot tireder than he does.' We started to walk over to the desk to collect our keys.

'That's most encouraging.'

'What shall we do this evening? Or do you want to sleep?' She was unselfish enough to keep anxiety entirely out of her voice, but when I said we'd go wherever she wanted there was an extra bounce in her stride. She decided on a two hour taxi ride to everywhere in the city she'd ever heard of that she hadn't managed to see that afternoon, followed by dinner in a second-floor glass-walled restaurant, looking down and across the lights of Broadway and Times Square. At eleven-thirty, when we got back to the Biltmore, she was still wide awake.

'What a fabulous, fantastic day,' she said in the lift.

'Good.'

'I'll remember it as long as I live.'

I smiled at her enthusiasm. It was a thousand years since I'd been as happy as that, but sometimes I could still imagine how it felt. That evening it had been quite easy.

'You are far from drizz,' she said, contentedly grinning.

'You'd be no great drag to be stuck in a lift with yourself.'

But the lift stopped unimaginatively at the eighth floor as scheduled and we walked along to our rooms. Her door was opposite mine.

I kissed her cheek. 'Goodnight, little Lynnie.'

Her brown eyes smiled serenely back. 'Goodnight, Gene. Sleep well.'

'You too,' I said. 'Kentucky first stop in the morning.'

It took four more days to find the girl in the photograph, though maybe I could have done it in two if it hadn't been for Lynnie. Privately aware that it wasn't necessary for me to do the job myself I dredged up a cast iron-sounding reason for having to accompany her to Lexington, and we flew down via Washington, which involved another quick taxi tour instead of a lengthy wait at the airport. Lynnie didn't intend to miss a thing.

Eunice met us at Lexington airfield and drove us to Midway, and after a prawn and avocado lunch lent me her car to go on my errand. I greased Chrysalis's ex-groom into going with me with twenty dollars of his employer's money, and took him off to Sam Hengelman's. The horse van, Sam said out of the corner of his mouth as he watched an old movie on a cyan-heavy colour set, was still in care of the police department. If I wanted to look at it, go talk to them.

At the police department a state trooper listened to what I had to say, said 'Yeah,' several times, consulted higher authority, and sorted out some keys. Higher authority turned out to be a good-looking detective in his twenties, and we all four repaired to the parking lot behind the police building, where the horse van stood in one corner.

Chrysalis's lad pointed out the stall the stallion had inhabited, and the state trooper came up with a successful conclusion to the expedition: four long shining bay hairs.

'From his mane,' said the groom authoritatively.

The detective kept two for the State and sent off

the other two special delivery to Walt at Buttress Life, and the groom and I drove back to Midway.

Eunice and Lynnie were both in the pool, and the rest of the day and night came close enough to my daydream on the plane, except that the sixteen hours' sleep shrank to six, but even that was spectacular by recent standards.

When Lynnie said over large cups of breakfast coffee the next morning that she wished I wasn't going, I very nearly didn't. If I'd stayed, Buttress Life would have paid the insurance and a load of grief would never have happened. Yet if I could go back to that cross-roads moment again I know I would inevitably make the same decision. Once a hunter, always a hunter: the inner compulsion hadn't loosened its grip: the quality they'd hauled me out of the Army for was too basic in my nature, and being what I was, what I am, slopping out of the chase was impossible. Keeble had known, I admitted wryly, that he had only to get me hooked.

'I must go,' I said, 'if I'm to find the horse.'

'Damn the horse,' Lynnie said.

I laughed at her. 'You've learnt quickly.'

'I like Eunice,' she said defensively. 'She doesn't shock me.'

I gathered from that that she certainly did, but that Lynnie would never admit it.

'But you will come back here? Before you go home, I mean?'

'I expect so,' I said.

She fiddled with her coffee cup, looking down. 'It's only a week since I picked you up at your flat, last Sunday.'

'And you've aged a year.'

She looked up quickly, startled. 'Why did you say that?'

'It was what you were thinking.'

'I know,' she said, puzzled, 'but I don't know how you do.'

'Crystal set in the attic. Intermittent though, unfortunately.'

'Just as well, if you ask me.' There was a healthy mockery on her laughing face. 'How would you like to be tuned in permanently to Eunice?'

Eunice herself trailed through the doorway at that moment wearing an electric blue wrapper and a manageable hangover. With both still in place, after two cups of coffee and a cigarette, she trundled Lynnie and me to the airport.

'Goodbye, you son of a bitch,' she said to me, as I stood beside her window. 'I guess you can come back any time you want to.'

Lynnie glanced at her sharply, with sudden speculation: growing up in front of one's eyes. I smiled goodbye to them both and walked away into the airport. From there I bus-stopped a thousand miles to Denver, and chartered a twin-engined Piper from a local firm for the last two hundred to Rock Springs.

The pilot chewed his nails savagely beside me all the way as if he were a dedicated auto-cannibal, and I arrived feeling sick.

On the hot late Sunday afternoon the little desert town looked lifeless. Shimmering air rose endlessly over the dump of abandoned rusting motor cars, a Greyhound bus rolled past with passengers staring like fish through its green glass windows, and sprinklers on the richer front lawns kept the parching heat at bay. At the bus station I learnt that old man Hagstrom's boy was the agent for Snail Express, but when I found old man Hagstrom, fanning himself in a rocker on the front porch of his small frame house, he said that his boy was out calling.

Hagstrom himself seemed to be glad to have company and told me to go inside and bring two beers out of the icebox. The icebox was in the living room, just through the screen door. It was a shambles of a room with sagging broken-spring chairs, dirty worn out rag rugs, a scattered assortment of cups, glasses, and bottles, all unwashed, and a vast new television. I took the beer out on to the porch, sat on the top step, and drank from the bottle, like my host.

The old man rocked, scratched himself, drank, and said vaguely that his boy would be right along, I could bet on it. I looked up and down the hot empty street. There were other shapes rocking gently in the shade of the porches, half invisible because many had the insect screens round the outside rails. From behind them they watched the world go by: only thing was, the world rolled past in automobiles and didn't stop to talk.

Two beers later, while old man Hagstrom was telling me how he personally would have dealt with the Saigon situation in '67, his boy rolled up in a pock-marked Chrysler. His boy was literally a boy, not more than eighteen: old man Hagstrom's grandson. He rubbed his hands down his grease-marked T-shirt and jeans, and held one out to me with as easy going a welcome as his grandfather's. I explained what I wanted.

'Sure you can look at the trailer,' he said, amiably. 'Now?'

'If you don't mind.'

'You're welcome.'

He waved me into his baking car and whirled it casually round a few corners, drawing up with a jerk outside a rickety looking gate set in a head-high wall. Through the gate, in a dusty area, stood four Snail Express trailers, all different sizes.

'That one,' I said, pointing to the largest.

'Came in last Saturday. I think. I'll look it up.' He unlocked a small brick-built office on one side, and I followed him in. Hot enough in there to please Satan.

'That's right, Saturday,' he said, consulting the ledger. 'Came from New York State, renting charge paid in advance for one week. The week wasn't up until Monday.'

'Do you remember who brought it here?'

'Uh, let's see. Oh yes. An old guy. Can't remember much about him. He had white hair, I guess.'

'What sort of car did he have, to pull the trailer?'

'I helped him unhitch . . . a station wagon, I think. Grey, mebbe.'

'It wasn't these two?' I showed him the photograph.

'Nope.' He was definite. As far as he knew, he'd never seen them. Had I asked his grandfather? I had.

He said he'd swept out the trailer, but I could look inside if I wanted to.

'Why did you sweep it?' I asked.

'Usually do. It was pretty clean already, though.'

I looked anyway. There were no bay hairs. Nothing at all to suggest that Chrysalis had ever been squeezed into it. The only suggestive thing about it was the way it was built: the roof opened outwards right along the centre line, to make the loading of tall objects easier. It had been worrying me that Chrysalis would not have walked into a tiny dark trailer: but one open to the sky was a different matter.

Old man Hagstrom's boy obligingly dug out the Hertz agent, who rented me an air-conditioned black Chevrolet with only five thousand on the clock. Overnight I added three hundred and thirty-four more, and drove into Gardiner for breakfast.

The road there had led through Yellowstone Park itself where the dawn had crept in mistily between the pine trees, and glimpses of lakes had looked like flat puddles of quick-silver. I had seen an ugly great moose, but no bears. Yogi was asleep.

I spent all morning walking round the town. None of the shops were selling the handkerchief, or had ever stocked any like it. The photograph produced no reactions at all. After a toasted bacon, tomato, and lettuce sandwich at a lunch counter I left Gardiner and went fifty-four miles to West Yellowstone.

The afternoon's trudge produced exactly the same absence of results. Hot, tired, and frustrated, I sat in the Chevrolet and wondered what to do next. No trace of Chrysalis in the trailer, even though it seemed likely it was the one the drivers had seen. No matching handkerchiefs at Yellowstone Park. Walt had been right. The trip was one pointless waste of time.

I thought of the long forest drive back through the park, the canyon gradients at midway, and the final hundred miles of desert to Rock Springs, and decided to put it off until the next day. Sighing, I found the best-looking motel and booked the best room they had, stood under the shower until the day's aches had run down the drain with the dust, and stretched out for a couple of hours on the kingsized Slumberland.

The waitress who brought my steak at dinner was large, loosely upholstered, kind natured, and with an obvious conviction that a man alone liked a bit of gossip. I wanted her to go away and let me eat in peace, but custom was slack and I learnt more than I cared about her complicated home life. In the end, simply to stop the flow, I pulled out the crumpled handkerchief and asked if she knew where I could get a new one like it.

She thought 'the girls' might know, and went off to ask them. Relieved, I finished my steak. Then she came back and doubtfully put the white square down beside me on the tablecloth.

'They say you might get one in Jackson. They do have bears on ashtrays and things down there. Down in the Tetons. A hundred, hundred-fifty miles. It's a holiday town, Jackson.'

I'd driven straight through Jackson the night before on the way up from Rock Springs, and seen only a small western town fast asleep. When I went back on the Tuesday morning it was buzzing with holiday-makers and local inhabitants, dressed all alike in cowboy clothes. Dude ranch country, I learnt. The main street was lined with souvenir shops, and the first one I went into had a whole pile of small white handkerchiefs with bears on.

CHAPTER EIGHT

The girl in the punt opened the ranch house door, walked halfway to meet me from the car, and greeted me with professional instant welcome.

'Mr Hochner? How nice to have you with us.'

'I'm glad you could take me at such short notice, with the Fourth coming up next weekend.' I shook her hand, putting a slight touch of German accent into my voice because it was easier for me than American if I had to keep it up for any length of time. It didn't seem altogether wise to be English.

'We're seldom full this early in the season.' She smiled as far up her face as her cheek bones while her eyes skimmed my clothes, car, and luggage. Only a hotel keeper's check up: it hadn't occurred to her that she'd seen me before.

'I'll show you straight to your cabin, if you like? Then you can freshen up and come along here to the ranch house for dinner later on. There will be a bell, to let you know when.'

I parked the car, and carrying my two suitcases, the

old one and the new one from Jackson, followed her along a grassy woodland track towards one of several small log cabins scattered among the trees.

She was tall and strong, and older than she had seemed on the river: twenty-six or twenty-seven, I guessed. The fair hair no longer hung childishly loose, but was combed up into a round topknot, leaving her neck cool and uncluttered. She wore dark blue Levis instead of the white trousers, but the pink shirt on top looked identical. One of the storekeepers in Jackson, the fifth I tried, had known her immediately when I had artistically let the photograph drop face up in front of him as I took money for a local map out of my wallet.

'Yola Clive,' he said casually, picking it up. 'And Matt. Friends of yours?'

'I'd thought of looking them up,' I agreed, sorting out bills. 'How do I get there, do you know? I haven't been to their place before.'

He obligingly gave me clear directions for a fifteen-mile drive, finishing, 'and the High Zee Ranch is the only place along there, so you can't miss it. But if you're planning on staying, I'd give them a call and make a reservation. It's a mighty popular place they run.'

'I sure will,' I said: and I did. I also bought some Levis and shirts and a pair of riding boots, and the suitcase to put them in. In cowboy country guns passed without comment: I added a heavy black tooled leather belt with a silver buckle, and the clerk didn't show any surprise at my wanting to make sure that the small-of-the-back holster I sometimes used would slot on to it.

Jackson preserved its own wild western flavour to the extent of a small authentic stage coach waiting in front of the drug store: but the sleepy disillusioned horses between the shafts looked a poor prospect against galloping redskins. Broad raised boardwalks edged with hitching rails ran along in front of the stores in the short main street, though the mud they had been built to avoid had long been metalled over. Motels with signs saying 'air-conditioning and central heating' were called 'Covered Wagon' and 'Rustlers' Hideout'. Jackson was an uneasy mixture of evolution and make believe, and clearly a success.

I sat in the sun on a hitching rail most of the afternoon: did a bit of thinking, and made two calls to Walt at Buttress Life.

Yola Clive led me round a neat stack of sawn logs, up two steps, across a minimal porch and through a screen door and a wood door into the cabin.

'Bathroom through there,' she said, pointing. 'And you'll probably need to light the stove in the evenings. The snows only melted here two or three weeks ago, and the nights are cold.' She smiled briefly and indicated a small tubful of a crumbly mixture which stood beside the squat black stove. 'Light the logs with two or three handfuls of that.'

'What is it?' I asked.

'Pep,' she said. 'A mixture of diesel oil and sawdust.' Her eyes glanced professionally round the room, checking that everything was in order. 'There's an ice machine out back of the kitchen, if you want to make drinks. Most guests bring their own liquor . . . We don't sell it ourselves. I expect you'll want to go riding tomorrow. We usually fix that up over dinner.' The half smile came and went, and Yola walked quietly away along the track.

Sighing, I investigated my quarters. There had been a reasonable compromise between age-old materials and modern construction, resulting in a sturdy two-roomed cabin with a pitch roof and varnished tree trunk walls. Two single beds stood on the polished wood floor in the main room, covered with patchwork quilts. A curtain across a half-shelved recess acted as closet, and the two upright chairs and the table were all home built. So, too, I discovered, were the towel rail, stool, and shelf in the bathroom. But the back-woods stopped short of the plumbing: and the lighting was ranch generated electric.

I unpacked on to the shelves and hangers, and changed from town clothes into Levis and a blue-and-white check shirt. The complete vacationer, I thought sourly: and buckled the gun belt round my waist.

After that for an hour I sat on the porch and looked at the view, which was good enough for a chocolate box. The Teton range of the Rocky Mountains stretched north and south, with dark green pine forests washing up from the valley to meet spotless snow-capped peaks. Along the bottom ran a sparkling thread of blue and silver, a tributary to the upper reaches of the one thousand mile Snake River: and between the river and the woods on whose edge my cabin stood, a wide stretch of sage brush and scrub was dotted with yellow weed-like flowers.

The woods around the cabin stood on the lower slopes of another ridge of peaks which rose sharp and high behind the ranch, shutting it in, close and private. The stream ran right along, in and out, but the only road into the narrow valley stopped dead in the parking area of the High Zee.

A bell clanged loudly up at the ranch house. I went back into the cabin and put on a sloppy black sweater which hid the Luger and looked reasonable at nine thousand two hundred feet above sea level, though the still persisting heatwave was doing a good job in the mountains too. Walking slowly along the dusty grass track I wondered if Matt Clive would know me. I certainly had no clear memory of his face on the punt, though I now knew it well from the photograph. It was unlikely, since his full attention must have been concentrated on Dave Teller, that he had taken much notice of me; but he might possibly have a sharper impression than Yola, as I had been closer to him when I went in after Dave.

I needn't have wondered. He wasn't there.

Yola sat at one end of a long golden wood table flanked by chattering well-dug-in ranch guests. Family groups, mostly, and three married couples. No singles except me. A bright well-coiffured mother invited me to sit beside her, and her hearty husband opposite asked if I'd had a long drive. On the other side of me a small boy told his parents loudly that he didn't like stuffed pancakes, and every face round the table looked sunburned, vital, and overflowing with holiday spirits. I battened down a fierce urge to get up and go out, to get away from all that jollity. I didn't see how I was ever going to make the effort to look as if I were enjoying myself.

By the end of the meal it felt as if my smile were set in plaster, rigid and mechanical to the extent that my face ached with producing it. But the hearty man opposite, Quintus L. Wilkerson III, 'Call me Wilkie,' seemed pleased to have a practically non-speaking audience, and made the most of it. I endured a splash by splash account of his day's fishing. His wife Betty-Ann had ridden to the lake with him, and then gone on into the hills in a party containing her two children, Samantha and Mickey. I heard about that too, from all three of them. They asked me to ride with their party the next day, and I wrenched my tongue into saying I'd be glad to.

I lasted out the coffee. The Wilkersons promised

to see me at breakfast, and Yola asked if I were comfortable in the cabin.

'Thank you, yes.' Remembering the German accent. Smile.

'That's fine,' she said brightly, her eyes sliding past. 'Ask if there's anything you need.'

I walked stiffly out of the ranch house and along the dark track to the empty cabin; leaned wearily against one of the posts holding up the porch roof and looked at the row of peaks glimmering palely in shifting moonlight, with streaky cloud across the sky. My head ached with a feeling of compression, as if my brain wanted to expand and fill up with air.

How could I go on like this, I thought. Dinner had been about as much as I could manage. I didn't know what to do about it. No use praying: no faith. If I went to a doctor I'd get a bottle of tonic and a homily about pulling myself together. There was absolutely nothing to be done but endure it, and go on with that until it got better. If I could only convince myself that it would in the end get better, at least I would have something to cling to.

Somewhere in the valley a stallion shrieked.

Maybe it was Chrysalis. If he wasn't actually on the High Zee Ranch I thought the chances very high that he was somewhere near. Maybe Keeble did know what he was doing sending me to find him, because it was evident that I could still function normally on the work level: concentration acted like a switch which cut out the personal chaos. If I concentrated twenty-four hours a day, life would be simple.

One trouble with that. It was impossible.

The ranch held upwards of a hundred and twenty horses. About forty of them were penned in a big corral near the main ranch house, saddle horses for the ranch guests to ride.

Breakfast had been early, but the fitting of guests to horses took some time, even though everyone except me had been there two or three days and knew which animal they wanted. The head wrangler asked me if I could ride, and if so, how well.

'I haven't been on a horse for nine or ten years,' I said.

He gave me a dead quiet one with U-shaped hocks. The western saddle seemed like an armchair after the postage stamp I'd been teethed on: and there were no new-fangled things like buckles for raising and lowering stirrups. The head wrangler unlaced the thong holding the three-inch-wide leathers to the saddle, slid them down two or three holes, and laced them up again. Good soft leather, which could go all day and not rub the horse.

Over to one side of the ranch house, past its green watered lawn, there was a smallish sturdily railed paddock of not more than an acre. I'd spent all breakfast looking out of the window at the seven horses in it.

Three mares, two small foals, two stallions. Both the stallions were bays, but one had a white blaze and was no thoroughbred.

'What are those horses over there?' I asked the wrangler, pointing.

He paused a second while he worked out how to put it delicately to an ignorant dude, and foreigner into the bargain, and then said, 'We breed most of the horses, on this ranch.'

'Oh, I see,' I said. 'Do you have many stallions?'

'Three or four. Most of these', he glanced round the patiently waiting mounts, 'are geldings.'

'That's a nice looking bay,' I commented.

He followed my eyes over to the small paddock again. 'He's new,' he said. 'A half-bred Matt bought in Laramie two or three weeks back.' There was disapproval in his tone.

'You don't like him?' I said.

'Not enough bone for these hills,' he said briefly, finishing the second stirrup. 'Now, is that comfortable?'

'Fine,' I said. 'Thank you.'

He nodded with casual friendliness and went to see to someone else. The wranglers differed from the dudes only in the matters of age and dress. They were all boys or young men between eighteen and thirty, several of them college boys working their vacation. The dudes were either parents or children; scarcely one in the twenties. No one, Betty-Ann Wilkerson told me knowledgeably, called cowboys cowboys anywhere except in films. Cowhand was possible, but the right word was wrangler. There were no cattle on the High Zee. The wranglers herded the horses, and the horses were there for the dudes to ride.

In the matter of clothes the wranglers were less flamboyant, less well pressed, altogether dustier. They had been up since five-thirty and other people's holidays were their hard work.

'They turn the horses out on the hills every night,' Wilkie explained, 'and go up and herd them down in the morning.'

We set off from the ranch in two parties, about twelve guests and two wranglers in each. Down over a flat wooden bridge across the narrow river, and up into the main Teton range opposite. Wilkie rode in front of me and Betty-Ann behind as we wound upwards through the woods in single file; and neither of them tired of talking.

'They turn the horses out on the hills over here because there isn't enough pasture in the valley to feed them.' Wilkie turned half round in his saddle to make sure I could hear. 'They go miles away, most nights. The wranglers fix a bell on to some of them, like cowbells in Switzerland, so that they can find them in the morning. The ones they put bells on are the sort of natural leaders, the horses other horses like to be with.' He smiled heartily. 'It's sure difficult to see them sometimes, with the sun shining through the trees and making shadows.'

What he said was true because we passed a group of three in a hollow later on, and I didn't see them until one moved his head and clinked his bell.

'They only bring in the number they need,' Betty-Ann filled in. 'They just leave the rest out, and maybe bring some of them in tomorrow, if they come across them first.'

'So sometimes a horse could be out for a week at a time?' I suggested.

'I guess so,' Wilkie said vaguely. He didn't really know. 'Of course, if they want one particular horse, the wranglers will go right up the mountain to find him, I do know that.'

'Anyone who can ride well enough can go up with the wranglers in the morning,' Betty-Ann said. 'But they *canter* up and down here instead of walk.'

The path was steep and also rocky.

'These horses are born to it, honey,' said Wilkie kindly. 'Not like the riding school horses back home.'

At eleven thousand feet the path levelled out on to a small tree-shaded plateau overlooking a breathtaking pine-wooded valley with a brilliant blue lake in its depths. The cameras came out and clicked excitedly. The chattering voices exclaimed over an order of beauty that demanded silence. And eventually we rode down again.

Yola asked me at lunch if I had enjoyed my morning, and I said without difficulty that I had. The Wilkerson children were calling me Hans and asked me to swim in the stream with them in the afternoon. Wilkie clapped me heartily on the shoulder and told me I was a good guy, and Betty-Ann had irritatingly begun looking at me in a way which would change her husband's mind about that instantly, if he noticed.

I left the lunch table last and whisked away a large slice of bread in a paper napkin. Alone in my cabin I unpacked some specially acquired groceries, filled one pocket with sugar cubes, and on the bread scooped out a whole tin of sardines. With the bread still held in the napkin I walked down through the sage brush and along to the mares' and foals' paddock, reaching it on the far side from the ranch house.

There I offered sugar in one hand and sardines in the other. The mares came and sniffed, and all chose sugar. The foals chose sugar. The bay with the white blaze chose sugar. The dusty half-bred that Matt bought two or three weeks ago in Laramie came last, less curious than the rest.

He sniffed at the sardines and raised his head with his ears pricked, staring across at the high Tetons as if hearing some far off sound, smelling some distant scent. His nostrils quivered gently. I looked at the splendid lines of bone in the skull, the gracefully slanted eye, the perfect angle of head on neck. He had the crest of a thoroughbred stallion, and the hocks of a racehorse.

He bent his head down to the sardines and ate the lot.

*

Yola and Matt Clive lived in a cabin of their own, separate from the main ranch house, which contained only the dining room, kitchens, sitting room, and wet day games room for the guests.

Yola backed an olive-drab pick-up with small white lettering on its doors out of a shady carport beside her cabin, and drove away down the dusty road. I stared after her, half amazed, half smiling. Full marks to the horse van drivers, I thought. They'd seen both the Snail Express van and the pick-up. They must have seen them both several times, but even so, they'd remembered.

Guests were allowed to use the telephone, which was located in the Clives' cabin. I strolled over there, knocked on the door, and found the place empty. Not locked, though in this case there was a key. There were no locks on any of the guest cabin doors: one could only bolt them on the inside, with a simple wooden wedge slotted into the latch.

A quick tour of the Clives' cabin revealed two separate single bedrooms, living room, kitchen, bathroom, and office. I planted three hypersensitive listening devices as invisibly as possible, and unhurriedly left.

After that I climbed into the Chevrolet and drove myself back to Jackson, where the telephone was more private. My call to Buttress Life lasted a long time, and Walt's contribution to the second part of the conversation consisted of gasps and protests of 'You can't.'

'Listen, Walt,' I said in the end. 'We're not policemen. I imagine your company would settle for the property back and no questions asked? And my brief is to restore Chrysalis to Dave Teller. Just that. Nothing more. If we start things the way you want, we'll end up with a lot of smart lawyers and most probably a dead horse.'

There was a long pause. 'All right,' he said slowly. 'OK. You win.'

He wrote down a long list of instructions. 'This is Wednesday,' I said, thinking aloud. 'Sunday morning. That gives you three clear days. Should be enough.'

'Only just.'

'Never mind,' I said soothingly. 'You can do most of it sitting down.'

Walt wasn't amused. 'And you, what exactly will you be doing?' he asked sarcastically.

'On a dude ranch,' I said reasonably, 'one dudes.'

At the Post Office I mailed off to him by express delivery six hairs from the mane of the sardine horse, and motored back to the grim business of acting the holiday I'd feared from the start.

The three days seemed eternal. Riding took up the mornings and most afternoons and that was the best of it. Meals continued to be a desperate trial. The nights were long. I wished that Lynnie could have come with me, because in her company the depression seemed to retreat, but she was Eunice's crutch, not mine. And her father, trust me as he might, would have found it hard to believe I would only ask for her daytime closeness. And maybe I couldn't have done it. So no props. No props at all.

Yola ran the ranch with a sort of super-efficiency which looked easy, juggling staff and guests into harmony without a single wrinkle of anxiety and without any show of aggression. The fair hair continued to be worn tidily on top. Her clothes were jeans and shirt and soft flat shoes. No boots: no masculinity. She radiated friendliness and confidence, and her smile never once reached her eyes.

She didn't go riding with her guests, and I never sat next to her at meals because most of the husbands and many of the wives conducted a dignified scramble for her favours, but on Thursday evening, when with several others I was drinking after-dinner coffee out in the open on the long porch, she dropped gracefully down into the empty chair beside me, and asked if I were enjoying my holidays, and was finding my cabin comfortable.

I answered with half-true platitudes, to which she half listened.

'You are young,' I said next, with great politeness, 'to own so beautiful a place.'

She replied to this small probe with frank ease. 'It belonged to my grandfather and then to my mother. She died a year or two back.'

'Has it always been a dude ranch? I mean, it seems a bit hilly for cattle . . .'

'Always a dude ranch,' she agreed. 'My grandfather

built it about forty years ago . . . How did you hear of us?'

I glanced at her unhurriedly, but she was merely curious, not suspicious.

'I asked in Jackson for somewhere good and fairly quiet, out in the mountains.'

'Who recommended us?'

'Just a man in the street.'

She nodded, satisfied.

'What do you do in the winter?' I asked.

There was a flicker in the eyes and a quick private smile on the mouth: whatever she did in the winter pleased her more than hotel keeping.

'We move down south. Snow completely blocks this valley from November through March. Most years it's May before we come back . . . We usually open the ranch the second week in June, but the canyons are often impassable then.'

'What do you do with the horses?'

'Oh, they go down to the plain, on a friend's ranch.'

Her voice was as strong and capable as the rest of her. I watched her eyes slide round towards the paddock with the mares and foals, and pause there calmly, and return to me. Expressionless.

I smiled her a force five version of an adults-only smile, and asked if she ever found it lonely, so far out in the wilds. To this mild but unmistakable come-on there was no reaction beyond a crisp shake of the head. I was the only man there not guarded by a watchful wife: Yola wasn't in the least bit interested.

I complimented her on the ranch food, and on the helpfulness of the wranglers. She said she was glad I was pleased. I yawned and apologized, and said it must be all the fresh air ... she'd heard it all dozens of times a year, said everything she'd said so often that she no longer had to think. No use on this occasion using any jolting technique to force out an unguarded phrase: jolting her was roughly the last thing I wanted to do.

After a while I stood up lazily and said I would turn in, and she gave me the usual meaningless half-way-up smile. She hadn't really seen me at all: wouldn't remember me in another month. Unless I inadvertently gave her cause.

The three bugs in her cabin worked on the audio-switch principle: any noise, and speech especially, which they picked up, automatically started the recording machine which occupied the back half of the ordinary looking transistor radio standing beside my bed. But there was little to overhear. Yola slept alone, and apart from one evening when she invited four of the guests in for a drink, the only conversations were telephone calls.

In my cabin each evening, warming by the squat black stove, I played back the day's 'take'. Nearly all the calls were to do with business: grocery orders, laundry, blacksmith's supplies, and future bookings.

But one call, on Friday evening, was worth all the trouble.

'Uncle Bark?' Yola's voice said, low and clear. One of the bugs was behind a picture of drooping roses on the wall over the telephone table.

'. . . honey.' The occasional word escaped from the receiver in return, but Yola must have been holding it close to her ear.

'Sure. Everything's fine here,' she said. 'Absolutely no kind of trouble.'

'. . . Matt? . . .'

'That's what I called about, Uncle Bark. Matt wrote me he's having to give up in Europe. He says he can't get near to you-know-who, they've got him holed up as tight as Fort Knox. So I guess we'll just have to keep everything under wraps for a while longer.'

'. . .'

'It sure is a nuisance, yeah. But as long as we get him to you before the snows come again . . .'

'. . .'

'How can we? You know it isn't built for that.'

'. . . stay . . .'

'We certainly can't send him down to Clint's with the others. We'd waste a whole year and he might break a leg or something.'

'. . . desert.'

'We don't want him at Pitts, it isn't built for it. But there's a good long time for Matt to arrange something.'

'. . . hadn't started.'

'Yeah, I'm sure you would. But it's too late now. How were we to know that something so goddam stupid would happen? Matt will probably be home some time tomorrow. I'll have him call you.'

She put down the receiver soon after that: and I wound back the tape and played the conversation over again. Two unsubstantial points emerged. If Dave Teller had been too obviously guarded, Matt would have realized that the punt episode was not considered to be an accident. And the something 'goddam stupid' which had somewhere or other upset the Clives' original plans might be that I'd been there to fish Dave out of the river, or might be something else quite different; something which had made the removal of Dave necessary in the first place. The horse had been stolen on June 15th, Tuesday, and Yola had asked the London hotel for Dave's weekend address on June 19th, Saturday. So what, if anything, had happened in the four days between? Something goddam stupid . . .

I told Yola after breakfast on Saturday morning that I had enjoyed my stay immensely and would be leaving the following day. She smiled the regulation smile without clearly focusing, and thanked me for letting her know.

'So if I could have my bill at breakfast tomorrow?' I suggested.

'Sure,' she said. 'But you can't stay over Monday for the Fourth?'

'I'm afraid not.'

She nodded, not caring one way or the other. 'I'll get it ready for you, then.'

The Wilkersons exclaimed over my going. 'You'll miss the barbecue,' Samantha said. 'And the float trip down the river.'

A local man took parties down the fast flowing Snake on black inflated rubber raft dinghies: one of the area's attractions, like the rodeo and the ski lift. The Wilkersons had asked me to join them. 'Maybe I'll come back next year,' I said. And maybe I wouldn't.

I looked after the children that afternoon while Betty-Ann went to the hairdresser and Wilkie drove to a distant lake for the fishing. They swam in the stream, where I refused to join them in case my head in the water jogged Yola's sleeping memory, and we fed sugar and handfuls of grass through the rails to the leggy foals in the little paddock. The rails were solid young tree trunks dove-tailed and nailed into even sturdier posts, and the gate was just as substantial. Its hinges were bolted through the gatepost, and a heavy padlock fastened it through two strong hasps. None of this strength was new.

Samantha and Mickey didn't think much of the sardine bay.

'Too spindly,' Mickey said. 'His legs would snap if he went up the mountain.' I looked across at the Teton range, the tops shining white in the hot sun. The sure-footed born-to-it ranch horses picked their way easily up and down the steep rocky paths over there, through the woods growing with flat huckleberry leaves, across the screes left from landslips, and on to the bare stony patches above the snow line.

'Why don't you stay till Monday night?' said Mickey. 'If you go tomorrow, you'll miss the fireworks.'

CHAPTER NINE

At one o'clock, early Sunday morning, I stood on the porch of my cabin waiting for my eyes to dilate, and listening to the night.

A slight wind, riffling the trees. A car horn, very distant. The faint hum of the electric generator in its special house. No sound from Yola's cabin. None all evening. Matt hadn't yet come home.

With some misgivings I had left my riding boots in the cabin, and wore only thin rubber-soled plimsolls, with a pair of socks on top. I walked quietly through the sage brush on the long way round to the little paddock, the spicy fragrance rising into my nose as I disturbed the silver-grey leaves. The half moonlight was enough to see by without a torch and streaky clouds made shifting shadows across the ground: it couldn't have been better if I'd sent in an order.

The padlock's strength was illusory. It had a simple lever movement inside which took me less than five minutes to fiddle open. No one could have heard the click of success. Nor the tiny squeak of the gate opening. I slipped through and distributed sugar to the mares and foals. The bay with the white blaze greeted this with a trumpeting whinny; but no lights went on in Yola's cabin or the wranglers' bunkhouse.

The sardine horse flared his nostrils at me but ate the sugar and let me slip over his head the simple rope halter I had come armed with. I spent some time rubbing his nose and patting his neck, and when I walked towards the gate he came with me docilely enough. I opened the gate and led him through, and the mares and foals quietly followed, their unshod hooves making dull little clops on the loamy ground.

The gentle procession went slowly across towards the river, over the flat bridge with hollow thuds, and up into the darkness of the pine woods. The mares soon stopped to graze, and the foals with them, but the bay stallion with the blaze suddenly realized he was free again, and crashed past me at high speed, squealing and cantering up the path and making as much noise as a train-load of football supporters. Anxious, heart-quickened moments passed: but still no reaction from below.

The sardine bay tugged hard to follow. I soothed him and steadied him, and we presently walked on. He picked his way too cautiously over the stones and corners of rocks sticking up in the narrow path, but I couldn't hurry him without risk; my neck prickled at the thought of being slung into a Wyoming jail for horse stealing; but it was nothing to the fear I had that Mickey might be right about those spindly legs.

In places all the way up the width of the path dwindled to two feet, with a wall of rock on one side and a steep slope on the other. Riding along them by day one simply had to trust that one's horse wouldn't tumble over the edge, as nothing could then have stopped a rock-strewn descent of two or three hundred feet. At these points there wasn't room to walk side by side with a horse one was leading: I inched up the path ahead of him, and slowly, cautiously, he put his feet delicately down between the bigger stones, and scrunched after me.

Two or three times we passed small groups of horses from the ranch, the cow bell clanking gently round the neck of the leader and betraying their presence. Their dark shapes melted into the jumbled background of woods and rocks, and the moonlight picked out only an eye, a rump, a swishing tail. The wranglers found them each morning by tracking, as the bells were only audible for a furlong. I'd had a long talk with one of the boys about tracking, and he'd shown me how they did it. They were going to be able to follow my way up the mountain as clearly as if I'd given them directions, and to tell the time I went by the amount of dew which formed in the hoof prints. The boy had shown me hoof prints, told me how many horses had gone by and when, and all I had seen were some scattered dusty marks. They read the ground like a book. If I tried to obliterate the sardine horse's hoof prints, I obliterated also any chance of the Clives believing he had wandered off by accident. The fuzzy outline of plimsolls under socks was, I hoped, going to pass unnoticed: nothing less was worth the discomfort of wearing them on such jagged going.

It took two hours to reach twelve thousand feet and to come to the end of the tracks I'd learnt in the past four days. From there it was a case of trusting my own nose. The drifting streaks of cloud made black shadows like pits across the rocks and several times I stood still and felt ahead with one toe to make sure that the ground was in fact still there, and I was not stepping straight off a precipice. The moon itself, and the cold mountain air moving against my right cheek, kept me going in the right general direction, but the dotted-line trail I had studied on the map proved more optimistic than actual.

The horse's legs stood up to it remarkably well. Mine had already had enough. Mountaineering was not among Civil Service requirements.

The peak of the Grand Teton rose to thirteen thousand seven hundred feet. The summit loomed very close. Patches of snow, half melted, exposed black looking banks of scree. I came suddenly across a narrow trail winding past them like an eel: people had walked along there recently, scraping into the snow. I had, with some luck, come the right way. The cold bit down under my black jersey and through the thin shirt underneath, and I wished I had had the sense to bring gloves. But it couldn't be a great deal farther: through the short canyon pass, and out the other side. I looked at my watch. The climb had taken nearly three hours and I was late.

It was darker in the canyon, but also invisible from the valley below. I took the small torch out of my jeans pocket, and shone it in front of my feet. Because of that, the whole expedition came unstuck.

A man suddenly rounded a corner a short way ahead and stood foursquare in the centre of the trail. Startled even more than I was, the horse backed instantly away, tore the rope out of my hand, pulled me flat over as I tried to hang on, and skipped sharply away along a narrow ridge branching off to the left.

Sick and furious I got back on my feet and turned to go after him. The man took a tentative step down the trail and called out.

'Gene?'

It was Walt.

I bit my tongue literally to stop the rage in my mind from spilling over him. There wasn't time for it.

'I saw you coming. The light,' he explained. 'I thought I'd come along to meet you. You're later than you said.'

'Yes.' I shut my mouth. There was half a million pounds loose in a death trap. My responsibility, and my fault.

The moon pushed out a feeble twenty watts. I

couldn't see the horse. The path he had taken in panic was a ledge eighteen inches wide with sheer rock on the left and a fierce slope of scree on the right. A gradient so steep that it was as dangerous as a straight down drop: and in its black invisible depths there would be the usual big slabs with upjutting edges.

'Stay here,' I said to Walt. 'And keep quiet.'

He nodded without speaking, understanding that the situation was beyond apology. His instructions had been expressly to wait for me at one arranged spot.

The ledge was thirty feet long with a bend to the left. I walked along it slowly, not using the torch, my left hand trailing along the rock wall, the grey light just enough to show the crumbly uneven outer edge.

After thirty feet the ledge widened into a saucer-shaped bowl three quarters surrounded by towering rocks. The sloping floor of the bowl led directly into the sharper slope of the scree. On the floor of the bowl, patchy snow and rough black pebble.

The horse was standing there, sweating. Quivering in every rigid limb. There was no way out except back along the ledge.

I stroked his muzzle and gave him four lumps of sugar, speaking gently to him in a voice much calmer than my feelings. It took ten minutes for the excessive tension to leave his body, and another five before he would move. Then I turned him carefully round until he was facing the way he had come.

Horses react instantly to human fear. The only

chance I had of getting him safely back was to walk round there as if it were a broad concrete path across his own stable yard. If he smelt fear, he wouldn't come.

Where the ledge began, he baulked. I gave him more sugar and more sweet talk. Then I turned my back on him and with the halter rope leading over my shoulder, walked slowly away. There was the faintest of protesting backward tugs. Then he came.

Thirty feet had never seemed so interminable. But an animal's sixth sense kept him from putting a foot over the edge, and the slithering clop of his hooves on the broken ground came steadily after me all the way.

Walt, this time, made no sound at all. I came across him standing motionless several yards up the intended trail and he turned without speaking and went on ahead.

Less than half a mile farther the path descended and widened into a broad sweeping basin: and there, where Walt had been supposed to meet me, waited another man, stamping his feet to keep warm.

Sam Kitchens. Holding another horse.

With a powerful torch he inspected every inch of the one I'd brought, while I held his.

'Well?' I said.

He nodded. 'It's Chrysalis all right. See that tiny scar up there, under his shoulder? He cut himself on a metal gate post one day when he was a two-year-old and a bit full of himself. And these black dots, sort of freckles, along that patch of his belly. And the way his hide grows in a whirl just there inside his hock. He always had clean legs. There's a mark or two on them now that wasn't there when I had him. But apart from knowing him from his general shape, like, I'd certainly swear to those other things in any court you'd like to mention.'

'Was the cut from the gate post bad enough to be treated by a vet?'

He nodded. 'Five or six stitches.'

'Good,' I said. 'Then off you go with him. And take good care.'

Sam Kitchens grinned. 'Who'd have thought I'd have seen him again up the Rocky Mountains in the middle of the night? Never you mind, I'll take care all right.'

He turned Chrysalis expertly round, clicking his tongue affectionately, and began the mile-long walk down to the Teton camping ground, to where he and Walt and Sam Hengelman had come in a horse box.

Walt said, 'It's too late for you to go back. Come with us.'

I shook my head. 'I'll meet you in Idaho Falls as we arranged.'

Walt moved uncomfortably. 'It's not safe to go back.'

'I'll be fine. You just get the two Sams cracking. They've got to be well on their way before dawn. They've got that bill of sale?'

Walt nodded, looking at the big mountain pony beside me.

'He cost five hundred dollars. One bay horse, no markings, entire, aged seven or eight. As ordered. That's what the bill of sale says, and that's what we've got in the van, if anyone asks. Sam Kitchens chose it. Said it was as near as you would get, without actually paying thousands for a blood horse.'

'This one looks fine. See you, then, Walt.'

He stood in silence while I levered myself on to the new horse's bare back and gathered up the reins. I nodded to him, turned away, and started back up the trail to the canyon.

Late, I thought. Almost too late, now. The wranglers would be high up in the hills by six, rounding up the horses. Dudes rode as usual on Sunday mornings. It was already five, and the first greyness of dawn had crept in as the moon faded. If they saw me out so early, I was in trouble.

At a jog trot, his sturdy legs absolutely at home on the terrain, the new horse took me back up into the canyon, past the fearful little ridge that Chrysalis had taken, and out on to the Clive valley side of the Tetons. From there down I looked out for a bunch of High Zee horses, but I was well below the snow line before I heard any of the bells.

There was a little group in a tree-filled hollow. They moved away at my approach, but slowly, and when I was among them and stopped, they stopped also. I slid off the horse I was riding, threaded my fingers through the mane of one of the High Zee group, and transferred the bridle from one to the other. Then, leaving Dave Teller's five-hundred-dollar purchase free on the hill, I pointed my new mount's nose homewards, and gave him a kick.

He knew the way, and he consequently could go much faster. The Wilkersons had told me the wranglers cantered down those steep rocky inclines, but until I did it I hadn't imagined what a hair-raising business it would be. The horse put his feet where I would have said no man could balance, let alone a quadruped, and when I turned him off the regular path he hardly slackened his pace. We went headlong downwards through pines and alders and groves of silver-trunked dead trees, back to the thicker woods with patches of grass underfoot, and more undergrowth of huckleberry and sapling. There was one sticky incline of black bog where a mountain stream had spilled out sideways on to a slope of earth, but my pony staggered across it, tacking downwards, sinking in to his knees at every step. Farther on, he crossed the tumbling stream itself, picking his way through a mass of underwater rocks, and lower still he went straight down a bare pebbly slope where the normal path ran from side to side in easier zigzags. Whippy branches caught at us under the trees, but I laid my head flat beside his ears, and where he could go, I went too.

The gentle dude rides had been no preparation for

this reckless descent, and the one or two point-to-points I'd tried in my teens were distant memories and milksop stuff in comparison. But skills learnt in childhood stay for ever: balance still came instinctively. I didn't fall off.

We kept up the pace until there was less than a mile to go, then I veered the pony along to the right, up along the valley and away from the bridge to the ranch.

The wranglers would no doubt follow him up there to round him up, but I hadn't time to do the whole detour on foot. It was too light and too late to get back into the ranch across the bridge. I was going to have to cross the stream higher up and go down to my cabin through the woods on the far side.

I slid off the pony nearly half a mile upstream, and took off the bridle. The rough brown hide was streaked dark with sweat, and he didn't look at all like an animal who had spent a peaceful night grazing. I gave him a slap and he trotted away, wheeling round and upwards, back on to the hill. With luck the wranglers wouldn't find him until he'd cooled down, especially as it wouldn't be him they'd be looking for.

I could hear the panic going on down by the ranch house as soon as I stepped cautiously out of the woods and began the freezing cold traverse of the stream. The stones dug into my bare feet, and the water splashed my rolled-up trouser legs. But as I couldn't from where I was see any of the buildings, I trusted that no one there could see me. The shouts came up clearly, and then the thud of several horses cantering across the bridge. By the time I was across the stream and sitting down to put on my shoes again, they were going up towards the woods, and I could see them. Six wranglers, moving fast. If they looked back, they could see my head and shoulders sticking up out of the stretch of sage brush.

A hundred yards of it between me and the safety of the trees on the ranch-house side of the valley. I lay down flat on the ground for a few exhausted minutes, looking up at the dawn-filled sky: a high clear pale blue taking over from grey. The tracks of the mares and foals and both the stallions led straight uphill. I gave the wranglers time to go some way after them, and then quietly got to my feet and slipped unhurriedly across the sage brush and down through the trees to my cabin.

It was ten past six. Broad daylight.

I pulled off my filthy sweaty clothes and ran a deep hot bath. Tiredness had gone down to the bone, and the water tingled like a friction rub on my skin. Relaxing, reviving, I stayed in it for half an hour.

The tape played back for me the heavy knocking on Yola's door and the head wrangler telling her that the mares and stallions were out.

'What do you mean, out?'

'The tracks lead down to the bridge. They're out on the hills.'

'What?' Yola's voice screeched as the full meaning hit her. 'They can't be.'

'They sure are.' The wrangler's voice was much calmer. He didn't know the size of the disaster: wasn't in the game. 'But I can't understand it. The padlock was fastened like you said it must be, when I checked around yesterday evening.'

'Get them back,' said Yola sharply. 'Get them back.' Her voice rose hysterically. 'That new stallion. Get him. Get him back.'

There were sounds after that of drawers being pulled roughly open, and a door slamming, and silence. Yola was out looking for Chrysalis. And, Chrysalis was on his way to Kentucky.

The ranch guests knew all about it, at breakfast.

'What a fuss,' Wilkie said. 'You'd think they'd lost the deeds to a goldmine.'

They had.

'I'm glad they found the dear little foals anyway,' Samantha said.

'They've found them?' I asked. The small paddock was still empty.

'They've put them in the barn,' agreed Mickey. 'With their mothers.'

'Someone left the gate unlocked,' Betty-Ann told me. 'Isn't it a shame? Yola's obviously in a fearful state.'

Yola had been in the dining room when I strolled in to breakfast, standing silent and rigid by the kitchen door, checking that all the guests were there, looking for signs of guilt.

Poise had deserted her. The hair was roughly tied with a ribbon at the nape of her neck and the lipstick was missing. There had been no professional reassuring smiles. A muscle twitched in the strong jaw and she hadn't been in control of the wildness in her eyes.

I ate a double order of bacon and buckwheat hotcakes with maple syrup, and drank three cups of coffee.

Betty-Ann opposite me lit a cigarette and said did I have to leave, couldn't I stay another few days. Wilkie gruffly said they shouldn't try to keep a feller. Wilkie had cottoned on, and was glad to see me go.

Strong footsteps came into the room from the door behind me. Betty-Ann looked over my head and her eyes widened.

'Why hello there,' she exclaimed warmly, transferring her attentions. 'How good to see you.'

Wilkie, I thought in amusement, should be used to it by now. But the Wilkersons' problems blinked out of my mind for ever when someone else called the new man by his name.

Matt.

Matt Clive spoke from behind my shoulder; a drawling bass voice under strict control.

'Listen folks. I guess you know we've had a little

trouble here this morning. Someone let out the mares and horses from their paddock over there. Now if it was any of you kids, we'd sure like to know about it.'

There was a short silence. The various children looked uncomfortable and their parents' eyebrows peaked into question marks.

'Or if anyone knows that the gate wasn't properly fastened yesterday at any time?'

More silence.

Matt Clive walked tentatively round the long table, into my line of sight. About Yola's age, Yola's height. Same jawline. Same strong body, only more so. I remembered the two bedrooms in their cabin: the ringless fingers of Yola's hand. Yola's brother, Matt. I drank my coffee and avoided meeting his eyes.

One or two of the guests laughingly mentioned rustlers, and someone suggested calling in the police. Matt said they were seriously thinking of it. One of the stallions was quite valuable. But only, of course, if it was absolutely certain that none of the guests had left the gate open by accident.

Sympathetic murmurs were all he got. He might indeed be brave enough, or desperate enough, to call in the police. But if he did, they wouldn't recover Chrysalis, who should by now be hundreds of miles away on a roundabout route, accompanied by a strictly legal bill of sale.

Matt eventually went away, trailing a thunderous aura and leaving the guests unsettled and embarrassed.

I asked the girl who waited at table if she could fetch my account for me, as I wanted to pay up before leaving, and after an interval she returned with it. I gave her cash, and waited while she wrote a receipt.

The Wilkerson family said their goodbyes, as they were hoping to go riding if any of the wranglers had come back from searching for the missing horse, and I walked unhurriedly back to my cabin to finish packing. Up the two steps, across the porch, through the two doors, and into the room.

Yola came out of the bathroom carrying a rifle. The way she handled it showed she knew how to use it. Matt stepped from behind the curtained closet, between me and the way out. No rifle for him. A shotgun.

I put on the puzzled act, German accent stronger.

'Excuse me. I do not understand.'

'It's the same man,' Matt said. 'Definitely.'

'Where's our horse?' said Yola furiously.

'I do not know,' I said truthfully, spreading my hands out in a heavy shrug. 'Why do you ask such a question?'

Both the guns were pointing steadfastly my way.

'Excuse me,' I said, 'I have my packing to finish. I have paid the bill. I am leaving this morning.'

'You're not going anywhere, friend,' Matt said grimly.

'Why not?'

'You get that horse back here, and then you can go. Not before.'

He was going to have a fine old time if he intended to keep a prisoner silent indefinitely on a ranch full of holiday guests.

'I can't get him back,' I said. 'I don't know where he is. Several friends of mine, however, do know where I am. They will be expecting me to be leaving here this morning.'

They stared at me in silent fury. Children in crime, I thought, for all their ingenuity. They had walked straight in with their guns without thinking clearly through. They were, however, lethal children, ruled by impulse more than reason.

I said, 'I am unlikely to go around saying "I stole a horse from the Clives." If you do nothing, and I now drive safely away, you may hear no more of it. That's the best I can offer. You will not, whatever you do, recover the horse.'

The only sensible course open to them was to let me go. But Yola's finger tightened on the trigger, and I reluctantly decided it was time for the Luger. Watching her, I saw a split second too late in the looking glass that Matt had taken a step behind me and was swinging his gun butt like a bludgeon.

He caught me solidly across the back of the skull and the patchwork quilt on the bed dazzled into kaleidoscopic fragments in my glazing eyes as I went down.

CHAPTER TEN

When I woke up it was pretty clear that I wasn't intended to be a hostage, but a corpse.

The cabin was full of smoke, and small flames rose in a long uneven swathe across the floor. I couldn't remember anything at first. Looked at the scene muzzily, half sitting up, my head dizzy and splitting with pain. The Clives, I thought. They'd emptied the whole tub of pep out into a straggling line, and set it alight. Sawdust and diesel oil burning slowly and billowing out unbreathable gases.

They'd laid me against the stove so that it would seem as if I'd fallen and hit my head on it. The empty pep tin rolled away from my foot as I tried to get up, and my hand brushed against a cigarette and a book of matches.

Most deaths in fires weren't caused by burns but by asphyxia. The cabin wouldn't burn down from fire on the floorboards: fire never burnt downwards, only up. The Clives were staging my exit for no better motive than revenge. And as an accident it was one of their poorer efforts.

Having staggered its way through those useless random thoughts, my brain cleared enough for me to decide it was high time to move if I was going to do anything about living. And I supposed I would have to.

I stumbled on to my feet, pulled the quilt off one of the beds, tottered into the bathroom with it and soaked it under the taps in the bath. Smoke was well down in my lungs, thick and choking. It's bloody stupid, I thought groggily, it's damn bloody stupid that boy-and-girl keep trying to shove me where I want to go, and I keep trying not to let them. Ridiculous. Ridiculous . . .

I found myself on my knees, half unconscious. The bath water still running. Pulled myself up a little, hauled out the dripping quilt, flung it over the worst of the fire. Silly, I thought. Much better to go out of the door. Tried that. Damn thing was stuck.

Window, then. Stuck.

Wrapped my hand in the curtain and pushed it through one of the panes of glass. Some air came in. The insect screen stopped more.

Down on my knees again. Terribly dizzy. A black hell in my head. Smelt the quilt burning, lifted it off one lot of fire, and on to the next. Damped it all out into a smelly black faintly smouldering path and felt old and weak from too much scrambling up and down mountains and deeply ill from the crash on the brain and too much smoke.

Opened the front of the fat black stove. Shapleigh, it said. Gradually the smoke began to clear away up its stackpipe while I lay in a poor state beside the cabin door and breathed the fresh air trickling in underneath.

Several eras later I stopped feeling like morgue material and the hammer in my head died to a brutal aching throb. I began to wonder how long it would be before Matt and Yola returned to make their horrified discovery of my death, and wearily decided it was time for action.

I stood up slowly and leaned against the door. They'd fastened it somehow from the outside, in spite of there being no lock: and it was simple enough to see when one's eyes weren't filled with smoke. The screen door opened outwards, the wooden door inwards. A small hook leading in through the latch was holding the two together. I pushed it up, and it slid away as the inner door opened.

My wallet lay on the table, not in my pocket. They'd been looking. Nothing for them to find, except their own photograph. They'd taken that. But they hadn't searched very far: the Luger was still in its holster at my back, under my outhanging shirt. I checked the magazine – still loaded – and put it back in place.

The only other thing I really wanted to take with me was my radio. I squashed down its extended antenna aerial and shoved it into my old suitcase on top of the things I'd packed before breakfast. Then, picking it up and fighting down the whirling chaos which resulted, I opened the screen door. Behind me the cabin lay in a singed shambles. Ahead, the comparatively short walk to the car seemed a marathon.

I might have made it in one if I hadn't felt any worse: but at the end of the woodland track, when all that was left to go was the open expanse of the car park, a wave of clammy sweating faintness seethed through me and I dropped the suitcase and leaned against a tree, waiting weakly for it to pass.

Yola came out of the kitchen door and saw me. Her mouth fell open, then she turned on her heel and dived back into the ranch house. For the rifle. Or for Matt. My hand closed on the pistol at my back, but I was very loath to use it. Too many explanations to authority would be involved, and I preferred to avoid them at this stage.

'Hello,' said a cheerful voice behind me. 'We thought you'd gone ages ago.'

I turned my wonky head and let my hand fall away from the gun. Mickey and Samantha were coming down the track from the branch which led to the Wilkersons' cabin.

'And I thought,' I said, 'that you'd gone riding.'

'The wranglers haven't brought in enough horses,' Mickey explained sadly.

'Are you sick or something?' asked his sister, coming to a halt and staring up into my face.

'A bit,' I admitted. 'I'd be awfully glad if you'd carry my suitcase for me, across to that black car.'

'Sure,' said Mickey importantly, and Samantha took my hand in motherly solicitude. With one child at each side I completed the trip.

It was the rifle Yola fetched. She stood with it stiffly in her hands and watched the children put the suitcase in the car and stand close to my window while I started the engine. An accidental drowning, an accidental smothering she could manage: but three public murders by shooting were outside her range. Just as well. If she'd lifted that rifle towards the children, I would have shot her.

'Bye,' they said, waving. Nice kids.

'Bye.'

I released the brakes and rolled away down the drive in a plume of dust, accelerating fast as soon as I hit the metalled road, and taking the main branch down to Jackson. If Yola thought of following in the pick-up, she didn't do it fast enough. Repeated inspection in the mirror showed no Clives chasing on my tail. The only things constantly before my eyes were bright dancing spots.

Through Jackson I turned north and west on the winding road to Idaho Falls. Along there the Snake River and the Pallisades Reservoir, sparkling blue against the dark pines, were stunningly beautiful. But my several stops weren't for appreciation: the cold sweating waves of dizziness kept recurring, like twenty-two over seven. I drove slowly, close to the side, never overtaking, ready to pull up. If I hadn't wanted to put a hundred miles or so between me and the Clives, I wouldn't have started from Jackson. Most of the time I wished I hadn't.

Walt was pacing the motel lobby like a frenetic film producer when I finally showed up at five-thirty in the afternoon.

'You are four-and-a-half hours late,' he began accusingly. 'You said . . .'

'I know,' I interrupted. 'Book us some rooms. We're staying here.'

He opened his mouth and shut it tight.

'I'm sorry,' I said, softening it, 'but I feel ill.'

'What's the matter?'

'Concussion.'

Walt gave me a searching look, booked the rooms, and even went so far as to carry my suitcase. I lay straight down on the bed, and he sat in an easy chair in my room and rubbed his fingers.

'Do you need a doctor?' he said.

'I don't think so. It's not getting any worse.'

'Well . . . what happened?'

'I'll give you some free advice,' I said. 'Don't ever let Matt Clive come within bashing distance of your head.'

The dizziness wasn't so bad lying down.

'Do you want a drink?' he asked.

'No . . . Let's listen to a tape recording instead.' I told him how to open the back of the radio and to rewind the reels.

'Neat little job,' he commented. 'Where did you get it?'

'Had it specially made, two or three years ago.'

Walt grunted, and switched on. The head wrangler banged on Yola's door and told her that the mares and stallions were out. Walt's face lifted into a half grin.

The recorder played twenty seconds of silence after each take, and began again at the next sound. The next piece was very short.

'Yola?' A man's voice, very loud. 'Yola! Where the hell is everybody?' A door slammed. Silence.

'That's Matt Clive,' I told Walt. 'He came back before breakfast.'

The voices began again. Yola speaking, coming indoors. '. . . say the tracks go straight up the hill, but he turned back at the high patch of scree and came down again.'

That was a bit of luck.

'They'll just have to go on looking,' Matt said. 'Yola, for God's sake, we can't lose that horse.' His voice was strained and furious. 'I'll go over to the house and see if any of those kids had a hand in it.'

'I don't think so. Not a darned one of them looks nervous.'

'I'll try, anyway.' His footsteps receded.

Yola picked up the telephone and made a call.

'That you, Jim? Have you seen any horse vans coming through Pikelet since last night? . . .

'Well no, I just wondered if you'd seen one. Not this morning, early? . . .

'No, it was just a chance. Sure. Yeah. Thanks anyway.' She put down the receiver with a crash.

Walt raised his eyebrows. 'Pikelet?'

'Couple of shops and a filling station where the Clives' own road joins the main road to Jackson.'

'Just as well we didn't . . .' he began, and then changed it to, 'Is that why you insisted on the long way round?'

'Partly,' I agreed. 'I wanted it to look as if Chrysalis had gone off by himself. I wanted to avoid them realizing he'd been deliberately stolen. Keep them guessing a bit, give us time to get well clear.'

The tape began again. Matt came back running.

'Yola. That man. That damned man.'

'What man?' She was bewildered.

'The man that pulled Teller out of the river. How long has he been here?'

Yola said almost in a whisper, 'Here?'

Matt was shouting. 'Here. Having breakfast. Staying here, you stupid bitch.'

'I don't . . . I don't . . .'

'I saw him at Reading too,' Matt said. 'He called to see Teller in the hospital. They let him in past all the watchdogs. I saw him looking out of the window. How the hell did he get here? Why in God's name didn't you spot him, you stupid, stupid . . . He's the one that's taken the horse. And I'll damn well make him bring it back.'

'How?' Yola said, wailing.

'Excuse me,' said the voice of the girl who waited at table. 'Excuse me, Miss Clive. Mr Hochner wants his bill.'

'There on the desk,' Yola said.

'Which is Hochner?' Matt, urgent.

'The German in cabin three.'

'Where was he sitting at breakfast? What does he look like?'

'He had his back to the door from the hall,' the girl said. 'He's wearing a blue-and-white check shirt, and he's quite tall and has dark brown hair and a tired sort of face.'

'Give him the bill then,' Matt said, and waited until she had gone. 'Hochner!' The voice was almost incoherent with rage. 'How long has he been here?'

'Since . . . Tuesday.' Yola's voice was faint.

'Get your rifle,' Matt said. 'If he won't give us that horse back . . . I'll kill him.'

There were small moving about sounds, and the tape went quiet. The time they had spent in my cabin telescoped into twenty seconds of silence; and the recording began again.

'He was right, Matt,' Yola said. 'We should have let

him go.' Her voice had gone quiet with despair, but Matt's still rode on anger.

'He had his chance. He should have told us what he'd done with Chrysalis.'

After a pause Yola said, 'He wasn't going to do that. He said so. Whatever you do, he said, you won't recover the horse.'

'Shut up,' Matt said violently.

'Matt.' A wail in her voice. 'He was right. We won't recover the horse and his friends will come looking for him, like he said.'

'They'll only find an accident.'

'But they won't believe it.'

'They won't be able to prove any different,' Matt insisted.

After another pause Yola said almost without emotion, 'If he got the horse clean away . . . if someone else has him now, and he's on his way back to Teller . . . they'll know we had Chrysalis here. We'll be arrested for that.'

'Hochner wasn't going to say he'd stolen the horse from here.'

'But you wouldn't listen.' Yola suddenly flared into anger of her own. 'He was right all the time. We should have let him go. We'd have lost Chrysalis . . . but this way we're in terrible trouble, they'll never believe he died by accident, we'll have the whole FBI here and we'll end up . . . we'll end up in . . .'

'Shut up,' Matt said. 'Shut up.'

'He might not be dead yet . . . can't we go and stop it?' Her voice was urgent, beseeching.

'And have him accuse us of attempted murder? Don't be such a fool. No one can prove it isn't an accident, can they? Can they?'

'I suppose not . . .'

'So you leave him, Yola. You just leave him. He had his chance. I gave him his chance . . . You just wait for some of the guests to see the smoke and come and tell you, like we said. Don't you try going up there. Just don't try it.'

'No . . .'

'And I'm going back on the mountain with the wranglers. Chrysalis went across the bridge. His tracks are there. Well . . . I'm going tracking. Mr Clever Hochner might be bluffing all along the line. He might have Chrysalis tied to some tree up there, and he might not have told anyone where he is, and no one will come asking.' He convinced himself that this view of things was reasonable, and in the end Yola halfway agreed.

'We'll have to tell Uncle Bark,' she said finally.

There was a blank pause while they considered this.

'He'll blow his top,' Matt said gloomily. 'After all that planning.'

'He'll have to know,' Yola said.

'I'll call him this evening, if we have to. But we might have found Chrysalis by then.'

'I sure hope so . . .'

Matt went away then on his search, and presently, after Yola had left to go back to the ranch house, there was continued silence on the tape.

Walt switched the recorder off and looked across at me with a complete absence of expression.

'What did they do?'

I told him.

'Would it have passed as an accident?'

'I expect so. Neat little picture: man lighting cigarette, throws match absentmindedly in tub of pep instead of waste basket, panics, spills the stuff, steps wildly back from flames, trips over stove and knocks himself out. Bingo.'

'Do you smoke, though?'

'Sometimes. They used my own pack from the bedside table. And my own matches. It was impulsive, unpremeditated. They just looked round and used what came to hand. They're quite good at it.'

'Lucky you woke up in time,' Walt said.

'I suppose so.' I shut my eyes and wondered how he would react if I asked him to go out for some codeine.

'I've worked with one or two people like you before,' he said. 'And I can't say I like it.'

'Thanks,' I said sardonically. No pills.

'With your kind,' he said, 'dying comes easy. It's living takes the guts.'

I opened my eyes. He was watching me steadily, his

sober face removing any possibility that he was intending to be funny.

'How are you on guts?' he asked.

'Fresh out.'

He sighed deeply. 'That figures.'

'Walt . . .' I began.

'It struck me first last night, on the mountain. You were sure anxious about Chrysalis, but you didn't give a goddam about falling off the top yourself. It made me freeze just to watch you leading him along that ledge . . . and you came back as calm as if it had been your own yard.'

He was apologizing, in his indirect way, for his startling appearance on the path.

'Walt,' I said, half smiling. 'Will you go get me something for a headache?'

CHAPTER ELEVEN

Eunice, Lynnie, Sam Kitchens, and stud groom Chub Lodovski leaned in a row on the rail of the stallions' paddock at Midway and watched Chrysalis eat Kentucky grass with opinions varying from Lodovski's enthusiasm to Eunice's resignation.

The half-a-million pounds' worth looked none the worse for his trip up the Tetons. Better than on the ranch, as Sam Kitchens had removed all the Wyoming dust from his coat on the journey back, and the bay hide shone with glittering good health in the sunshine. There wasn't, Lodovski assured me, the slightest chance of his going missing again.

Batteries of photographers and pressmen had come and gone: the stallion had been 'found' straying on the land of a friend of Dave Teller's about thirty miles from where he had disappeared. All the excitement was over.

I walked back to Dave's house with Eunice and Lynnie, and Eunice poured me a drink which was four-fifths whisky and one-fifth ice.

'Who put you through what meat grinder?' she said. 'You look like a honeymoon couple on the tenth night.'

Sam Hengelman had driven into Midway with Chrysalis at lunchtime (Tuesday). I had flown to New York with Walt the day before, and had just back-tracked to Lexington, in time to catch the tail end of Eunice interviewing the press. Several of that hard bitten fraternity had tottered out past me with pole-axed expressions and Lynnie had been halfway through a fit of giggles.

I made inroads into the hefty drink.

'I could do with a good long sleep,' I admitted. 'If you could give me a bed? Or there's the motel . . .'

'Stay here,' Eunice said abruptly. 'Of course you're staying here.'

I looked from her to Lynnie. I couldn't stay in the house with one alone: perfectly proper with both. Silly.

'Thanks, then. And I must call Dave, in England.'

Dave, still in hospital, sounded incredulous.

'I heard it on a news flash, not half an hour ago,' he said. 'Chrysalis just plain turned up.'

'He sure did,' I said dryly.

'Where had he been?'

'It's a long story,' I said, 'and wires have ears. But the expenses stand right now at somewhere near six thousand three hundred dollars. Is that enough for you, or do you want to go on for some answers?'

'To what questions, fella?' He sounded uncertain.

'To why Chrysalis was hi-jacked, and why you fell in the river. And another thing: do you want Allyx back?'

'For God's sake . . . do you know where he is?'

'No. But maybe I could find him. However, if I do, and we get as positive an identification as on Chrysalis, the insurance money on Allyx will have to be repaid to Buttress Life. That will be the equivalent of buying him all over again. He's three years older now, and you'll have lost three crops of foals. He may not be a good proposition for you or your syndicate any more. In which case you might prefer not to have him found. It's up to you.'

'Jeez,' he said.

'Will you think it over, and call back?' I suggested. 'Your wife and Lynnie are filling me up with food and drinks, and I guess I'll be staying here tonight. But if you want me to go on, will you clear it with Keeble? I'm due back at my desk at nine AM next Monday morning, and I might not make it.'

'Sure,' he said, somewhat weakly, and I handed the receiver to Eunice.

'How's it going, honey?' she said, and I took a good swallow, put my head back on the chair, and listened to her long-married-wifely conversation with my eyes shut.

'Don't ask me how he did it, Dave, I don't know. All I know is he rang from New York yesterday afternoon and asked me for the name of any close friend of ours who was influential and respected, preferably high up in horsebreeding circles, and whose word would be taken as gospel by the press. So, after a rake around I said I guessed Jeff Roots fitted the bill; and lo and behold Chrysalis turned up on Jeff's land this morning . . . Yeah, the horse is as good as new; wherever he's been they've treated him right . . . Look, Dave, surely enough's enough? I heard what Gene said about finding Allyx. Well, don't do it. We need Allyx like a dose of clap. And your boy here is no goddam Hercules, a puff of wind would knock him off, the way he's come back . . . Lynnie's fine, sure. We're taking a trip tomorrow out to California. I'll measure up the curtains for the new place, things like that, and Lynnie can have some days on the beach and maybe try some surfing with those de Vesey boys. So look, why don't we take Gene with us, huh? . . . Sure, I've made reservations at The Vacationer in Santa Barbara . . . they're bound to have another room . . .'

I listened to her plans with disappointment. If I wanted to laze anywhere, it was right where I was, on the Midway Farm. By the peaceful pool in the quiet green garden, sleeping, drinking, and looking at Lynnie.

Eunice put down the receiver, and we had dinner, and late in the evening Dave rang through again.

'Gene?' he said. 'Now listen, fella. Apart from curiosity, is there any good reason for finding those answers you talked about?'

'Forestalling repetition,' I said promptly.

'No more stolen stallions and no more attacks on me?'

'That's right.'

There was a pause.

'I'll buy the answers, then,' he said. 'If you can get them. And as for Allyx . . . if you think there's any chance of finding him alive and vigorous, then I guess I'm morally obliged to give you the go-ahead. I'd have to syndicate him all over again, of course. He'll be twelve now. That would give him only about six to eight more years of high potency . . . But his get from before his disappearance are winning all over Europe. Business-wise I'm not too happy about those three lost years. But blood-wise, it would be criminal not to try to get him back.'

'All right,' I said. 'I'll see what I can do.'

'What you spent on finding Chrysalis is less than his fee for covering a single mare. You've a free hand again for Allyx.'

'Right,' I said.

'Sim Keeble says you've got seven days' extension of leave. Something about it being due to you anyway, from a week you were entitled to at Christmas and didn't take.'

'I'd forgotten about that.'

'I guess I could fix it with him for more, if the extra week isn't enough.'

'If I haven't finished by then I'll have failed anyway, and might as well go home.'

'Oh.' He sounded disappointed. 'Very well, we'll leave it like that for the present.' He cleared his throat. 'Eunice didn't seem to think you looked too well.'

'The boy on the punt who knocked you out did the same thing for me.'

'Gene!' His voice was shocked.

'Yeah. Don't tell my boss I'm that incompetent. Though come to think of it, he knows.'

He laughed. 'When you find that boy again give him a one-two from both of us.'

'Sure,' I said. But I'd been taught my job by cerebral people who didn't reckon a screener would ever have to fight for his life, and by the time I proved them wrong I was too old to become expert at boxing or judo, even if I'd liked the idea, which I didn't. I had learnt instead to shoot straight, and the Luger had in the past three years extricated me unharmed from two sticky situations. But in a stand up hand-to-hand affair with that young bull Matt Clive I would be a five hundred to one loser, and 'giving him a one-two from both of us' in any physical sense was a very dim possibility indeed.

'Keep in touch, fella,' Dave said.

'Sure,' I answered again, meaning it as little: and we rang off.

Curled opposite in a tomato armchair, Eunice said gloomily, 'I gather we're stuck with that bloody Allyx.'

'Only if we find him.'

'Oh, you'll do that, blast you.' Her bitterness was so marked that Lynnie stared at her. Too young to understand, I thought, that it wasn't me particularly that Eunice wanted to hurt, but life in general.

They went upstairs shortly afterwards murmuring about California in the morning, and I switched off the light and sat in near darkness, finishing the fourth of Eunice's massive ideas on drink and working out the questions I would ask the next day. I could find Allyx on paper, if I were lucky: but he could hardly turn up loose after three years. Three weeks had been strictly the limit. The whole thing might have to be more orthodox, more public. And I wouldn't again, I decided mildly, put myself within accident reach of the murderous Clives.

After a while I deserted the last half of the drink and wandered upstairs to the spacious air-conditioned room Eunice had given me. With a tired hand I switched on the light inside the door, and yellow pools in frilly shades shone out on brown and gold and white furnishings.

One splash of jarring bright pink. Eunice herself, in a fluffy trimmed wrapper, was lying on my bed.

I walked slowly across the thick white carpet and sat beside her on the white spotted muslin coverlet.

'What do you want?' I said gently.

'What do you think?'

I shook my head.

'Does that mean no?' Her voice was abruptly matter of fact.

'I'm afraid it does,' I said.

'You said you weren't queer.'

'Well . . . I'm not.' I smiled at her. 'But I do have one unbreakable rule.'

'And that is?'

'Not to sleep with the wives . . . or daughters . . . of the men I work for.'

She sat bolt upright so that her face was close to mine. Her eyes had the usual contracted pupils of the quarter drunk.

'That includes Lynnie,' she said.

'Yes. It does.'

'Well, I'll be damned. You mean that night you spent in New York with her you didn't even try . . .'

'It wouldn't have been much good if I had,' I said, half laughing.

'Don't you believe it. She never takes her eyes off you, and when you were away she talked about nothing else.'

I stared at her in real surprise. 'You must be wrong.'

'I wasn't born yesterday,' she said gloomily. 'She has two photographs of you as well.'

'What photographs?' I was staggered.

'Some her brother took. That day on the river.'

'But she shouldn't . . .'

'Maybe she shouldn't,' Eunice said dryly. 'But she does.' She swung her legs carelessly around to sit on the edge of the bed beside me and I saw that for someone bent on seduction she had come well wrapped up.

'You expected me to say no,' I said.

She made a face. 'I thought you might. But it was worth a try.'

'Eunice, you're nuts,' I said.

'I'm bored,' she said explosively, and with an undoubted depth of unbearable truth.

'That puts me into the golf and bridge category.'

She was still playing games.

'At least you're goddam human,' she said, her mouth cracking into a smile. 'More than you can say about most men.'

'What do you like best about moving to California?' I asked.

She stared. 'Your mind's like a bloody grasshopper. What has that to do with sex?'

'You tell me, and I'll tell you.'

'For God's sake . . .' But she made some effort at concentrating, and in the end came up with the answer I had been most expecting.

'Fixing up the rooms, I guess.'

'You did all these . . .' I waved my hand around, embracing the house.

'Yeah, I did. So what?'

'So why don't you start in business, doing it for other people?'

She half laughed, ridiculing the idea, and half clung

to it: and I knew she'd thought of it in the past, because I hadn't surprised her.

'I'm no bloody genius.'

'You have an eye for colour. More than that: for mood. This is the most comforting house I've ever been in.'

'Comforting?' she said, puzzled.

'Yeah. Laugh, clown, laugh. That sort of thing. You can fill other people even though you feel empty yourself.'

Tears welled up in her grey-green eyes, and she shut the lids. Her voice remained normal.

'How do you know?'

'I know.'

After a pause, she said, 'And I suppose what it has to do with sex is that interior decorating would be a suitable sublimation for a middle-aged woman whose physical attraction is fading faster than her appetite . . .' The bitterness came from long acquaintance with the jargon and its point of view.

'No,' I said mildly. 'The opposite.'

'Huh?' She opened her eyes. They were wet and shiny.

'Playing games is easier than working.'

'Spell it out,' she said. 'You talk in goddam riddles.'

'Sex . . . this sort of casual sex . . .' I patted the bed where she'd lain, 'can be a way of running away from real effort. A lover may be a sublimation of a deeper need. People who can't face the demands of one may opt for passing the time with the other.'

'For Christ's sake . . . I don't understand a bloody word.' She shut her eyes and lay flat back across the bed.

'Thousands of people never try anything serious because they're afraid of failing,' I said.

She swallowed, and after a pause said, 'And what if you do bloody fail? What then?'

I didn't answer her, and after a while she repeated the question insistently.

'Tell me what you do if you fail?'

'I haven't got that one licked myself, yet.'

'Oh.' She laughed weakly. 'Oh God. The blind leading the blind. Just like the whole bloody human race.'

'Yeah.' I sighed and stood up. 'We all stumble along in the dark, and that's a fact.'

'I don't know if you'll believe it, but I've been utterly bloody faithful to Dave . . . except for this . . .'

'I'm sure of it,' I said.

She got to her feet and stood swaying slightly.

'I guess I'm tight.'

'Better than loose,' I said smiling.

'For God's sake, spare me goddam puns at one o'clock in the morning. I suppose if you're looking for that so and so Allyx there's no chance of you coming to California?'

'I wish there were.'

'Goddam liar,' she said vaguely. 'Goodnight.'

She made straight for the door and didn't look back.

I drove them to the airport in the morning. Eunice had lent me her car and the house for as long as I needed them, and had passed off her overnight visit with one sarcastic dig at breakfast.

'Better undersexed than sorry.'

'What?' said Lynnie.

'Eunice is offering a solution to the population explosion,' I explained.

Lynnie giggled. Eunice showed me a double row of teeth and told me to pass the cream.

When I'd seen them off I followed a local road map and Eunice's inaccurate directions, and eventually arrived at the Perry Stud Farm, home of Jefferson L. Roots, chairman, among other things, of the Bloodhorse Breeders' Association. A houseboy in a spotless white coat showed me through the house and on to the patio: a house made of large cool concrete boxes, with rough-cast white walls and bare golden wood floors. The patio was shaded by a vine trained across a trellis. There was a glass and metal table, and low comfortable lounging chairs around it. From one of these Jeff Roots extricated himself and held out a welcoming hand.

He was a thick man with a paunch which had defied health farms, and he worried about his weight. His manner had the gentle, deprecating ease of the really tough American; the power was inside, discernible but purring, like the engine in a Rolls. He was dressed in a tropical-weight city suit, and while I was there an efficient girl secretary came to remind him that time and his connection to Miami would wait for no man.

'A drink?' he suggested. 'It's a hot day already. What would you like?'

'Lime juice?' I asked. 'Or lemon.'

I got lime, squeezed fresh on to crushed ice. My host drank sugar-free tonic water and made a face over it.

'Just the smell of french fries and I'm a size larger in shirts,' he complained.

'Why worry?' I said.

'Ever heard of hypertension?'

'Thin people can have it too.'

'Tell that to the birds . . . or rather, tell it to my wife. She starves me.' He swirled his glass gloomily, ice and lemon rising perilously to the rim. 'So, anyway, Mr Hawkins, how can I help you today?'

He pushed a folded newspaper across the table and pointed at it with an appreciative smile.

'Chrysalis cocooned,' the headlines said. And underneath, in smaller letters, 'High price stallion loses liberty, corralled at Perry, reshipped to Midway. And are the mares there glad, or are they? Our tip is syndicators breathe again.' There was a picture of Chrysalis in his paddock, some mention of Dave's leg, and a few snide remarks about the police and the local horse folks who hadn't been able to spot a million dollars at ten paces.

'Where did you rustle him up from?' Roots asked. 'Sam Hengelman wouldn't say. Most unlike him.'

'Sam was an accessory to a conjuring trick. A little matter of substitution. We left a horse and took a horse . . . I guess he didn't want to talk himself into trouble.'

'And naturally you paid him.'

'Er, yes,' I agreed. 'So we did.'

'But I gather from your call that it's not about Chrysalis that you want to see me now?'

'No. It's about Allyx.'

'*Allyx*?'

'Yes, the other stallion which . . .'

'I know about all that,' he interrupted. 'They turned the whole state upside down looking for him and they found just as much trace as they did of Chrysalis.'

'Do you by any chance remember, ten years ago, another horse called Showman?'

'Showman? Showman? He got loose from a groom who was supposed to be exercising him, or something like that, and was killed in the Appalachians.'

'How certain was the identification?'

He put his tonic water down carefully on the table.

'Are you suggesting he's still alive?'

'I just wondered,' I said mildly. 'From what I've been told, they found a dead horse two years after Showman vanished. But although he was in a high state of decomposition, he'd only been dead about three months. So it easily might *not* have been Showman, just somewhat like him in colour and size.'

'And if it wasn't?'

'We might just possibly turn him up with Allyx.'

'Have you . . .' he cleared his throat. 'Have you any idea where they . . . er . . . might be . . . turned up?'

'I'm afraid not. Not yet.'

'They weren't . . . wherever you found Chrysalis?'

'No. That was only a shipping station, so to speak. Chrysalis was intended to go on somewhere else.'

'And at that somewhere else, one might find . . .?'

'There's a good chance, I think.'

'They might have been shipped abroad again. Down to Mexico or South America.'

'It's possible; but I'm inclined against it, on the whole.' Uncle Bark, whoever he was, lived somewhere in the States. Yola had not needed to call the overseas operator to get through to him, on the telephone. She hadn't even made it person to person.

'The whole thing seems so extraordinary,' Roots said, shaking his head. 'Some nut going around stealing stallions whose value at once drops to zero, because he can't admit he's got them. Do you think some fanatic somewhere is conducting experiments. Trying to produce a super-horse? Or how about a criminal syndicate all getting their mares covered by bluest blood stallions at donkey prices? . . . No, that wouldn't work, they'd never be able to sell the foals for stud, they wouldn't be able to cash in on the blood lines . . .'

'I think it's a good deal simpler than either of those,' I said, smiling. 'Much more down to earth.'

'Then what?'

I told him.

He chewed it over and I drank my lime juice.

'Anyway,' I said. 'I thought I'd try along those lines, and see if it leads anywhere.'

'It's fantastic,' Roots said. 'And I hope to God you're wrong.'

I laughed. 'Yes, I can see that.'

'It'll take you months to plough through all that work yourself . . . and I don't suppose you have too close a knowledge of the thoroughbred scene over here . . . so why don't I get you some help?'

'I'd be very grateful.'

There was an outside extension telephone close to his chair. He lifted the receiver and pressed buttons. I listened to him arranging with the publishers of a leading horse journal for me to have the run of their files and the temporary services of two long-memoried assistants.

'That's fixed, then,' he said, standing up. 'The office is on North Broadway, along in Lexington. I guess you'll let me know how you make out?'

'I certainly will.'

'Dave and Eunice . . . they're great guys.'

'They are.'

'Give her my best,' he said, looking at his watch.

'She's gone to California . . .'

'The new place?'

I nodded.

'Crazy idea of Dave's, moving to the coast. The centre of the bloodstock industry is right here in Lexington, and this is the place to be.'

I made the sort of non-critical, non-committal noise in my throat necessary on such occasions, and Jeff Roots thrust out a rounded hand.

'I have this stockholders' meeting in Miami,' he said, apologetically, and he walked with me through the house to where his secretary waited in a Cadillac parked beside Eunice's Toronado Oldsmobile.

At the newspaper offices, I found, anything Jeff Roots wanted done was done whole-heartedly and at the double. My two temporary assistants proved to be an elderly man who spent most of his time compiling an annual stallion register, and a maiden lady in her fifties whose horse face and crisp masculine voice were easy to take, as she had an unexpectedly sweet smile and a phenomenal memory.

When I explained what I was looking for they both stared at me in dumb-struck silence.

'Isn't it possible?' I asked.

Mr Harris and Miss Britt recovered themselves and said they guessed so.

'And while we're at it, we might make a list of

anyone whose name or nickname might be Bark. Or Bart, perhaps; though I think it's Bark.'

Miss Britt promptly reeled off six names, all Barkleys, living in and around Lexington.

'Maybe that's not such a good idea,' I sighed.

'No harm in it,' Miss Britt said briskly. 'We can make all the lists simultaneously.'

She and Mr Harris went into a huddle and from there to the reference room, and were shortly up to their elbows in papers and books. They told me to smoke and wait, which I did all day.

At five o'clock they came across with the results.

'This is the best we can do,' Miss Britt said doubtfully. 'There are well over three thousand stallions at stud in the States, you see. You asked us to sort out any whose fees had risen steadily over the past eight or nine years . . . there are two hundred and nine of them.' She put a closely typed list in front of me.

'Next, you wanted the names of any stallions who had been conspicuously more successful at stud than one would have expected from their own breeding. There are two hundred and eighty two of those.' She gave me a second sheet.

'Next, you wanted to know if any of this year's two-year-olds had proved conspicuously better at racing than one would normally have expected from their breeding. There are twenty-nine of those.' She added the third list.

'And lastly, the people who could be called Bark . . .

thirty-two of them. From the Bar K Ranch to Barry Kyle.'

'You've done wonders,' I said sincerely. 'I suppose it's too much to hope that any one farm is concerned on all four lists?'

'Most of the stallions on the first list are the same as those on the second. That stands to reason. But none of the sires of the exceptional two-year-olds are on either of the first two lists. And none of the two-year-olds were bred by any of the Barks.' Both of them looked downcast at such negative results after all their work.

'Never mind,' I said. 'We'll try another way tomorrow.'

Miss Britt snorted, which I interpreted as agreement. 'Rome wasn't built in a day,' she said, nodding. Mr Harris seemed to doubt that this particular Rome could be built at all with the materials available, but he turned up uncomplaining at nine the following morning, and they both dived in again, on new permutations.

By noon the first two lists had been reduced to twenty. We all adjourned for a sandwich. At two the searching began again. At three ten Miss Britt gasped sharply and her eyes went wide. She scribbled quickly on a fresh piece of paper, considered the result with her head on one side, and then looked across to me.

'Well . . .' she said. 'Well . . .' The words wouldn't come.

'You've found them,' I said.

She nodded, only half believing it.

'Cross-checking them all by where they raced, their years of purchase, their markings and their approximate ages, as you asked . . . we came up with twelve possibles which appeared on the first two lists. And one of the sires of the two-year-olds fits your requirements and comes from the same farm as one of the first twelve. Er . . . do you follow me?'

'On your heels,' I said, smiling.

Mr Harris and I both joined her and looked over her shoulder at what she had written.

'Moviemaker, aged fourteen years; present stud fee ten thousand dollars.

'Centigrade, aged twelve years; this year's stud fee fifteen hundred dollars, fee next year twenty-five hundred.

'Both standing at Orpheus Farm, Los Caillos.

'The property of Culham James Offen.'

Moviemaker and Centigrade: Showman and Allyx. As clear as a frosty sky.

Stallions were normally booked for thirty to forty mares each breeding season. Forty mares at ten thousand dollars a throw meant four hundred thousand dollars every year, give or take a live foal or two. Moviemaker had cost one hundred and fifty thousand dollars at public auction ten years ago, according to Miss Britt's researches. Since then Offen had been paid somewhere near two-and-a-half million dollars in stud fees.

Centigrade had been bought for a hundred thousand dollars at Keneland sales. At twenty-five hundred a time he would earn that hundred thousand next year alone. And nothing was more likely than that he too would rise to a much higher fee.

'Culham James Offen is so well regarded,' Miss Britt said in consternation. 'I simply can't believe it. He's accepted as one of the top rank breeders.'

'The only thing is, of course,' said Mr Harris, regretfully, 'that there's no connection with the name Bark.'

Miss Britt looked at me and her smile shone out sweet and triumphant.

'But there is, isn't there? Mr Harris, you're no musician. Haven't you ever heard of Orpheus in the Underworld . . . by Offenbach?'

CHAPTER TWELVE

Walt said 'For God's sake' four times and admitted Buttress Life might be willing to send him from coast to coast if Allyx were the pot of gold at the end of the rainbow.

'Los Caillos is a short distance north-east of Los Angeles,' I said. 'I thought of staying a bit farther north, on the coast.'

'If you like.'

'Come to The Vacationer, Grand Beach, Santa Barbara, then. I'll meet you there tomorrow.'

He repeated the address. 'Who's paying?' he said.

'Buttress Life and Dave Teller can fight it out between them. I'll put the motel on Teller's expenses. Can you wring the fare out of your office?'

'I guess so.' His sigh came wearily over the wire. 'My wife and kids aren't going to like it. I was fixing to take them on a picnic this Sunday.'

'Postpone it a week,' I suggested.

'It's been postponed twice already, on your account.'

'Oh.'

After a short pause, he said, 'Around six, tomorrow, local time. That do?'

'That would do very well.'

'See you,' he said briefly, and put down his receiver with a crash. I returned the Teller instrument more kindly to its cradle and surveyed the green and tomato room.

Nothing to do.

Mixed a drink with precision, and drank it. Wandered down to the pool, thought about a swim in the dusk, and couldn't be bothered to undress. Went back to the house, and ate a dinner cooked and served by Eva, who chattered so long in her pleasure at having someone to speak to in her own language that I heartily regretted I'd ever used it. Wished desperately she would stop and go away, and when at last she did, that was no good either.

Tried to read and turned six pages without taking in a word. Wandered restlessly again into the black velvet deep green garden, and sat in one of the chairs by the pool, looking at darkness inside and out. Unreasonable, I thought drearily, that I shouldn't have recovered normally from losing Caroline, that I didn't value the freedom other men envied, that I couldn't be content with all I had: cruel that depression was no respecter of status or achievement and struck so deep that no worldly success could alleviate it.

Great fame, universal honour, droves of personal friends had demonstrably failed to save a whole string of geniuses from its clutches, and every year it bagged its thousands from unimportant people like me who would never see their name in print or lights, and didn't necessarily want to. Probably depression was an illness as definite as jaundice, and one day they would inoculate babies against it. I supposed I could count myself lucky not to have had it in its acute form, where its grey-black octopus tentacles reached out and sucked into every corner of the spirit until quite quickly life became literally unbearable, and the high jump suddenly presented itself with blinding clarity as the only logical, the only possible relief.

I wouldn't come to that day, if I could help it. I would *not*.

The Vacationer was right down on the beach, with the sound of the bright blue Pacific creeping in a murmur under the transistors, the air-conditioning, the civilized chatter, the squalling of children, and the revving of cars. There were no ocean rooms left. Walt and I, next door to each other, overlooked the parking lot.

Eunice and Lynnie were out when I arrived and still out when Walt checked in at six, but they were back when I went down with him for a drink before dinner. I had left a note at the desk for Eunice, but I hadn't told Walt she would be there. He stopped dead in his tracks when he saw her sitting with Lynnie, and turned on me a narrow-eyed composite glance of dislike and anger. If I'd told him she was to be with us, he wouldn't have come: he knew that I knew it. He was entitled to his rage.

Eunice was, however, the wife of a very good client of his firm. He swallowed his feelings like a pill, and chased them down with a double bourbon in silence. Eunice and Lynnie were on frosted looking daiquiris and happy with it. They both looked marvellous, with honey-brown skin and a languorous and sun-filled way of moving. Eunice wore fluorescent green with bits of gold at anatomical points like ears, wrists, and feet. Lynnie had acquired a locally grown hot pink-orange tunic, and the few straps of her sandals seemed to be made of polished semi-precious stones. Even Walt, after a while, couldn't take his eyes away from them for long.

We had dinner outside, under a trellis lit by hundreds of tiny multi-coloured lights, on a shallow terrace which led directly out on to the sand. Eunice's language was for once as soft as the sea breeze, and consequently as a social evening it developed into a reasonable success.

Over the coffee I asked Eunice with a casualness which drew a piercing glance from Walt, 'Have you by any chance heard of a racehorse breeder called Culham James Offen?'

'Heard of him,' she said. 'Of course I have. Everyone has.'

'I haven't,' Walt said flatly. One couldn't expect complete capitulation. He was doing very well.

'I mean, everyone in the bloodstock world would have heard of him,' Eunice explained without obvious patience. 'He has that terrifically successful stallion Moviemaker. And Dave says one ought to think of sending mares to another one of his, Centigrade . . . The first crop of foals is winning two-year-old races this season all over the place. But quite apart from that,' she smiled broadly, 'I guess we'll be seeing a good deal of him from now on.'

'Er . . . why?' I asked diffidently.

'Our new place is right next to his.'

Walt's mouth fell open and I stopped stirring my coffee.

'What did you say?' I said, feeling my eyes go blank, as I knew they always did under shock.

'Our new place, where we're moving to, is right across the road from Offen. We can see his paddocks from our bedroom windows.' I gaped in fascination at Eunice while she outlined in such blissful ignorance the reason for the attempted murder of her husband. He himself had told me that the executors of the late Davis L. Davis had accepted his tender for the farm only recently, during the week before our momentous trip on the river. So the something 'goddam stupid' which had happened to Yola and Matt Clive's scheme was that they had discovered that of all the people on earth it was to be Dave Teller who was to be Offen's new close neighbour. They had discovered it *after* they'd hi-jacked the horse, or they wouldn't have gone ahead with the plan.

'Why are you laughing?' Eunice asked, frowning. 'What's so funny?'

'It's not funny,' I agreed, straightening my face, 'Far from it. Do you know Culham James personally?'

'Not yet. Does it matter?' She still looked puzzled.

'It would be wiser not to make close friends with him in too much of a hurry.'

'Why not?'

'Might prove a prickly flower.' I had a mental vision of Dave looking out of his bedroom window day after day, looking over to the paddocks where Chrysalis and Allyx were let out to graze. He might never have recognized them. But also he might. Culham James simply couldn't take the risk. Yola and Matt had flown immediately to England to dispose of Dave a long way from the real scene of danger.

While Allyx remained at Orpheus Farm and Dave continued making active plans to move alongside, the explosive situation would still exist. Though Matt Clive might have given up temporarily, I fervently hoped that Radnor-Halley wouldn't let their vigilance slide a millimetre. A call to Keeble would be wise . . . even at California–London rates.

'I'm going for a walk on the shore,' said Lynnie, kicking off the pebbly sandals. 'Who's coming?'

I beat Walt to it by quicker reflexes, and collected

a grim look from him as I left him alone with Eunice. Lynnie remarked on it, grinning as we ambled silently away on the trickling sand.

'He's put off by the bloodies,' I explained. 'That's all.'

'She says it less often over here,' Lynnie commented. 'And she doesn't drink, except one or two before lunch, until after we've changed in the evening. Why is that, do you think?'

'She's escaped from the Lexington cage.'

'That heavenly house . . . a cage?'

'Uh huh.'

'The new one isn't half so beautiful,' she protested.

'It will be, when Eunice has finished. And then the walls will close in again.'

'Another cage, do you mean?' She sounded uncertain.

'Another cage,' I agreed.

'Life can't be just escaping from one cage and ending up in another,' she said explosively, repudiating violently so bleak a vision.

'Everyone lives inside bars,' I said. 'The trick is not to want to get out.'

'Stop it,' she said in distress. 'I don't want to hear that.'

'They used to keep linnets as pets,' I said. 'But there aren't any linnets in cages any more. Budgerigars instead. You'll be all right, little linnet.'

'I never know when you're being serious.'

'Always.'

'But half the time what you say is so . . . so crazy.'

'Life is serious, life is crazy. Anything crazy is serious, and everything serious is crazy . . . I'll race you along to that beach hut.'

She beat me to it in her bare feet, and leaned against the rough wooden wall laughing and getting her breath back while I tipped half-a-ton of sand out of my shoes. We walked on a little farther, and then sat down in the warm night and looked out across the shadowy peaceful ocean. No land between us and Japan, half a world away.

'Did you come out here to be with . . . us, or to find Allyx?' she said.

'Both.'

She shook her head. 'You brought Walt. That makes it to find Allyx.'

'Walt would have chosen to stay somewhere else,' I said, smiling. 'So California for Allyx, Santa Barbara for you. Satisfied?'

She murmured something unintelligible, and we sat in silence while she scuffed sand into a heap with her toes.

'Will you find him, do you think?' she asked in the end.

'Allyx? We might do.'

'When, roughly?'

'I don't know. Tomorrow, maybe.'

'And then . . . you'll go home?'

'I guess.'

'Back to an office . . .' She swept out an arm, embracing the wide sky. Back to an office, I thought coldly: and to the perpetual digging into people's privacy, to the occasional snaring of a bent applicant, to drizzle, to Putney, to the vacuum of the flat. To, in short, my normal life. The trick was not to want to slip through the bars.

'What are you going to do, now that you've left school?' I asked.

She sucked in a breath. 'After this, all the old things seem horribly dreary.'

'They'll soon give Dave a walking plaster . . .'

'I *know*,' she wailed. 'Don't think I don't know. I was supposed to be starting a secretarial course in September . . . I utterly don't want to, any more. Why can't everyone just live on the beach and be warm all the time . . .' She rocked with her arms laced round her bent up knees.

'Not enough beach.'

She giggled. 'You are just about the least romantic man alive. Comes of being a civil servant, I suppose. Like Daddy.'

In time we walked back along by the edge of the sea and paused when we came level with the motel. She put her hand on my arm and simply stood there waiting. I kissed her forehead, and then her nose, and finally her mouth. It was all very gentle, and utterly unnerving.

'This is no good,' I said, taking my hands from her shoulders. 'No good at all.'

'I've been kissed before,' she said anxiously. 'I really have.'

'That isn't what I meant,' I said, half laughing. 'You'd qualify for a diploma. No . . . it's just, little Lynnie, that we're a long way from home . . . and I never kiss brunettes more than once on a Friday.' I turned away towards the motel and jerked my head for her to follow. The best resolutions in the world would come a cropper faced with something like Lynnie, and immediate flight was the only course. It didn't seem to be popular with Lynnie herself, but I couldn't help that. I walked her briskly up the beach and made a joke about what Walt would be saying to Eunice, and we arrived in reasonable order to find that it was nothing: they were sitting across the table from each other in a miles-apart silence. Eunice gave us a long cool look and Walt one of disillusion, and Lynnie quite unnecessarily blushed, confirming their obvious suspicions. The harmless little walk hadn't been a good idea from any one of four points of view.

Walt and I drove quietly into Orpheus Farm the following morning. He did the talking: a thoroughly professional piece of work, insurance patter at the double. A survey for new fire regulations, he glibly explained, necessitated us seeing over the entire establishment.

We saw. Every stall in every barn, every hay loft, every straw bale, every inch. We saw Moviemaker. We saw Centigrade. We made a great many notes.

Culham James Offen himself escorted us round the coolest barn containing his four prize stallions. A great deal of self satisfaction sat on his shoulders like an impervious duck's-back mantle. I considered this with uneasy suspicion.

Uncle Bark was not only a man in his fifties with white hair, but he had a grey station wagon in a third of his large garage. I saw Walt giving it a sidelong glance. Undoubtedly it was Uncle Bark who had delivered the Snail Express trailer to old Hagstrom's boy at Rock Springs; and very likely Uncle Bark who had followed Sam Hengelman's van along the turnpike. Impossible to prove, though, at this distance.

The colour of his hair was premature. Very few wrinkles marked the smooth suntanned face, from which white eyebrows stood out like a bracket of snow, nearly meeting over the nose. His eyelashes were also white, but the albino non-pigmentation stopped short of the eyes: not pink, but a clear pale blue.

He carried his head stiffly on a thick muscular neck, and the large body beneath the airy white shirt looked solid more than soft. Not a man to ignore in any company. A physique which teemed naturally with success: and success had given him an arrogance of expression where a decent humility would have been more fitting.

The whole farm had the high gloss of money-no-object. Mathematically precise white-painted wood railings ringed the paddocks, and the approach to the Spanish-style house was landscaped with watered lawns and palms and an occasional bed full of spiky red flowers with sharp purplish leaves. We didn't penetrate the house: Walt's fire insurance only stretched to the stabling.

After we'd seen the stallions Offen handed us over to his stud groom, a fair, surprisingly young man he called Kiddo, who had a drawling western voice and an air of having been born without urgency. Every second word was 'uh', and his walk was thirty-two frames a second; slow motion.

'Been here long?' I asked him, as he pointed out the spotless foaling stalls.

'Five or six months,' he said, showing no resentment at a personal question; good natured, unsuspicious, no sign of nerves.

'You must be good, to get a job like this so young,' I congratulated him.

After a pause he said, 'I got a feeling for horses, see? Mares, they foal down nearly always at night. Comes from having to give birth in the dark out in the wild, you understand?'

'Why in the dark?' asked Walt, puzzled.

Another pause. Not for a deliberate choice of what or what not to say, I realized, but just a moment of waiting while the instinctive knowledge coalesced into words.

'They drop 'em by day, some hungry hyena comes along and kills the foal in the first half hour. Foals, now, they're readier to run at birth than most other critturs, but you've got to give 'em a half hour to dry off.'

'But they don't have to run, here,' Walt protested.

'Nature don't know that,' Kiddo pointed out reasonably. 'Another thing, mares mostly drop their foals pretty quick. Don't take some of them no time at all. And then, see, I always know when a mare's ready, and most often I go to the stall and make sure she's doing all right.'

'How do you know?' I asked, fascinated.

A much longer pause. Then he said, 'I don't know how I know, I got a feeling for it. I just wake up some nights and think, that Rose is about ready, and I go on out to her, and maybe there she is, not needing a bit of help, or maybe with the cord round the foal's neck, strangling it. I bin with horses, see, all my life.'

'Where were you before you came here?' I asked.

'Uh . . . all over. Had a job in Lexington a while back, but they said I didn't keep good time turning up at work.' He grinned suddenly, a big mischievous lighting-up of the passive patient face. 'Then . . . uh . . . I was with a feller in Maryland . . . he had a barn was falling down and honeysuckle breaking his fences and creeping into his windows, but he sure had some pretty mares and one of them was the dam of the horse who won the Preakness a year back. Though I don't go to the races, myself.'

'Where after Maryland?' I asked.

'Uh . . . here. I seen this ad in the *Blood Horse*, and I wrote. It was a joke, mostly. I never expected to hear a word, knowing this was a big place and everything. But Mr Offen, it seems he didn't want no great business man, just someone with a feeling for the mares . . . and he's keeping me on, he says, though there was two before me he let go after they'd been here a month.'

It didn't seem to worry him. He had the God-will-provide nature which doesn't understand anxiety and never stores up winter nuts. Not that he had any need to. His 'feeling for mares' was in fact priceless: he would probably never cash in on it as he could but he'd never want for a job.

Kiddo watched us go in the same calm friendliness with which he'd shown us round. Walt and I agreed on the way back to Santa Barbara that he was only potentially an opponent. Loyalty might be given to Offen if he demanded it, but at present Kiddo had no idea what was going on.

'Unless,' Walt said thoughtfully, 'he's a brilliant actor.'

I shook my head. 'He wasn't acting. None of the signs.'

Walt looked at me curiously, taking his eyes too long off the road. 'Can you always tell?'

I smiled. 'That's one of those unanswerable questions. I've a feeling for it, like Kiddo with his mares. But if it lets me down sometimes, how am I to know?'

'You'd know soon enough when secrets started leaking to the other side,' Walt pointed out. 'Have you ever passed as clear anyone who turned out to be a spy?'

'Yes.'

'How often?'

'Once.'

'In your first year, I suppose,' Walt said with mild sarcasm.

'In my second year. He was the first serious spy I had to deal with, and I didn't spot him. The counter-espionage chaps turned him up six months later when he'd done a good deal of damage, and the press made the usual scathing remarks about the feebleness of our screening system.'

'Which you took to heart,' Walt said dryly.

'I guess so.'

He drove a mile and then said, 'And now you're so good at it that they beat you up. What do you think about things when that happens?'

'That there's a big fish coming down the pipeline and they want me out of the way.'

'So you look all the harder.' A statement, not a question.

'You might say so. Yes.'

'They'll kill you one of these days.'

I didn't answer. Walt flicked a glance sideways and sighed. 'I suppose you don't care.'

'There are a lot of others in the department.'

Walt drove into Santa Barbara without another word, where we joined Eunice and Lynnie in the terrace restaurant for lunch. They had, they said, bought that morning the big bright dangling earrings which swung with every turn of their heads. Lynnie's were scarlet, Eunice's acid green; otherwise identical. Still friends, I thought in some relief. Still in harmony. Whether Eunice would do a small chore for me was, however, another matter.

We had clam chowder with shrimp to follow, and Lynnie said with all this seafood she'd be growing fins. During coffee, when she stood up restlessly and said she was going down to the sea, it was Walt, after a pause, who said he would go with her. She looked at me questioningly, worriedly, and then turned and walked quickly off with him, talking a good deal too brightly.

'Don't you hurt that child,' Eunice said fiercely.

'I don't want to.'

'You're too bloody attractive.'

'Yeah. Charm the birds off the trees,' I agreed sardonically. 'Little wives spill their husbands' secrets into my bloody attractive ears.'

She looked shocked. Quite a change, I thought, from dishing it out.

'You mean you . . . *use* it?'

'Like a can opener. And as a catalyst. Who doesn't? Salesmen, politicians, actors, women, all using it like mad.'

'For God's sake . . .' Her voice was faint, but she was also laughing.

'But not on Lynnie,' I added wryly.

'You didn't need to, I guess. Dragging Dave out of the Thames was a lot more effective.'

I watched Lynnie's and Walt's backs as they reached the tide line.

'So that's why . . .?' I said, almost to myself.

'Hero worship,' Eunice said with barbs. 'Does it give you a kick?'

'Like a mule's in the stomach . . .'

She laughed. 'It's not that you're so madly handsome in any obvious way.'

'No,' I agreed with truth, 'I'm not.'

She looked as if she were going to say more and then thought better of it. I jumped straight in while her mind was still half flirting, knowing, and despising the knowledge, that in that mood she was more likely to do what I asked.

'Has Lynnie still got those photographs of me?'

'Don't worry,' she said sarcastically. 'In a fire, she'd save them first.'

'I'd like Culham James Offen to see them.'

'You'd like *what*? What are you talking about?'

'About you and Lynnie driving over to pay a neighbourly call on Culham James this afternoon, and easily, dearest Eunice, you could tell him about me pulling Dave out of the Thames, and Lynnie could show him my photograph. Especially the one of me sitting by a table outside a pub. That group of all of us.'

She gaped and gasped, and then started thinking.

'You really can't be as pleased with yourself as all that . . . so for God's sake, why?'

'An experiment.'

'That's no answer.'

'Earning my keep at The Vacationer.'

A look of disgust turned down her mouth.

'Finding that bloody horse?'

'I'm afraid so.'

'You don't mean . . . surely you can't mean that Offen has anything to do with it?'

'I'd like to make sure he hasn't.'

'Oh, I see. Well, I guess that's not much to ask. Sure. I'll get Lynnie to come with me.'

'And tell him I'm looking for Allyx.'

She gave me a straight assessing stare, and said, 'How about Chrysalis?'

'Whatever you like. Say that Dave employed me to get him back.'

'I don't know why I'm doing it.'

'More interesting than golf?' I suggested.

'Is it a game?' She was sceptical.

'Well . . . like hunting bears,' I smiled.

'Oh, yes.' She nodded sardonically. 'A sport.'

CHAPTER THIRTEEN

I parked a hired car in some scrub off the road leading to Orpheus Farm, and smoked a rare cigarette. The fierce afternoon sun roasted through the metal roof and a water mirage hung in a streak over the dry road. A day for lizards to look for shade. They'd run out of air-conditioned heaps at the hire firms: I'd had to take one of those old fashioned jobs where you breathed fresh air by opening the window. The air in question was as fresh as last week's news and as hot as tomorrow's.

At five past four Eunice and Lynnie passed unseeingly across my bows, heading back to Santa Barbara. I finished the cigarette and stubbed it out carefully in the flaked chromium ashtray. I looked at my fingernails for ten minutes. No special inspiration. At half past four I started the car, pointed its nose towards Orpheus, and went to call on Uncle Bark.

This time I drove straight up to the house and rang the ornate bell. A houseboy came: all on the same scale as at Jeff Roots's. When he went to find Culham

James I followed quietly on his heels, so my host, even if he had meant to, had no chance to say he was out. The houseboy opened the door on to a square comfortable office–sitting room and Culham James was revealed sitting at his desk with a green telephone receiver to his ear.

He gave the houseboy and myself a murderous glare between us which changed to reasonable affability once he'd got control of it. 'I'll call you later,' he said to the telephone. 'A Mr Hawkins has this minute arrived . . . that's right . . . later then.' He put down the receiver and raised his eyebrows.

'Did you miss something this morning?' he asked.

'No . . . should we have done?'

He shook his head in mild annoyance. 'I am merely asking the purpose of this return visit.'

'My colleague and I wanted answers to one or two extra questions about the precautions you take against fire, especially as regards those two exceptionally valuable stallions . . . er . . . Moviemaker and Centigrade.'

Under his suntanned face, behind the white bracket of eyebrows, Culham James Offen was beginning to enjoy a huge joke. It fizzed like soda water in his pale blue eyes and bubbled in his throat. He was even having difficulty in preventing himself from sharing it: but after a struggle he had it nailed down under hatches, and calm with a touch of severity took over. We went solemnly through the farce of fire precautions, me leaning on his desk and checking off Walt's solid sounding inventions one by one. They mostly had to deal with the amount of supervision in the stallions' barn at night. Whether there were any regular patrols, any dogs loose on watch, any photoelectric apparatus for detecting opacity, such as heavy smoke?

Offen cleared his throat and answered no to the lot.

'We have the extremely expensive and reliable sprinkler system which you saw this morning,' he pointed out. 'It is thoroughly tested every three months, as I told you earlier.'

'Yes. Thank you, then. I guess that's all.' I shut my notebook. 'You've been most helpful, Mr Offen.'

'You're welcome,' he said. The joke rumbled in his voice, but was coloured now with unmistakable malice. High time to go, I thought: and went.

When I got back to The Vacationer some while later I found Eunice and Lynnie and Walt sitting in a glum row behind empty glasses. I flopped into a chair opposite them and said, 'Why the mass depression?'

'You're late,' Walt said.

'I told you not to wait dinner.' I caught a passing waiter on the wing and arranged refills all round.

'We were considering a search party,' Eunice said.

I looked at all three of them more carefully. 'You've been comparing notes,' I said resignedly.

'I think it's terrible of you . . . *wicked*,' Lynnie burst out. 'To have made me go and deliberately . . . *deliberately* . . . put you in such frightful danger.'

'Lynnie stop it. I wasn't in any danger . . . here I am, aren't I?'

'But Walt said . . .'

'Walt needs his brains seen to.'

Walt glared and compressed his mouth into a rigid line. 'You didn't tell me you'd arranged for Offen to know you were the man who took Chrysalis. And you didn't tell me the Clives had tried to kill Mr Teller.'

'And you didn't tell *me*,' Eunice added, 'that the couple in the background of the photograph Lynnie showed Culham Offen had tried to kill you too.'

'Or you'd never have let Lynnie show it to him?'

'No,' she said slowly.

'Just as well I didn't.'

'And you deliberately misled me by saying you wanted to clear Offen. It wasn't true.'

'Er . . . no. But I did want you to behave naturally with him. And anyway, why all the fuss?'

'We thought . . .' Lynnie said in a subdued voice. 'We almost thought . . . as you were gone so long . . . that you . . . that they . . .'

'They didn't,' I pointed out obviously, smiling.

'But won't you please explain why?' Lynnie said. '*Why* did you want me to give you away like that?'

'Several reasons. One was to make Dave safer.'

'I don't see how,' Eunice objected.

'By letting Offen know, and through him the Clives, that we could prove the Clives were in England and beside the Thames on the day of Dave's accident.

Murder by accident is only a good idea as long as there's no apparent motive and the murderers have no apparent connection with the victim. We've shown them that we know their motive and their connection, and they must now be aware that if Dave were killed they would be the first suspects. This makes it less likely they will try again.'

'Crikey,' Lynnie said, 'Go on.'

'When Walt and I went to Orpheus Farm this morning saying we were making a survey for new fire precautions, Offen wasn't worried. He didn't know me from Adam then, of course. It was before you showed him my photograph. But he showed no anxiety at all about two strangers turning up on a pretext that he didn't even bother to check. None of the edginess one might have expected if he'd just had one stolen horse pinched back from him, and was in possession of two others standing in his barn. I didn't like it. It didn't feel right.'

'He hasn't got them,' Eunice said with relief. 'I was sure it couldn't possibly be right that Culham Offen would steal horses. I mean, he's *respected*.'

Walt and I exchanged a glance of barely perceptible amusement. To be respected was the best cover in the world for fraud. Fraud, in fact, could rarely exist without it.

'So,' I said, 'I thought it would be helpful if he knew for certain that I was especially interested in Moviemaker and Centigrade, and that I wasn't in fire insurance, but was the man he had to thank for losing Chrysalis. When I went back, after you two had left, he still wasn't worried. On the contrary, he was enjoying the situation. It amused him enormously to think that I believed I was fooling him. I asked him a lot of questions about the security precautions surrounding Moviemaker and Centigrade, and he was still completely untroubled. So,' I paused, 'it's now quite clear that the two horses standing in his barn called Moviemaker and Centigrade are in actual fact exactly what he says: Moviemaker and Centigrade. He isn't worried about snoopers, he isn't worried about me making clumsy preparations to steal them. He must therefore be confident that any legal proceedings will prove the horses to be the ones he says they are. He'd ambush me if I tried to steal them, and have me in real deep trouble, which would be to him some small compensation for losing Chrysalis.'

Walt nodded briefly.

Eunice said obstinately. 'I think it only proves that you're barking up the wrong damn tree. He isn't worried simply because he isn't guilty of anything.'

'You liked him?'

'Yes,' she said. 'He was bloody sweet.'

Lynnie nodded. 'I thought so too.'

'What did he say when you showed him the photographs?'

'He just glanced at them at first,' Lynnie said. 'And then he took them over to the window. And then he asked me who had taken them, and where, and when. So I told him about the day on the river, and about you and Dave going under the weir . . .'

At the side of my vision Eunice gave me an I-told-you-so smile.

'. . . and he said one or two nice things about you,' Lynnie finished. 'So I told him you came over here to look for Chrysalis, and somehow or other you found him.'

'He asked where you found him,' Eunice nodded. 'But we didn't know. I said you were now trying to find Allyx, and it certainly didn't worry him. I'm sure you must be wrong.'

I smiled at her. She didn't want the horse found, and as an ally she was as reliable as thin ice on a sunny day. I didn't intend to tell her anything in future which I wasn't prepared to have passed on to Offen. Like most law abiding citizens she had not grasped that a criminal mind didn't show, that an endearing social manner could co-exist with fraud and murder. 'Such a *nice* man,' the neighbours say in bewilderment, when Mr Smith's garden is found to be clogged with throttled ladies. 'Always so pleasant.'

Eunice, propelled by a strong semi-conscious wish for him not to have Allyx, might tell Offen anything, simply because she couldn't visualize a 'sweet' man being deadly. She might also tell him anything propelled by the same impulse which had made her point a gun at me.

'Let's have dinner,' I suggested; and Eunice and Lynnie went away to freshen up.

Walt looked at me thoughtfully, then raised his eyebrows.

I nodded. 'I put a bug on the underside of his desk, two feet from the telephone. I was late back because I was listening. He called Yola and told her about my visit but there wasn't much else. I left the set hidden, and came back here.'

'Do you mean it, that those two horses really are Moviemaker and Centigrade?'

'Sure. He bought them, remember. Openly. At bloodstock sales. And obviously he's kept them. I suppose he never could be certain that some ex-owner would turn up for a visit. Those horses will have been tattooed inside their mouths with an identity number when they first began to race. They have to be, over here, don't they? It'll be quite easy to establish that they're the right two.'

'You don't think Mrs Teller's right . . . that he never had Showman and Allyx after all?'

'I'll play you his call to Yola some time. He had the foresight to whisk those horses away from Orpheus when we got Chrysalis. He was more or less waiting for something like our visit this morning. No flies on Culham James, I'm afraid. Er . . . Walt, did you give Eunice and Lynnie any details about our jaunt in the Tetons?'

He looked uncomfortable. 'I was annoyed with you.'

'What exactly did you tell them?'

'Not much. I was horrified at Lynnie having shown Offen that picture of the Clives, and when Mrs Teller said you'd planned it I said you must be mad, they'd tried to kill you once already.'

'And you told them how?'

He nodded, not meeting my eyes.

'Did you tell them about the bugs and the wireless set?'

'No.'

'It's important, Walt.'

He looked up. 'I didn't mention them.'

I relaxed. 'How about our mountain walk?'

'No details.'

'Place?'

'I'm pretty sure I mentioned the Tetons.'

Nothing there that would hurt.

'How much did you say about Showman and Allyx?'

'I told them that you'd worked out through the stud books that Offen must have them.'

'Did you say the words "Uncle Bark"?'

He shook his head. 'I'd forgotten about that.'

I sighed. 'Walt. Mrs Teller doesn't want Allyx found any more than she wanted Chrysalis. Let's not entrust the state of the nation to the Indians.'

He flushed a little and compressed his mouth. Eunice and Lynnie came back shortly after, and, though we all four had dinner together it proved a taciturn and not over-friendly affair.

Walt rode up to my room for a conference after the coffee.

'How do we find them?' he said, coming bluntly to the point and easing himself simultaneously into the only armchair.

'They've made us a gift of them, in one way,' I said thoughtfully. 'We can send a bunch of lawyers in to query Moviemaker and Centigrade's identity, and get it established beyond doubt that the two Offen showed us are in fact those two horses. He'll be keen for them to do it: and once he's done it, he'll be stuck with them. We will meanwhile do another little vanishing trick with the other two and start our own identification parade on our ground. Once they are established as Allyx and Showman, Offen cannot possibly claim them back.'

'Two objections,' Walt said. 'We don't know where Allyx and Showman are. And if we find them, why not get lawyers into the act right away? Why go to all the danger and trouble of taking them?'

'Same as Chrysalis,' I pointed out. 'The first sign of any real trouble, and they'd be shot. It's not illegal to kill a horse and whisk it smartly off to the dog food people. And vastly more difficult to identify a dead one. Impossible, I'd almost say, for the degree of certainty we need here.'

'Even if we take them, and establish their identity, and everything goes smoothly, Offen will still be raking in those colossal stud fees of half a million dollars a year, because we'd never be able to prove that for the past ten years Showman has been siring every foal that's down in the book as Moviemaker's . . .'

I smiled. 'We'll do something about that, once we've sorted out the rest.'

'Which brings us back to square one,' Walt said flatly. 'Where the hell do we start?'

I perched on the window sill and looked down sideways into the brightly lit car park. Coloured bulbs on the face of the motel raised rainbow shimmers on glossy hard tops and struck me as a deeply melancholy commentary on human achievement. Yet I wouldn't have wanted to live without cars or electricity . . . if I'd wanted to live. My room was only two floors up, with none above. Too near the ground. I'd known of a woman who'd jumped from five and bungled it. A gun was better . . .

'Well?' Walt said insistently.

'I'm sorry . . .?' I said vaguely, turning my head back to him.

'Where do we look?'

'Oh . . . yes.'

'On the ranch?'

'Very doubtful, don't you think? They must know that's the first place we'd think of.'

'There's a lot of land there,' he said. 'And a lot of horses to lose them in.'

I shook my head. 'They'd have to keep them in a paddock close to the house. All the rest of the ranch is well named Rocky Mountains, and they couldn't turn them loose for fear of them breaking a leg. We'd better check, though.' I stared unseeingly at the carpet. 'But I guess the horses are with Matt. Offen is at Orpheus Farm, and Yola is tied to the ranch seeing to about thirty guests, so where's Matt?'

'Where indeed,' Walt said gloomily.

'He and Yola don't spend their winters on the ranch because the valley is blocked by snow. She told me that they go south . . . On one of those telephone calls she told Offen they couldn't keep Chrysalis at a place called Pitts, because it wasn't suitable. But that was when they didn't know we were after them . . . when it wasn't an emergency.'

'So somewhere south of the Tetons we find this Pitts, and Matt and the horses will be waiting for us?'

'Yeah.' I smiled briefly. 'Sounds too easy.'

'Easy!' Walt said.

'They must leave a forwarding address for mail,' I pointed out. 'They live a conventional law-abiding life with a longstanding business to give them obvious legal means of support. There must be dozens of people in Jackson who know their winter address.'

'Our Buttress agent could get that, then. First thing in the morning.'

'Fine.'

Walt levered himself out of the armchair and hesitated.

'Come along to my room,' he said. 'I've got a bottle.'

I wasn't sure that I wanted to, but he smiled suddenly, wiping out all resentments, and one didn't kick that sort of olive branch in the teeth.

'Be glad to,' I said.

The smile went deeper and lasted along the passage to his room, which was almost identical to mine. The window looked out on the same cars from a slightly different angle, and he had two armchairs instead of one. There was a bottle of Old Grandad on a round tray with glasses and a water jug, and on his bedside table stood a leather-framed photograph. I picked it up idly while he went to fetch ice from the machine along the passage. Walt with his family. A good-looking woman, a plain girl in her early teens, a thin boy of about ten: all four of them smiling cheerfully into the lens. He came back as I was putting them down.

'I'm sorry about the picnic,' I said.

'Next week will do just as well,' he said. 'We've got the whole of the summer, I guess.'

We sat in the armchairs, drinking slowly. I didn't like bourbon much; but that wasn't the point. He talked casually about the split-level ranch-type house they'd moved into the year before, and how his daughter got along just fine with the folks next door, and how they'd had trouble with the boy's health, he'd had rheumatic fever . . .

'How about your own future, with Buttress Life?' I asked.

'I've gotten about as high as I'll get,' he said with surprising honesty. 'There's only one more step up that I really want, and that's to chief investigator, claims division, and that'll come along next year when the present guy retires.'

He poured more drinks, rubbed his thumb slowly over the round fingertips, and said Amy and the kids were asking him for a pool in their back yard, and that Amy's mother was a problem since Amy's father died last fall, and that he hadn't caught a single ball game last season, he'd been that busy . . .

We sat for more than an hour without mentioning the horses once. He yawned finally and I uncurled myself from the soft chair, putting down the third time empty glass. He said goodnight sleepily with easy friendliness and, for the first time since I'd known him, without tension. Back in my own room, undressing, I wondered how long it would last. Until I made the next unpopular suggestion, I supposed. I didn't know whether to envy him his enclosing domesticity or to feel stifled by it. I did know that I liked him both as a man and as a working companion, moods and all.

*

The Buttress Life agent in Jackson came through with the Clives' winter address within twenty minutes of Walt calling him: 40159 Pittsville Boulevard, Las Vegas, Nevada.

I remembered Yola's smile at the thought of winter. Las Vegas explained it. Yola liked to gamble.

'What now?' Walt said.

'I'll go on out there and take a look.'

'Alone?' There was a certain amount of anxiety in his voice, which I interpreted as a desire not to be left in Santa Barbara with Eunice.

'We need you here,' I said placatingly. 'And don't tell her where I've gone.'

He gave me a sharp glance. 'I won't.'

We drove in the hired car out to Orpheus Farm, where I showed him where I'd hidden the radio tape recorder between three rocks, with its aerial sticking up through the branches of a scrubby bush. The nearest neatly railed paddock was only feet away; the house, about four hundred yards. We picked up the radio and parked a short distance down the road.

'Supposing he sees us?' Walt said, watching me wind back the reel.

'He'll only think we're watching the farm routine, to know when to pinch Moviemaker. The radio will pick up the bug in his office from at least a quarter mile, but it gets fainter after that. It has to work on the air-vibration system. Not such a good amplification as electricity. Do you ever use them?'

'Bugs?' He shook his head. 'Not often. Cameras with telescopic lenses are better. Catch the claimants walking around on their paralysed legs.' Satisfaction echoed in his voice. Like me, a rogue hunter to the bone.

Smiling to myself, I switched on. Cutting in and out, Culham James' various conversations filled three-quarters of an hour of tape time, but nothing he said was of any use to us. I rewound the reels again and we put the radio in among the rocks, Walt agreeing that he would come back after sunset and listen to the day's take.

He drove me then to the Los Angeles airport, where I hopped on a plane to Las Vegas, arriving mid afternoon. The desert hit like a gust from an oven when they opened the plane doors, and from a nearby building the usual lighted numbers proclaimed to the populace that in the shade, if they could find any, it would be 108.

The air-conditioning at the edge of town motel I booked into was turning itself inside out under the strain, and the Hertz man who presently took my money admitted that this was a little old heatwave, sure thing. Had to expect them, in July. The inconspicuous Pontiac he hired me was this time, however, a cooled one. I drove around for a while to get my bearings, and then took a look at Pittsville Boulevard.

The high numbers ran two miles out of the town, expensive looking homes along a metalled road with the desert crowding in at their rear. The Clives' house was flanked by others on both sides: not near enough to touch, but too near for the invisible stabling of stallions. The place on Pitts wasn't suitable, as Yola had said.

It was low and white, with a flat roof and a frame of palms and orange trees. Blinds and insect screens blanked out the windows, and the grass on each side of the drive was a pale dry biscuit colour, not green watered like its neighbours. I stopped the car in the roadway opposite and looked it over. Not a leaf moved under the bleaching sun. Ten minutes ticked away. Nothing happened in the street. Inside the car, with the engine stopped, the temperature rose like Christmas prices. I started up again, sucked in the first cold blast from the air-conditioner, and slid on along the way I was heading.

A mile past the Clives' house the metal surface ended, and the road ran out across the desert as a dusty streak of gravel. I turned the car and went back, thinking. The comparative dead-endedness of Pittsville Boulevard explained the almost total lack of traffic past the Clives', and also meant that I couldn't drive past there very often without becoming conspicuous to the neighbours. Keeping a check on an apparently empty house, however, wasn't going to get me much farther.

About five houses along on the town side of the Clives' there was another with water-starved brownish grass. Taking a chance that these inhabitants too were away from home I rolled the Pontiac purposefully into the palm-edged driveway and stopped outside the front door. Ready with some of Walt's insurance patter, I leant on the bell and gave it a full twenty seconds. No one came. Everything was hot, quiet, and still.

Strolling, I walked down the drive and on to the road. Looking back one couldn't see the car for bushes. Satisfied, I made the trip along to the Clives', trying to look as if walking were a normal occupation in a Nevada heatwave: and by the time I got there it was quite clear why it wasn't. The sweat burnt dry on my skin before it had a chance to form into beads.

Reconnoitring the Clives' place took an hour. The house was shut up tight, obviously empty. The window screens were all securely fastened, and all the glass was covered on the inside with blinds, so that one couldn't see in. The doors were fastened with safe-deposit locks. The Clives had made casual breaking-in by vagrants nearly impossible.

With caution I eased round the acre of land behind the house. Palms and bushes screened a trefoil-shaped pool from being overlooked too openly by the neighbours, but from several places it was possible to see the pools of the flanking houses some sixty yards away. Beside one of them, reminding me of Eunice, a woman in two scraps of yellow cloth lay motionless on a long chair, inviting heatstroke and adding to a depth of suntan which would have got her reclassified in South Africa. I moved even more quietly after I'd seen her, but she didn't stir.

The rear boundary of the Clives' land was marked by large stones painted white, with desert scrub on the far side and low growing citrus bushes on the near. From their windows, brother and sister had a wide view of hills and wilderness; two miles down the road neon lights went twenty rounds with the midday sun, and the crash of fruit machines out-decibelled the traffic. I wondered idly how much of Uncle Bark's illicit proceeds found their way into Matt and Yola's pocket, and how much from there vanished into the greedy slot mouths in Vegas. The stud fees went around and around and only Buttress Life were the losers.

On the way back to the motel I stopped at every supermarket I came to, and bought two three-pound bags of flour from each.

From a hardware store I acquired a short ladder, white overalls, white peaked cotton cap, brushes, and a half-gallon can of bright yellow instant drying paint.

CHAPTER FOURTEEN

Walt listened to what I had to say in a silence which hummed down the telephone wires more eloquently than hysterics.

'You're crazy,' he said at last, sounding as if he seriously meant it.

'Can you think of anything else?'

After a long pause he said grudgingly, 'Nothing quicker.'

'Right, then. I'll fix everything this end and give you a call in the morning. And let's hope it works.'

'What if it doesn't?'

'Have to try something else.'

Walt grunted gloomily and hung up.

I spent an hour at the airport, and then went back to the motel. The evening oozed away. I played some roulette without enthusiasm and lost backing black against a sequence of fourteen reds; and I ate a good steak listening to a girl singer whose voice was secondary to her frontage. After that I lay on my bed for a while and smoked, and kept the blues from crowding in too close by thinking exclusively of the job in hand.

At two I dressed in a dark green cotton shirt and black jeans, went downstairs, stepped into the car, and drove along Pittsville Boulevard to 40159. The town itself was wide awake and rocking: the houses along Pitts were dark and silent. With dimmed lights I rolled quietly into the Clives' driveway and stacked the bags of flour close to the front door. Then, holding the car door but not shutting it, I eased the Pontiac back along the road and parked it in the driveway of the same empty house that I had used in the afternoon. Again, not wanting any neighbours to remember hearing a car door slam, I left it ajar, and walked back to the Clives'.

The night was warm and gentle with a deep navy blue sky and stars like fluorescent polka-dots. Two miles away the blazing lights of Vegas raised a bell-shaped orange glow, but among the palms and orange trees the shadows were thick and black and comfortably concealing.

The Clives' was only the latest of a great many houses I had broken into. My short cuts to truth were scandalous by all public and private standards, and Keeble rarely asked how I got my information: and as I would have had the press, the police, and public opinion all balefully against me if I'd ever been caught, A gag on eggs would have been clumsy in comparison.

Law-abiding citizens never knew I'd been their guest. For the Clives', however, I had alternative plans.

Wearing surgeons' rubber gloves, and with my shoes stuck through my belt to the left of the Luger, I worked on the lock on the back door, and after not too bad a time, considering its complexity, the two sets of tumblers fell sweetly over, and the house was mine.

Inside, the air was stale and still, and dust sheets draped the furniture, looking like pale boulders in the dim light of my torch. The rear door opened into a spacious hall which led straight through to the front. I walked across, unbolted and unfastened the front door, brought in the bags of flour, and left the door ajar, like the one I'd come in by: the value of always being prepared for instant flight had been drummed into me by an ex-burglar who had once neglected it.

I went into the bedrooms. Large separate single bedded rooms again for Yola and Matt, and a guest bedroom, with a bathroom to each. I pulled all the covers off the furniture and flung on to the floor everything they had left in the chests and closets. Over the resulting mess in each room I shook six pounds of self-raising flour.

In the kitchen I emptied on to the floor a packet of soap flakes, a packet of rice, some cereal and four pounds of brown sugar, which were all lying handy in the pantry. I unlocked the pantry window and unfastened its outer screen, leaving both open: and as an afterthought tumbled some canned fruit off the shelf beneath it, to show that the intruder had come in that way.

In the spacious living room I again removed all the covers, put every ornament and small loose object in a heap on the floor, and flung flour over them and around the whole place. A smaller cosier room, facing the road, contained a desk full of papers, two large bookshelves, and a well-filled sewing box. Together the jumbled contents made a splendid ankle-deep mess on the floor. Pounds of flour fell over everything like snow.

It was while I was tearing open the last bag, ready for a final scatter round the hall, that I heard the distant police siren. Frozen, I doubted for a second that it was for me: then considered that either a too watchful neighbour had seen my torch in chinks through the blinds, or else that the Clives' complicated locks weren't their only protection, and that they had a direct burglar alarm line to the police.

Without wasting much time I shut the front door and heard the lock engage. Emptied the last bag of flour over a plastic flower arrangement on a table in the hall. Flitted through the rear door and clicked it shut behind me. Thrust the torch into my pocket.

The siren wailed and stopped at the front of the house. Doors slammed, men shouted, boots ran. Someone with a megaphone urged me to come out with my hands on my head. The edges of the house were outlined by a spotlight shining on its front.

With bare seconds to spare before the first uniform appeared in silhouette around the corner I reached the nearest of the bushes flanking the trefoil pool and dived behind it. Being quiet enough was no problem, as the law were making an intimidating clatter all around the house, but staying invisible was more difficult. They brought another spotlight round to the rear and shone it full on the house. The shuttered windows stared blindly and unhelpfully back, reflecting the glare almost as far as my cover.

Lights appeared in neighbouring houses, and heads stuck like black knobs out of the windows. I eased gently away past a few more bushes and thought I was still a great deal too close to a spell in the zoo.

A shout from the side of the house indicated that they had found the open pantry window. Four troopers altogether, I judged. All armed to the teeth. I grimaced in the darkness and moved another few yards with less caution. I wasn't going to give them any forefinger exercise if I could help it, but the time was running out.

They were brave enough. One or more climbed in through the window and switched on the light. I more rapidly crossed the last stretch of garden, stepped over the white-painted stones, and headed straight out into the desert.

Five steps convinced me I needed to put my shoes on. Ten steps had me certain that the only vegetation was prickly pear, and close-ranked, at that. I should imagine I impaled myself on every one in the neighbourhood.

Back at the Clives' they had temporarily stopped oohing and ahing over the mess, and were searching the grounds. Lights moved round the next door houses as well. If they went five along and found the car, things would get very awkward indeed.

I had meant to be safely back in my motel long before I called the police early in the morning to say that I was a civic minded neighbour who had just seen a prowler coming out of the Clives' . . .

When they showed signs of shining the light out towards where I was stumbling along I lay down flat on the ground and listened to the thud of my heart. The spotlight beam flickered palely over the low scrubby bushes and outlined the flat spiky plates of the prickly pears, but in the shifting uneven shadows that they threw, I reckoned I must be just another clump. There was a good deal of shouted discussion about whether it was necessary to take a look-see in the desert, but to my relief no one came farther out than the boundary stones. Gradually, frustrated, the dazzle and commotion retreated and died away.

The lights inside the Clives' house went out. The police car drove off. The neighbours went back to bed. I got to my feet and brushed off the surplus of dry sandy earth. What with that and flour dust even the blindest cop would have little difficulty in buttoning me on to the crime.

With more care than on the outward trip I headed back towards the houses, but at an angle I hoped would bring me near the car. The sooner I beat it from that little neck of the woods, the better . . .

I stopped dead.

How might one catch a prowler? Just pretend to go away, and wait somewhere down the road, and when he thought everything was safe, he'd come carelessly along and fall into your waiting hands like a ripe plum.

I decided not to drive back towards Las Vegas from that quiet cul-de-sac. Just in case.

At the fifth house along, everything was quiet. I cat-footed through the grounds, around the house, and took a distant look at the car. Still there. No trooper beside it. I stood in the shadows for longer than was probably necessary, then took a deep breath and risked it. I completed the steps to the car and peered in through the window. Empty. Made a quick cautious tour of the row of spiky low-growing palms hiding it from the road.

Nothing. No irate shouts. All quiet. Car undiscovered. Sighing with relief, the vision of the malicious Clives dancing at my trial fading a little, I pulled wide the already open door and folded like an understuffed rag doll into the driving seat. For five minutes I did nothing more energetic than to breathe freely, and enjoy it.

There remained however the problem of telephoning to Walt: and I chewed it over thoughtfully while absent-mindedly pulling prickly pear needles out of my legs.

I was a fair hand at wire tapping, when I had the kit: but it was in Putney. No doubt there would be a telephone in the empty house alongside. But I wasn't sure that I wanted to risk this house too being directly connected to the police, if that was what had happened at the Clives'. On the other hand, I had been in the Clives' house twenty minutes before the police showed up. Yet they might be quicker, on a second call.

After half an hour I pulled on the rubber gloves, climbed out of the car, and picked the front door lock. It turned all right, but unfortunately the prudent householders had also used bolts. Always a toss up which door of the house people bolted. I walked round to the rear, and let myself in. There was a telephone on a table in the hall. I walked over to it, then turned, retraced my steps, left the door ajar, went round to the car, started up, and drove quietly away in the dead end direction, not stopping until I was off the metalled road on to the gravel, and round a couple of bends. I switched off the light and smoked a cigarette.

Another half hour passed. No lights went on along by the houses; no police sirens, no disturbances at all. I drove gently back, parked in the same spot as before, went round into the house, and called up Walt.

He wasn't amused at being woken at 5 AM.

'A slight change of timing,' I said apologetically. 'The police have already seen the mess.'

He drew in a sharp breath. 'They didn't catch you!'

'No.' No point in telling him how close it had been: he hadn't approved of my going in at all.

'I suppose you want me to come now, then?' he said, with resignation.

'Yes, please. As soon as you can. Leave the car keys at the inquiry desk at Los Angeles airport, and I'll pick them up. The helicopter pilot I've engaged at Las Vegas is Michael King. He's expecting you. Just ask for him. The helicopter radio will pick up the frequency of the bug I've got with me, so you won't need to bring my recorder. Was there anything on the tape today?'

'Yesterday,' Walt corrected. 'Not much. I went over after dinner last night and ran it through. Offen had a friend over. There was two hours of just ordinary yapping. I didn't get back here to bed until one.'

'When this is over you can sleep for a fortnight.'

'Yeah?' he said sarcastically. 'Tell it to the marines.'

He put down his receiver with less of a crash than usual. Smiling, I took out a five dollar bill and left it stuck half under the telephone. Then I let myself out, relocked the door behind me, and went back to the car.

Three hours uneventfully went by. Night changed to day. The air temperature began its morning climb. A few energetic birds sang: and I smoked another cigarette.

Soon after eight a patrol car went up the road, siren fortissimo. Pittsville Boulevard woke up. I eased out of the car, walked carefully down towards the road, and tucked myself invisibly between a palm and a bush, from where I had a clear view of everyone driving up towards the Clives'.

From along the road I could hear several excited voices, most of them children's: and a small boy and a girl came past close to me doing an Indianapolis on their tricycles.

Several cars drove down from the houses, all with men alone, going in to Las Vegas. One woman followed. Three women came the other way, all looking eager. At nine-thirty two men drove in from Vegas, one of them adjusting a large folding camera: the local press.

An hour later a quiet-engined helicopter drifted over and landed out of sight behind a fold of hill.

At ten-fifty the hawk came to the lure.

A sky blue convertible Ford, with the hood down. Matt, driving fast, hunched with anger. Youth, strength, and fury, knotted into one callous personality. Even in a speeding car the impression came across with the solidity of a shockwave. Standing on his brakes flamboyantly late, he screeched down from sixty to nil outside his own house, scattering children like pigeons.

Satisfied, I got stiffly to my feet and went back up the drive to the car. There I removed from the boot the white overalls, white cotton gloves and a cap, and put them on, along with a pair of sunglasses. With a screwdriver from the tool kit I opened the tin of paint and gave the oily yellow contents an encouraging stir; cleaned and replaced the screwdriver, and rested the paint lid gently back on the tin. Then, picking it up by its handle with my right hand, and carrying brushes and ladders with my left, I strolled out on to the road, and along to the Clives'.

Matt's Ford stood at the door at a crooked angle to the patrol car. A good many people were still standing around, staring and gossiping in the sun. I meandered slowly through them and took a closer look at the blue convertible, and then withdrew discreetly to the edge of the proceedings.

Taking the bug out of my pocket, I talked to Walt, hoping he could hear. He couldn't answer: it was strictly one way traffic on the midget transmitter.

'Do you read me, Walt? This is Gene. Our young friend came in his own car, not a hired one or a taxi. His name is on the registration. Pale blue new Ford convertible, at present with the top down. Grey upholstery. Nevada plates, number 3711–42. I'll do the paint if I possibly can, though he may deal with it, of course; and I'll put this bug in the car. When he starts up, you'll hear him. Good luck. And for God's sake don't lose him.'

Indirectly, vaguely, I again approached the car. No one took any notice. I was merely one of the time-passing onlookers, a workman who wasn't working. Several of the children and some of their mothers had seen the state of the well-floured rooms, and thought it a dreadful shame. I leaned my ladder against the rear wing of the blue convertible, put the brushes and paint pot down casually on the flat surface of the boot, and mopped not too imaginary sweat off my face and neck.

Some of the blinds in the Clives' house had been raised, so that in places one could see into the house. No one was looking out. I stretched a hand over the side of the car with the bug in my palm, and felt its sucker cling snugly under the glove shelf.

Still no faces at the windows.

I said to the nearest little boy, 'Someone told me the intruder got in through the pantry window, round that corner.'

'No kidding?' he said, his eyes wide.

'Sure thing.'

He told his mother. They went to look. Nearly everyone followed them, especially as someone nudged the press photographer, who said he would take a picture.

I took a last comprehensive look at the windows, turned to walk away, and with a quick backward flip of a gloved hand, tipped over the can of paint. The lid came off. The can rolled slowly across the flat top of the boot and clanked heavily to the ground. The result was a bright broad spreading pool of yellow on blue, and a proper lake on the gravel.

I was out on the road when the first child saw it and ran after me.

'Your paint's tipped over, mister.'

'Yeah, I know. Don't touch it. Don't let anyone touch it, huh? I'm just going to fetch the stuff to get it off.'

He nodded importantly and ran back, and I made it safely along to the hired car, and drove away in peace towards Las Vegas, taking off the useful cap and gloves as I went. Back at the motel I showered, changed, packed, and paid my account; drove to the airport and returned the car to the Hertz agent: kept a very wary eye open in case Matt Clive had decided to travel by air; ate a much needed sandwich, and caught the first plane out to Los Angeles.

When I collected the car keys at the inquiry desk, there was a note from Walt as well.

> You're one great crazy guy. And don't think I don't realize what you risked. If you're reading this, I guess you've made it, and aren't behind bars. My pal in the CIA told me you could be relied on to do mad things, and boy, he was right. What do you use for nerves? Count me strictly out, next time.
>
> Walt.

Surprised, and not ungrateful that he should have bothered, I slipped his letter into my pocket and drove into the city to look for a good place for tape recorders. I managed in the end to hire for one week an elaborate recorder which would play at the ultra slow fifteen-sixteenths of an inch per second, the speed of my own, and with it sitting on the passenger seat beside me, pointed my nose towards Orpheus Farm, Los Caillos. Then I removed the full reel from the radio recorder and fixed it up with another: no one appeared to have disturbed it in its bush and boulder hiding place, and as far as I could tell, no one saw me come and go.

Lynnie and Eunice were just walking up from the beach when I got back to The Vacationer: but they both greeted me with ten degrees of frost and went straight on past, murmuring that they guessed they would see me at dinner.

Slightly puzzled, shrugging, I carried my bag and the recorder up to my room, rewound the tape I had collected, and started it to run through while I took off my city suit and turned the air-conditioning to high.

Yola rang up, in great agitation. The houseboy answered, and went to tell Offen, who was still in bed. By great good fortune the houseboy neglected to go back to replace the downstairs receiver when Offen lifted the bedroom extension, and the bug in consequence had picked up the whole conversation.

'I've had a call from the cops in Vegas . . .'

'Don't shout, Yola. I'm not deaf.'

She didn't listen. 'Some vandals have wrecked the

house at Pitts.' She really minded: there was grief as well as anger in her voice.

'How do you mean, wrecked?'

'They say everything in the house has been thrown on the floor, and flour and sugar and stuff have been tipped over everything. They want to know what's been stolen, they want me or better Matt to go down there and deal with it . . . and I can't, Uncle Bark, I simply can't. We've got thirty-two people in, and I can't possibly get away. Matt will have to go.'

'But Matt . . .'

'Sure,' she wailed. 'Do you think I don't *know*? But he'll have to. Those horses won't die if he leaves them for a few hours. It's much farther for me, I'd be away at least two days. It's *hopeless.* Everything's gone wrong since we took that damn Chrysalis.'

'And if you remember,' Culham James said tartly, 'that was your and Matt's idea. I always said it was too soon after the last one. You and Matt have been too greedy ever since you found out.'

'Relatives ought to share their good luck, not to keep it to themselves.'

'So you're always saying.'

Nothing like a little blackmail to cement a family together, I thought in amusement. Offen had been happy with his half million a year, it seemed: but Matt and Yola, stumbling on the honey pot, had been in a hurry for more. Impulsive, ingenious, greedy Clives; if they had only been content with a share from Showman and Allyx, Offen would never had been found out.

Yola glossed over the longstanding squabble and returned to the current disaster. 'I didn't get Matt's number. What is it?'

'I haven't got it here, it's in my book downstairs . . .'

'Well look, will you call him? Tell him to get right on over, the cops will be there waiting. Tell him to call me from there and tell me what gives . . . I can't bear it if those bastards have stolen my mink wrap . . . and there's all that money in the safe . . .'

'Better face up to it that it's gone,' Offen said, with the tiniest trace of malice.

'They might not have had time,' Yola said. 'The alarms go off when anyone goes in the den, and there isn't supposed to be time for anyone to find the safe and open it before the cops get there. We paid enough for it . . .'

It had been their bad luck that by the merest chance I had left the den until last.

Yola disconnected, and after the twenty second gap on the tape, Uncle Bark called up Matt from the downstairs telephone. Matt's comments were mostly inaudible though detectably explosive. He agreed to go to the house, but nothing Offen said gave any clue as to where Matt was at that moment. It appeared only that he was somewhere within a reasonable radius of Las Vegas, as he was going to be able to drive there, see to things at the house, and get back in time to feed the horses in the evening: which narrowed it down to somewhere in an area of roughly a hundred and fifty thousand square miles. A pocket handkerchief.

A brief telephone conversation of no interest followed and then, presumably in the afternoon, Offen had switched on his television set to watch a racing programme. As far as I could tell from spot checks, it had used up the whole of the rest of the four-hour playing time.

Sighing, I switched off, and went downstairs. Lynnie and Eunice, dressed in dazzling colours, were drinking daiquiris and watching the Pacific sunset. I got another cool welcome and monosyllabic replies to my inquiries about their day.

Finally Eunice said distantly, 'Did you have a good time in San Francisco?'

I blinked. 'Yes, thank you.'

They relapsed into a longer silence which was broken only by a waiter coming to tell me I was wanted on the telephone.

It was Walt.

'Where are you?' I said.

'Las Vegas airport.'

'How did it go?'

'You can relax,' he said comfortably. 'The horses are on a small farm in a valley in Arizona, out beyond Kingman. We landed there and I asked around some. Seems the couple who own the farm don't make much of a living, but last week they said a friend was giving them a trip to Miami, and a young fellow would be looking after the place while they were away.'

'That's great,' I said with emphasis.

'The paint made it easy. We heard him yelling blue murder when he saw it, but I guess it had dried on by then and he couldn't get it off, because it was way past midday, and I'd begun to worry that he'd gone already and we hadn't heard him or that they'd picked you up planting the bug . . . anyway, we took off when his engine started, and the yellow splash was easy to see from a height, just as you said. He went right through Las Vegas and out on to the Hoover Dam road and across into Arizona. I kept the binoculars on him and we never flew near enough for him to notice us, I'm certain of that. He went up a winding graded road into the hills south-east of Kingman, and that was it.'

'You've done marvels.'

'Oh, sure. It was simpler than we were prepared for, though. You could hear the bug pretty clearly through the helicopter's headsets as high as two thousand feet, and we could have followed him in the dark if we'd had to, especially as he had his radio on for most of the way. We could hear music and news broadcasts now and then.'

'Are you coming back tonight?'

'Yeah, there's a plane in a half hour from now. But it'll be better than midnight when I get in.'

'I'll be awake,' I said. 'And just by the way, Walt,

what did you tell Eunice and Lynnie I was doing in San Francisco?'

He cleared his throat. 'I said you had some unfinished business there.'

'What sort of business?'

'Uh . . . like . . . er . . . female.'

'Thanks,' I said sarcastically. 'You're a right pal.'

Something very like a laugh lingered in my ear as I disconnected.

CHAPTER FIFTEEN

Lynnie and Eunice talked brightly to each other over dinner and I sat making plans for the next day and didn't listen. Politely after coffee we parted for the night, and at eleven I drove out to Orpheus with a fresh reel for the receiver in the rocks, and brought back the one I had fitted earlier.

Walt came back into my room as I was running it through, and we both listened to Culham James Offen talking to Matt and then to Yola.

Yola was a better bet from our point of view, because her angry feminine voice scattered higher sound waves out of the receiver, and one could imagine Uncle Bark holding it inches away out of deference to his eardrums.

He was doing his best to soothe her. 'Matt says it could have been worse; some of these vandals have thrown molasses and preserves and even sewage around in people's houses . . .'

'He says the whole place is *covered* in flour . . . it'll take weeks to clear up.'

'It'll vacuum quite easily, won't it? It's not sticky and it doesn't stain.'

But she couldn't be consoled, even when he reminded her that the money was safe, and that her mink wrap hadn't been stolen.

'But Matt says', she wailed, 'that it was *white.*'

'Flour will shake out . . . and might even clean it.'

'You don't understand.'

'Sure I do, Yola,' he said patiently. 'You feel like it was you who was assaulted, not your house. You feel dirty and furious and you'd like to kick the bastards who did it. Sure, I know. We had thieves in here once, when your Aunt Ellen was alive. They stole all her rings, and she said it was like being raped.'

They talked about the break-in for a good while longer, and Walt raised an eyebrow and remarked that I seemed to have gotten reasonable revenge for that clap on the head.

We were both yawning by the time Offen was through for the evening. The last half hour consisted of him telling his houseboy his plans and requirements, and none of these betrayed any anxiety or uncertainty. Culham James was confident, and I was glad of it. Worried men patrol their defences.

Walt went off to bed, and although I hadn't slept at all the previous night I woke again after only three hours. The coloured lights on the outside of the motel threw prismatic reflections on the ceiling. I stared up at them, trying to make patterns and shapes, trying any silly ruse to stop my mind from nose-diving into the pit. The tug of the unfinished chase was very faint, and whether Allyx and Showman ever sired another foal seemed a matter of supreme unimportance. Fraud, theft, attempted murder . . . who cared?

I had left the Luger in its belt holster across the room on a chair. Neither the Clives nor Offen were likely to come creeping through the night to do me in, and my usual enemies were six thousand miles to the east. The only danger lay in myself, the deadliest enemy of the lot. The theory that going to bed with the gun out of reach would lessen its magnetic temptation was proving a dreary flop.

One more day, I thought in the end. Anyone could manage just one more day. If you said that firmly enough every night, one might even finish the course.

Dawn crept up on the coloured bulbs and washed them out. I took a shower and shaved, and admitted that I had seen healthier looking men than the one in my reflection.

Walt came along to my room when I was midway through orange juice and coffee at eight-thirty. 'What you need,' he said, eyeing this, 'is some good solid food.'

'I don't feel hungry.'

His eyes slid to my face and away. 'Come on down and eat with me.'

I shook my head. 'I'll wait for you.'

He wouldn't go alone. He ordered hot-cakes and eggs and coffee from room service, and we got straight down to business while he demolished them.

'It'll take two and a half days for Sam Hengelman to get to Kingman,' I said.

He nodded with his mouth full.

'He was starting early this morning,' I went on, 'I called him last night, after you'd been through from Las Vegas. He's driving the van himself, and he's coming alone. That means his journey time will be longer, but it seemed better that way from the secrecy point of view.'

'Did you tell him it was another snatch?' Walt said doubtfully.

I smiled. 'I engaged him to come and collect a horse belonging to Dave Teller. He asked if we were likely to be collecting this one in a lonely place at night, and I said yes, we probably would.'

'And he didn't back out?'

'He merely remarked that he had no great objection to an easy buck if I would assure him he couldn't go to jail for it.'

Walt wiped errant egg off his chin. 'And could he?'

'I couldn't tell him it was impossible. Odds of a thousand to one, I said. He said a thousand bucks against one chance of going to jail wasn't enough.'

Walt laughed. 'So how much is he coming for?'

'Fifteen hundred, plus the normal hiring fee, plus expenses.'

'Not bad for one week's work.' He paused, stirring sugar, then said tentatively, 'What do you get out of this yourself?'

'Me?' I said in surprise. 'I've no idea. Three weeks' heatwave instead of the English summer . . .'

'Didn't you negotiate a fee?'

'No.'

'How come?'

'It didn't occur to me.'

His face crinkled into a mixture of emotions with what appeared to be amazement and pity coming out on top.

'How about you?' I said.

'I'm not on vacation,' he pointed out. 'I get a pretty good salary, and also a cut of everything I save the company.'

'So Chrysalis has been worth the extra work?'

'At a million and a half, are you kidding?' Walt looked at me earnestly. 'Look, Gene, I'm going to give you one half of that cut . . .'

'No,' I said, interrupting. 'I don't want it.'

'You know darned well I wouldn't have found that horse, not in a million years. Nor got him back alive so quickly. And as for these other two . . .'

'You keep it for your kids,' I said. 'But thanks, anyway.'

He would have gone on insisting, but I wouldn't

listen, and after two attempts he gave it up. In the back of my mind, as I outlined what I suggested we should do next, there lingered a bitter suspicion that I hadn't accepted his gift because it would be a selfish waste if I didn't stick around to spend it. I had rejected any strings of conscience tying me to life. The death-seeking force was up to another of its tricks.

'A pincer movement, I think,' I said. 'Or rather, a simultaneous attack on two fronts.'

'Huh?'

'Keep Culham James Offen's attention riveted on the Moviemaker and Centigrade he has on his farm while we spirit away the others.'

'Er, quite,' Walt agreed.

'You can take Offen,' I said.

'And you take the horses?'

I nodded. Walt considered what might happen if we exchanged roles, and didn't argue.

'What are the chances of finding out which company Matt insures the Las Vegas house with?'

Walt thought about it. 'Our agent there might be able to. But why?'

'I . . . er . . . would rather take those horses when I know Matt is safely away.'

Walt smiled.

'So,' I went on, 'it shouldn't be too difficult to get him to go back to the house on Pitts. Say for instance his insurance company required him to make an inspection of his security arrangements and sign some document or other, before they would renew full cover? We know from the telephone calls to Offen that Matt and Yola have a safe in the den with a lot of money in it. Matt won't want to be uninsured for more than a minute, after having one break-in already.'

'We couldn't ask his company to do that . . .' Walt paused and looked at me with suspicion.

'Quite right,' I nodded. 'You can. You know all the jargon. As soon as we hear from Sam Hengelman that he has reached the Arizona border, you can start the spiel on Matt.'

'From here?'

'Yes. Ask him what time would be convenient for him, but try to manoeuvre him into coming late in the afternoon or early evening, say six or seven. Then it would be dark when he got home, and late, which should hamper him a bit when he finds the horses are gone . . . he might even stop off in Las Vegas for a couple of hours at the tables.'

Walt said thoughtfully, 'I reckon I'd better go to the house on Pittsville and meet him.'

'No,' I said abruptly.

He looked at me. 'You'd thought of it?'

'You are not going anywhere near Matt Clive.'

'And why not?'

'You want a split skull or something?'

'Like webbed feet.' The smiled hovered. 'All the same, what is Matt going to do when he arrives at his house and no insurance man turns up? What would you do? Call the company, I guess. And then what? He discovers no one in the company knows anything about him having to come back to the house, and he starts thinking like crazy. And if I were him I'd call the local cops and get them whizzing out to the farm for a look-see. You didn't see the road there from Kingman. But I did. There are no turnings off it for the last ten miles to the farm. What if you met the cops head on, you and Sam Hengelman and two stolen horses?'

'He wouldn't risk calling in cops.'

'He might reckon that if he was losing everything anyway, he'd make sure you went down as well. And I mean down.'

Every instinct told me not to let Walt meet Matt Clive.

'Suppose he won't make a late appointment?' he said. 'When I grant most of the company would have gone home, and it would be more difficult to check. Suppose he insists on three in the afternoon, or even the next morning? Do you want to snatch those horses by day?'

'Not much. But it would take him at least two hours each way. Add an hour for waiting and checking. Even if he called the police, it wouldn't be for three hours after he left home. We'd have been gone with the horses for two of those.'

Walt obstinately shook his head. 'The limits are too narrow. A horse van won't be liable to do better than thirty miles an hour on the farm road, if that much. You have to go into Kingman, which is in the opposite direction from Kentucky, and then round and across Arizona . . . there aren't too many roads in that state, it's mostly desert. The police could find you too easily.'

'Down through Phoenix . . .'

'The road to Phoenix twists through mountains, with hairpin curves most of the way.'

'I don't want you walking into an empty house with Matt Clive.'

He looked at me without expression. 'But you would go. If he didn't know you, I mean.'

'That's different.'

'How?' he said, half insulted, half challenging.

I looked at him sideways. 'I bet I can run faster than you.'

His forehead relaxed. 'You're in pretty good shape, I'll give you that. All the same, I'm going to Las Vegas.'

He'd manoeuvred me into not being able to persuade him against it on the grounds of safety; and from all other points of view it was a good idea. Against my instinct I agreed in the end that he should go.

'I'll drift on out tomorrow and look at the farm beyond Kingman,' I said. 'I suppose you couldn't see whether there were any other horses there besides the two we're after?'

He looked startled. 'You mean there might be another identification problem?'

'Perhaps. Though I'd say it's certain our two have Moviemaker's and Centigrade's stud book numbers tattooed inside their mouths. They would have to, to satisfy visiting grooms, for instance, that their mares were being mated with the right stallion. But I've never seen then . . . Showman and Allyx. If there are other horses there, it'll simply mean going round peering into all their mouths until I find the right ones.'

Walt raised his eyes to heaven. 'You make everything sound so darned easy. Like it's only five miles to the top of Everest, and everyone can walk five miles, can't they?'

Smiling, I asked him for precise directions to the farm, and he told me.

'And now this end . . .' I said. 'How many strings can you pull with the Los Angeles fraud squad?'

'Not many,' he said. 'I don't know anyone out there.'

'But with Buttress Life behind you?'

He sighed. 'I suppose you want me to go and dip my toes in the water?'

'Jump right in,' I agreed. 'Talk your way to the top chap, and tell him Buttress Life suspect that Moviemaker and Centigrade are Showman and Allyx. Get everything nicely stirred up. Make Offen prove beyond any doubt that the two horses at Orpheus literally are Moviemaker and Centigrade.'

He nodded. 'OK. I'll start this morning. Have to go a little carefully, though, or Offen will come up so fast with a libel suit that we'll wonder what hit us.'

'You must be used to ducking.'

'Yeah.'

I gave him the page Miss Britt had written out for me in Lexington.

'Here are the figures. No one can question these, not even Offen. You might find them useful in getting the law moving.'

He tucked the paper into his pocket and nodded, and shortly after, with the habitual martyred sigh, levered himself out of his chair and ambled on his way.

I sat and thought for a while but got nowhere new. There was going to be little else for me to do but wait and watch for the next few days while Sam Hengelman rolled his way two thousand miles across the continent.

When I went down to lunch I found Eunice and Lynnie sitting in cool bright dresses under the dappled shade of the sea-facing terrace. Their hair was glossy and neat, their big earrings gently swinging, their legs smooth and tanned, the whites of their eyes a detergent white.

They didn't get the lingering scrutiny they deserved. With them, equally crisp, equally at ease, sat Culham James Offen, Uncle Bark.

All three seemed a scrap disconcerted when I folded myself gently on to the fourth chair round the low table on which stood their long frosted drinks.

Offen and I nodded to each other. There was still in his manner the superior, self-satisfied amusement he had treated me with at his house. Reassuring. Lynnie smiled, but with a quick sidelong glance at Eunice to make sure such treachery hadn't been noticed. Eunice had on an 'I-am-your-employer's-wife' face, which didn't wipe from my mind, nor hers, I imagine, the memory of the fluffy pink wrapper.

'We thought you'd gone to LA with Walt,' Lynnie said.

Eunice gave her a sharp glance which she didn't see. 'We ran into Mr Offen in the lobby here, wasn't that extraordinary?'

'Extraordinary,' I agreed.

Offen's white eyebrows went up and down in an embarrassment he couldn't entirely smother.

'It sure has been a pleasure,' he said, 'to get to know you folks better.' He spoke exclusively to Eunice, however.

She had warmed again to the charm he had switched on for her, and gave me the tag end of a scornful glance. How could I, she inferred, imagine this nice influential citizen could be a crook.

'How are Matt and Yola these days?' I said conversationally.

Offen visibly jumped, and a blight fell on the party. 'Such charming young people,' I said benignly, and watched Eunice remembering what had happened to Dave, and also perhaps what Walt had told her about their attack on me. 'Your nephew and niece, I believe?'

Offen's pale blue eyes were the least impressive

feature in his tanned face with its snow-white frame. I read in them a touch of wariness, and wondered whether in prodding Eunice to face reality I had disturbed his complacency too far.

'They would sure like to meet you again,' he said slowly, and the heavy ill-feeling behind the words curdled finally for Eunice his milk-of-human-kindness image.

'Are you expecting them within the next few days?' I asked, dropping in the merest touch of anxiety.

He said he wasn't, and his inner amusement abruptly returned. I had succeeded in convincing him I would be trying to remove his horses from Orpheus pretty soon now; and shortly afterwards he got purposefully to his feet, bent a beaming smile on Eunice, a smaller one on Lynnie and a smug one on me, and made an important exit through the motel.

After a long pause Eunice said flatly, 'I guess I was wrong about that guy being sweet.'

We ate an amicable lunch and spent the afternoon on the beach under a fringed umbrella, with the bright green-blue Pacific hissing gently on the sand. Out on the rollers the golden boys rode their surfboards, and flat by my side little Lynnie sighed to the bottom of her lungs with contentment.

'I wish this could go on for ever,' she said.

'So do I.'

Eunice, on the other side of Lynnie, propped herself

up on one elbow. 'I'm going to take a dip,' she said. 'Coming?'

'In a minute,' Lynnie said lazily, and Eunice went alone. We watched her tight well-shaped figure walk unwaveringly down to the water, and Lynnie said what I was thinking. 'She hardly drinks at all now.'

'You're good for her.'

'Oh sure.' She laughed gently, stretching like a cat. 'Isn't this heat just gorgeous?'

'Mm.'

'What are all those scars on you?'

'Lions and tigers and appendicitis.'

She snorted. 'Shall we go in and swim?'

'In a minute. What did you and Eunice and Offen say to each other before I arrived?'

'Oh . . .' She sounded bored. 'He wanted to know what you were doing. Eunice told him you and Walt were cooking something up but she didn't really know what. And . . . er . . . yes . . . he asked if Walt was really an insurance man, and Eunice said he was . . . and he asked other things about you, what your job was and so on, and why you were out here with us . . .'

'Did Eunice tell him I got her to show him that photograph on purpose? Did she tell him that I was certain that the horses he has at Orpheus Farm are Moviemaker and Centigrade?'

Lynnie shook her head.

'You're quite sure?'

'Yes, absolutely. Would it have been a nuisance if we had?'

'A fair way to being disastrous.'

'Don't worry then. He was only here about a quarter of an hour before you came down, and all Eunice said was that you were er . . . er . . . well her actual words were, some dim bloody little office worker on vacation.' Lynnie laughed. 'She said her husband had been grateful to you for saving his life and was paying your bill here, and that all you seemed to be interested in at present was a girl up in San Francisco.'

I looked down to where Eunice's head bobbed in the surf and wondered whether she'd given him perfect answers from design or bitchiness.

'What's she like?' Lynnie said.

'Who?'

'The girl in San Francisco.'

'You'd better ask Walt,' I said, turning my head to look at her. 'He invented her.'

She gasped and laughed in one. 'Oh good! I mean . . . er . . . then what were you really doing?'

'Ah, well,' I said. 'Now that's something I'd hate Eunice to have told Culham Offen.'

She lay looking back at me steadily for several seconds. So much more assurance, I thought idly, than on that day on the river, when she had still been a child.

'Is that why you've told us practically nothing? Don't you trust her?'

'She's never wanted the horses back.'

Lynnie blinked. 'But she wouldn't . . . she wouldn't have ruined on purpose what you're trying to do. After all, you're doing it for her husband.'

I smiled and she sat up abruptly and put her arms round her knees.

'You make me feel so . . . *naïve*.'

'You', I said, 'are adorable.'

'And now you're laughing at me.'

I wanted impulsively to say that I loved her, but I wasn't sure that it was true. Maybe all I wanted was an antedote to depression. She was certainly the best I'd found.

'I'm going away again in the morning,' I said.

'To San Francisco?'

'Somewhere like that.'

'How long for?'

'Two nights.'

'This is your last week,' she said, looking out to sea.

The thought leapt involuntarily, *if only it were* . . . I shook my head abruptly, as if one could empty the brain by force, and climbed slowly up on to my feet.

'There's today, anyway,' I said, smiling. 'Let's go and get wet.'

Walt came back at seven with dragging feet and a raging thirst.

'Those detectives from the DA's office will scalp me if they find out we're only using them,' he said gloomily, up in my room. 'Two of them have agreed to go out to Orpheus Farm tomorrow, and I'm meeting them on the LA road to show them the way. Day after tomorrow, some guy from the bloodstock registry office is going out. I got the DA's office to call him and fix it.'

'Couldn't be better.'

Walt recharged his batteries with Old Grandad and said, 'So what's new with you?'

'Offen came here on a fact-finding mission.'

'He did *what*?'

'Came looking for answers. Got some real beauties from Eunice which won't help him any, and went away believing we'd be back on his doorstep pretty soon.'

'I guess', Walt said, 'that he wanted to know if we'd called it off and gone home, and whether it was safe to bring those horses back again. It's days since he saw any sign of us. Must have been like sitting on an H-bomb with a tricky firing pin.' He swallowed appreciatively and rolled his tongue over his gums. 'He'll get all the action he wants, tomorrow.'

When he plodded tiredly off to shower before dinner, I telephoned Jeff Roots.

'How was Miami?' I said.

'Hot and horrible, and I gained four pounds.'

Commiserating, I thanked him for his help with the newspaper files and told him that owing to Miss Britt we had found the two stallions.

'I wish I didn't believe it. Are you certain?'

'Yes.'

His sigh was heartfelt. 'We'd better start proceedings . . .'

'I've . . . er . . . already started them. We may in a day or two have two horses on our hands which will need to be stabled somewhere eminently respectable while their identity is being investigated. Owing to the length of time they've been lost, it may take a couple of months to re-establish them. Where would you think it would be best to put them?'

After a pause, he said, 'I suppose you're asking me to have them here?'

'Not really,' I explained. 'Too much of a coincidence after Chrysalis, perhaps. I'd thought rather of a more official place . . . I don't know what you have.'

'I'll think of something.' He coughed slightly. 'There won't be anything illegal about their recovery?'

'No more than for Chrysalis.'

'That's no answer.'

'There shouldn't be any trouble with the police,' I said.

'I guess that'll have to do,' he sighed. 'When do I expect them?'

'If all goes well, they should reach Lexington on Sunday.'

'And if all doesn't go well?'

'You'll have no problem.'

He laughed. 'And you?'

'One more won't matter.'

CHAPTER SIXTEEN

For most of thirty hours I sat in the mountainous Arizona desert and looked down at Matt Clive leading a boring life.

Like his sister, he was capable, quick, efficient. He watered the stock and mended a fence, swept out the house and fed the hens; and spent a great deal of time in the largest barn on the place.

I had found myself a perch among the rocks on the east-facing side of the valley, half a mile off the dusty road to the farm. At nearly three thousand feet above sea level the heat was bearable, though the midday sun blazed down from nearly straight overhead, and eggs would have fried on the sidewalks if there had been any. Desert plants were designed to save themselves and no one else: at my back grew a large agave, its central stem rising six feet high with flat outspreading flowers turning from red to brilliant yellow. For leaves it had razor-sharp spikes springing outwards from the ground in one large clump. Stiff; angular; not a vestige of shade. The spindly buckhorn and the flat devil's fingers would have been pretty useless to a midget. I folded myself under the overhang of a jagged boulder and inched round with the meagre shade patch until the sun cried quits behind the hill.

Showman and Allyx had to be in the big barn: though I saw no sign of them, nor of any other horses, on the first afternoon.

By air to Las Vegas and hired car to Kingman had taken me all morning, and at the last fork on the way to the farm I'd had to decide whether to risk meeting Matt head on on the road or to walk ten miles instead. I'd risked it. Ten miles there was also ten miles back. The car had bumped protestingly off the road two miles short of his farm, and was now out of sight in a gulley.

Binoculars brought every detail of the meagre spread up clear and sharp. The small dilapidated house lay to the left, with the big barn on the right across a large dusty yard. Along most of a third side of the rough quadrangle stretched an uneven jumble of simple stone buildings, and behind those the rusting guts of two abandoned cars lay exposed to the sky.

Maintenance was at a minimum: no endemic prosperity here. The owners scratched for a living in a tiny valley among the Arizona hills, existing there only by courtesy of the quirk of rock formation which had brought underground water to the surface in a spring. The small river bed was easy to follow from where I sat: grass and trees circled its origin, sparse paddocks stretched away to sagging fences on each side of its upper reaches, a corn patch grew beside it near the farm buildings, and lower down it ran off into the desert in a dry wide shallow sandy trough. Heavy rain would turn it every time into a raging torrent, as destructive as it was vital. High behind the house, dominating the whole place, a huge onion-shaped water storage tank sat squatly on top of a spindly looking tower.

Mile after mile of plain dark poles stretched along the road to the farm, carrying an electric cable and a telephone wire, but civilization had fallen short of refuse collection. A sprawling dump at one side of the big barn seemed to consist of a brass bedstead, half a tractor, a bottomless tin bath, the bones of an old wagon, a tangled heap of unidentifiable rusting metal, and roughly fifty treadless tyres of varying sizes. Filling every crevice among this lot were bottles and empty food cans with labels peeling and jagged lids mutely open like mouths. Over the top the air shimmered with reflected heat.

Matt had already spent at least a week in this ugly oasis. Walt shouldn't find it too hard to persuade him to make an evening visit to Las Vegas.

I watched until long after dark. Lights went on and off in the house, and Matt moved about, visible through the insect screens because he didn't draw any curtains. If, indeed, there were any.

Cautiously at some time after one o'clock, when all

the lights on my side of the house had been out for more than two hours, I picked my way down to the farm. The night was still warm, but as the only light came from the stars it was black dark on the ground, and with agave clumps in mind I reckoned my torch held lesser risk.

I reached the farmyard. Nothing stirred. Quietly, slowly, I made the crossing to the barn. Matt in the house slept on.

No padlocks: not even bolts. There weren't any. The wide door of the barn stood open; and with this invitation, I went in. Inside, the barn was divided into six stalls along one side, with feed bins and saddlery storage racks along the other. Here and everywhere else dilapidation and decay were winning hands down: everything my torch flicked over looked in need of help.

Four of the stalls were empty, but in the two central ones, side by side, stood two horses. Gently, so as not to frighten them, I went over, talking soothingly in a murmur and shining the torch beam on the wall in front of their heads. Their eyes in the dim light rolled round inquiringly, but neither gave more than a single stamp of alarm.

The first one tried to back away when I shone the torch into his mouth: but an exceedingly strong looking head collar and a remarkably new chain kept him from going more than a few feet. I ran my hand down his neck and talked to him, and in the end got my inspection done. The tattooed mark, as often, was none too clear: but discernibly it was 752:07. The registration of Moviemaker.

The tattoo on the second horse was more recent and also clearer: the registration number of Centigrade.

Satisfied, I gave them each a friendly slap, and with great care left the barn. Matt still slept. I hesitated, thinking that enough was enough, but in the end went down to the end of the farmyard to take a quick look through the other buildings. In one only, a deep narrow garage, was there anything of interest: a car.

It was not Matt's pale blue convertible, but a tinny black saloon three or four years old. My flashlight picked out a piece of paper lying on the passenger seat, and I opened the door and took a look at it. A copy of a work sheet from a garage in Kingman. Customer's name: Clive. Work required: Remove yellow paint from Ford convertible. Further instructions: Complete as soon as possible.

I put the paper back on the seat and shone the light over the dashboard. A small metal plate screwed on to it bore the name of the garage in Kingman: Matt had rented this car while his own was being cleaned.

Outside, everything was still, and feeling like a shadow among shadows I went quietly out of the farmyard and along the dusty road towards Kingman. It seemed a lot farther than two miles to the flat stones I had left one on top of the other as a marker, and even after I had reached them it took me quite a while to find the hidden car and get it back on to the road.

It was well after three when I called Walt. He sounded resigned, but he'd known it would be some time in the night.

'Are they there?' he said.

'They are. They're quite unguarded, and there's only Matt on the place. How about things your end?'

'Oh.' Amusement crept in. 'Offen was full of offended dignity. Didn't know how anyone could suggest he was engaged in fraud; that sort of thing. It didn't impress the DA's squad at all, because they get that sort of bluster every time. Made them all the keener, if anything. They had quite a long session with him, all fairly polite but definitely needling. Artists, they are. From our point of view Offen said nothing significant except for one little gem. The DA's guys asked to see the stud groom. That's Kiddo, remember? The one who told us about the mares foaling at night?'

'I remember,' I said.

'Well, it seems it's a slow time around studs just now, and Kiddo went off on vacation the day after our first visit.'

'He didn't say anything about that when we were there.'

'He sure didn't. Offen says Kiddo will be back in three weeks. By then, I guess, he expects to have had Moviemaker and Centigrade identified as themselves, and then when the dust has settled he can bring

Showman and Allyx quietly back, and it'll be safe for Kiddo to return. I guess Offen didn't know which way he'd jump, and booted him off out of trouble.'

'I'm sure you're right,' I said. 'Anything interesting on the tape?'

'I've been listening to that damned machine until I'm bored to death with it,' he said wearily. 'Today's run was mostly the DA's men talking to Offen, so I heard all that twice over. He then called both Yola and Matt and told them about it, and he sounded pretty pleased with the way things were going. I'd say Matt was a mite annoyed at having to stay where he is: Offen was telling him not to be stupid, what was a week or two with so much at stake. Also Yola must be wanting Matt back, because Offen smoothed her down with the same spiel.' Walt paused and cleared his throat. 'What would you say is the relationship between Matt and Yola?'

Smiling into the receiver I said, 'Such thoughts, Walt, from you!'

'It's possible . . .' he said uncomfortably.

'It sure is. But there's nothing to indicate it except for their not being married.'

'Then you don't think . . .?'

'I'd say they're certainly centred on each other, but how far it goes I couldn't guess. The only time I've seen them together they've had their hands full of punts and guns.'

'Yeah . . . well, maybe crime is how it takes them.'

I agreed that it probably was, and asked him if he'd got Matt set up for the insurance meeting.

'I sure have,' he said with satisfaction. 'I called him this afternoon. It must have been soon after he'd been talking to Offen, I guess, because he seemed to be glad enough to be given a reason for going to Las Vegas. I suggested six PM which sounded all right, but he himself asked if I could make it later.'

'He'll probably want to feed the horses about then, when the day gets cooler,' I said. 'And those horses would come first.'

'Yeah. At three million for two, they sure would. It beats me why he doesn't guard them every minute.'

'Against what?' I said.

'You got a point,' he conceded. 'Only us. And we're obviously concentrating on the two at Orpheus. Right?'

'Right.'

'Anyway, Matt said could I make it later than six, and we agreed in the end on nine. That should mean he'll take that gander at the roulette tables on his way home, and maybe give us most of the night to get the horses clear.'

'Good,' I said. 'That's fine. But Walt . . .'

'Yes?'

'Take care.'

'Go teach your grandmother,' he said, and I smiled wryly and asked him if he'd heard from Sam Hengelman.

'Sure, he called this evening, like you asked. He'd reached Santa Rosa in New Mexico and he was going on to Albuquerque before stopping for the night. He said he'd be in Kingman by four or five tomorrow afternoon . . . today, I suppose, technically . . . and he'll meet you at the Mojave Motel. I told him the return trip wouldn't be starting before eight, so he's going to take a room there and catch a couple of hours' sleep.'

'Thanks, Walt, that's great,' I said.

'We're all set, then?' There was a hint of unease in his voice, and it raised prickles again in my early warning mechanism.

'You don't have to go to Las Vegas,' I said reasonably. 'We've time enough without it.'

'I'm going,' he said. 'And that's that.'

'Well . . . all right. I think we could do with a checkpoint, though, in case anything goes wrong. Let's say you wait in the lobby of the Angel Inn from eight to eight-thirty tomorrow evening. That's where I stayed. It's right on the edge of Las Vegas, but it's an easy trip to Pittsville Boulevard. I'll call you there sometime during that half hour; and if I don't, you stay put, and don't go out to Matt's house.'

'OK,' he said, and although he tried, there was distinct relief in his voice.

We disconnected, and I ate a sandwich and drank coffee at an all night lunch counter at the bus station before returning to my hired car and pointing its nose again towards the farm and the hills. The two flat stones came up again in the headlights, and re-stowing the car in its former hiding place, I finished the journey on foot.

Back in the shelter of the same jagged rock I tried for a time to sleep. There was still an hour or more before dawn, and the sun wouldn't be too hot for a while after that, but in spite of knowing that I'd get no rest at all during the following night, my brain stayed obstinately awake. I supposed an inability to sleep on open ground surrounded by cacti and within yelling distance of a man who'd kill me if he had a chance could hardly be classed as insomnia in the ordinary way: but I had no illusions. That was precisely what it was. The restless, racing thoughts, the electrical awareness, the feeling that everything in one's body was working full steam ahead and wouldn't slow down; I knew all the symptoms much too well. One could lie with eyes shut and relax every muscle until one couldn't tell where one's arms and legs were, and still sleep wouldn't come. Breathe deeply, count all the sheep of Canterbury, repeat once-learnt verses; nothing worked.

The sun came up and shone in my eyes. Inching out of its revealing spotlight I retreated round the side of the rock and looked down to the farm through the binoculars. No movement. At five-thirty Matt was still in bed.

I put down the glasses and thought about a cigarette. There were only four left in the packet. Sighing,

I reflected that I could easily have bought some in Kingman, if I'd given it a thought. It was going to be a long day. All I'd brought with me beside the binoculars was a bottle of water, a pair of sunglasses, and the Luger in my belt.

At seven-thirty Matt came out through the rickety screen door of the house, and stood in the yard stretching and looking around at the cloudless cobalt blue sky. Then he went across to the barn and poked his head briefly inside.

Satisfied that the gold was still in the bank, he fetched buckets of water and joined it for long enough to muck out the stalls and see to the feed. After a time he came out with a barrowful of droppings and wheeled it away to empty on the far side of the barn, out of my sight.

The hens got their grits, and the calves in a near compound their ration of water, and Matt retired for his breakfast. The morning wore on. The temperature rose. Nothing else happened.

At noon I stood up for a while behind the rock to stretch my legs and restore some feeling to the bits that were numb from sitting. I drank some water and smoked a cigarette, and put on the sunglasses to circumvent a hovering glare headache: and having exhausted my repertoire except for a few shots from the Luger, folded myself back into the wedge of slowly moving shade, and took another look at the farm.

Status quo entirely unchanged. Maybe Matt was

asleep, or telephoning, or watching television, or inventing systems for his trip to Las Vegas. He certainly was not doing much farming. Nor did he apparently propose to exercise the horses. They stayed in their stalls from dawn to dusk.

By two I knew intimately every spiny plant growing within a radius of ten feet of my rock, and found my eyes going far oftener to the broad sweep of desert on my left than to the dirty little farm below. The desert was clean in its way, and fierce, and starkly beautiful. All hills and endless sky. Parched sandy grey dust and scratchy cactus. Killing heat. A wild, uncompromising, lonely place.

When I first felt the urge just to get up and walk away into it I dragged my eyes dutifully back to the farm and smoked the second cigarette and thought firmly about Matt and the horses. That only worked for a while. The barren country pulled like a magnet.

I had only to walk out there, I thought, and keep on going until I was filled with its emptiness, and then sit down somewhere and put the barrel of the Luger against my head, and simply squeeze. So childishly easy; so appallingly tempting.

Walt, I thought desperately. I couldn't do it because of Walt and the unfinished business we were embarked on. The horses were there in front of me, and Walt and Sam Hengelman were on their way. It was impossible just to abandon them. I hit my hand against the rock and dragged my mind back to the farm and the night ahead. And when I'd gone through that piece by piece I concentrated one at a time on Yola and Offen, and Eunice and Dave Teller, and Keeble and Lynnie, trying to use them as pegs to keep me believing that what I did mattered to them. That anything I did mattered to anybody. That I cared whether anything I did mattered to anybody.

My hand had been bleeding. I hadn't even felt it. I looked dispassionately at the scraped skin, and loathed myself. I shut my eyes, and the desolation went so deep that for an unmeasurable age I felt dizzy with it, as if I were in some fearful pitch black limbo, with no help, no hope, and no escape. Spinning slowly down an endless shaft in solitary despair. Lost.

The spinning stopped, after a while. The internal darkness stayed.

I opened my eyes and looked down at the farm, only half seeing it, feeling myself trembling and knowing that there wasn't much farther to go.

Matt came out of the house, walked across the yard, took a look into the barn, and retraced his steps. I watched him in a disorientated haze: those horses in the barn, what did they matter? What did anything matter? Who cared a sixpenny damn about blood lines, it would all be the same in a hundred years.

Dave Teller cared.

Let him.

Dave Teller cared a ten thousand dollar damn what happened to them.

Crystal clear, like distilled water logic, it occurred to me that I could give us both what we wanted if I postponed my walk into the desert until later that night. I would pack the horses off with Hengelman, and instead of driving back to Kingman after him, I would set off on foot, and when it was nearly dawn, and everything looked grey and shadowy, and the step would be small . . . then . . .

Then.

I felt, immediately after making this firm dccision, which seemed to me extremely sensible, a great invasion of peace. No more struggle, no more fuss. My body felt relaxed and full of well-being, and my mind was calm. I couldn't think why such an obvious solution hadn't occurred to me before. All the sweat and sleeplessness had dissolved into a cool, inner, steady light.

This stage lasted until I remembered that I had once been determined not to reach it.

After that, creeping in little by little, came the racking conviction that I had merely surrendered, and was not only despicable but probably insane.

I sat for a while with my head in my hands, fearfully expecting that with the false peace broken up and gone, back would come the shattering vertigo.

It didn't. There was only so great a tiredness that what I'd called tiredness before was like a pinhead on a continent. The dreary fight was on again; but at least I'd survived the bloodiest battle yet. Touched bottom and come back. I felt that after this I really could climb right out, if I went on trying.

A long way to go. But then, I'd have all the time I needed.

CHAPTER SEVENTEEN

I had cramp right down both legs. Matt came out of the house and I woke up to find that the shade patch had moved round while I hadn't. When he went into the barn I started to shift the necessary two yards and found my muscles in knots.

The shade wasn't much cooler, but much better cover. I sat in it waiting for Matt to come out of the barn and for my legs to unlock. What they needed was for me to get to my feet and stamp about: but if Matt caught sight of anyone moving so close to him the whole project would lie in ruins.

He fetched water for the horses, for the calves, and for the hens. I looked at my watch, and was horribly startled to see it was nearly six. It couldn't be, I thought; but it was. Four hours since I last checked. Four hours. I shivered in the roasting air.

Matt brought the empty muck barrow around and into the barn, and came out with it filled. For the whole afternoon I'd fallen down on the surveillance, but looking back I was fairly sure nothing had changed at the farm. Certainly at this point things were as they had been: Matt had no helpers and no visitors, and when he left for Las Vegas the horses would be alone. For that piece of certainty I had been prepared to watch all day, and a poor job I'd made of it.

Matt shut the barn door and went into the house. Half an hour later he came out in a cream-coloured jacket and dark trousers, a transformation from his habitual jeans and a checked shirt. He opened the doors of the shed containing the car, went inside, started up, and drove out across the yard, round the bend on to the road, and away over the desert towards Kingman.

Satisfied, I finally got to my feet. The cramps had gone. I plodded tiredly off to the two-mile distant hidden car, and wished the night was over, not beginning. I hadn't enough energy to lick a stamp.

Matt's dust had settled when I followed him along the empty road, but when I got into Kingman he was still there. With shock I saw him standing outside a garage I was passing, and I drew into the kerb fifty yards on and looked back. The black saloon he had hired and his own blue Ford were both standing there in the forecourt. An overalled girl attendant was filling the Ford's tank from the pump, and Matt was looking in snatches at his watch and exhibiting impatience. Seven-twenty; and a hundred miles to Las Vegas. He would be a few minutes late for his appointment with Walt.

Slumping down in my seat I fixed the driving mirror so that I could watch him. He paid the girl for the petrol and hopped into his car over the top, without opening the door. Then he pulled out on to the road, turned in my direction, and went past me with his foot impressively on the accelerator. I gently followed for a while at a respectable distance, content to keep him only just in sight, and turned back to the town once he was conclusively topping the speed limit on Route 93 to Las Vegas.

Outside the unprosperous looking Mojave Motel Sam Hengelman's horse van took up a sixth of the parking space. Inside, they told me that he had arrived at four-thirty and was along in Room 6, sleeping. I left him to it, because we couldn't move anyway until I'd phoned Walt at eight, and went into the bus station for some coffee. It came in a plastic carton out of an automat, black but weak. I drank it without tasting and thought about some food, but I wasn't really hungry enough to bother, and I was too dirty and unshaven for anywhere good. Until after eight I sat on the bus station bench staring into space, and then used the bus station telephone to get through to Walt.

He came on the line with little delay.

'How's things?' he said.

'Matt left Kingman for Las Vegas at seven-thirty, so he will be a little late.'

'Left Kingman?' Walt sounded surprised.

I explained about Matt changing cars.

'I suppose his Ford wasn't quite ready when he got there. Anyway, he's coming in that, not the hired one.'

'Are you all right?' Walt said hesitantly.

'Of course.'

'You don't sound it.'

'Sam Hengelman's here,' I said, ignoring him. 'He's asleep along at the Mojave Motel. We'll start as soon as I get back there and wake him up.'

'It's all safe at the farm?' He seemed anxious.

'Deserted,' I assured him. 'Has been all yesterday, all last night, and all today. No one around but Matt. Stop worrying. You just see Matt and put on your act, and then head straight back to Santa Barbara. As soon as Sam's clear of the area I'll follow you. See you for breakfast about twelve hours from now.'

'Right,' he said. 'Well . . . keep your nose clean.'

'You too.'

'Sure thing. It's not me that's nuts.'

The line clicked clear before I found an answer, and it left me with a vague feeling that there was more I should have said, though I didn't know what.

I knocked on Sam's door at the motel, and he came sleepily stretching to switch on the light and let me in.

'With you in a minute,' he said, reaching for his shoes and looking round for his tie.

'Sam, you don't have to come.'

'Eh?'

'Go back to sleep. I'll go and fetch the horses. That way you won't be so involved.'

He sat on the edge of the bed looking down at the floor. 'I'm still driving them to Lexington?'

'Unless you want out. Leave the van, and fly home.'

'Nope.' He shook his head. 'A bargain's a bargain. And I may as well come all the way. That van's none too easy in reverse . . . don't know that you could handle it.'

I half smiled and didn't argue. I'd wanted him with me, but only willingly, and I'd got that. He knotted his tie and brushed his hair and then took a sidelong glance at my own appearance, which fell a ton short of his. He was a fleshy man of about fifty, bald, pale-skinned, and unexcitable. His nerves, I thought, were going to be at least equal to the evening's requirements.

'Let's go, then,' he said cheerfully. 'I paid in advance.'

I followed him across to the van and climbed up into the cab. Sam started the engine, told me he'd filled up with gas when he'd first reached Kingman, and rolled out south-east on the road to the farm. His broad face looked perfectly calm in the glow from the dashboard, and he handled his six-stall horsebox like a kiddicar. He went eight miles in silence, and then all he said was, 'I'd sure hate to live this far from town, with nowhere to get a beer.'

We passed the third of the three side roads and started on the last ten uninhabited miles to the farm. Three miles farther on Sam gave an alarmed exclamation and braked from his cautious thirty to a full stop. 'What is it?' I asked.

'That gauge.' He pointed, and I looked. The needle on the temperature gauge was quivering on red.

'Have to look see,' he grunted, and switched off the engine. My thoughts as he disappeared out of the cab were one enormous curse. Of all hopeless, dangerous places for his van to break down.

He came back and opened the door my side. I jumped down beside him and he took me round to show me the exhaust.

'Look,' he said unnecessarily. 'Water.'

Several drops slid out, glistening in the light of his torch.

'Gasket,' he said, putting into one word the enormity of the disaster, and what he thought of fate for trapping us in it.

'No water in the radiator,' I said.

'Right.'

'And if we go on, the engine will seize up.'

'Right again.'

'I suppose you don't carry any extra water in the van?'

'We sure do,' he said. 'Never travel without it.'

'Can't we pour some in the radiator . . .?'

'Yeah,' he said. 'We can. There's two gallons. We can pour in a quarter, and go three miles maybe before it's all leaked out, and then another quarter, another three miles. Four quarts, twelve miles. And that's it.'

Thirteen miles out from Kingman. We could just about get back. Seven to the farm. We could refill the radiator at the farm, but Sam couldn't set out on his two thousand mile journey with a stolen cargo in a van emptying like a dry dock.

'There's an extra gasket, of course,' he said.

'A spare one?'

'Sure. Always carry a full set of spares. Never know where you're going to need them. Universal joints, big ends, carburettors, I carry them all. Anyone with any sense does that.'

'Well,' I said in relief, 'how long will it take you to fit the spare?'

He laid the engine bare and considered it in the torch light.

'Cylinder head gasket. Say three hours.'

'*Three hours!*'

'Won't take much less,' he said. 'What do you want to do?'

I looked at my watch. Eight-fifty. Three hours made eleven-fifty; and if we then went on to the farm and picked up the horses we couldn't be back through Kingman until one-fifteen.

Matt would reach Pittsville Boulevard by nine-thirty, and finish his insurance business long before ten. If he drove straight home again he would be on the farm road at midnight. If Sam changed the gasket, so would we.

If Matt stopped to play the tables, he would be at

least an hour later. His clothes had suggested he would stop. But whether for one hour or six, there was no way of telling.

'Change the gasket,' I said abruptly. 'Then we'll see.'

Sam nodded philosophically. It was what he would have done in any case if the van had broken down anywhere else, and without more ado he sorted out what he wanted and started unscrewing.

'Can I help?' I said.

He shook his head and clipped his torch on to a convenient spar to give a steady working light. There seemed to be little haste in his manner, but also no hesitation and a good deal of expertise. The heap of unplugged parts grew steadily on a square of canvas at his feet.

I walked away a few steps and felt for the cigarettes. Two left. I'd still forgotten to buy more. The smoke didn't help much towards making the next decision: to go on, or to go back.

I'd already gambled on Matt staying to play. If it had been Yola, I would have felt surer that it would be for most of the night: but her brother might not have the fever, might only want a short break in his boring stint with the horses. How short? How long?

The decision I came to, if you could call it that, was to wait and see what time Sam restarted the engine.

The night, outside the bright pool by the van, was as dark as the one before. The stars glittered remotely, and the immensity of the American continent marked their indifference to the human race. Against such size, what did one man matter? A walk into the desert . . .

Carefully I pinched out the end of my cigarette and put the stub in my pocket. A good criminal, I thought wryly: I'd always been that. I had a job to do, and even when I'd finished it, I was going for no walks into the desert. I was going back to Santa Barbara, to have breakfast with Walt and Eunice and Lynnie. The prospect at that moment seemed totally unreal, so far were thc Arizona hills from the lush coast, so far had I been into the wasteland inside me.

I went back to Sam and asked how it was going. He had the cylinder head off and was removing the cracked gasket.

'So, so,' he said calmly. 'I'm breaking the record.'

I did my best at a smile. He grunted, and said he could do with a cup of coffee, and I said so could I. We hadn't brought any.

He worked on. The air was still warmer than an English summer and he wiped sweat off his bald forehead with the back of a greasy hand. The light shone on his thick stubby fingers, and the click of his spanners echoed across the empty land. The hands on my watch went round in slow fractions. The gasket was wasting the night. And where was Matt?

After two hours Sam's spanner slipped on a nut and he cursed. In spite of his calm, the tension wasn't far from the surface. He stopped what he was doing, stretched upright, took three deep breaths and a look at the night sky, and waited for me to say something.

'You're doing fine,' I said.

He sniffed. 'What'll happen if they catch us here?'

'We won't get the horses.'

He grimaced at my non-answer and went back to his task. 'What have you been doing all day?'

'Nothing. Sitting still.'

'You look half dead,' he commented. 'Pass me those two washers, will you?'

I gave him the washers. 'How much longer?'

'Can't say.'

I stifled the urge to tell him to hurry. He was going as fast as he could. But time was ticking away, and the postponed decision had got to be made. Turning my back on the tugging desert I climbed up to sit in the cab. Eleven-twenty. Matt could be a bare quarter of an hour out from Kingman. Or glued to the green baize and the tricky numbers in Las Vegas.

Which?

For a long half hour I looked out of the back windows while no helpful telepathic messages flowed through them. A straightforward gamble, I thought. Just decide if the winnings were worth the risk.

An easier decision if I'd come alone: but if I'd come alone I couldn't have mended the gasket.

At eleven-forty Sam said gloomily that he was having to fix the water pump as well. It was sticking.

'How long?'

'Another twenty minutes.'

We stared at each other in dismay.

'Go on then,' I said in the end. There was nothing else to do.

I left the cab and walked restlessly a short way back along the road, fearing every second to see Matt's headlights and wondering how best to deal with him if we had to. I was all for stealing from him what wasn't his, but not for damaging his skin. He, however, would have no such inhibitions. There would certainly be blood. Not fair to make it Sam's.

At two minutes past midnight he called out that he had finished, and I walked quickly back to join him. He was pouring water into the radiator, and screwed on the cap as I came up.

'It should be OK now,' he said. His hands were covered in grease and his big body hung tiredly from the shoulders. 'Which way do we go?'

'On.'

He nodded with a wide slicing grin. 'I figured you'd say that. Well, I guess that's OK by me.'

He swung up into the cab and I climbed in beside him. The engine started sweetly at first try, and switching on his headlights, he released the brake and eased away along the road.

'If anyone catches us here from now on,' I said, 'duck.'

'Yeah?'

'Yeah.'

'Tell you something,' he said comfortably. 'I swing a mean left hook.'

'The chap we'd be taking on goes for the head. But with a club of some sort in his fist.'

'Nice guys you play with,' he said. 'I'll remember that.'

We covered the remaining distance at a good speed and in silence. The horsebox crept round the last corner and its headlights flickered over the farm ahead. I put my hand on Sam's arm, and he braked to a halt a short way from the yard.

'Switch off, would you? Lights too,' I said, and jumped quickly down from the cab to wait a few precious seconds until my eyes and ears got used to silence and dark.

No lights in the house. No sound anywhere except the ultra-faint ringing vibrations of limitless air. The calves and hens were asleep. The horses were quiet. I banged on the cab door and Sam switched his headlights on again before climbing down to join me. The bright shafts lit up the back of the house and wouldn't shine straight into the horses' eyes when I led them from the barn. Over on the shadowy side of the yard the open doors of the shed where Matt had kept his car yawned in a deep black square. The jumbled rubbish dump just in front of us threw surrealistic shadows across the dusty ground, and its smell of decay brushed by our noses.

Sam swept it all with a practised glance. 'Not much of a place.' His voice was as low as a whisper.

'No . . . If you'll unclip the ramp, I'll go fetch the horses. One at a time, I think.'

'OK.' He was breathing faster and his big hands were clenched. Not used to it, after all.

I hurried down towards the barn. It wasn't far; about forty yards. Now that we were totally committed my mind raced with urgency to be done, to be away, to be safely through Kingman before Matt came back. He could have been on the road behind us, be rushing at this moment across the desert to the farm . . .

What happened next happened very fast, in one terrifying cataclysmic blur.

There was an urgent shout behind me.

'Gene!'

I turned, whirling. There were two sets of headlights where there should have been one.

Matt.

The voice again, yelling. 'Gene! Look out.' And a figure running down the yard towards me.

Then there was a roar behind me and I turned again and was met full in the eyes by the blinding glare of two more headlights, much closer. Much closer.

Moving.

I was dazzled and off balance and I'd never have got clear. The running figure threw himself at me in a rugger tackle with outstretched arms and knocked me over out of the way, and the roaring car crashed solidly into the flying body and left it crumpled and smashed and lying on top of my legs.

The car which had hit him turned in a wide sweep at the end of the yard and started back. The headlights lined themselves up like twin suns on their target and with a fraction of my mind I thought it ironic that now when I'd decided not to, I was going to die.

Half sitting, half kneeling, I jerked out the Luger and pumped all of its eight bullets towards the windscreen. I couldn't see to aim straight . . . my eyes were hurting from the glare . . . Not that bullets would do any good . . . the angle was wrong . . . they'd miss the driver . . . By the time I fired the last one the left headlight was six feet away. I uselessly set my teeth against the mangling, tearing, pulping collision . . . and in the last tenth of a second the straight line wavered . . . the smooth side of the front wing hit the back of my shoulder, the front wheel ran over a fold of my shirt, and the rear wheel gave me a clear inch.

Almost before I realized it had missed me, the car crashed head on into one of the buildings at my back with a jolting screech of wood and metal. The bodywork crumpled and cracked. The stabbing lights went black. The engine stopped. Air hissed fiercely out of a punctured tyre.

Gasping, dreading what I would find, I leaned over the heavy figure lying on my legs. There were more running footsteps in the yard, and I looked up hopelessly, unable to do any more. I'd used all the bullets . . . none left.

'You're alive!' The voice came from the level of my ear, the man kneeling. Sam Hengelman. I looked at him in a daze.

'I thought . . .' I said, with no breath, '. . . this was you.'

He shook his head. 'No . . .'

He helped me raise and turn the man who'd saved me; and with sickness and unbearable regret I saw his face.

It was Walt.

We laid him on his back, in the dust.

'Look in the car,' I said.

Sam lumbered silently to his feet and went away. I heard his footsteps stop and then start back.

Walt opened his eyes, I leaned over him, lifting his hand, feeling with surging hope for his pulse.

'Gene?' his voice mumbled.

'Yes.'

'He didn't come.'

'Didn't . . .?'

'Came to help you . . .'

'Yes,' I said. 'Thanks, Walt . . .'

His eyes slid aimlessly away from my face.

'Christ,' he said distinctly. 'This is it. This is . . . really . . . it.'

'Walt . . .' His hand was warm in mine, but it didn't move.

'Sod it,' he said. 'I wanted . . . I wanted . . .'

His voice stopped. There was no pulse. No heartbeat. Nothing. Nothing at all.

I put gently down on the ground the warm hand with the rounded fingertips, and stretched out my own, and shut his eyes. It should have been me lying there, not Walt. I shook with sudden impotent fury that it wasn't me, that Walt had taken what I'd wanted, stolen my death . . . It would have mattered so little if it had been me. It wouldn't have mattered at all.

Walt . . . Walt . . .

Sam Hengelman said, 'Is he dead?'

I nodded without looking up.

'There's a young guy in the car,' he said. 'He's dead too.'

I got slowly, achingly, to my feet, and went to look. The car was a blue Ford convertible, and the young guy was Matt.

Without caring, automatically, I took in that the car had smashed the right-hand door of the garage shed and ploughed into the wall behind it. Most of the windscreen was scattered in splintered fragments all over the inside of the car, but in one corner, where some still clung to the frame, there was a finger-sized hole.

Matt was lying over the steering wheel, his arms dangling, his eyes open. The skull above the left eyebrow was pierced and crumpled inwards, and there was blood and hair on the chromium upright which had held the windscreen. I didn't touch him. After a while I went back to Walt.

'What do we do?' Sam Hengelman said.

'Give me a moment . . .'

He waited without speaking until eventually I looked up and down the yard. Two sets of headlights still blazed at the way in.

'That's Walt's car up there?'

'Yeah. He drove up with the devil on his tail and jumped out and ran down after you . . .'

I turned the other way and looked at the dark garage.

'The young guy must have been in there all the time, waiting for us,' Sam said. 'He came roaring out and drove straight at you. I couldn't have stopped him . . . too far away. Walt was halfway down the yard . . .'

I nodded. Matt had been there all the time. Not in Las Vegas. Not on the road. Lying in ambush, waiting.

He hadn't passed us on the road, and there was no other way to the farm. He must have gone back ahead of us. Turned round on the road to Las Vegas and driven back through Kingman while I was sitting in the bus station waiting to telephone to Walt.

But why? *Why* should he have gone back? He hadn't seen me following him, I'd been much too far behind, and in any case I'd left him once he was safely on the highway.

It didn't matter why. It only mattered that he had.

Sam Hengelman looked down at Walt and summed up the mess we were entangled in.

'Well . . . what the heck do we do now?'

I took a deep breath.

'Will you fetch that torch of yours?' I asked, and he nodded and brought it from his van. I went with it over to the Ford, and took a longer, closer look. There wasn't much to see that I hadn't seen before, except for a bottle of bourbon that had been smashed in the impact. The neck and jagged top half lay on the floor to Matt's right, along with several smaller pieces and an uneven damp patch.

I walked into the garage and looked at the Ford from the front. It wouldn't be driving anywhere any more.

The big torch lit up clearly the interior of the deep shadowy garage. Quite empty now, except for a scatter of cigarette stubs against the left-hand wall. Matt had been smoking and drinking while he waited. And he'd waited a very long time.

The bullet hole faced me in the windscreen and left me with the worst question unanswered.

I'd have to know.

I stood beside Matt and went over every inch of his body down to the waist. He'd taken off the cream-coloured jacket and was wearing the checked shirt he'd worked in. There were no holes in it: no punctures underneath. His head was heavy. I laid it gently on the steering wheel and stepped away.

None of the bullets had hit him. They'd only smashed the windscreen and blinded him, and he'd slewed a foot off course and run into the wall instead of me, and his head had gone forward hard against the slim metal post.

Slowly I returned to where Sam Hengelman stood beside Walt. He drooped with the utmost dejection and looked at me without hope.

'Did you unclip the ramp?' I asked abruptly.

He shook his head. 'Didn't have time.'

'Go and do it now. We're taking the horses.'

He was aghast. 'We can't!'

'We've got to. For Walt's sake, and your sake, and Dave Teller's sake. And mine. What do you propose? That we call the police and explain what we were all doing here?'

'We'll have to,' he said despairingly.

'No. Definitely not. Go and let down the ramp.'

He hesitated unbelievingly for a few seconds, and then went and did as I asked. The horses stood peacefully in the barn, apparently undisturbed by the racket, the shots, and the crash. I untied the nearest, Showman, and led him quietly up the yard and into the van.

Sam watched me in silence while I tied him into one of the stalls.

'We'll never get away with it.'

'Yes we will,' I said, 'as long as you take these horses safely back to Lexington and never tell anyone,

anyone at all, what happened here tonight. Blot it out of your mind. I'll let you know, when you get back, that you've nothing to worry about. And as long as you tell no one, you won't have.'

The broad fleshy face was set in lines of anxiety.

'You've collected two horses,' I said matter-of-factly. 'An everyday job, collecting two horses. Forget the rest.'

I returned to the barn, fetched Allyx, and loaded him up. Sam still hadn't moved.

'Look,' I said. 'I've . . . arranged . . . things before. There's a rule where I come from – you take a risk, you get into a mess, you get out.' He blinked. 'Walt threw himself in the way of that car,' I said. 'Matt didn't intend to kill *him* . . . You didn't see a murder. Matt drove straight into the wall himself . . . and that too was an accident. Only two automobile accidents. You must have seen dozens. Forget it.' He didn't answer, and I added brusquely, 'The water can's empty. You can fill it over there.'

With something like a shudder he picked up the container and went where I pointed. Sighing, I checked that he had brought three days' fodder for the stallions, which he had, and with his help on his return, shut the precious cargo up snugly for their long haul.

'You don't happen to have any gloves around?' I asked.

'Only an old cotton pair in the tool kit.'

He rooted about and finally produced them, two

filthy objects covered with oil and grease which would leave marks on everything they touched, as tale-bearing as fingerprints. I turned them inside out and found they were thick enough to be clean on the inside. Sam watched wordlessly while I put them on, clean side out.

'OK,' I said. 'Will you turn the van, ready to go?'

He did it cautiously as far away from Walt as he could, and when he'd finished I stepped with equal care into the car Walt had come in, touching it as little and as lightly as possible, and drove it down into the yard, stopping a little short of the screen door to the house. There I switched off the engine and lights, put on the brake, and walked back to talk to Sam where he sat in his cab.

'I've three jobs to do,' I said. 'I'll be back as quick as I can. Why don't you just shut your eyes for a couple of minutes and catch a nap?'

'You're kidding.'

I concocted a replica of a smile, and a fraction of the tension in his face unwound.

'I won't be long,' I said, and he nodded, swallowing.

With his torch I surveyed the yard. The Luger was an automatic pistol, which meant it threw out the cartridge after each shot. No one would find the spent bullets, but eight shiny metal shells scattered near Walt's body were something else. Seven of them winked in the light as I inched the torch carefully round, and I collected them into my pocket. The eighth remained obstinately invisible.

Thc cjection slot had been on the side of the gun away from Walt, but the cases sometimes shot out straight upwards instead of sideways, and I began to wonder if the eighth could possibly have travelled far enough over to be underneath him. I didn't want to disturb him: but I had to find the little brass thimble.

Then, when I'd decided I had no choice, I saw it. Bent and dusty, partly flattened, no longer shining. I picked it up from the spot where I had been half-lying in the path of Matt's car. He had run over it.

After that I attended to the ground itself. Tyre marks didn't show on the rough dusty surface, but the hoof prints did to some extent. I fetched a broom of twigs from the barn and swept them out.

The garage was next. I punched through into the car the remaining corner of the windscreen with its significant bullet hole, and I picked up every one of the cigarette stubs which told where and how long Matt had waited. They went into a trash can standing a few yards along from the house door.

Matt hadn't locked the house when he went out. I went in to look for one essential piece of information: the address of the place, and the name of its owner. The torchlight swept over the threadbare covers and elderly furniture, and in one drawer of a large dresser I found what the farmer used for an office. The jumble of bills and letters gave me what I wanted. Wilbur

Bellman, Far Valley Farm, Kingman. On the scratch pad beside the telephone, Matt had written a bonus. In heavy black ballpoint were the simple words: 'Insurance 9 PM.'

Before leaving I gave the big dilapidated living room a final circuit with the torch and the beam flickered over a photograph in a cardboard folder standing on a shelf. Something about the face in it struck me as familiar, and I swung the torch back for a second and closer look.

The patient passive face of Kiddo smiled out, as untroubled as it had been when he told Walt and me about Offen's mares. Loopy unformed writing straggled over the lower half of the picture. 'To Ma and Pa, from your loving son.'

If Offen had sent his stud groom to Miami to join his parents, Kiddo's loyalty to his employer was a certainty. I almost admired Offen's technique in furnishing himself in one throw with an obscure hideout for the horses and a non-talking employee.

After the house there remained only Walt. Nothing to do but to say goodbye.

I went down on my knees beside him in the dust, but the silent form was already subtly not Walt. Death showed. I took off one glove and touched his hand: still warm in the warm air, but without the firmness of life.

There was no point in saying to him what I felt. If

his spirit was still hovering somewhere around, he would know.

I left him lying there in the dark, and went back to Sam.

He took one slow look at my face and said in an appalled voice, 'You're not leaving him there?'

I nodded, and climbed up beside him.

'But you *can't* . . .'

I simply nodded again, and gestured to him to start up and drive away. He did it with a viciousness that must have rocked the stallions on their feet, and we went back to Kingman without speaking. His revulsion at what I had done reached me in almost tangible waves.

I didn't care. I felt only one grim engulfing ache for the man I'd left behind.

CHAPTER EIGHTEEN

Lynnie put her brown hand tentatively on mine and said, 'Gene . . . what's the matter?'

'Nothing,' I said.

'You look worse than you did when you came back with Chrysalis. Much worse.'

'The food doesn't agree with me.'

She snorted and took her hand away. We were sitting on the sea terrace, waiting for Eunice to come down for dinner, with the sun galloping the last lap to dusk and the daiquiris tinkling with civilized ice.

'Is Walt back yet?' Lynnie said.

'No.'

'He's a funny man, isn't he?' she said. 'All moods and glum looks, and then suddenly he smiles, and you realize how nice he is. I like him.'

After a pause I said, 'So do I.'

'How was San Francisco?' she asked.

'Foggy.'

'What's the matter?'

'Nothing.'

She sighed and shook her head.

Eunice arrived in a cloud of yellow chiffon and clanked her gold bracelet as she stretched for her drink. She was cheerful and glowing; almost too much to bear.

'Well, you son of a bitch, when did you crawl in?'

'This afternoon,' I said.

'So what's new?'

'I've given up trying to find the horses.'

Eunice sat up straight with a jerk. 'For crying out loud!'

'I'll be starting home soon. Tomorrow evening, I expect.'

'Oh no,' Lynnie said.

'Oh, yes, I'm afraid so. The holidays are over.'

'They don't look as if they've done you much good,' Eunice observed. 'So now how do you deal with it?'

'With what?'

'With flopping. With not making out.'

I said wryly, 'Look it smack in the eye and dare it to bite you.'

'It probably will,' said Eunice sardonically. 'It'll chew me to bloody bits.' She drank the second quarter of her drink and looked me thoughtfully over. 'Come to think of it, it seems to have done that to you already.'

'Maybe I'll take up golf.'

She laughed, more internally relaxed than I'd ever seen her. 'Games', she said, 'are a bore.'

When they went in to eat I couldn't face it, and drove off instead to fetch the tape recorder from the rocks at Orpheus Farm. The short journey seemed tiresomely long. It had been nearly four hundred and fifty miles back to Santa Barbara from Kingman, and neither bath, shave, nor two hours flat on the bed seemed to have had any effect.

Back in my room at The Vacationer I listened to the whole of the tape's four-hour playing time. The first conversations, two or three business calls, were from the previous morning, after Walt had put in a new reel. Then there was almost an hour and a half of an interview between Offen and a man from the Bloodstock Registry Office. They had already been out to see the horses, and Offen was piling proof on proof that the horses in his barn were veritably Moviemaker and Centigrade. A groom who had cared for Centigrade during his racing days was asked in to sign a statement he'd made that he recognized the horse and would if necessary swear to its identity in any inquiry.

The bloodstock man apologized constantly that anyone should have doubted Offen. Offen enjoyed the scene, the joke rumbling like an undertone. After they'd gone he laughed aloud. I hoped he'd enjoyed it. He wouldn't be laughing much for a long time to come.

Next on the tape was a piece of Offen giving his houseman instructions for replenishing the drink stocks, then an hour's television programme. And after that, Matt telephoned.

I couldn't hear his voice at all, only Offen's replies, but they were enough.

'Hello, Matt. . . .

'Slow down, I'm not taking this in. Where did you say you were? . . .

'What are you doing on the road to Las Vegas? . . .

'Well, I can see the house must be insured. . . .

'You found *what* under the glove shelf? . . .

'How do you know it's a homer? . . .

'All these minute transmitters are a mystery to me . . .

'Who could have put it there? . . .

'I don't follow you. What was that about yellow paint? . . .

'But the police said it was vandals . . .

'All right, Matt, don't shout. I'm doing my best. Now let's get this clear. You were fumbling for a pack of cigarettes and you dislodged this . . . thing. Bug, whatever you said. And you're worried now that Hawkins and Prensela put it in your car, and that they used that and the yellow paint to follow you, so that they know where you've been staying, or maybe. Is that right? . . .

'Matt, I think you're blowing this thing up too big . . .

'But did you actually *see* a plane following you? . . .

'Well, yes, sure, if you think you should go back, go

back. The horses are far more important than the insurance on the house. But I think you're wrong. Hawkins and Prensela have been concentrating on Moviemaker and Centigrade here, they've stirred up the DA's office from LA and the bloodstock registry, and it's been a three ringed circus here for the last couple of days. They wouldn't have been trying to find any horses anywhere else, because they're sure they're here in the barn . . .

'Well, I don't *know* who could have planted the bug . . .

'Yeah. All right. Go on back, then . . .

'Call me in the morning . . .

'Goodnight, Matt.'

The receiver went down, and for a few seconds there were the indistinct noises of Offen going over the conversation again in his mind, punctuating it with 'umphs' and small doubtful grunts.

I switched the tape off temporarily and thought bitterly about Matt finding the bug. I hadn't had a chance to remove it: on my first night visit to the farm the car in the garage had been the one he'd hired while his own was being cleaned of paint. But neither had I looked upon it as a very great hazard, because the little capsules were light and clung tightly. It had been long odds against him groping for cigarettes while driving in the dark, and dislodging it. I hadn't taken it into account.

Some time on his way back to the farm it must

have struck him that the insurance appointment might be phoney; that if we had tricked him into going to Las Vegas once already, we might be tricking him again. If we'd got him out of the way, it could only be to take the horses. So he'd wait; in the dark, ready to spring.

He must have begun to think, when he'd sat out the three hours it took to mend the gasket, that Uncle Bark was right and he was wrong: but all the same he'd gone on waiting. And, in the end, we had come.

I switched the tape on again for the rest. The whole night had been telescoped into the few seconds' silence, because when Offen made his next call it was clearly morning.

'Yola, is that you?'

A faint clacking reached the bug. Yola's higher pitched voice disturbed more air.

'Have you heard from Matt?'

'...'

'No, he said he'd call me this morning, and he hasn't. I can't get any answer from the farm.'

'...'

'Well, not really. He called me last night because he had some crazy idea Hawkins had traced the horses ...'

A loud squawk from Yola.

'Something about a listening bug and yellow paint.'

Yola talked for some time and when Offen answered he sounded anxious.

'Yeah, I know he found the first one when we thought that was impossible . . . do you really think Matt may be right?'

'. . .'

'Yola, that's right out. Why don't you go yourself?'

'. . .'

'Close the ranch then. Send them all home.'

'. . .'

'Look, if you're right, if Matt's right . . . say when he went back last night the DA's men were sitting there waiting for him? Say they're sitting there right now, waiting for me to turn up and see why Matt doesn't answer his calls? No, Yola, I'm not walking into that farm and find I have to answer questions like what am I doing there, and what are those two horses in the barn, with Moviemaker and Centigrade's registrations tattooed inside their lips? I'm not going.'

'. . .'

'Matt may be off on some plan of his own.'

'. . .'

'No. I'll give him today. If I haven't heard from him by morning I'll . . . well, I'll think of something.'

Yola's final remark was loud, and I heard it clearly. Full of anxiety, full of anguish.

'If anything's happened to Matt . . .'

The end of the tape ran off the reel, and I switched off the recorder. For Yola, as for Walt's wife, life would never be the same again.

I went to bed and lay awake, feeling feverish from

lack of sleep. Relaxed every limb, but my mind would have none of it. It was filled too full, as it had been all day, of a picture of Walt still lying on his back in the farmyard. The sun had risen and blazed on him, and set again. He would have no shelter until tomorrow. I couldn't sleep until he had. I tried to, but I couldn't.

On my way back to Santa Barbara I'd stopped for coffee and a handful of change, and I'd telephoned to Paul M. Zeissen in the Buttress Life office on Thirty Third Street. It had been nearly 6 PM New York time. Zeissen was preparing to go home for the weekend. I was a little worried, I told him, about Walt. He had gone to do some life insurance business on a farm in Arizona, and I hadn't heard from him since. Zeissen and I talked it over for a few minutes in unurgent civilized tones, and arranged finally that if I hadn't heard from Walt by morning, Buttress Life would ring the Arizona State Police in Kingman, and ask them as a favour to go out to the farm, just to check.

In the morning I would ring Zeissen at his home. By noon, perhaps, the Kingman police would reach the farm. They would read the story: insurance salesman arrives for appointment, gets out of car. Matt Clive, hurrying back to meet him, swings into the yard, sees a dark figure too late, hits him, runs straight on into the wall because judgement suspended by horror at collision. Matt, with whisky inside him, and a bottle in the car. Inside the house the 9 PM insurance appointment written in Matt's hand. And nothing else. No horses. No suggestion of visitors. No sign that it could have been anything but a tragically unlucky accident.

Matt had been good at accidents.

So was I.

I lay on my stomach on the beach all morning while Lynnie sat beside me and trickled sand through her fingers. Eunice had gone to Santa Monica, down the coast.

'Are you really going home this evening?' Lynnie said.

'First hop, yes.'

'Would you mind . . . if I came with you?'

I stirred in surprise.

'I thought you wanted to stay here for ever.'

'Mm. But that was with you . . . and Eunice. Now you're going . . . and Eunice hasn't been here much this week, you know. I've spent ages all on my own, and there isn't that much to do on a beach, when you do it every day . . .'

'Where had Eunice been?'

'Santa Monica, like now. There's some place there she spends all her time in, where they import vases and bits of sculpture and expensive light fittings, and things like that. She took me there the day before yesterday . . . I must say it's pretty gorgeous. Marvellous fabrics, too.'

'She might feel hurt if you just pack up and leave her.'

'Well, no. I mentioned it to her before she went this morning, and honestly I think if anything she was relieved. She just said if I really wanted to go, OK, and she would probably be moving down to Santa Monica in a day or two anyway.'

'If you really want to, then. I'm catching the night flight to Washington . . . I've a visit to make in Lexington tomorrow morning. After that, back to New York, and home.'

'You don't mind if I tag along?' She sounded a scrap uncertain.

'Come to think of it,' I said, 'you can wake me at the stops.'

We had a sandwich for lunch which I couldn't eat, and at two the girl from the reception desk came to say I was wanted on the telephone. Paul M. Zeissen told me in a suitably hushed voice that the Arizona police had been most co-operative and had gone to Bellman's farm as asked, and had found Walt dead. I made shocked noises. Zeissen said would I pack Walt's things and send them back? I said I would.

'I suppose,' he suggested diffidently, 'that you and he had not completed your other business?'

'The horses?'

'One horse. Allyx,' he said reprovingly. 'Showman was insured with another company.'

'Oh . . . yes. Allyx should be in circulation, safe and

authenticated within a month or so. I expect the Bloodhorse Breeders' Association will be getting in touch with you. Walt worked very hard at this, and it was entirely owing to his efforts that Buttress Life will be recovering most of the million and a half it paid out.'

'Where did he find the horse?'

'I can't tell you. Does it matter?'

'No . . .' he said thoughtfully. 'Goods back, no questions asked . . . we work on that principle, the same as any other company.'

'Right then,' I said. 'And you'll of course pay his commission to his widow?'

'Uh . . . of course. And naturally Walt had insured his life with us . . . Mrs Prensela will be well provided for, I feel sure.'

Provided for. Money. But no Walt. No picnic.

I said goodbye to Zeissen and went slowly back to Lynnie. When I told her Walt was dead, she cried for him.

Upstairs, when I packed his clothes, I lingered a good while over the framed photograph of him with Amy and the kids, and in the end put it in my suitcase, not his. It could hardly be the only photograph his wife would have of him, and I didn't think she'd worry much if it didn't return with his baggage.

Eunice came back tired and abstracted from Santa Monica, and after absorbing the shock of Walt's death was unaffected when Lynnie told her over early dinner that she was going home with me.

'Much better to travel with a man to look after you, honey,' she agreed absent-mindedly: and then, giving me a more characteristic sharp glance, added, 'Don't let him get up to any tricks.'

Lynnie sighed. 'He wouldn't.'

'Huh,' she said, but without conviction, and then asked me, 'Will you be seeing Dave when you get back?'

I nodded. 'Very soon after.'

'Tell him then, will you, that I've found a darling little business in Santa Monica. They're looking for a partner with some capital, to open another branch, and if the accounts are right I'd like to do it. I'll write to him, of course, but you could explain . . . I guess you could explain better than anyone.'

'I'll explain.'

She said she was too tired to come all the way back to Los Angeles to see us off, and we said goodbye to her in the lobby, where she kissed Lynnie and then me on the cheek with a quite surprising strength of feeling.

Lynnie said, as we drove away, 'I'll miss her. Isn't that extraordinary. I'll really miss her.'

'You'll come back.'

'It won't be the same . . .'

I returned the hired car to the Hertz agent at the airport, we caught the plane to Washington, and I made up on parts of the way for the three nights without sleep. Lynnie said at Lexington that she could quite see why I needed someone to wake me at the stops.

We went in a taxi to Jeff Roots's house and his teenage daughters took Lynnie off for a swim in the pool while I sat with him under his vine-covered trellis and thought how cool and substantial he looked in his bright open-necked Sunday shirt.

'Sam Hengelman should reach Lexington some time this afternoon or early evening,' I said. 'He'll call you to know where to take the horses.'

'That's all fixed,' Roots nodded.

'Would you give him a message from me?'

'Sure.'

'Just tell him everything's OK: that I said so.'

'Sure. You are, aren't you, one hundred per cent certain that those two definitely are Showman and Allyx?'

'One hundred per cent. There isn't the slightest doubt.'

He sighed. 'I'll get the identification started. Though who is to know Showman after ten years? A bay with no markings . . . and only a four-year-old when he came from England.' He paused, then said, 'Have you any suggestions as to how we can start prosecuting Offen for fraud and theft?'

I shook my head. 'I'm not a policeman. Not interested in punishment, only prevention.' I smiled briefly. 'I came to get the horses back. Nothing else. Well . . . they're back. I've done what I was engaged for, and that's as far as I go.'

He eyed me assessingly. 'Do you want Offen to go on collecting huge stud fees, then?'

'He won't,' I said. 'Not if someone starts a quick rumour immediately that both Moviemaker and Centigrade have been suffering from an obscure virus which will certainly have affected their virility. Owners of mares can be quietly advised to insist they don't pay any stud fees until the foals have shown their quality. After that . . . well, Offen does legally own Moviemaker and Centigrade, and he's entitled to the fees they earn on their own merits.'

'You're extraordinary,' he said. 'Don't you want to see Offen behind bars?'

'Not passionately,' I said. Offen had enjoyed his prestige almost more than his income. He would be losing both. And Yola . . . she was going to have to work hard, without Matt, and probably without the expensive house on Pitts. Bars seemed superfluous.

He shook his head, giving me up as a bad job. 'We'll have to prosecute, I'm sure of it. I'll have to get the lawyers to see about it.'

He called the houseman to bring our drinks, and merely sighed when I said I'd as soon share his sugar free tonic.

We sipped the well-iced innocuous stuff and he said again that Offen would have to be prosecuted, if only to provide a reason for Allyx and Showman having disappeared for so many years, and to account for tattoo marks inside their mouths.

'I can see you would think that,' I said. 'I also think you'll have a terrible job proving that any of the mares booked to Moviemaker and Centigrade were actually covered by Showman and Allyx. I didn't find Showman and Allyx on Offen's farm. I doubt if anyone would testify that they were ever there. Certainly Offen would deny it, and go on denying it to the bitter end. It's his only hope.' I paused. 'I did manage to get some tape recordings, but unfortunately, even if they could be used as evidence, they are inconclusive. Offen never mentioned Showman or Allyx by name.'

Roots stared gloomily into space.

'This makes it difficult,' he said. 'What you are in fact saying is that we know Offen switched the stallions, because of the tattoo marks, but no one will be able to prove it?'

I looked down to where Lynnie was jumping into the pool in a big splash contest with Roots's daughters. Her lighthearted laughter floated up, carefree and very young.

'I wouldn't try,' I said. 'Rightly or wrongly I decided to repossess the stolen goods by stealing them back. First, so that Offen would have no chance of destroying them. Second, so that there shouldn't be years of delay while lawyers argued the case, years of the stallions standing idle, with their value diminishing day by day and their blood lines wasting. Third, and most important, that there should be no chance of Offen getting them back once the dust had settled. Because if he had any sense he would swear, and provide witnesses to swear, that the horses in dispute were two unraced halfbred animals of no account, and he'd explain the tattoos on their lips by saying he'd used them to try out some new type of ink. What more likely, he would say, than that he should repeat the numbers of his two best horses? He could make it sound a lot more reasonable than that he should have stolen two world famous stallions and conducted a large scale fraud. He has great personal charm.'

Roots nodded. 'I've met him.'

'Showman and Allyx were being looked after by Offen's nephew,' I said. 'Offen can say he'd lent him two old nags to hack around on, and he can't imagine why anyone would want to steal them.'

'He could put up an excellent defence, I see that,' he admitted.

'His present stud groom is innocent,' I added. 'And would convince anyone of it. If you leave things as they are, Offen won't get Allyx and Showman back. If you prosecute him, he may.'

He looked shattered, staring into his glass but seeing with experienced eyes every side of the sticky problem.

'We could try blood tests,' he said at last.

'Blood tests?'

'For paternity,' he nodded. 'If there is any doubt about which horse has sired a certain foal, we take blood tests. If one disputed sire's blood is of a similar group to the foal's, and the other disputed sire's is different, we conclude that the foal was sired by the similar sire.'

'And like in humans,' I asked, 'you can tell which horse could *not* have sired which foal, but you couldn't say which, of a similar blood group, actually did?'

'That's right.'

We thought it over. Then he said cheerfully, 'If we can prove that none of the so-called Moviemaker foals could in fact have been sired by Moviemaker, but could all have been sired by Showman, we'll have Offen sewn up tight.'

'Couldn't he possibly have made sure, before he ever bought Moviemaker, that his and Showman's blood groups were similar? I mean, if he's a breeder, he'd know about blood tests.'

Roots's gloom returned. 'I suppose it's possible. And possible that Centigrade and Allyx are similar too.' He looked up suddenly and caught me smiling. 'It's all right for you to think it's funny,' he said, wryly matching my expression. 'You don't have to sort out the mess. What in God's name are we going to do about the Stud Book? Moviemaker's . . . that is, Showman's . . . get are already siring foals, in some cases. The mix up is in the second generation. How are we ever going to put it straight?'

'Even if,' I pointed out, trying hard to keep the humour out of my voice and face, 'even if you prove Moviemaker couldn't have sired the foals he's supposed to have done, you can't prove Showman *did*.'

He gave me a comically pained look. 'What other sire could have got such brilliant stock?' He shook his head. 'We'll pin it on Offen in the end, even if we have to wait until after Showman and Allyx have been re-syndicated and their first official crops have won as much stake money as all the others. Offen wouldn't be able to say then that they were two halfbred nags he'd given his nephew to hack around on. We'll get him in the end.'

'The racing scandal of the year,' I said smiling.

'Of the year? Are you kidding? Of the century.'

Lynnie and I flew from Kennedy that night on a Super VC 10, with dinner over Canada at midnight and breakfast over Ireland three hours later. I spent the interval looking at her while she slept beside me in her sloped-back chair. Her skin was close textured like a baby's, and her face was that of a child. The woman inside was still a bud, with a long way to grow.

Keeble met us at Heathrow, and as usual it was raining. Lynnie kissed him affectionately. He went so far as to shake my hand. There was a patch of stubble on his left cheek, and the eyes blinked quickly behind the mild glasses. Santa Barbara was six thousand miles away. We were home.

Keeble suggested a cup of coffee before we left the airport and asked his daughter how she'd enjoyed herself. She told him non-stop for twenty minutes, her suntan glowing in the grey summer morning and her brown eyes alight.

He looked finally from her to me, and his face subtly contracted.

'And what have you been doing?' he said.

Lynnie answered when I didn't. 'He's been with us on the beach a good deal of the time,' she said doubtfully.

Keeble stroked her arm. 'Did you find the horses?' he asked.

I nodded.

'All three?'

'With help.'

'I told Dave I'd drop you off at the hospital when we leave here,' he said. 'He's still strung up, but he hopes to be out next week.'

'I've a lot to tell him, and there's a lot he'll have to decide.' The worst being, I thought, whether to carry on with his move alongside Orpheus Farm, or to disappoint Eunice in her new found business. Nothing was ever simple. Nothing was easy.

'You don't look well,' Keeble said abruptly.

'I'll live,' I said, and his eyes flickered with a mixture

of surprise and speculation. I smiled lopsidedly and said it again, 'I'll live.'

We stood up to go. Instead of shaking hands Lynnie suddenly put her arms round my waist and her head on my chest.

'I don't want to say goodbye,' she said indistinctly. 'I want to see you again.'

'Well,' I said reasonably. 'You will.'

'I mean . . . often.'

I met Keeble's eyes over her head. He was watching her gravely, but without disquiet.

'She's too young,' I said to him, and he knew exactly what I meant. Not that I was too old for her, but that she was too young for me. Too young in experience, understanding, and wickedness.

'I'll get older,' she said. 'Will twenty-one do?'

Her father laughed, but she gripped my arm. 'Will it?'

'Yes,' I said recklessly, and found one second later that I really meant it.

'She'll change her mind,' Keeble said with casual certainty.

I said, 'Of course,' to him, but Lynnie looked up into my eyes and shook her head.

It was late afternoon when I got back to the flat. The tidy, dull, unwelcoming rooms hadn't changed a bit. When I looked at the kitchen I remembered Lynnie making burnt scrambled egg, and I felt a fierce disturbing wish that she would soon make some more.

I unpacked. The evening stretched greyly ahead.

I sat and stared vacantly at the bare walls.

If was a grinding word, I thought. If Sam Hengelman had taken longer to mend that gasket, Walt would have found us on the road and would have stopped us going to the farm. If Sam had mended it faster, we'd have reached the farm well before Walt, and Matt would have killed me, as he'd meant.

If I hadn't decided to recover the horses by stealing them, Walt would be alive. They might collectively be worth nearly five million dollars, but they weren't worth Walt's life.

I wished I'd never started.

The grey day turned to grey dusk. I got up and switched on the light, and fetched two objects to put on the low table beside my chair.

The Luger, and the photograph of Walt with his wife and kids.

The trouble with being given a gift you don't really want is that you feel so mean if you throw it away. Especially if it cost more than the giver could afford.

I won't throw away Walt's gift. Even if Lynnie changes her mind, I'll survive.

Tired beyond feeling, I went to bed at ten. I put the Luger under the pillow, and hung the photograph on the wall.

And slept.

DICK FRANCIS

Come to Grief

'This is Francis writing at his best'
Evening Standard

Sid Halley, the ex-champion jockey turned investigator who appears in *Odds Against* and *Whip Hand*, is back. In *Come to Grief* he faces new dangers, new deeply demanding decisions.

Sid Halley has uncovered an obnoxious crime committed by a friend whom he – and everyone else – has held in deep affection. On the morning set for the opening of the friend's trial, at which Sid is due to be called as a witness, other people's miseries explode and send him spinning into days of hard, rational detection and heart-searching torment.

Troubled, courageous and unwilling to admit defeat, for Sid Halley it is business as usual.

Winner of the Edgar Allan Poe award for best crime novel of the year.

'Dick Francis is firmly in the saddle and leaving the opposition standing . . .'
Sunday Telegraph